THE CRONE OF LIGHT'S END

THE CRONE OF LIGHT'S END

THE ERWAIN TRILOGY

MARIAH STILLBROOK

Published in the United States by Creative James Media.

www.creativejamesmedia.com

978-1-965648-14-8 (trade paperback)

First U.S. Edition 2025

For Liv, always.

But also, for all the dreamers. For those who grew up still peering over shoulders in search of 'Gobble-uns,' faeries, and gnomes. For all of you who never stopped believing in magic even when they told you to.

Yes, this is for you too.

$\maltese$ I $\maltese$

Lantern's Edge

I t was the kind of day that children look forward to. Not a cloud in sight; the sky so blue one could almost get lost in it and find the darkness that is space.

The midnight soil under the grass was still just damp from last night's rain, and the earth that Malina and Dora laid upon seemed happy. Their hands were clasped as they looked up at the sky—the sun like a tunnel of light streaming down over their freckled faces. Their features were similar, but they weren't identical twins. They'd been seeded from separate eggs.

"The test is coming," Malina said. "I feel it in my bones."

Dora blinked away the unruly UV rays beating down into her golden irises, and over her brown skin. "'Tis because we are to be eight next week. That is when it happens."

Malina squeezed her hand. "How do you know?"

"Because Teddy told me."

Teddy, the son of Vera, was one of their mother's followers.

Teddy's family hadn't borne any twins, but his mother's sister had.

"Did he tell you what happens . . . where the loser goes?"

Dora's face remained neutral.

Their mother, never a woman to portray softness, even in the eyes of her own children, had never sugar-coated the fate of her girls. They had been the product of a ritual that their coven practiced many years ago. Their mother, the high priestess, was driven by a spell of her own creation. One that required two seeds from the same womb. Two witches from which they would take the power from one and harness it into the other. There would be a test, and the winner would attain the power.

The ritual their coven performed had produced three sets of twins. The movement of power from one vessel to the other had yet to work. Dora and Malina were the third and final set. As for what happened to the other two twins who lost their battles, their mother never mentioned those details.

Dora licked her cherry red lips and replied to her sister's inquiry. "Teddy didn't know what happened to the loser."

She sensed Malina's head roll in her direction; her little dark eyes on her. "But *you* know, don't you?"

She did.

Dora had forever known things that Malina hadn't. Both had been born witches, but that didn't mean they excelled at the same practices. Malina had always had a natural tendency when it came to healing, while Dora had a fierce intuition that could even cause her mother to tremble. But Dora had always been very sneaky not to let her mother know how much authority she was actually carrying.

"It doesn't matter," Dora said. "You'll win."

Malina was rolling her head softly back and forth in the happy grass. "No. You've always been the stronger one."

The word 'truth' slipped through the barrier Dora had tried to put up in the corner of her skull.

"Strength is all in one's mind," she replied. "You believe me to be the stronger one so I am. That is all. You must believe in yourself, Malina."

Malina opened her mouth to reply but she was never given the chance, for in that moment their mother walked out from their small stone cabin that sat on a hill overlooking the lake in Forest's Peak—the chosen settlement of their people. Their home, specifically, had been the meeting place of their coven for several years. A coven that had been growing steadily, and though Dora didn't know what it meant, she'd heard someone spit out the word cult once upon a time.

"Dora! Malina! 'Tis time for tea!"

The girls sighed before begrudgingly rolling to their stomachs and slowly coming to their knees, and eventually their feet.

"Must we?" Malina said with a pout. "'Tis such a beautiful day. I'd fancy a swim."

Their mother stood as a statue in her blood red skirt that flowed around their wooden porch. The day was hot, but still her arms and neck were covered by the lacy shirt she wore in black. The fragile material did nothing to soften her features.

"You will swim another day," she answered as the girls ran past the wooden sign in front of their house. The name of their coven and a statement to those who got too close, burned into it. She was not the sort of crone who sought out those in need of remedies; she was not a healer, and unless it was coven related, she did not like visitors. Lantern's Edge was a fitting title . . . it was, in fact, the light's end. Her girls ran over the porch and into their quaint home, taking their seats around the wooden table for their daily lesson on tea leaves.

Before she turned to face them and follow their lead, their mother took one last look ahead of her, at the lake. Its stillness reflecting the overly bright sun the day had given them. Inside the cabin, Dora watched her mother as she sat in the ordered fashion: with her spine erect and her hands laced together just behind where her wand and tea laid. As she waited, she heard the woman's thoughts.

Yes, you or your sister will swim another day. In just a few short days to be exact.

The crone turned and faced her girls, her cheek bones a little more severe than usual; actually, Dora noted, her elbows seemed pointier than ever also. Their mother was beginning to thin out . . . her features were looking less human. Did it have something to do with the rise in animal deaths they'd been witnessing around their home the past few new moons? The faery deaths? Dora's gaze remained focused straight ahead as she tried to keep her thoughts quiet. However, it seemed her mother's followers were getting hungrier and thirstier. There'd been rumors that the coven was feeding directly from the earth.

The woman's skirt followed her like a pool of blood as she took one step at a time, like a trained ballet dancer, then came to stand before them. Looking down at her daughter, she said to Dora, "Is there something you'd like to ask me?"

Dora had trained herself to remain neutral. "No."

Malina kicked her ankle under the table.

"No, *what?*" Their mother specified.

They weren't to call her mother. And to be fair, it wasn't hard not to. The only love the girls had ever known had come from each other. Perhaps that was why they were so close— why Dora felt protective over Malina.

"No, Crone." The woman's head began to sink down until

her eyes were level with Dora's. She needn't say anything more, Dora was already well versed in what lines she needed to repeat and when. "No, Crone of Light's End."

The left side of the woman's lips curled up in such a way that caused Dora's stomach to turn.

"That's better." The woman stood back up then made her way to her seat. She snapped her fingers and waited for the teapot she'd been heating over the stove to float over to where they were seated. As soon as it was within her grasp, she began to pour the boiling water into the cups sitting before her daughters.

"Now then, girls, you know what to do."

Dora and Malina met one another's stares for just long enough to allow the diminutive communication to peak, then each set of eyes dove into the tea before each little hand gripped the porcelain handle of her teacup and began to sip.

As Dora slurped the concoction, she set her thoughts into action. She wasn't ignorant; she knew the power her mother had conjured—the innocence she'd sucked on to get to where she was. It wasn't enough to be clever around her. No, one had to be exceptional at both magic and wit. Good thing then, that Dora was good at both things. Malina, though, she lagged. All Dora could hope for was that her sister could prove to be more than ordinary, to follow the instructions she'd given her thus far. Because if Dora knew one thing to be true, it was that in one week's time, if their mother had her way, there would only be one of them left standing. She couldn't let their mother know that she was helping Malina. If the Crone of Light's End was left with the weaker version and their magic didn't bind together as was planned, then she would kill whoever was left.

As it was, there were two things Dora was sure of: she wouldn't let her mother turn her into a monster and she wouldn't let her sister die. What the Crone didn't know, and didn't need to know, was that Dora had already set her own plans into action.

"Well then, girls, what do we have?" asked their mother once their cups had been drained.

Dora inconspicuously held her breath as Malina handed over her mug. It was all Dora could do not to send hexes her sister's way as Malina's hand trembled as she handed over the cup.

Regardless of whether the tenor in her daughter's handling of their fine porcelain bothered their mother, the woman showed no mention of it. Instead, she narrowed her eyes into what was left of the brew. The tea was a combination of green leaves, ground up apple seeds, and rosemary. It had energy, clarity, and wisdom; it was a brew made to let the truth be out.

Dora remained still, quietly breathing tendrils of smoke in and out of her nostrils. Had Malina done as she asked? Had she buried herself far, far down in the depths of her soul and thought only of fire?

"Hm," said their mother, her features softening just a smidge. But whatever she'd read in the remains of Malina's tea, she didn't declare. At least not right away. Instead, she turned to Dora as she set down one mug and reached for another. "Let's see what yours has to say, shall we?"

Dora took another deep breath through her nose as she sat up taller. She worked hard on her appearance, as she mustn't ever look as if she were plotting or pretending.

"Ah," said their mother with a firm shake of her head. "Here we are again, Dora." She took a second to reach for Malina's mug before setting both results under her child's nose. "What do you see, child?"

They'd been at this for weeks, but it wasn't until last time that Malina finally found her strength.

Dora stated what she'd said just three days ago.

"Smoke and embers."

"Whose belong to who?"

"The smoke is mine and Malina's is trying to grow into fire."

"Yes," answered their mother.

It was Dora's turn to kick her sister under the table, for Malina's expression did not at all match what she'd managed to conjure. The girl looked terrified.

"I'm sorry," Dora whispered.

Their mother wasted little time plucking the wand from her side and slashing it through the air. Dora cringed as the skin along her cheek parted and blood began to seep from the wound.

As her hand found her face, their mother stepped back from the table. "What did she do wrong, Malina?"

Dora just stared at her twin, willing her to answer correctly.

"She—She apologized."

Again, the woman slashed the air, adding a second future scar to Dora's small, innocent face. "And what did you do wrong, child?" she asked Malina.

This time Dora's sister took a second to gather herself before stating, "I stuttered."

Their mother picked up their mugs and threw them to the ground.

"One week away, girls. We are one week away from your test and all you're bringing to the table are theatrics and feces." She bent down and glared at each of them equally. "I would not embarrass me if I were you. I will have a strong witch in my company, or I will have none at all. Are we clear?"

Both girls nodded before the woman exited the cottage, leaving them to themselves.

As soon as they were alone, Malina jumped over to Dora's side and picked up her wand, preparing to help heal her face.

"No," Dora said, shooting out a hand before her sister could do any such thing. "Leave it."

"Why would you want to keep the pain?"

"Those who have walked through fire need proof so that they can show the world how strong they once were."

Malina dipped her chin and raised her brows. "I thought you wanted me to be the strong one."

Dora reached for her twin's hand and squeezed it. "I don't want you to be, I need you to be."

All Dora had ever wanted was for her sister to survive and maybe even have a shot at having a life of her own. But even through all her brilliance, Dora was but a child. She saw the here and now and never thought about the future.

Those scars, they were just the beginning.

In the years to come, they would still be a part of her, though no one would see them. The only thing she would dare to keep would be her name, but by that time, the Dora the old village had known would have been long forgotten. Not buried, but not important. Not a friend, maybe your foe . . . just like she'd planned.

Makayla

"Ms. Wood, would you please take the stand?"

I stood from my seat, my hands coming to smooth the fabric of my wool pants. They were gray with tiny white specks, and they paired perfectly with the long-sleeved white button-up I'd chosen to go with them. The outfit was, of course, from The Boxed Professional. I'd received the outfit months ago but had saved it specifically for a day grand enough to meet the expectations of he, she, or they who had designed each component.

The cuffs had red stitching carefully crafted into the satin fabric. It was late eighties meets the late nineties, and it was fabulous. My white wedge Mary Janes topped off the outfit in such a glorious way that I would have expected applause if I was anywhere else in the world. Anywhere else but in this room surrounded by wooden walls, as brown as the paper bag my mother had given me not that long ago to find my breath.

I stepped up onto the carpeted stair and prepared to lay my hand over a book I didn't care one way or the other about, but what was waiting for me was something a little different.

The clerk walked forward, his face covered in a porcelain mask, and he was draped in periwinkle robes. His hair was strikingly white and as he lifted his arms up—the object I was to swear upon in his hands—I noted his skin was the color of wet sand.

"Do you, Ms. Wood of the house of Wood, declare to the court that everything you are about to say is true? That you will hide nothing and reveal all."

My hand appeared before the blade in his hand. The Sword of Avalon. And I placed it over the golden silver blade.

"Ms. Wood?" the clerk asked when I said nothing. "Do you declare the truth?"

"My name is Makayla Wood—"

"Do not forget the entire title."

Rage filled my veins at the interruption. My hand squeezed the blade so hard that blood began to seep from the cracks made between my digits. "*My name is* Makayla Wood Koehaias, also known as Lala Abberwockey Koehaias of the Erwain descent."

As if no blood had been shed and this was all a very normal occurrence, the clerk remained still. "Do you declare the truth and nothing but the truth, so help you Loral?"

The sword was in my hand and my blood was now inside the sword. It was speaking to me, like a little child who had just been fed from its mother and was making the time to show how grateful it was.

Fly. Fly. Fly.

I shut out the nonsensical whispers that had come from the blade and looked from my bleeding hand still clenched around the sword and up to the masked clerk. "I'm not supposed to be here."

"I thought this is what you wanted," said the clerk.

I turned and looked out into the courtroom. It was empty save for two birds, perched on Helene's statue.

"How did that get here?" I asked, pointing to the likeness of my aunt, now forever etched in stone.

"We thought it best that your family be present."

"Where are my mom and dad . . . my other parents? Naomi and Philip."

"I believe they are in the middle of a snorkeling tour at the moment," stated the clerk.

"Right," I said.

Toby had them taken away. They didn't know a single thing about what had happened, about what I'd seen in so little time. Of the queen I'd become . . . or not become. I suppose for that achievement to happen, I would still need to slay Sebastian Loral, even if the majority of his kingdom wanted him dead as much as I did. Even if he wasn't the actual problem, but a symptom of the evil that had infiltrated the land like an enchanted farm of termites.

My eyes deviated to the chair that was supposed to be the stand. It was a throne carved from white marble. Without affirming my truth, I stepped away from the clerk—taking the sword with me—and had a seat. Before me, there were no sparkling waters, no Pool of Aeslin. No, that water source had been drained along with all the magic imprisoned inside it. What swam before my feet was something a little different, and just as odd.

"What am I looking at, sir?"

The clerk folded his hands behind his back and stood straight as an arrow. "The beyond, my lady."

"What beyond?"

"Makayla."

I looked out into the courtroom, following the voice of my birth father. As I did, one of the birds transformed into the lanky person of Tanker Abberwockey. He was dressed in a sunflower jumper and silver sandals.

"Hi Dad."

He smiled, the only way Tanker Abberwockey would be able to smile. "It's time to come back to reality."

I shook my head. "I don't think I can do that."

"You have worlds depending on you, daughter."

"I don't think I can handle what happens when it's all over."

His ear met his shoulder. "You're too smart for your own good. Do I send a thank you or a hexogram to Naomi and Philip on behalf of those brains of yours?"

The Sword of Avalon was getting heavy in my lap. "I didn't get it from them."

Tanker stood taller, his eyes a little glossier than they'd been a moment ago. "You can't keep hiding in here, Makayla. Maude gave you that book of spells for survival, not for you to get lost in your own mind."

"This is a dream," I lied.

He shook his head sharply. "No, it's not. You're not asleep, and you're not in your right mind. This is not the moment to escape, Makayla. Not when you are in a strange new land."

I deviated my jaw while turning my gaze away from my faery birth father. "It's lonely there."

"You are with Petal and Sir Toby."

I returned my attention to him. I wasn't sure if I should be thanking him or regretting knowing him. The beyond was right there—but a drop in the bucket away.

"What happens if I fall?"

Tanker sighed. "I think you know."

I caressed the Sword of Avalon with a single finger; there were no longer any traces of my blood on the blade or my hands. "If it leads to where I think it leads, then why would Maude have had this sort of spell in her Book of Shadows?"

Tanker reached forward and placed his hands over the nearest chair. "There is no such thing as a perfect flower. Sure, from all purposes it may appear to be the most beautiful creation known to all creatures, but perhaps when it smiles it is missing a tooth, or when it sings it quickly becomes known to everyone around it that it is tone deaf—"

"In the world I knew for a very long time flowers didn't do or have those things."

He wrinkled his forehead. "That you knew of."

"Right," I whispered.

"Even if everything about the specimen was perfect, its roots could be frayed." He shifted his feet. "What I'm trying to tell you, daughter of mine, is that everyone loses their spark from time to time, and your birth mother was no exception." He paused, waiting for me to lift my chin in his direction. "Once a spell is written in one's book, it is not a proper thing to remove it. The pages tell the story of the magic maker; to alter one's book is to tell lies about their life."

I lowered my eyes to the opening at my feet. It wasn't frightening in the very least. If anything, it was more terrifying to think that I had no qualms about slipping away from what seemed like an impossible life and into—what? Nothing. Everything.

"No," I said softly, still gazing into the churning clouds, and if I concentrated on it hard enough, the falling stars. "I can't fall."

I returned my gaze to Tanker, only to find a gentle smile lining his face. I waited for him to speak, but what else did he have to say? He and I both knew I didn't have it in my heart to give up—to fall into the abyss of wherever this portal would take me. I'd been a fighter ever since I was born.

Still, there was something I couldn't fathom facing. Not just yet.

My lashes fluttered. "*He's* different now."

Tanker closed his eyes only to reopen them. "Yes." He knew of who I spoke.

"I saw my king murdered only to reappear moments later."

Again, his response was limited. "Yes."

And then came the words I'd never thought I'd say out loud. "I don't know what I'm doing."

Tanker just continued to smile. "Welcome to life, Makayla."

And then he was gone.

Soon after that, the walls began to drain of color, the portal at my feet began to shrink and the clerk at my side started walking towards his exit.

"Wait," I called to his back.

He turned around and faced me. His eyes looked wet from where they peered at me from behind the porcelain mask.

"What happens now?"

"The same thing that happens every time, Miss Makayla. You will return to where you were before you came here."

"And then what?"

He shook his head. "I don't know. It is not my journey."

"I still don't know what to do."

His wet eyes fell to the sword in my lap. "The answers are right there. I believe it's already begun speaking to you. Open your ears, my queen. Open, hear, heal."

And then he was gone.

The room fish-eyed, then shifted to the left and right as if it were a painting someone was tipping back and forth before me.

"Makayla."

The courtroom had emptied out. It was only the sword and me.

"Makayla—hey."

Bits of light began to tear through the court and my retro business attire became the purple dress I'd gotten from Esmerelda Waukine, back before my best friend was taken and made into an elf, and before my other best friend was transformed into something malicious.

"No . . ." I whispered.

I wasn't ready to go back. Why couldn't I just stay in the courtroom forever? Or at the very least for just a few moments more.

As the room I was using continued to tear apart, the throne I sat upon became Petal, the sword returned to where it had gotten accustomed to hanging by my side, and Toby's arms warmed me as they hugged my middle.

"Do you need me to land, Sir Toby?" Concern overfilled Petal's voice.

"No," I answered in his place, the cool wind slapping my cheeks as we flew through the purple clouds. "I've returned."

Toby didn't hesitate to squeeze my back tighter to his chest and I tried not to let the moisture find the corners of my eyes. His lips sent shivers to meet my heart beats as he whispered into my ear, "Are you sure you're okay? That was the third time."

I turned my cheek into his lips. "Yes. I'm sorry—I won't do it again."

I could feel it in him, the need to say more. To try and fix the fraying edges of every cell in my body. Even my wings had been shaky lately. When he pulled back and let the subject go, I loosed a breath.

The Great Beyond was a spell I'd come across before Cee-Cee and Jeremy and I had been transported into Garlandia. The description read like a dream, but Maude's notes had described the spell as an escape. I'd never used it, but I'd stared at the words long enough that the prose had become embedded in my mind. The photographic memory didn't hurt, either.

During our first day in this world—in this place lit by the same sun but through a purple filter—I'd been unable to deal. Too much had happened; my eyes had seen too much. And so I left.

The great beyond didn't appear until the second time I was in the daydream spell. This was the first time I had seriously contemplated falling into it. That alone was probably enough to tell me something. The spell should be left alone from this point on. Sandpapered from my mind like a stain on wood.

I turned my attention back to our surroundings.

The purplish hue of the noon day sun should have been an impossible thing. Just as the violet dirt and blue-green native grass should have been but an imaginary drawing in a child's room filled with plush animals and wooden blocks. This world was a brother, sister, or cousin of Garlandia, as well as the only world I'd thought I'd known for the first seventeen years of my life. Worlds but a finger's slip away through the transparent curtain that kept one from the other. Like the emotions we keep housed in these vessels we call bodies.

Was any of this real? Was I still in Lucy Armstrong's office, my heart beating too fast—my breaths hard to capture? Was I but an anal-retentive git, as my birth father once called me, just lying on the floor, dreaming, while the ambulance came to revive me?

No. It was far too vibrant and alive to be a delusion, and these sentiments floating around inside me had far too much texture to be synthetic or part of a fictional prose. This heaviness in my chest, like a storm brewing somewhere too far away to know how disastrous it had the potential to be, was something that couldn't be imagined. Only felt.

There was no need to question why this dark cloud had seeped into my heart and was now spreading through my veins with every beat of the organ's drum. Marrying my king had stitched the tear in my side back together, but the reunion couldn't possibly fix what laid before me. I had Avalon's sword. I alone was to figure out where it was leading us and where we could find further instructions pertaining to taking down the disease that had infiltrated Garlandia over two hundred years ago, taking first Sebastian Loral then the freedom of his people.

Why couldn't I just be a normal girl planning a birthday party?

I'd turned eighteen yesterday. I'd gained another year around the sun as Toby and I hung onto Petal's mane while her hooves left the ground and she flew over the endless ocean belonging to this world. I hadn't mentioned it; it seemed far less important on the scale of things that ranked higher than the stars in the sky. Since I'd found my wings again, I hadn't heard mention of a single birthday celebration. I wasn't sure if Garlandians cared about birthdays (I mean, they did live forever*ish*), or if it was just the wrong time to be happy about anything. Either way, I hadn't said a word about it.

"Town below!" Petal shouted, craning her head back so we could hear her over the wind. "We're going to start the descent!"

Toby's arms tightened around my waist as the Pegasus's wings slid out to the sides, gliding us slowly down from the height we'd taken. I hadn't seen even a hint of a town below; then again, I'd been 'wandering' for much of the flight.

Sure enough, as we lowered beneath the pink clouds for the first time in hours, a beach materialized below, and though it sounded far too human of a description—a beach town spread out before us.

"Where are we?" I questioned.

Petal once more threw her head back just enough to answer. "I am at as much a loss as you and Sir Toby, but one truth that transfers between the worlds is this: if you are searching for treasure, then there is no better person suited to your inquiry than a local."

Toby leaned in and whispered in my ears. "She means to say that she has no idea where we are, so we'll need to ask around."

"Right," I whispered too softly for even my ears.

I wished so badly just then that we *were* treasure hunters. Tanned shoulders and sun-bleached hair. Fly by the seat of our pants free people who had found an old, weathered map leading us to this land. But we weren't, and if anything, we had the treasure with us in the form of the blade that had brought us here. It had taken us from Garlandia into this world encased in violet. It had taken us on a three-day journey where we took turns between the land and sky, searching for any claim to life. We'd survived from currants, coconut water, and ninny fish we'd caught off a small island on day two.

Petal's hooves hit the ground a few times, our heads jolting back rudely and dust swirling round our shoulders, before her wings disappeared and a swift canter became a gallop, which then turned into more of a strut. She'd landed just before a wooden sign made from beechwood; the name of the town burnt into it. Lorelei.

"That's an interesting name for a beach town," I said.

"Not when the king rules from under the sea," Petal retorted, dipping her nose and coughing. It had been a long journey. Days on her back with very little to eat. We were

smelly, dirty, and though we were surrounded by purple water
—thirsty enough to drain a lake.

"Slow down for a minute," Toby said. As soon as she did,
he jumped off, holding out a hand for me to take. When we
were both on solid ground, he added, "We are just fine
walking from here. You've carried us long enough."

Petal didn't argue.

As we walked over the gravel path we'd landed upon, the
gravel turned to stone and the town began to open before us.
Since we'd arrived on the top of a hill, it was easy to see down
and into Lorelei's layout. There were roads and houses—
shops. And if I wasn't mistaken, there were even surfers
stretching out their boards over the gentle waves.

Toby had grasped my hand as we walked down the hill,
the Sword of Avalon swinging softly by my side. As we tread
down the hill, he pointed his free hand in the direction of a
small hut of a building hugged by two larger ones.

"We should start there—looks like a pub."

"I will break away before we get there if you do not mind,
Sir Toby. I would like to find a trough, and if I am lucky enough,
I may be able to come across some answers in my own way."

"Of course," Toby answered.

But just as Petal was about to turn in the opposite
direction, the sky darkened to a midnight-colored pansy, and
the wind picked up around the three of us, causing our hair to
whip around our faces. The clouds fell from the sky, shielding
our view of the growing waves. Petal whinnied and my wings
began to creep up behind my back—my fingertips gracing the
handle of Avalon's sword.

"Keep your hands off it," said a voice from the impending
fog that had rolled in over the course of mere seconds.

My hand froze just over the sword's hilt.

"Who goes there?" Toby shouted over the emergent wind.

The face of an elf—or something like an elf—walked through the purple and blue haze. His body was covered in a sheath of seaweed, his skin blueish-gray, and his hair long and black. It was his teeth that really got me. Sharp . . . like the miniature mouth of a shark.

He didn't answer, instead, his eyes—like green beads made from glass—fell to the sword hanging from my belt. As my jaw unhinged, my words choked up somewhere between the back of my throat and where they needed to flow outward. Petal hissed, and Toby took a fighting stance.

"I wouldn't do that if I were you, cousin," the man said, his speech clearly directed at Toby. I hadn't even noticed as my king pulled out his wand. And then, before this ocean elf was able to heed another warning, the mist cleared just enough to reveal an army of elves—or *some* elf-like species— ready and at the wait for whatever they were here for.

And then a realization found me. As a slow gasp fell from my lips, I knew. They weren't here for us as much as what we'd brought into this world. And they weren't elves . . . at least not entirely. They were mermaids.

$%$ 3 $%$

Dora

The sun had just laid to rest and the moon had found its shadow. Dora looked more like a witch than ever; her entire body swathed in a deep velvet hooded cape, the color of the deep end of a lake. It wasn't a matter of being recognized—no one came to the sacred ground. It was rumored to be laden with curses. Dora was prepared to disappear quickly if the moment called for it.

The air had a metallic quality; it stung the nostrils and caused the heart to pick up its pace. Ever since Garlandia had fallen to this new disease, those with any intelligence had figured out that to fight was suicide. Therefore, one had better learn how to fly, even without wings. Dora had been around long enough to have figured out how to get away in a pinch.

It wasn't just the vampires that had infected the land, not even that of the occasional Morcai that was rumored to have been seen. Though she had not ventured that way, she had on good authority that the castle had now been infiltrated by witches, followers of The Robes. Their numbers weren't large enough to qualify for an army, but there were more of them than there should have been. The war between Dankas and Lanakes was still raging, however it had been taken to only the soil; the castle was now witches' domain. Everybody else had either run away or they were hiding in the forest.

The travel ban no longer existed, but that didn't mean there weren't still plenty of forest citizens biding their time. This was home to so many; it was of no surprise that both faeries and elves refused to leave until there was absolutely no other choice.

As for the jesters, it was only the ones who had sided with the Robes who hunted in the forest. The ones under the instruction of the queen's first real knight—Foxfire—they were finding nourishment from other sources. The Robes took charge of the castle during the day and let the guard shift to the Minx dragons at night. It was a first, for as long as Dora had lived in Garlandia, never once had dragons been brought to the grounds, let alone the Bathar Minx. The Bathar creatures did not fare well here; it was too humid for one (Minx preferred a dry climate), and it was simply not their world, for two. But the witches did not care about that. The beasts stood for power. The Robes, if anything, were after only that.

Dora had taken a chance—leaving Anastacia, or the *priestess*, to her own devices. The tea she'd brewed should have started taking effect shortly after she left Lantern's Edge. If that soul was as susceptible to Dora's sleepy time concoction as she was in her previous life, then Dora could expect to arrive back home to one passed out witch. The worst thing would be if Anastacia did not drink it and chose to skulk behind Dora's heels as they scampered over the forest floor.

But Dora had been heavy handed with the honey and passionfruit—two things the priestess had never been known to turn away. At least back in the days when she'd still been eating some *regular* food.

Dora peered under the hood of her cape, veering slowly to the side as if she was rooted to the shallow opening between the blackened trees. Nobody in Garlandia knew the real story as to why the witches claimed this ground as sacred. As to why it was to be left alone. Only Dora knew that it wasn't truly haunted, for any traces left behind from the Bahidicaras were contained. Well, until recently.

A snake caught by the moonlight slithered up the trunk of the nearest tree, capturing Dora's attention, until the presence of another body shifting onto the grounds behind her caused her eyelids to fall. Her fist grappled for the velvet robe hanging around the glass vials that never left her belt, and an icy breath left her chest.

She reopened her eyes to find that her visitor was sheathed in the obscurities that came with night. Though she could not see who it was who had discovered her secrets, she was brutally aware of one thing.

"You are not fey."

"No."

The voice was like cyanide. It stung the insides of her ears for moments afterwards. Dora had been in character for hundreds of years; this was the first time her limbs dared to betray her as they began to shake.

The fluttering messenger had arrived just that day and its message had been tricky: *Meet me at the sacred ground once the sun has found its coffin. I would be your soldier, Dora of Light's End. That is if you will have me.*

Tricky, yes. Did this someone intend to truly stand by her, or were they using her for personal gain? One thing was for sure, whoever this was knew of her past. Otherwise, they wouldn't have used her mother's title when addressing her.

"H—How did you conjure the butterfly?" It was usually something that was only done by the wand of a faery. Or by a witch who was hundreds of years old.

"It is amazing what you are capable of once death finds you," said the shadow creature.

A small cry left Dora's lips as the figure stepped out of its silhouette and onto the sacred ground. She recognized him immediately, though his skin had grown the color of fungus since she'd last set her eyes upon his flesh.

Dora's chest rose as she struggled to portray the strength she'd used to stay alive all this time. "Who are you here on behalf of?"

His chin moved to one side while his eyes veered to the other. "Why do you assume I am here in place of someone?"

Her thoughts came to a screeching halt. "If you are not, then tell me. Why are you here?"

The stranger offered a question in place of an answer. "Where is he?"

"Who?"

"Loral." His voice cracked as he stated the name.

Her voice was barely more than a whisper. "Why do you care?"

Loral had become nothing more than a fugitive. Considering what was now running free over the Garlandian grounds, the king now posed about as much of a threat as a runaway toddler who had been maddened by its inability to express its frustrations. He wasn't only wanted for his betrayal—the way of the land would not allow a new ruler to sit upon the throne until the last was terminated.

Dora's back stiffened as her visitor continued to stand eerily still. When he spoke, she lost her breath. "The flowers don't just speak with their mouths; they send messages through their roots. Visions of the past . . . of the present. The future. I've seen it . . . how this land was both saved and destroyed by your magic."

The sensation of a soft rain coming down to tickle the flesh overcame the witch. "You've been shown." Two questions chased one another around in her mind: how much of the past had he seen and whose side was he on? And then a third grew from the first two . . . could he tell which side she was on?

He said nothing. Had he been reborn with the realization that the teachings of his people were born of nothing more than a cult? Or did tar still coat his heart? As they stood apart over the sacred ground, the snake continued to slither around the tree.

Dora dared to take a step in her summoner's direction. As she did, her skin changed color under the pale moonlight. Ivory became light ebony. Ever so slowly, she pulled away her hood, a pair of golden eyes peering from what had once been Garlandian blue. It felt good to be herself.

Her visitor remained committed to his lack of expression. "How come you never changed your name?"

Her head slowly swayed from left to right. "It was all I had left."

The two stood in silence, the moon washing over them like the sun finding fresh snow the day after a heavy storm. Finally, the one with the ability to call on the butterflies, walked forward. Dora rooted herself like the trees she envied as he reached out a pale hand and let his too long fingers grace the scars on her cheek.

"It was the Crone who did this to you."

"Yes."

"And the Crone was your mother."

"In blood, perhaps. But I've never thought of her that way." Dora blinked and returned her glamour. The moment her hair returned to blonde and her skin paled—the second the scars were hidden—his hand fell away. However, the chill he'd instilled upon her skin stayed.

"Dora of Lantern's Edge, I summoned you because I want to know."

She waited, but when he said no more, she asked, "Want to know what?"

"What is my role?"

She raised her brows, her eyes averting back and forth as though it was an obvious thing. "I was under the impression that you were fairly confident about where your game piece was settled over this board."

His hesitation was palpable. And then it occurred to her, he was just as unsure about her stance as she was about his. "I was born to lead the . . . village."

His reluctance at naming that village told Dora everything she needed to know.

She inhaled a deep breath through her nose. Normally, during a venture such as this one, she would tap into the mind of her opponent. Figure out whether he, she, or whoever it may be standing before her was being truthful. But it was difficult to tap the mind of the undead. This left her with two options: bow out or trust. She desired so very much to take that first option, but—

"I do not beg, but I *will* ask you not to run, Dora."

She did not hesitate with her reply. "I see you've acquired some telepathy."

He did not muse.

"Fine," she finally stated with a firm jaw. "Your butterfly. Is it prepared to fly through the worlds?"

The soldier didn't flinch. "I don't see why it wouldn't be."

"The fey spend much time grooming the butterflies they call upon. 'Tis not a task to take lightly."

"Rasha will be fine."

Dora's eyes widened. "You've named her?"

"She already had a name."

Her chest lifted. "Okay."

She blinked three times while his eyes remained too open.

"Why would Rasha need to leave this world, witch?"

Tread carefully, she quietly reminded herself. "My associate and I are readying to make our move. But what we seek is no longer in this world."

"You're gathering the . . . other details."

"Yes." It was the truth.

"And then what?"

She'd been careful to allow only that bit of information to surface; the rest was guarded. Buried at the bottom of the lake where she'd once been expected to die.

She chose her next words carefully. "What do *you* think?"

His stony expression didn't waver. "I think you're the daughter of one of the most hideous priestesses there ever was." He paused as if waiting for her to reply, but not even a muscle in her cheek moved out of line. "I think you have more power than she ever could have dreamed of having on her own, and I think it would be frightening to have to go up against you."

"But you would."

"Again, Dora, it was what I was bred for."

"To go up against me?"

He no longer needed to breathe to survive, but still, he raised his sharp nose up to the sky and inhaled deeply. "I was bred to remove any and all threats."

Both were quiet for quite some time. Finally, Dora dared to speak. "You've a decision to make, it seems. I shall leave you to it." She folded her hands together as the bottom of her cape began to dance along the ground. "We will communicate through Rasha. I have met her; therefore I know how to find her if I need to correspond with you. And if you need me, send her."

"You do not fear that I may get in your way?"

She kept her gaze steady. "My fear was taken away a long time ago."

From there, Dora began to fade, the fibers of her cape pulling her back to where she belonged.

"Wait."

She held onto the energy surrounding them over that cold, black ground. "Yes?"

"Is it true what they're saying? That Makayla Wood yields creation?"

She pierced his eyes with her own. "Yes."

He seemed to chew on the inside of his cheek. "And she has the Sword of Avalon."

"That she does," Dora stated matter-of-factly.

For a moment it appeared as if he was trying to remember how to smirk. "You're not going to tell me a single thing, are you?"

"No, I am afraid not."

"Very well," he said, with a slight lift of his chin. But just as Dora began to creep away, he stopped her once more. He very slowly held out his arm, then pulled up the sleeve of his tunic. All that was there was pale, bluish skin. "I used to visit my mother when I was a young boy; I thought maybe she would want to see me . . . she never cared to. She was vile and she marked me. The evidence of what I lived through is no longer there."

A wave of something akin to being maternal washed over Dora as she looked down at the boy's arm. Boy? Man? Monster? That was something she couldn't yet define. Ever so gently, she reached for his wrist and held it in her hand.

"Your mother scarred you too?"

"Yes," was all he said.

"We aren't that different after all."

The next part he said in a voice that could've been covered in tears, if only he knew how to cry. "Perhaps not."

An easy smile found Dora as she patted his arm. "It may not be visible" —she raised her free hand to touch her cheek — "but your scar is still there. It is part of you, part of your story, and no one can take that away. No magic can undo it. That pain is yours. It is your strength."

For the first time since they'd arrived in this place, his expression changed. He appeared almost lost. "Is that what feeds you—revenge?"

"No," she said with a shake of her head. "Retaliation is what those like your king swore by. I am simply trying to put things back the way they were before my head was shoved under the water. I am fulfilling the orders given to me by my—"

Footsteps interrupted her final words. A jingle jangle.

Vampire jesters. They were not afraid of the sacred grounds for they were already as cursed as one might hope to be. And if Dora was sure of one thing, she knew that if they were this far out into the brush that they were only out to satisfy their hunger.

Dora held tight to her maybe friend, or possible tricky enemy for but a moment longer. "Rasha will be our tie. Goodbye for now."

A mere second later she was gone.

Dora slipped the hood from over her head as she walked through the enchantment between the frigid grounds of the dark forest and the memory she'd inhabited for years on end. A very small weight had been lifted from her chest, for as eternally wicked as that moment could have turned—it hadn't.

She was just sliding her arms out from her cloak when *that voice* cut into her like a blade that had been sitting in fire.

"Where have you been?"

Dora lifted her chin just in time to find herself caught in the spider's web. "Out."

The girl blinked then turned her head to the side so slowly that one could almost hear it creak. "Out?"

"Yes." *The damn tea hadn't worked.*

The girl yawned.

Or perhaps it had worked, and for just long enough.

Dora retrieved her wand from under her robes and held the tip of it against her hand, carefully depositing a thick black glittery gel into her palm. Once there was enough to deliver, she showed it to the girl. "Dark matter, from the burrow near the last or first frozen lake in this land. We may need it where we are headed tomorrow."

Anastacia held her gaze over the shadowy substance for long enough to grind her teeth. Then, much to Dora's relief, she lifted a hand to cover her mouth again before turning back towards Lantern's Edge.

"Fine. I'm going back to bed. I'll see you in the morning."

"Yes," Dora replied, siphoning the dark matter back into her wand. She kept it there for emergencies. You never know when you might need something heavy to distract the observations of others.

She waited until the girl was two steps into the memory to follow suit. That had been lucky and there was no room in the future for luck. To hesitate at all would be suicide. Dora had to move forward with the intent to conquer. Otherwise, this world and all the others would be more than at risk. They would inevitably fall to destruction and eventually dissolve.

"We leave first thing," the girl said, mainly because she needed to have the last word. She hadn't changed a bit.

"Yes," Dora answered. "As soon as the rest of our party arrives, we will be through the folds."

The girl's pink hair swung around her face as she turned to face Dora. "What?" she asked, short and snippy.

Dora's relaxed expression didn't budge. "I've already mentioned that we have a guard. You didn't think we'd be traveling light, did you? Where we are headed, two will not do. We will need a body for each element. Otherwise, survival will not be in the cards."

The priestess narrowed her eyes. "Gloria found her way there alone."

Dora shook her head. "Gloria found her way to the pass, but if you think she traveled through the Enclave Mountains with but her broom and wand, you are mistaken. She'd have hired a guard to get her to her destination." It was a believable story.

The girl was silent for a moment longer, no doubt dissecting Dora's challenging statement. Finally, regardless of whether she believed her or not, the girl allowed a sharp tongued, "Fine," to slip between her teeth, the caps of which had already started to look more predatory than usual. "In the morning, then," she said, once more heading for the cottage.

Dora only nodded. She knew better than to add the final note. She had but one shot to do that and that time was far from before her. Instead, she tucked her wand into her side and prepared to head into the cottage as well.

She would watch over the priestess as she slept and retrace the steps she'd been drawing out for years. She would not sleep; she had not been able to rest ever since her little head had resurfaced from that black lake.

Your eyes shall not rest until the roots are pulled from the ground and burned to dust, not until that dust is evaporated and the air is stilled. Only then will you be granted the ability to turn off.

They were not words to live by, they were instructions. Orders that Dora had been waiting over two hundred years to fulfill. She was closer to the end than ever, and all she could think about as she followed the body of the young girl—two souls inhabiting its shell—was what it would be like to sink not only into sleep after all this time, but what it would be to simply not exist any longer.

4

Makayla

We'd gone from royalty to prisoners; these soldiers had wasted little time escorting us to what I'd heard one of them refer to as the temple of the sea. It was a platform of white marble that appeared from the ocean like an underwater spaceship. The oceanic soldiers—the mer—stood around us in their most human form (which would not have been enough to keep the fear from the hearts of the people I grew up around), and in each of their hands was a staff worthy of impaling the greatest of white sharks.

All I could think, even through all the madness shuffling its way through my thoughts, was whether this served as Lorelei's court room. Were there lawyers in this world? Or at least something like that. Was there justice? Or was this environment just as corrupt as Loral's?

Petal, Toby, and I were on display in the middle of the floating platform. We'd been corralled onto this thing as a group, the rustic blades of more than one merman and maid pointed at our heads. Our audience wasn't only the mer people, but it seemed that the entire population of Lorelei had come out to the shore to check on the disturbance. There were easily a hundred or more beach bums, some with pointy ears and others with wings, standing around over the light purple sand. And out in the vast distance, as far as the eye could see into the purple ocean, were dragons—dare I even say it: baby dragons. I'd only realized they were young after watching one of their mamas fly out from behind a large grouping of trees and swoop up her babe from the tides. The beasts were red, blue, green, purple, iridescent—they were all colors and every color, and they were magnificent. I couldn't believe we had yet to see them, considering we'd already been traveling for days. Then again, if they were both land and sea creatures, that would explain it. For this was the first time we'd been near enough to a large body of land.

I attempted to draw myself away from the amazing spectacle and redirect my attention to our captors. They were all so similar in shape and stature, but there were a few subtle differences. Like humans, their facial features differed from one to the other; and though their skin was predominantly silver and blue, there were variations between light and dark. Some had long dark hair that hung in beaded braids, while others had locs. Their clothes were made from seaweed, magically wrapped around their body. Just like humans, some seemed more aware of fashion than others. The man who I'd decided was their leader—the same male who had first spoken to us through the mist—wore seaweed pants and a seaweed buttoned up shirt. A seasuit. All their feet were bare.

With my wings at attention—not that I'd have been able to fly away with the force field encasing the platform—I attempted for the fifth time since we'd been ushered onto this thing, to clear up the misunderstanding.

"Will someone *please* hear us out. This sword was given to me by Aeslin, a witch who—"

"This sword was stolen! It belongs to this ocean," proclaimed a merman a few rows behind his leader. He made a fist and shook it in my direction. "No faery or elf should have been given this blade, and it should have especially been kept away from those who consider themselves witches."

"It wasn't in the hands of any of those creatures. It was *given* to Titania!" I shot back with my teeth bared. I had far too much on my plate; this entire ordeal was nothing more than an unnecessary nuisance. Speaking to these aquatic aliens was like trying to communicate with a brick wall. They weren't listening, and when they did speak, all they did was throw out the same accusations.

"The sword belonged to Avalon," stated the same mer.

I rolled my eyes. "She's dead."

There were several gasps from the people of the sea.

"We do not use that word," the mer leader stated.

I half expected Toby to push his arm out before me and come front and center to attempt and clear up this mess, but he had stayed a shoulder behind me from the moment we'd been corralled onto this thing. In fact, ever since he'd returned from the dead, he'd been . . . *different*. I turned my cheek so that I could meet his eyes for a solid, salty breath. He did nothing more than reach for my hand and give it a squeeze.

Our conversations had been light during our travels through this new world. We'd all seen enough horror and heartache in and out of that castle before leaving Garlandia that we had been just fine treading silently over the waters and through the clouds via Petal's back, but Toby had stressed at one point that this was *my* journey. This sword had found *me* and what happened next needed to go through my soul. He was but a guard. A keeper . . . Titania's keeper.

My feet remained rooted as I turned back around to face the soldiers once more. "Okay, whatever. Avalon has simply returned to the eth—" I stopped. This wasn't working, I needed a new strategy. I crammed my eyes shut and pleaded with the ghost of Titania to help get me through this. And then, out of nowhere, the words came. My eyelids fluttered back open. "The Bahidicaras." Every single one of them gasped. "Good, so you've heard of them." I didn't wait for the backlash, instead I spoke over the chatter rumbling through the group of sea creatures. "These cultists caused the gods and goddesses to send down their children. Avalon and Titania were amongst these hidden warriors." I held my breath as I sorted through my words. "Sometime between passing from this life to the ether, Avalon gave Titania her sword. This sword," I said, gently tapping the hilt still tied to my side. "I don't know why Avalon did this, and to be honest I'm still learning about this taboo group of otherworlders also referred to as the bad village, but I do know for a fact that this sword was used against *our* faery queen and her mate; and that it has been waiting for me to find it and bring it back here." I scanned the fierce faces of those around us, searching for some kind of recognition that what I was saying wasn't complete bullshit. However, no one even dared to breathe. At least the rumblings had died down, and if anything, I finally had their attention.

At long last, there was movement.

"The sword wasn't forged here," came a voice from the crowd. Female. Very slowly the crowd parted, and a thin mermaid thoughtfully made her way towards us. Her silver cheekbones were so sharp that it was as if shadows could fit inside. However, her teeth looked normal, not like all the other rows of mini shark teeth directed our way, and her pixie haircut was a striking white. My thoughts wandered for a split second, and I wondered if she'd had her teeth filed so they looked less offensive. Also, she almost immediately reminded me of someone, but before I could think too hard on that, she spoke again. "The sword arrived with Avalon. As legend states, she was not born, but delivered. It was the sword that cut her heart in half and eliminated her ability to swim with our kind, for that sword" —her gaze shot to the blade then back up at me— "is the only weapon that can take out a deity or a deity's offering."

The words balanced over my tongue for a moment before I set them free. "A deity's offering?"

The mermaid sunk in closer to where Petal, Toby, and I were grouped together in a prisoner's keep. "Your Titania and our Avalon were never born of our worlds; they were dropped from the sky like tears. The sword was given to Avalon so that when the time came, they could use it to take out the enemy then return to where they belonged. Only the sword would allow them to reform into their highest energy." She paused and the only sound came from that of the waves sloshing just below the platform. "Our Avalon, her heart was pierced too early. The sword taken."

"That may be the case," I offered, "but regardless of what you believe, Titania didn't steal the sword. It was given to her." At least that was the story I'd been told.

The world stopped breathing for a millisecond as the mermaid lowered her right ear to her shoulder. Her eyes narrowed and I could almost hear her thoughts churning.

I was confident, that if anyone might try and save us, maybe it could be this mermaid. I dared to move a toe forward an inch. As I did their leader tensed.

"You just said that Titania and Avalon were dispersed in the same way," I said, caution laid over me like honey. "Children of the gods, here, to save these worlds from a sinister practice that was getting out of control. They were on the same team." My lips came together as I warned my heartbeats to calm down so that I could recall Aeslin's message, for she had told us to come here, and she wouldn't have done that just to send us to our graves. "I am not saying that your Avalon wasn't murdered; I cannot speak to that. All I know is that the faery queen was in possession of this sword and that she was aware it had once belonged to her cousin."

"She stole it!" A merman spat out from about three rows back.

My gaze immediately deviated in his direction. "Titania had no reason to steal it. As far as Titania knew, the enemy had been defeated and she was ready to rule Garlandia with her king."

"That isn't right," the mermaid said, except her words weren't damning. The way she said it, she seemed to be trying to sort through the details as much as I was. "If Titania had been aware that the mess she'd been sent down to fix was cleaned up, she would have reached back up for the stars and asked them to take her home. She would not have remained for love; Gaia would not have allowed it." The mermaid fixed her gaze tighter around my own. "For her to be setting up camp could have meant only one thing: that the threat was still very much alive."

Over the sloshing of the violet waves, a searing cry erupted from one of the baby dragons playing in the sea. As his mother flew out to grab him, I let my fingers brush against the hilt of the sword. Almost immediately I was brought back to my latest daydream—sitting on the stand, hovering before the great beyond with Avalon's sword resting over my legs. It had spoken to me then . . . it had a voice. And that's when it hit me.

Very carefully, so none of the sea creatures would jump forward, I wrapped my sweaty palm around the hilt, and I pleaded. The sword had only spoken to me once, and only in that spell. What it had said had been borderline nonsense, but still, it had a voice.

Please. If you can help me, now is the time.

But nothing happened. Nothing apart from the leader taking a step closer.

"Remove your hands from that blade," he seethed.

"Give her a chance," the mermaid with whom I'd been speaking said before he'd even finished his last word.

The leader's cheek snapped in her direction. "Layla, can you not see that this faery is stalling? That she is plotting to take what's left of our Avalon and use it for personal gain?"

I couldn't help myself. "Wait—what? That's not at all what I'm doing." I pointed at the mermaid named Layla. "She just said it herself, that the weapon was sent with the offspring so that they may return after they'd fulfilled what they'd been sent here to do! It was never anyone's but theirs. It doesn't belong here, it doesn't belong anywhere but with—"

"Silence!" he demanded, shooting a very unkind look in my direction before returning his attention to the mermaid. "The sword belongs with the sea."

Oh my goddess, it was like the definition of insanity up here on this platform.

"This *sword* doesn't belong here," I repeated, stabbing a finger down at the platform. "I haven't come to this place to return it—at least not without answers." As heat rose to my cheeks, I accidentally gripped the blade too harshly and it cut into my hand. "Shit!" I exclaimed, pulling away my palm only to find that my blood was seeping *into* the sword.

Fly.

The whisper found my ears and my ears alone. I raised my gaze to meet the leader's. His eyes were hardened, and he looked like he was about to pounce.

Fly.

My brows furrowed without my permission, but there was

no time to dwell on uncertainties. The soldier who was closest to us, this nameless entity who seemed to be leading this force, said to whoever was ready and willing, "Take it from her." His knuckles whitened as his grip tightened around his own weapon. "Take it from her then kill them all."

"No," said the one mermaid who had dared to walk forward and address us herself.

The merman's head moved so slowly in her direction. "Back in formation, Layla."

But the mermaid stood taller, the seaweed wrap encasing her body growing into a fitted suit guaranteed to turn more than a few heads at the right catwalk. Her sharp nose turned up in the air and she gestured to the sword by my side with her chin. "No one here has it on any authority that Avalon's wishes were for the sword to be kept here. If what this faery is saying has any veracity, then we should be pondering over her speech. For the Bahidi—"

"Stop." The merman more than glared at her. "What has gotten into you? I won't be spoken to like this, especially not by the likes of you."

For a moment it appeared that we were no longer the attraction. Every bit of attention was gathered over the shoulders of this leader and to whom he was busy sneering at.

Layla—and what a beautiful name that was—didn't show an ounce of fear or regret as she repeated, "Fine. Take the sword. What's stopping you?"

As the two stood off face to pale blue face, the water under our platform began to grow agitated, as if the gods themselves were stirring this giant pot we called earth.

The leader sliced through the air with his staff before setting his sights back on me, then stated stiffly, "We are the rulers of the sea and land. Our voice is the end all, and I am the speaker of our company. Anyone who dares stand with these fugitives can rest assured that their fate will match theirs." He then held out his staff to the nearest soldier and once it was out of his hands, he squared himself off with our party of three once again. Toby and Petal leaned in closer to me as the merman began to strut over to where the three of us were on display. When next he spoke, he reached his left hand forward. "As previously stated, the sword belongs to the sea, and my people and I *are the sea.*"

"Luke," said the mermaid called Layla.

Their leader hissed, snapping his head back at her. "Quiet, you're already on thin ice." And then he began reaching once more for the sword that hung around my belt.

"I beg of you to see reason!" yelled the mermaid once more.

Though the gossip around the platform was growing as steadily as the waves, no one else dared stand up to their leader. I, in fact, had chosen to remain still as well. Not because I didn't intend to fight, but because I instinctually felt rooted. That, and the sword was, like, talking to me. It kept telling me to fly. Didn't it understand that I would if I could?

The waves had grown so unruly that as soon as Luke was within a foot of where Petal, Toby, and I stood, a large splash jumped onto the platform. Still unfazed, hypnotically almost, the mer leader reached his pale blue hand out—his eyes hungry and teeth bared. But just as he got close enough to touch Avalon's sword, a white flare, like lightning, erupted from the blade and hit him in the chest, knocking him to the ground.

I yelped and fell back against Toby, just as Petal's wings flew out to the sides and knocked out at least five sea creatures. Staffs rose as merpeople scattered out of formation —a cluster of them coming to their leader's side. In the scuffle there was but one who didn't move, who kept her eyes on me like molasses coating bark. And then, in the time it took me to blink, she tapped her foot before falling through the platform.

Petal whispered heatedly to Toby and I. "Get ready to fly, Miss Makayla. Sir Toby, take hold of her hand."

The rest unfolded like flares going off one after another. Waves grew around the platform, and it began to spin and rock. The sheer forcefield that stood as a barrier between us and the sea was no longer visible. The soldiers standing around their leader began to lose their balance, while those who had been leaning over their commander swayed and fell —their staffs rolling into the angry waves. Seaweed outfits breaking away and floating like debris over the tides. Legs becoming tails.

Amidst the chaos, Luke—his hands grappling for anyone within reach—lifted his head and tried to offer a weak command. "Don't let them go!"

But it was too late, our wings were lifted.

Toby held on to my waist as Petal and I lifted over the heads of the soldiers, our wings fluttering in place only for a second before taking off for land. We'd gotten no further out than a few hundred yards when a green, iridescent dragon sidled up beside us—Layla perched on its neck as if she was riding a giant horse.

"Follow me!" she yelled.

There was no time to question the bizarre circumstances, or to place bets on whether she was with us or against us—or take into account that her face eerily matched that of an elf who had once upon a time spit at my feet. There was hardly time to swallow the panic that had set in around the beating of my heart.

I turned to Toby, who simply nodded, then called to Petal

whose wings were thumping loudly next to us, "Into the wild we go!"

Petal nodded, and from there we flew into and above the forest that separated Lorelei from the sea.

5

Makayla

The dirt was somewhere between dark purple and red when our hooves and feet finally met the ground. We landed in a clearing just large enough for the dragon Layla was riding to fit between the trees. Trees that reminded me more of the forests I'd seen in the human world. They were silent—I couldn't believe I'd become accustomed to having them speak—and they were taller, thinner. Just another alien race awaiting us along our travels.

The mermaid slipped from the dragon's scaly back to the earth as swiftly and gracefully as a ballerina, then patted its back. "Thank you, Shell. Off you go now, back to your herd. Take the back way so as not to be seen."

The dragon nodded its heroic head then lifted from the ground and was off before any of us had even a second to take note of the fact that an actual *dragon* had been flying alongside us. Truly, though, I was most likely the only one exceptionally taken by the creature. Petal and Toby had seen such beasts before. In fact, it had been a baby dragon that had lit Toby's home on fire when he'd been but a child.

As the magnificent creature rose through the trees and its wings spread out once more, my gaze still strapped to its underbelly, I directed my next line to Layla, "They have names?"

"Of course they do," she answered. "Why wouldn't they?" I lowered my attention back to her, observing as she pulled at the seaweed wrap that served as her clothes—tearing at the sleeves until they were gone, exposing a set of thin, pale blue arms.

"I don't know," I replied, my brows lifting. "Did you name them or—"

"She was named by her mother, obviously," Layla retorted, absentmindedly. "Now come on, my people don't often leave the sea, but they will for that." Her gaze shot to the blade hanging from my side before lifting to meet Toby's stare, then Petal's. "We stay on foot—they'll be expecting us to fly to get there faster."

"And where is there?" I asked.

"A place they know not of, but they'll be tracking us any and every way they know how. I know a certain someone who can help," she said, before turning east and setting foot through the trees.

I looked to my king who had stayed eerily silent through all the day's adventures. He did nothing more than reach for my hand and take it into his own, then smiled. I sighed, then followed our mermaid ally, alongside my husband and his Pegasus.

"We can trust her, right?" I said quietly.

"Yes," Toby answered. Hearing his voice was enough to light up the organ beating steadily in my chest. Even though he was right here with me, I still somehow missed that second heartbeat he'd placed in my chest while we'd been separated.

Petal leaned down and chomped on some native grass, chewed it noisily then swallowed. In a very unladylike manner, she spit through her teeth then added, "The lady of the sea is not coded like the others. She stands out of formation. She is to be trusted."

Layla turned only her cheek back at us as she continued to walk over the forest floor barefoot. If it bothered her, she didn't show it. "All accurate, except the lady part."

Petal coughed. "Excuse me. I did not mean to offend."

"Seriously?" she said, shooting an interesting look Petal's way. "You'll have to work harder than that to offend me."

She continued marching forward, the bark on the long, skinny trees darkening the further into the forest we got, and though it was nearly an impossible thing to notice, as there was not much light, the air had a sparkling quality. Like fog, yet not fog. More like mist made from glitter.

"It's enchanted," Toby mused, as if reading my mind.

"The whole forest?" I questioned.

"Yes," Layla said, from up ahead. "Those who live here do not like strangers crossing into their wood. Most would pass through here without seeing any trace of life."

"Most?" Petal said.

"Yes. Don't worry, I know the combination to get through it."

This new acquaintance had her quirks. I wanted details, all of them; but I could sense that to keep from getting bitten I needed to tread lightly. Also, I was still caught up on this dragon business.

"Are the beasts—are they telepathic?"

"What beasts?" Layla said without turning around. She easily made her way over two trees that had fallen, one toppled over the other like it had ended its life to be with its companion.

"Those like Shell."

She was quiet for a few beats. Finally, she said, "In general, I suppose you could call them that. But really, they only communicate with those who know which way they like to move."

"What?"

Toby snickered and I sneered at him.

Petal cleared her throat then said, "She's implying—I'm sorry, are you male or female?"

"I can breed," Layla answered, "but I don't associate as just one gender." She paused and seemed to be assessing the terrain before us. After a long pause, she added dryly, "I am woman, hear me roar, but please don't disregard the masculine that lives inside me as well."

"Right," Petal said. "Well then, what Layla is saying is that a dragon communicates with movement, whether it is its own species or a different breed. But dragon dancers are rare, for only a chosen few understand how to translate their routines."

"Their routines?" I repeated under my breath. Then a little louder, I stated, "Like a dance?" Before any of them could answer, my thoughts shifted back to Helene. "You mean they speak to dragon dancers?"

"Yes," both Layla and Petal said together.

I looked up at Toby who shot me a sly grin and squeezed my hand tighter.

"Does that mean that you're one?"

Layla, her gaze still locked somewhere out in the distance, answered in a cool manner, "Do you really think that Shell would have allowed me on her back otherwise?"

"I wouldn't kno—"

"Silence," she said quietly but with force as she held up her arm in our direction.

I bit down over the side of my cheek. Being silenced wasn't something I enjoyed. Still, as much as I wanted to debate her demands and question her authority, she'd saved us. Petal and Toby trusted her, and she seemed to be following some sort of direction. Or searching for it in any case.

Finally, after minutes of standing over thin ice, she finally jetted out a finger. "There! It was just there. Did anyone else see it?"

"See what?" I questioned, as I stood on my toes and tried to search through the spiky bushes through which she was pointing.

"Was it the rabbit?" Petal asked.

"Yes. Though it's not a rabbit. Come," she said, waving us along with her. As we strutted forward, cautiously, she began clicking her tongue and making another sound comparable to a bird chirping.

"What is it?" I whispered to Toby.

Before he could answer, Layla said, "It's a pooka. It changes its appearance so often, I never quite know what to look for. Plus, it's ornery, so we have to catch it."

"It's a goblin," Toby said into my ear.

"Don't call it that—it hates that," Layla spat over her shoulder. She was taking large strides through the brush. Overgrown bushes with bright pink and purple flowers were popping up all around us.

Toby rolled his eyes, then continued. "The creatures can change their appearance at will or become invisible. Many fey communities use them as guardians."

"Its name is Robert," Layla said in an agitated tone.

Petal snickered.

"Is something funny?" Layla asked her.

"No." Petal cleared her throat for the second time then gave both Toby and I a humorous look. "Not at all, my manly woman friend."

Layla simply shook her head and muttered so softly that if it hadn't been for the silent forest, we wouldn't have heard her at all, "Damn these old-fashioned souls." Then loud enough not to be mistaken, she added, "You know, things are changing. We can be whoever we want to be nowadays."

"Oh, please don't mistake me for being ignorant, Layla," Petal said, speaking out in her own defense. "I am all for diversity. We've all just been locked down for so long . . . One forgets what the colors look like when they aren't all faded away. But just so you know, your shine is quite beautiful. And handsome."

The mermaid was quiet, tracking the pooka for another minute or two, before she finally spoke back. "Thank you."

The reply was short, and if I wasn't mistaken, maybe the closest to sweet that Layla was capable of being. However, the sincerity of the moment faded just as quickly as it arrived, when all of a sudden the bushes to the right of us shook and a bit of white and yellow light shot up into the air before diving back into another bush to the left of us.

We froze. Petal's right front hoof balanced just a foot over the ground, my breath caught in my lungs, and Toby's hand became a smidge tighter around my own. My jaw began to unhinge, but before I could utter even the slightest fragment of speech, Layla's arm shot back in my direction as if she was hyper aware of any and all movements.

"Don't . . . move," she said, before deliberately moving one toe forward. Her next breath was geared at the pooka. "Robert? I know it's you. I've come to order some pies."

Silence followed, and I was beginning to think we'd all decided to keep from breathing. I was just rehearsing the images of what a pooka or goblin could possibly look like when the bush it last dove into shook again. This time, the creature showed itself. Ornery or no, it sure did appear sheepish.

"Hello," Layla said, her gaze falling over the golden light that had now taken the form of a rabbit standing on its hind legs. The pooka simply remained in its spot. "I need to order ten pies from Aunt Sue at Tapioca and Burch."

The pooka made two twitchy noises in the back of its throat and shook its head.

Layla didn't waste any time reacting. "Wait, what day is it? Thursday. Shit—I need to order seven pies then."

The pooka's nose moved up and down quickly three times before the creature exploded into diamonds of light, each particle disintegrating into nothingness right before our eyes. My mind was working at warp speed, trying to keep up with the illusions I was experiencing, when Layla turned her cheek to us and motioned with her head for us to follow.

"Robert's gone and become transparent, but we don't need him any longer. Come."

Petal was slightly ahead of Toby and I as our feet crunched over the remnants of sticks and other forest droppings. As we allowed her to stay a shoulder ahead of us, I asked, "What did it do? Nothing looks any different. I thought the pooka was supposed to let us in."

Before Layla could answer, Toby beat her to it. "I think it did."

And that's when it began to happen. It was much like the first time I entered Garlandia—as soon as Mort had decided to let us in, even though my mother's baked mud cakes were easily the worst dirt pastries known to gnome-kind. It hadn't been that long ago, really, that I'd been standing before that mailbox, my wings tied up behind my back, and the world had shifted between the street I grew up on and the one to which I'd been born.

Except this wasn't quite the same. If anything, it was quite the opposite.

When I'd entered Garlandia, the world became the forest. Here, as we walked forward into this secret realm, the forest floor changed to sand, and paved roads appeared along with the sound of light traffic.

Trees faded, and in their place, cottages—much like the structures we'd seen in the town of Lorelei—before the mer people had stolen us away to their sea platform like we were savages. A male faery, but not like any faery I'd ever seen in my neck of the woods, rode by on a purple scooter. He was lanky and tall, folded up on the small motorbike like a paperclip. His ears were long and pointy, as was his nose, and his wings were so sheer I had to squint to see that they were there at all. About a block up three children were having a game of keep away with an orange ball. Surely they weren't *human* . . . but if they weren't, their appearance could've fooled me.

"What is this place?" I muttered, soaking it all in. We'd somehow found ourselves along a sidewalk, businesses to the right of us and the street to the left—more small buildings on the other side.

"It's a secret district of Lorelei," Layla said matter-of-factly. "It formed long ago, when things sort of" —she paused — "took a dive. This isn't a place one might find on a map. One must know about it to enter, and even then, it is very protected."

"So it's a safe land," I supposed out loud. Like Raton.

"I guess you could say that," Layla retorted. "Goods are traded in the main township, but this is where the humans and the Reefs prefer to live. Over the years many other species have joined the village."

"Reefs?" Petal said, shock lining the edges of her voice. "I was under the impression that the Reefs had all but died out."

"No," Layla replied, numbness surrounding the word like an aura. "That was but a rumor spread for the sake of survival."

By this point, my head was spinning. I'd taken to using the clomping of Petal's hooves to keep my heartrate settled at a steady pace.

"What are Reefs?" I asked.

"Ancient fey," Toby said softly into my ear.

Layla paused from her fearless stroll through the village to pierce my eyes with hers. "The priestess found the Reef's quite tasty. Anyone with wings like theirs while she was living, fled."

I'd just unhinged my jaw to ask *all sorts of questions* when Layla pointed to a sign a few feet away. A chalkboard announcing the day's special: Lavender Honey Boba Tea and Rosemary Muffins.

"This is us," she said.

I knew it was stupid the second I said it, but still, the words fell from my mouth. "Is this where we're picking up the pies?"

I couldn't see her face, but I just knew that Layla was rolling her eyes. "There are no pies. That was the code to get in." And then she turned her heel sharply into the coffee shop, which looked like any other hipster dive in small town America. Just before she was all the way in, she popped her head back out. "Sorry," she said to Petal, "you'll not fit. Do you mind waiting?"

"Not as long as you buy me a muffin," said the Pegasus. "Though I was truly looking forward to pie."

Toby reached out and patted his old girl's face. "We'll buy you twelve as soon as we get the chance."

Petal nearly purred.

"There's a fountain around the corner," Layla stated. "You may drink from it."

Petal nodded, then began to back off so that Toby and I could follow Layla.

"See you in a few," I said to Petal just before turning into the shop.

Cool air and the scent of butter and sugar, along with fresh chopped herbs, hit me in the face as we entered the small facility. It was inviting and the notes of something both new to my senses and familiar stung my nostrils. I knew what it was even before I saw the signage for it: Fresh Licorice Root from the Garlandian Hills.

I immediately thought of Maude.

And then I saw her.

Blythe. At least that's what her name tag said.

Her lavender hair was trimmed into a pixie cut. Her skin was the color of Toby's, and her ears were just as long. Just like the faery we'd seen on the way in, she had a pair of sheer wings trying to hide behind her back. Her eyes were violet and as they fell over my shoulders, an invisible sharp rain seemed hit the bare skin around my face, neck, and arms. Toby's hand fell from my mine, and he drifted a step behind me as the faery's gaze centered in on Layla before traveling to the blade hanging from my leather belt.

"Dammit, L," said the faery with a heavy sigh. "What are you about to get me into?"

The bag I'd been carrying for so long—the one that hung crossed over my body and contained the only two things that meant anything to me anymore: the secret stone Toby had made for me and Maude's spell book—it grew heavier, and I could have sworn the stone warmed from inside of it. But I never took the chance to check, for before anyone could utter a single added word, my knees buckled, and I fell to the ground. Out cold.

6

Lantern's Edge

Malina and Dora were off the hook from reading more tea leaves for the time being. There were other things their mother needed to deal with, such as growing her coven. She already had more followers than most places of worship, but she needed more. She *desired* more.

The 'meet and greet' at Lantern's Edge was sponsored by the upcoming test Malina and Dora would be participating in. Before each test, the coven did this: reached their claws into the witch population and combed through them, searching for new followers. More energy to add to their growing power. But it wasn't just witches any longer who had been seeking out Forest Peak. Any creature, great or small, yearning for a new adventure, had entered the realm of Lantern's Edge, and the priestess gladly took anyone willing to pledge.

The news of the coven was spreading near and far, via

speech, wands, and wind. It was from this chatter that sent a certain pair of sisters to Dora's cottage that day. There was much discussion about what was happening over by Lantern's Edge. Much talk that this was no ordinary coven. Even the gods had gotten involved, or so some had said.

Dora's wound refused to heal, and she had no mind to magic the gashes on her cheek shut. Out of all the potential pledges who entered their humble home that day, it was but one set of sisters who took the time to come and question Dora about the incident.

Unlike many of the souls who came to this end of the forest, the energy coming from the sisters was whole, and they seemed fair and neat. Nothing like the *creatures* who flocked to their mother as if she'd been born of stardust.

"Oh dear," said one of the sisters. "Look at this tiny goddess. She's been opened up." The witch bent down and brought her delicate hand up to fit under Dora's chin. "What has happened, little one?"

Dora desperately desired to reach for Malina's hand and pull herself and her sister into this woman's chest. There was a feeling there—one she'd not felt before. If she'd been let out into the world, further than the lines her mother had firmly rooted into the earth, the barriers she and Malina weren't to cross (for the world outside of Forest Peak was not for them) she may have understood what she was feeling. A maternal instinct from someone bred to save. A witch who understood the oath some magic makers took upon their adolescence; harm none.

"Sisters," Dora stated, looking from one to the other. She may have had a young face but still she knew— "You do not belong here."

"Of that much we can clearly see," whispered the one hanging around the side of the other.

The one cupping Dora's chin with her hand, speaking

softly to the little witch, stated, "We've come only because we've heard whisperings. The grounds are beginning to darken around this patch of forest. Reefs are going missing. And more recently, humans."

"Humans?" Dora speculated.

That wasn't their mother's style; the priestess had only ever really had a taste for the magic that ran inside of the Reefs. However, she had been known to drain the occasional squirrel when she was incredibly hungry, and the *things* she was creating could very well have acquired certain tastes. Who was to say their practices hadn't gotten as far as feeding from humans?

"She said nothing of that," Dora cursed under her breath.

It was not surprising, though, that more Reefs were disappearing. It *was* surprising that the ancient fey still wandered towards Forest Peak at all—what, with all the faeries gone missing. Then again, a broken soul is a broken soul and as they lived and breathed, there were Reefs at Lantern's Edge that very moment. Dora knew that if the Reefs who had sauntered into their home in curiosity of what this coven was offering didn't pledge, they still would not leave. Instead, their screams would echo against the stars later in the night. Honestly, Dora wasn't sure which fate was worse.

Clearly taken aback by Dora's last words, the witch nearest her clung even closer as she asked, "Who said *nothing of that*? Your mother?"

Dora swallowed and the woman finally removed her hand from her chin, bringing both appendages to the young girl's shoulders.

"I suppose that is what one might call her," Dora answered. The sisters each reached for the gaze of the other. "She, um . . . she feeds from the earth, amongst other things."

A dark cloud may as well have fallen upon them. The

sister holding Dora's shoulders spoke gravely. "What do you mean by that, little one?"

Dora shrugged, her gaze roaming to find that Malina was in the corner of the kitchen, her back to a wall, watching as the priestess shook the hands of the new batch of followers she'd invited into her home.

Heat reached into Dora's tear ducts, but she'd been trained not to cry. In response to what she'd just said, she attempted to clarify what she'd meant about her mother feeding from the earth. "Just that, blood and energy feed her . . . but not like the creatures of the night. It is a decision to do so, not a need. At least it didn't used to be." The small girl's eyes flitted back and forth, catching sight of her mother. The priestess still hadn't noticed that she was speaking so closely to visitors. She and her sister were to be nothing more than ornaments. Punishment would find them otherwise. In a much smaller voice, one beneath that of a whisper, Dora stated, "As if she's been running dry for days on end, she drains the soul of the earth as if it is a lake."

"Castonia," Dora heard the other sister whisper.

The one holding Dora's shoulders closed her eyes as if she could shut off what she'd just heard. Then, returning her attention to the child, she said rather quickly and with a warm smile that seemed to be dripping with hesitance. "That's your sister over there, yes?"

Dora followed the witch's hasty gesture, then nodded.

"Perhaps the two of you should come with my sister and me. We have an extra room and I've been told I make a fine meal."

An array of fireworks went off in Dora's mind and for the smallest half second, her heart warmed. But it wasn't ever a dream that would come true. Not only would the priestess hunt them like rabbits, but she'd already ensured that Malina and Dora's feet would only be able to trek over the lines she'd written above the soil. They weren't her daughters; they were her ingredients. And she wasn't willing to lose them.

"I—we can't." Dora lowered her head until her chin hit her chest. "I'm sorry."

The witch named Castonia looked up at her sister. "What are we to do?"

Dora observed as the other one placed a hand over her chest. "I am unsure, sister. This is far worse than we could've imagined. We must go inform the others—help the humans, and whoever else needs safety, migrate away—"

"Excuse me."

A searing blade slashed through Dora's flesh, across her middle. And this time she would not bleed. This time, it was only a feeling her mother sent to her so that she would mind her manners, so to speak. Or not to speak—that was truly the intention. The child became stiff and backed away from where Castonia was kneeling before her. The good witch rose, as she and her sister stared bullets into the woman known to all as the priestess, or as some had been starting to call her, the Crone of Light's End.

"Madame," said the witch who Dora had yet to find a name for. "Thank you so much for opening your door. We've heard much about your organization."

"Yesss," said the priestess. "And from where do you hail. You and your—"

"Sister," answered the witch. "We are here from the other end of the forest."

"Ah." The priestess roped her bony knuckles together in front of her stomach. "You are ruled by the fishes."

Even Dora knew it was a derogatory punch in the direction of the sea creatures who reigned over the beach town. Their territory reached as far as the trees before Forest Peak; where they lived had yet to have a ruler, though the priestess was working her way to the top swifter than a panther before its next meal.

The sister who'd been speaking with Dora's mother, pursed her lips together. "Yes, the mer rule our land and we've never had issue with the arrangement."

The priestess curled her lips into a wretched smile. "I've been told Pontus has sent his daughter to watch over the sea and surrounding land. My following has even mentioned that she plans to trouble herself with a trip into our wood. Seems unheard of, for she is the same age as my girls. Have you heard of such a tale?"

"Her name is Avalon," said the one named Castonia. "And she will direct her energy where it is needed."

"Avalon," repeated the priestess, as if it were a sweater that she was sizing up to try on.

Dora could have cut the tension arising between her mother and the two sisters with a hex. Part of her wanted to reach for Malina and run off with the witches, cursed to remain on Forest Peak ground or not—but the other part of her knew it would only end in death. The sisters would do all they could to aid in getting her and her sister to safety, but they were not just up against a dark cloud. What the priestess brought into this ring was more like a tsunami laden with waves of fire. Then again, the only way out *was* death. At least that was what she assumed.

"I do believe we've outstayed our welcome, sister," said the unnamed witch. "'Tis time we depart." She laid her eyes over the priestess. "Thank you for the invitation."

"You're most welcome, sisters," purred the priestess, before she took Dora's shoulders into her grasp and pulled her in as if she cared for her more so than a mere magical prop. "Please, tell your fish friends that I said hello."

"And who may we address you as?" questioned Castonia.

The priestess narrowed her eyes, homing in on the title

she'd been trying out on her followers, but she was stopped before she could finish her speech.

"Yes, we've heard you called that, madame," said the other sister. "What we seek is a name."

"Oh," said the priestess, chuckling softly under her breath. "For that, my dears, I will need pledges."

Dora willed the sisters to look down, to catch her shaking her head softly. But it was an unnecessary thing. For the sisters were too smart to fall for such trickery. The villagers who had joined the ranks of those in this coven had a tendency to break away from the shore and move closer to the dark wood, and there had been some who had attempted to keep both lives going. The witches, fey, and elves who had pledged themselves to the cause known as Light's End had started to appear . . . different. Like this woman before them, it began with their bones. Sharp edges, black smudges around their eyes. But unlike this *priestess* who stood before them, it had worsened. Billy Squire, a field elf from the edge of town had lost all his golden hair and his spine was beginning to bend. He'd been such a nice young elf, but he was already losing the grasp he had over his farm, and it was rumored that he was soon to be moving permanently closer to this part of the forest. Tents were going up, even hermitages. The sisters had seen it for themselves as they flew close to the ground, their gazes craned over their broomsticks, and now that they were here, they were aware that it wasn't just loose talk that had been spreading like wildfire. This was truly a cult. The gods had been correct to shed their tears.

The unnamed witch reached for her sister. "I think we'd better think on it. But please, do something about your daughter's face. The poor dear looks as though she's been bleeding for days. Last I knew only a hex from a wand could make a wound fail to clot."

Dora felt a fist come around her heart and squeeze it until

it could not beat as the sisters slowly backed away. This time it wasn't from her mother . . . it was just a side effect of having emotions.

The sisters freed themselves from the grounds known as Lantern's Edge and used their brooms to get overhead quicker than a finger snap. It was only then that Malina sunk away from where the new recruits were roaming from room to room, shaking hands and preparing for the night's bonfire where the Crone would introduce them to what she called the tunnel. Of course, it wasn't really *the tunnel*, for she had no rights to such a majestic thing. But she was very talented when it came to theatrics and delivered a very convincing testimony.

Almost no one ever left after that.

"Crone," came the little voice of Dora's twin.

Their mother, still gripping Dora's shoulders so stiffly that if the child's skin hadn't been covered by a dress it would have been punctured, peered down at the little girl as if she carried fleas. "What is it, Malina?"

"What *is* your name? You've never told us."

Dora's eyes shut of their own accord. If there was one question you didn't ask—

"Don't you have anywhere else to be right now?" the priestess barked, causing Malina's eyes to grow and her lips to quiver.

Don't.

Malina looked to her twin, then quickly cinched herself back up.

"Now then," the priestess said, heat emanating from every pore in her body. "Fix these gashes up." She pushed Dora away and into her sister's arms. "We don't walk around with blood on our faces." Then more to herself than her daughter's, she added, "At least not when it is our own."

Once it was just the two of them, Malina pulled out her

wand and began to stitch up Dora's face. "You've left it too long; it will scar."

"I don't care," Dora retorted.

"Who were those women anyway?" Malina asked, running the tip of her wand over the gashes until Dora's face stopped bleeding and the wounds came together and turned pink.

"Our last chance at freedom."

Malina's eyes nearly popped out of her skull for the second time. "Then why did you let them fly off?"

"Because," Dora said, turning to watch their mother greet the newcomers as though they were simply entering the home of a woman hosting a cookie walk. "She would have killed them, and we wouldn't have gotten away."

She'd heard one of the new recruits speaking of this same character that the sisters mentioned. Avalon of the sea. *She came armed with a special sword.* Once the priestess's back was turned Dora took her sister's hands in hers and brought her into a corner unmanned by visitors.

"What is it?" Malina cried out, stubbornly retrieving her hands back and folding her arms across her chest.

"I've had a thought. I think I know how to make this all go away. Unfortunately, it's not going to be able to be a joint effort. Mother will have a witch either way—we can't both be that witch."

Malina's expression dulled. She didn't like talking about this. More than that, she often refused the conversation.

Dora gripped her sister's shoulders and stared into her eyes with urgency. "For once, sister, do not run. I need you to hear me. Only one of us is going to survive that test and that one of us will become *her* witch. Whoever is left will be filled with the other's power, this means whoever is left will be double the witch. Perhaps even stronger than her. The creatures of the sea cannot make it here; the priestess has ensured just that. It's possible even Avalon won't be able to cross the curses. But if *you* can get to the sea and to Avalon, then perhaps—"

"Dora," Malina said, water gripping the sides of her eyes—her chest risen. "Why does it have to be me?"

"Because," Dora said, her own breaths getting stuck in her lungs. "I've spoken to Hecate. I've prayed with my hands together under the moon while mother was asleep. I've asked her to show me the way."

"And—And what does she say?"

Dora's lips sealed together for a full ten seconds before she replied. "She said that when the time comes that you should win."

Malina's little brow furrowed. "She said no such thing. You're lying."

Dora shook her head. "I would not lie. Not about Hecate."

Once Malina agreed to what she'd said, the little girl strolled off in the direction of the front door. The lake . . . Malina was heading off to the lake. As soon as she was alone, Dora peered over to where the priestess was making casual conversation with a couple of Reefs from the edge of Lorelei. They had in their possession a small child. The young fey caught sight of Dora looking at her and waved her little hand in her direction. Dora waved back, trying to conjure a weak smile.

Unable to watch what was happening unfold, she exited the home from the back, trampling out to the stream that ran behind the house. As she stuck her little brown fingers into the water, she relaxed her forehead and tried to calm her frolicking heart.

It was true that she had prayed under the moon, that she had spoken to Hecate. But as of yet she had not heard from the mother of their bloodline. The plan she was forming was hers and hers alone. From the horror that was building around and inside the tree line that they called their own, she was keen to believe there were no such things as gods and goddesses. That Hecate was as much a myth as this supposed Avalon, the daughter of Pontus.

"Still, I beg of you to hear me, Hecate. If you are there, guide me. Give me strength. Aid me in the fight against evil. From this bad village . . ."

And for the first time in so very long, she allowed a tear to free itself from where she'd been taught to hide it. It burned as it fell from her scarred cheek and into the dancing water. And for a second, she thought she saw it sparkle—like it was shining just for her. But if it did, it did so for only a fleeting moment, then swam away.

7

Dora

The sun didn't always shine the brightest into the memory of Lantern's Edge, but that morning, as Dora took her final steps down the old wooden slats that she'd grown up running up and down alongside her twin, she took a moment to appreciate the slivers of white and yellow that warmed her cheeks the instant they contacted her skin. Somewhere, under the glamour, her real color soaked it in. It wasn't long before a cloud moved in, however. Perhaps not literally, but the occurrence did block the sun from over her shoulders.

"*What* are they doing here?"

Dora didn't hesitate, nor did she take the time to turn and face the girl as she retorted, "I told you, we will not be traveling alone." She inhaled a breath of magicked air and took her final step over the faded green and brown grass below.

"I am aware of what you said," the girl mimicked in a snotty tone that matched her face. "What I'm pointing out is that you failed, conveniently I might add, to mention who you hired to aid us in our fight."

"Oi!" Dora hollered out to the two elves waiting for them just inside the confines of the memory. She flew a single pale hand into the air that could have looked like a white flag from any distance. "Stay where you are—we'll come to you!" Then, pulling at her long dress, the crushed velvet cape she'd worn the night before now thrown over her person, she spoke over her shoulder once more. "Trust is expensive. Heime is a longtime ally."

"He is in cohorts with those who share the ring with Makayla Wood," the girl sneered.

"Is that a problem for you?" Dora shot back, all the while still marching towards the two elves. "You've repeatedly mentioned how little the faery means to you in your quest." She could see the girl's vexed expression without having to turn around and lay eyes over it, and that alone brought the warmth of the sun back to her skin.

The girl's face was still puckered as she stated feverishly, "Even if we can trust Heime, why did he have to bring *him*?"

"Bally?" Dora couldn't help but let slip a bit of amusement as she said the name. Without waiting for an answer, she added, "He is Heime's apprentice. Where one goes the other must follow."

The girl snagged Dora's elbow and pulled her back to her as though she was on a leash. Forcing her to look into those dark, soulless eyes, the priestess spoke. "This had better not be some sort of plotting on your end."

Dora remained impassive. "I assure you, I want this over and done with as much as you do."

The girl's grip over Dora remained firm, as did her jaw,

before she finally muttered, "Don't forget who's working for who."

Dora blinked only twice. "Never."

Dora snatched her arm back into her side and motioned for the girl to follow. When they were close enough to the elves, she waved in acknowledgement. "Good morning, you two. Did you have any issues getting here?"

"No," Heime replied with his ever-present poker face. "I remembered the way."

"Good," Dora nodded, before laying her gaze over the young boy who had recently found himself in the position of an elf. "And how are you fairing these days, Bally?"

"Good. Thank you, Dora."

Dora noted how different the boy was since his name had been Jeremy. The magic of the forest looked good on him; she hoped that once this was all over, he would accept it for the rest of his days.

With his hands tucked into his pockets, his attention moved from Dora to her associate, and without pause, he retracted his hands and began to lunge forward to wrap them around the girl. Dora and Heime shared a look as the girl stood as still as one of Loral's stone statues.

The boy paused once he realized that his friend wasn't returning the affection, and as he slowly backed up and studied her face, he cocked his head to the side. "Cee-Cee? What's wrong?"

It was quick, like light dancing over the surface of a lake's ripple, but it *had* been there. *She* had been there. And Dora was near positive that Bally, or Jeremy, had seen it too. Seen *her*. His friend.

The girl combed back a pink curl that had fallen into her eye. "Please don't call me that."

Bally scoffed. "Don't call you what? Cee-Cee?" Her lips

pursed tightly together. "*Okay.*" He turned and looked questionably at Dora and Heime. "Well, I guess that's that."

Dora licked her pink lips before squeezing Bally's shoulder. "We are so glad you are here with us. Now come, let's be on with it. We have a long journey ahead."

"Right," Bally said, allowing Dora to herd him and the others out through the sparkling veil that separated the forest from Lantern's Edge.

No one spoke as they trudged forward, and no one argued when Dora acted like she had caught a rock in her shoe and bent down as if she was digging it out. No one saw a thing as she retrieved her wand from inside her cloak and pointed it at the memory, extinguishing its existence from where it had hovered over this part of the forest for too many years.

From there, they began their journey. As they trekked on, Dora noted yet again how different Bally's posture was from the first time she'd spied him on that day Makayla Wood had taken her friends to the farmer's market for the first time. The boy named Jeremy—his shoulders were usually rolled forward. But as Bally, his shoulders were rounded down and back, his chin lifted. *This is good*, the witch of Lantern's Edge thought to herself. *For where we are going, uncovered shadows could most definitely be the death of someone.*

❧   8   ❧

Makayla

"Makayla Wood, we must stop meeting this way."

What the hell—

"What am I doing back here?" I asked, searching around the empty court room. The same room, in fact, that I'd been finding myself in every time I repeated the words that took me to the Great Beyond. This time, however, I hadn't set any ball in motion to bring myself here. And this time, it was just Tanker and me, sitting in the front row of the jury box. He was wearing a magician's cape and a construction worker's hard hat, which incidentally he'd added some bling to. "Are those rhinestones?"

His smile brightened. "Yes. Thank you for noticing them; took me the better part of a night to glue them on. It just sparkles more when you do it by hand." If we survived all this, I was going to need to get Tanker a Bedazzler. "And per the reason for you being here, had you read the fine print, you may have noted that your mother made a point to warn herself and anybody else who might go after this spell, that this sort of magic has a mind of its own. It's quite emotional. Uh, what some might even label as unhinged."

My forehead wrinkled as I thought over what he was implying. "You mean to say that this place may keep pulling me back, even when I don't want to come?"

"I'm afraid so."

"For how long?" I asked gravely.

He shrugged his shoulders. "As long as you need it, I suppose."

My jaw dropped and I stared at the empty spot where the judge should've been. "Well that—I mean, that's completely nonsensical. I've never *needed* it—"

"That's not what your heart told the spell as you brought it back to life."

I faced my birth father, or this version of him that my mind had created to cope with the things I couldn't handle in the real world . . . or worlds. "So what? Now I am at the mercy of this magic?" When he didn't answer, I scoffed and placed my hands over my knees. "This could be a real problem."

Tanker's hand covered mine and my eyes closed. It was almost cruel that I could feel the same blood that ran through my veins running through his between our skin.

Without reopening my eyes, I asked, "How do I keep this from happening?"

Tendrils from his soul wrapped around me like a blanket. "Well daughter, I believe if you read through that book your mother gave you, you may find that the 'episodes' are frequently associated with your heartbeats."

I wrapped my free hand around my head and sighed. "This is my paper bag."

He leaned in. "I'm sorry, what was that? Say again."

I swiveled in my seat so I could face him. "It is where I come to remember how to breathe when it gets too hard."

"Oh yes, that." He nodded and crow's feet appeared around his eyes. "You're just so smart, Makayla."

"Thanks," I said with a gentle sigh, "but I don't think if I was truly that smart I would have gotten myself into this mess to begin with."

Tanker looked at me as if all the answers were already within my grasp. "Makayla, brilliance doesn't mean you don't feel pain."

I dragged my tongue over my lips and nodded softly. "Except, just now—I wasn't feeling anxious or anything. I was just standing there, in a coffee shop, looking at some Reef faery. This shouldn't have happened."

His demeanor quickly changed—the tops of his wings suddenly erect. "A Reef. Exquisite. How I would love to come across a Reef." He used his free hand to scratch above his brow. "Did the faery say something that made you react in one way or another?"

"I mean—no. At least I don't think so." I decided it was a good time to scratch the skin above my own brow. "Something about the way her eyes set into mine though . . . it was like my dust froze . . ." My words trailed off as I thought about it. Everything had happened so fast that I hadn't had a chance to speculate over the odd occurrence. Suddenly the room tilted, and even though his hand was still hugging mine, I couldn't feel it. And then the courtroom began to fade, as did my birth father's voice as he tried to say something. I focused on his lips, watching the way they moved. He was trying to communicate, but I was being pulled away too fast to catch his speech—something about my wand, and—well, I couldn't hear the rest. And then—

"She's back!"

And oh, the headache that came with waking. I groaned as one of my hands immediately went to the back of my head.

"Banged it pretty good when ya fell," said the faery looking down at me. It was the one named Blythe. My heart raced as I looked back at her.

The Reef, or whatever she was, held up the small jar in her hand. It was then I noticed Toby and Layla were on the other side of me, Toby's hand around mine.

"Told ya, this shit'll wake the dead," the faery said to the two of them.

"What happened—what is that?" I asked, staring at the clearish violet balm she must've put under my nose. I could still smell it, whatever it was. Like angry lilies and . . . urine?

"Scaldron bile. It's super gross but we used to have this human working here who had this condition where she fainted a lot. One of the witches brought it by and it works as well as she claimed it would. Anyway, ya good, queenie? I gotta get back to my post."

"Um, yeah. Thanks," I said, using Toby's hand to pull myself up before gradually coming back up to standing. My legs were a little shaky, but I seemed to have all my pieces still intact. I pulled at each of my wings just to make sure.

"You okay?" Toby whispered into my ear as he hugged me into his side.

"Yeah—it was just—" I met his eyes. I couldn't tell him the truth; we had enough to worry about without my announcing that I'd played around with shaky magic and was dealing with the repercussions of that. "I think my body is just running on empty, you know."

"Of course," he answered.

"Well, we're in the right place for that," Layla added. Strumming her fingers over the counter, she looked to Blythe who had taken her spot back behind the register. "As much sugar as you can throw at us, please. These guys have been through a few days at sea."

"You got it," the faery said, stacking plates with butter rolls and flaky pastries onto the pick-up counter. "Denise!" she called out. A second later a very short female—*something* —came over and climbed up a little ramp next to the counter before collecting her food.

As soon as I turned to face Toby, he mouthed the word 'dwarf.' My eyebrows met the ceiling as I nodded. Apparently, I still had a lot to learn about what other creatures there were living inside these worlds.

🙰

Through discovery, I found that Sip N Sit was the name of the coffee shop we were frequenting. Toby and I sat across from Layla in a mismatched corner booth of the establishment. I wasn't sure if the patrons entering and exiting this place knew who Toby and I were, but from the side glances and heated whispers between pairs of elves, fey, and apparently humans, it was obvious we were offering some sort of entertainment.

I had yet to understand why this mermaid stood apart from the rest, but I had to figure that if she was going to harm us, she would have already done so. Trust was hard to come by these days, and I wasn't about to press Avalon's blade to her throat after she'd saved us from certain death. Instead, I ate and listened as she filled in the holes pertaining to our whereabouts. I'd just learned this town, or safe land, had no name; the citizens felt safer that way.

Since Blythe was our place to stay for the night, and she still had an hour left of her shift, we had some time to spare. Which was perfect, seeing as we hadn't had time to meet our escort properly. As Layla spewed out information, I sipped from the fresh licorice root I'd ordered—and *man* did I need the extra energy. I was seriously starting to drag.

"As you know, Lorelei has been through some things," Layla was saying.

I cocked a brow. "How so?"

She copied my expression, peering into my eyes like she was searching for something she'd lost.

"I've not told Makayla the whole of it," Toby said. He hadn't touched the bear claw or green tea that sat before him. As long as we'd been on our mission inside this purple world, he'd been sacrificing any food we found so that Petal and I would have a chance to refill our energy. He said the spell he'd used to come back altered his appetite. I, on the other hand, had scarfed down an entire cinnamon roll and couldn't stop looking at the beet salad the elf at the table next to us was eating.

Layla's gaze narrowed. "By the gods, Tobias. She carries Titania—she of all fey should know—"

"I've told her about the Bahidicaras, but as for their origins . . . I hadn't yet gotten to that part."

Layla shook her head and set down the orange roll in her hand. Her eyes shifted to mine. "*Here.* It was here that the madness began."

All the air left my lungs.

"How could you not tell her that?" Layla demanded, returning her attention to Toby. "You've been in our world for nearly three days now."

I leaned in, my hand resting protectively over Toby's leg under the table. "We've been surviving. There wasn't a lot of room for storytelling." And for most of the time that we'd been in this world, I'd been absent. One foot dangling over the ledge, teetering over that great beyond. It wasn't my king's fault.

My stomach growled and bile crept up my throat as Layla's sharp eyes sunk into mine. I was still so hungry—I felt sick.

"For the love of sand crickets, go get yourself one of those salads," she spat out, rolling her eyes. "I can hear your damn guts churning from over here."

"But we don't have any—"

"Here," she said, holding out a silver coin.

Normally, I might've refused the charity, but if I didn't get something more than empty calories in my body soon, I wasn't sure I'd make it. The next time I passed out, it *would* be for lack of nutrients. "Thanks," I said, reaching for the coin and ducking out of the booth.

As I stood in line, I kept one eye trained over Toby and Layla. They were whispering heatedly . . . but that wasn't the true reason for the unease pooling in my intestines. Layla's face. It had been eating away at me ever since I'd first set eyes on it. She looked just like—

"Hey again."

My attention was suddenly captured by the faery named Blythe. "Uh, hey," I said, holding up the coin. "Is this enough to get one of those beet salads? They look great."

Dimples grew on either side of her wide lips as she held out her smooth palm. "Yeah."

"Great," I said, dropping it into her hand.

I roped my hands together in front of my stomach. There was a wonky energy stuck between us as she opened the register and dumped the coin in it. So as usual, I made it more awkward. "So, um, looks like you're coming with us?" I bounced up on my toes then back down. After we'd been seated, Layla had explained that Blythe knew the terrain we were headed for better than anyone.

"Apparently," the faery answered back with a playful grin.

"So, um, how did you know who we were?" At least I

assumed she knew who we were, because of the way she'd spoken to Layla when we arrived.

At that, the grin evened out and she looked at me like I had snakes coming out of my head. "Seriously?" When I didn't jest, she shook her head and reached behind her for a fresh beet salad that the cook had made in seconds. "You do know who you are, right?"

My eyes flitted to the corner then back. "I mean—yeah. But I guess I just sort of thought only the creatures of Garlandia knew who I—"

She set the salad down before me then leaned in over the counter, putting her nose mere inches from mine. "*Everyone* knows who Makayla Wood is. Everyone."

"Oh." I reached down and grabbed a beet, tossing it into my mouth. I couldn't wait.

The faery named Blythe watched me, then sunk back down to her side of the counter, grinning even wider than she'd already been guilty of doing. "Shit man, you really are a trip, aren't you?"

I now had a whole mouthful of greens and the tastiest citrusy dressing I'd ever tasted in my mouth. Covering my lips with my hand, I tried to reply, "I'm just really hungry."

She chuckled as she passed me a fork. "Here. You're not in Garlandia—you don't have to eat with your hands."

"Thanks," I said, receiving the food weapon and nodding in appreciation as I began to take a step back. "We'll talk more in a little bit."

She bit down over her bottom lip and raised her lavender brows. I bumped into the next person in line as I tried to turn towards our table. At first the faery boy looked ticked off, but when he saw my face, his expression fell, and he apologized and even bowed his head a little.

By the time I sat back down at our table, I'd taken three

more hefty bites. I lifted the water glass nearest me to my lips and drained it.

"Better?" Layla asked, after I'd scarfed down the rest of the salad.

"Nearly," I said, taking a bite of Toby's untouched bear claw. Finally, my stomach was feeling a little better, and once and for all I was going to ask the question that was feeding from me like a starved Morcai. "If we are going to be working together, I need to know, what made you decide to trust us?"

She didn't even blink. "I assume you've come to know by now that *everyone* knows your story, lost Erwain."

"I'm starting to understand that, yes."

Toby put his hand on my leg. It felt an awful lot like he was anchoring me.

"Well, we have stories of our own here in this world. Unfortunately, they aren't the kind of tales a mother tells her child before bedtime." Her gaze lowered to her bluish hands before reaching back up to give me her full attention. "A large portion of elves have descended from two forces placed on this planet as an experiment from the hands of the gods. Though there are some, obviously, who hail from other lineages, many reflect a family tree that dates back to either—"

"Danka or Lanake," I whispered.

"Yes." Her eyes drifted from mine to Toby's.

"She knows only the barest of details about the two brothers," Toby stated.

Layla nodded before setting her gaze back on mine. "Danka and Lanake were torn from each other when they were very little, placed in separate corners and raised to be rulers. Danka's darkness began to show itself around puberty and Lanake's light, as it was always apparent, only grew brighter as he aged. The brothers ruled separately, and to shorten this narrative, I'll sum it up—there was a great and horrible war. Danka's main drive was to rise to the power of the gods." She paused and dipped her chin. "Sound familiar?"

My voice was a little raspier than I'd intended, but still, I nodded and said, "Yes." What she was describing sounded very much like the goal of the Bahidicaras.

"Long story short, Danka was finally taken down and Lanake became like a savior."

Something pinged in my head, and I turned to my king. "Didn't you say Lanake's soul was absorbed by the Bahidicaras?"

He nodded just as Layla said, "Yes, and believe me, we'll get to that. But for now, this is me answering your question, which to remind you was *why I am helping you*." She waited for my signal to go on. When my chest had slowly lowered, she heaved a sigh and continued. "Danka may have been exterminated, but as is the way of the world, pieces of him were left all around us. The brothers each had many children over the years. As you may expect, Danka's offspring tended to veer towards the dark spectrum while Lanake's descendants ran off in the direction of love and light. A lot of healers have Lanake blood. I'm saying all of this to you, Makayla, because I need you to understand. Even today there are individuals running around whose bloodlines reach very closely to the top of the family tree headed by Lanake and Danka."

My attention was completely absorbed by what she was saying. Hinged forward in my seat, I had to pause and take action to remove the fingernail that had found its way between my top and bottom teeth. My thoughts were reeling in trepidation over where this was going and my stomach was already sour at the thought of it.

"Now then, let me fast forward for a moment. Danka is dead, Lanake is now dead. The Bahidicaras usurped Lanake's soul and then they disappeared, and it is important to understand my wording, because that's what happened. They weren't dissolved—*they were just taken care of for the moment*." She paused . . . waiting for me to acknowledge her. After I'd given a hesitant nod, she went on. "As with any cult, once it was gone, secondhand followers began to come to the surface. Their numbers were small and they practiced with caution. Eventually, as the years began to creep up around them, they decided it was time to make their move.

"They elected a leader. A new priestess. Her name was Savannah. By this time, King Loral had been ruling Garlandia for many years; rumors of his tyranny and untouchable magic had leaked into every world. This interested Savannah very much, for the type of magic he was exhibiting as a protection for himself was eerily similar to the sort of untouchable magic used by the priestess of the Bahidicaras. Still, this was not the sole reason Savannah rode her broom between the lands. She went to Loral because she'd heard of his tracking system."

Static settled into my ears. "I thought every kingdom had one of those."

"No," Toby said. "My uncle is the only one to have had one made."

"It is an absolute invasion of one's privacy and the only reason to have that at all is in the case of genocide," Layla affirmed.

I bit down over my lip. Of course, how had I not put that together in the first place?

"Savannah met with King Loral. She faced him and his throne and she unfurled her plan unto him. Her followers, namely the Robes of Lorelei—"

I gasped.

"Have you heard of them?" Layla asked.

I was sure my face was as pale as Petal's mane. "Yes," I whispered.

Layla flicked her brows to the ceiling. "Savannah and her *Robes*—" She colored the word in a muddy brown. "They believed that the priestess would return, for no one had ever come across any evidence that she'd truly been dissolved. It was their belief that her spirit was still very much alive and that all it needed to reincarnate was a signal. They intended to create a diversion that might allow her to find her way back from whatever dark corner she'd been sent to."

My teeth were clenched and my fists tight as I asked, "And how exactly does one signal to the worst soul *ever* that they should come back to life?"

"Simple. Create someone just as terrible, or at least with the capability to be just as. Seed them, plant them, then wait for them to hatch." Layla took a sip from her water. She appeared thoughtful. "King Loral helped Savannah track down someone who had the capability to help her plant that seed. He had the tools to help her navigate through every world until she was able to find the exact male specimen she'd been seeking."

Next to me, Toby became rigid. Up until that very moment it had seemed to me that he'd always known everything, but his tension suggested otherwise. "No . . ." he said softly. "You're not inferring that—"

Layla raised a single brow. "Let me finish."

His chest rose, but he softened his neck and nodded. I returned my hand to his knee.

"Most of Danka's children didn't survive the war where their father was killed, because for the most part, they fought for him. Still, just because one is born to darkness, doesn't mean that is the destiny they must follow, and there was one son of Danka who didn't fit in with the pack and quietly parted ways with his family when no one was looking." She began to draw circles over the table with her finger, following the invisible designs with her eyes as she did so. "He was forgotten almost immediately by almost everyone. But that didn't mean he wasn't still alive—blending in with society as if he didn't have the mark of one of the most evil rulers *ever* running through his veins. Imagine Savannah's surprise when she found that this very elf lived only but a hop and a skip from where her coven met so often inside the woods just off the shore of Lorelei."

"No way," I gasped.

"Way," Layla said. "From there, it was so easy for her that it was almost cruel. She used her witchy ways to not only find this elf but seduce him. His name was Roose by the way, and he was but a common beach bum. He had a little hut near the ocean where he sold homemade surf boards. He loved the sunrise and—" Her words came to an abrupt halt as she turned away, wiping at one of her eyes as if she'd gotten something stuck in it. Still unable to look our way, she picked her speech back up. "—and the sunset. I think the sunset was his favorite, but he always told me that it couldn't compete with the morning because that was when the scaldrons would sing."

"The scaldrons . . ." I noted.

"Baby dragons," she said, the ghost of a smile on her face. She faced us again but didn't look up. "He could hear them sing. He was a dragon dancer too."

Shit. Where was this going?

"Savannah got pregnant with Roose's child, and when the baby was born, the Robes encircled the child and brought their absolute worst. They used the baby's DNA to summon the spirit of the priestess they so desired to return to this planet; they offered the child to her. They suggested it could be her counterpart, or if she did not want that, that he could be her second. Through Loral, they had an in with the government—this time they could start at the top."

"Wait a second," I said, throwing up a hand. "These witches thought they could summon the priestess of the Bahidicaras simply by offering a baby to her?"

"Not a baby—not by the time the priestess would come of age in her own new body."

"Right," I muttered. "So she couldn't just jump into a fully grown body—she had to reincarnate from birth."

And if this was going where I thought it was, then she had. Apparently, Savannah's plan had worked; if not, this was all a very strange coincidence.

"Yes," Layla said, in answer to my question. "Except no one can manifest the sort of magic the Robes of Lorelei were churning without leaving a scent, and as they weren't that far into the woods, it wafted directly to the beach and into the waters where the mer caught wind of it. The mer council followed the stench of the off magic directly to Savannah's cottage, but Lorelei is small, and word reached her coven before my kind could get to her.

"Savannah disappeared with the child and the Robes dispersed, going into hiding and awaiting the day that the priestess gave notice that she was back." Layla shook her head softly. "No one believed what they'd done had worked. Perhaps if they had, things would be different right now." She sighed. "Anyway, Savannah had enough time to return to Loral's side and deposit her child into his arms. She explained what she'd done and what this child represented. She also told him that the Robes of Lorelei would be keeping one eye on him at all times; that the priestess they'd summoned had the power to undo even him if he didn't agree to the terms, which were: raise the child, make him a knight, and ensure he had a place in line for the throne of Garlandia. Having political pull was a bonus they weren't willing to barter for."

I gulped. I now knew what was coming, and from the sick look on my king's face, so did Toby.

"After her child was delivered, Savannah returned to Lorelei. She was demented enough to believe that the priestess would return and reward her soul for what she'd done. That even if and when the mer killed her, that her soul would be given refuge. She was brought in and given a sentence worse than death, her punishment was a slow rot in a cavern so deep in the earth that not even the demons would be able to find her. But if they thought she was going to go quietly, they were wrong. Remember, she was demented, and as they cursed her, she shouted to them all the name of the father of her child and then she went on to declare to all who would listen as to *who* he was."

"A direct descendant of Danka," I whispered.

Layla's hand came to her face and her thumb brushed over her lips as she said, "They killed him . . . and then they killed one of their own." Layla's haunting eyes raised. "My mother was his mate. She knew his secret identity but never cared. She knew he wasn't evil. She didn't know that he'd been seduced by another female until Savannah announced it to the world; and incidentally neither had he. Savannah had used a charm that left his memory faded from the events of the night she'd used to seed her womb."

"Gods be damned," Toby muttered under his breath.

"Yes," Layla said, her eyes now more than watering. "I came to your aid not only because I believed your story, but because my people had already turned on me. My whole life I've been looked down upon because I'm a half breed, but after they murdered my mother, they put me on probation until they could figure out what to do with the half mer half elf with Danka blood."

I reached over the table and touched her hand. "Oh my god, Layla."

"Just because I am Danka's granddaughter doesn't mean that I am evil. I want to end this as much as you do, even if that means killing my brother."

All the air I'd ever breathed left my chest. "And your brother is—"

"Rally," Toby stated under his breath.

Layla looked to my king. "Yes, I am afraid that is the truth I've been readily unwinding."

9

Dora

The Enclave Mountains were known to travelers only as *morte d'evit*. The phrase was from a very ancient elfin language which translated to death is inevitable. Witches, elves, faeries, and a variety of other creatures had attempted to cross the cracked earth that led towards the sharpened cliffs and summit of those unclimbable hills, but no one had ever returned from their journey to claim that they'd been the first to make it to the top. Still, Dora had seen it in Cee-Cee's tea leaves the day her and Makayla Wood had first entered the memory of Lantern's Edge. The girl's mother, Gloria—one of the last living veins that laid claim to Hecate blood—she was there, in those mountains.

And to win this fight, she was needed.

The Enclaves lived in the northwest, between the worlds. The Garlandian castle was to the east of the forest, so they were lucky that they didn't need to travel past the dragons and cultists. But still, the journey wasn't made for unsoiled hands and feet. They would get there, Dora was sure of that, but it wasn't going to be a cake walk.

"Tell me, Dora," Heime hollered over his shoulder. He was in the lead. Bally and the girl between them while she took the place of the caboose. "Your employer, does he or she know where we are headed?"

Dora kicked at a dead lizard in the path and squinted up at the sky. They'd been walking steadily for a few hours now, and just as she'd expected the sky was beginning to turn on them.

"My employer knows everything," she stated.

Dora had a reputation; she had from the moment she stepped foot out of the sacred ground and into the Garlandian forest. Call it a survival tactic, call it insurance— either way, she'd used it like a second skin from the moment she entered the new realm.

Only the king knew where she came from, and *no one* ever asked who she worked for. There were assumptions of course, but that was where it ended. From the moment she'd spun that memory from her wand and used it as her permanent residence, Garlandians quickly began to regard her as taboo. There were rumors, oh yes there were. Rumors that she worked for *the* Crone. Nobody ever spoke of any of this out loud, at least out of doors, but there were speculations that this crone was none other than the Crone of Light's End . . . and *that* crone, if she was indeed somehow still 'around,' wasn't one that anyone dared to give any attention to. For attention led to energy and energy was fuel. Anybody who knew anything knew that to give that kind of evil any sort of gas money was the same as setting off a nuclear war. The world would come to an end.

Dora had chosen Heime to come along with them on this trek because he was the only one who had ever offered her anything akin to friendship, and though he never said so, she knew he didn't believe the rumors. Whenever he spoke of her 'employer' there was a catching glint in his eye that told the witch he didn't believe she had an evil bone in her body.

She had also chosen Heime because of his protégé. Yes, Bally was just as important to this mission as Dora's reputation. Even if the poor boy *was* still learning how to walk on those gangly legs. He'd grown about an inch or so taller since his transformation.

"'Tis a gamble," Dora muttered.

All three of their heads turned just a smidge back to where her words were catching up with them.

"What's that?" Heime grunted. His vision aligned with a cloud beginning to churn above their heads.

Dora stared up at the formation and blinked. As she did, lightning pierced the eye of the storm and the funnel evaporated back into the sky. A fog was starting to fall upon them. "'Tis a gamble!" she shouted up to him. Then added a bit more softly, "What we are doing is a gamble."

She looked forward and caught the eye of the young elf named Bally. In that fleeting look she saw all she needed to. Uncertainty, dread, and loss—but for whatever reason, there wasn't fear. Was it the transformation that had wiped the thin layer of sweat from his brow? Regardless, Jeremy was now Bally, and Bally was a necessary ingredient for what she needed to get this cake to rise. An anchor, or so one might say.

A strong wind blew across their faces as they began to tread up a rocky hill. The forest was now to their backsides and the last of it was fading away. In the distance, blue skies turned gray, and dirt began to rise from the earth.

Heime paused at the top of the hill, using his hand as a visor against the waning sun. "Do you mean to say that what we are doing may not be in favor of the gods?"

Dora walked past the girl then Bally, stopping only when she was shoulder to shoulder with Heime. "I don't think the gods have anything to do with this, old friend." She stared out into the dirt storm that was kicking up on the pass. "Where we are going, 'tis godless."

Heime's gaze followed the wind as the world became mad, then slowly let it fall to Dora's arm, dangling next to his. With his forefinger and thumb, he felt the fabric of her cape. "What is this made from? I dabble mostly in leather, but I must say, I've never come across a fabric such as this."

Dora's lips scrunched up to the side as her blue irises danced. "No Heime, you wouldn't have come across it. Not ever."

From there, she took the lead, refusing to acknowledge the fact that she could feel the girl pressing into her thoughts, trying to pick apart her memories so that she might fill in the many gaps she'd come back into her consciousness with. But those holes weren't going to get filled in, not until the last minute. Not if Dora had anything to do with it.

10

Lantern's Edge

There wasn't a cloud in the sky, yet the canvas that served as their backdrop was the color of an oyster. The unseen goddess who had gifted her blood to those who called themselves witches was hovering over the young child. Dora was wrapped in a garb that could have been confused for an old potato sack. Her brown arms and legs were lanky; if all went as planned, she would not be given the opportunity to grow old enough to acquire any more meat on those bones. If left to that of the lake, the heaviness of the waters would crush her. It was what the priestess was counting on.

The sky may have been dreary, but the light reflecting from the child's golden irises was as white as a champignon mushroom against the dark earth. And her stare, though vacant to most, was anything but. This girl was fierce. A tad reckless, perhaps, but not for any inane reason. No, she did not aim to lose the test because she feared what might become of her. She did so because she loved.

Because she loved.

Such a simple thing, but a choice that had caught the attention of someone she should be glad to know one day.

The test was the same as it always was. In dreams they may come—these trials set forth by she who deemed herself above the status of a mere high priestess. Twice the test had been administered; two other sets of twins within the coven. Dora and Malina were the third and final set of twins. This time the high priestess—the *Crone*—was determined for the ritual to work. Though even she had been befuddled to find that when her girls woke from their dreams that Malina was the one to claim fire . . .

⁂

The girls hadn't known what was coming, which was why Dora had been practicing. She'd already decided that Malina's nerves were going to be a problem, so she took it upon herself to practice magic that was well above her pay grade.

Dora and Malina only knew magic as far as it had been taught to them. White magic was foreign, and lessons happened only during coven meetings. The Crone had her followers babysit and educate, for she just didn't have time for those sorts of things. One such governess was Betty Willow, a witch from the human world who had been led into Forest Peak when the Crone came to round up many of them who had been sentenced to the hanging trees. Dora had trusted Betty because Betty hadn't seemed too keen on what was going on in this part of the wood; the young girl had even heard the woman state that death may have been better. Betty didn't stay—she fled with a few of the others before taking the oath. But before that, Dora had been blessed to have learnt some things from her. One of those being, that not only was it illegal for witches to share power, but that the gods had taken away such an allowance many moons ago. For to share power meant that a coven could put all their eggs into one basket, and as Betty had said, "What if those eggs were bad?"

Dora had known that everything her mother stood for was against the law. So far it hadn't mattered because it wasn't working. Still, Dora knew the second her mother realized how to share, or more preferably, how to receive power from others, that the world would be over. And the last thing Dora could allow, was for her mother to discover that *she* could, in fact, for reasons the small witch couldn't possibly know, delegate her power.

"How might someone have the ability to share their magic?" Dora had asked Betty before the witch left her side.

"Oh my," answered the witch. "I don't know, Dora. I suppose if the gods saw something in that individual, they might offer that gift."

That was just one day in more than she could count that Dora realized she was different.

Dora had kept her 'gift' quiet. While Malina slept, she cautiously practiced. It was so effortless that it caused her to feel that she was doing everything all wrong. The process was simple—hold Malina's hand and concentrate. From there, her power could flow into her twin—bright light flowing from one set of veins to the other. Taking it back was just as easy.

When the time came for the test, Dora simply nodded her head curtly to Malina as their mother 'tucked them in' for the first time. Or tied them down, more like. They'd already been given their instructions: sleep, proceed with the test, wake. The tea they'd been given ensured that their eyes grew heavy and that the girls would find their dreams simultaneously.

It happened sooner than later. Dora and Malina materialized over the beach before the lake on their property. Malina came to in a panic and Dora ran to her from where they'd been planted about twenty feet apart.

"Is she here, the Crone?" Dora asked, looking all around. But though the lake was indeed the same one that stood before Lantern's Edge, there was nothing else around them for miles.

Just as Malina started to say, "I don't think so," the water in the lake began to ripple and before their eyes rose the reddest dragon they'd ever seen. In truth, the first one they'd seen this close. For dragons didn't often come to Forest Peak, at least in this world, they much preferred mountain terrain or the water.

Dora knew the beast was female before it ever opened its mouth, and for a moment she forgot all about the test and how her sister shook in her arms. She was purely entranced by how beautiful this massive creature was. Not an ounce of fear could be found within her, and without her permission, her heart lit up.

"My, my, my. 'Tis two young little female nymphs who stand before me this time, but unlike the first two sets of twins, I can plainly see who it is who can understand me."

Dora loosed a ragged breath as Malina shivered.

"Is it going to eat us?" Malina asked.

It was all Dora could do to turn her head from the amazing fortress, its skin like a waterfall of rubies. Still, she twisted her features and looked to her twin. "Can't you hear her?"

"Of course I can hear her," Malina retorted. "She's roaring like mad!"

Dora moved her head slowly in the creature's direction. The dragon seemed to be watching them both with intent.

"She does not hear you!" Dora shouted to the dragon.

"She does not," bellowed the beast.

"Is that the test?" Dora hollered.

The dragon stared down at her and blinked, one eyelash could have been the size of the tallest tree trunk in all the land. "'Tis a dragon dancer the priestess seeks."

"Why?" Dora questioned.

"Obvious, isn't it?" When Dora didn't answer, the dragon sighed, causing the water to ripple and the earth to shake. "Not only does a dragon dancer denote strong magical ability, but only someone like you, Dora, can ask me for what your priestess desires."

By now, Malina was nearly in shreds. "What's going on?" she whispered heatedly into her sister's ear.

Dora hastily told her to hold on, then returned her attention to the glorious beast. "What does she desire?"

They could have swum across the lake in the time it took the dragon to answer. "A bit of my fire."

Every cell in Dora's body went numb as a life-threatening "NO" left her lips.

The dragon stilled and turned its giant head to the side. "You're different than the others."

"Could they not hear you?" she asked.

"One of the two other sets could sort of hear me, but not as clearly as you do. 'Tis not a common thing. No one has yet to take back my breath."

Dora thought over this information. No one had passed her mother's test yet . . . still the priestess had clearly done away with one child from each set of twins. It was detestable.

Dora peered up at the beast. "Do you know what she plans to do with it—your fire?" As far as Dora knew, dragon's breath was one of the most sought out spell ingredients. Difficult to attain and usually only used in dark magic. It had the capability to undo even the meanest, stiffest of enterprises.

"I am the product of a conjuring, child. My existence was pulled here just as yours. I know only what this spell has told me."

At some point Dora had started to stand taller, Malina still shaking in her arms. "Did you have a choice in this matter?"

"One always a choice."

"We didn't," Dora stated.

The dragon narrowed her eyes.

Dora stretched out her neck as she posed her next question. "Did you know that you were aiding in the schemes of one of the vilest persons in this world?"

Again, the dragon took her time answering. "I did not." She turned her head to the other side, then asked matter-of-factly, "Are you going to ask for my breath, Dora?"

And that's when all the air left Dora's lungs. "No," said the young witch, the word riding the last of her breath. "She is." And then she closed her eyes and transferred her power.

When Dora reopened her eyes, the world looked different. There were less layers, the wind had no words, and the dragon wasn't as pretty. In fact, she was damn near terrifying. What had once been rubies were now metallic scales with serrated edges. Smoke exited the beast's nostrils and every bone in Dora's body was telling her to run. Next to her, Malina had grown about an inch taller just from straightening out her hunched back, and she was staring up at the creature in the lake as if she'd just come across an angel in the sky.

It was Dora's turn for her jaw to drop as her sister spoke in a strange tongue and the dragon roared. What felt like ages later, a fireball erupted from the dragon's mouth then floated down and spread out until it was small enough to glide into Malina's mouth as if she was swallowing a burning snake. When it was over, the light Dora had given to Malina came back to her, and once more the dragon, as well as the world around them, was beautiful.

"What's just happened?" Dora asked, staring down at her hands which were still fluttering with light as her power became comfortable back in her skin.

Malina looked shaken to her core. "She said you *did* have a choice, and that—that you chose right. That Hecate would be proud. What—What did you choose, Dora?"

A tear ran down her cheek for the second time in her life. Her chin lowered as her jaw fell open. The dragon winked at her as she began to sink back into the lake, and even though the words weren't spoken out loud, Dora still heard them. *Good luck, Dora. You now know my name.* And just like that she did. Rosaline. *What a fitting name*, Dora thought.

Call on me whenever you wish, child. The fire will stay with the one you love just as your heart has asked.

The dragon was gone. Dora was just starting to wipe away her tear when her sister forced her to look her in the eyes. "Dora, what did you choose?"

The child looked deep into Malina's eyes. "Love, I suppose."

And then they woke.

⚜

The Crone had been speechless. The test was nothing if not accurate and the dragon's breath was truly authentic. The results could not be appealed. And though it seemed wrong—not because it was a disgusting thing she was doing, but because she had been sure Dora would return with the breath—the Crone marched her daughters to the lake's shore that very morning after the twins woke. The whole time she did, Dora could hear the Crone's thoughts. She wanted to drain the child of all her magic, sip on her blood like a fine wine—

for the magic stirring within this witch she'd created was the most salivating of all the bloodlines she'd ever scented . . . like it had been deposited directly from their goddess into Dora's veins. But she couldn't; it would go against the spell she'd been using and the risk in ignoring written magic was too far great to mess with.

"'Tis time, Dora," the priestess stated as they stood before her daughter's grave.

Dora didn't even flinch. Eight was a very young age to understand the world as it is, but Dora had never been all that usual for a child. Another reason her mother, if one could even call the woman that, had been slightly ajar when Malina had risen victorious from their test. For the sake of intellectuals, Malina couldn't even hold a wand properly. Somehow, the Crone just knew—*that fire* had belonged in Dora's keep. But again, even if it was all wrong, there was no going back. One didn't go against spun magic, not unless they were after a curse. Though this sort of magic could very well have been viewed as an execration to the craft regardless of whether it was being worked in a straight line or down a rocky, curvy path strewn with poisonous serpents. This magic, itself, was a curse.

Dora didn't say a word after her mother spoke. She did not shed a tear. Not even as Malina reached for her hand to give it a squeeze.

"Stop that," their mother chirped, snagging the young girl's hand away from her sister's. "You were not bred to shed your feelings upon one another. This is work."

Bred, Dora thought. What an appropriate word that was. They had not been seeded for the sake of a mother and father wanting to extend their family, nor had they been conceived from any sort of love at all. No, it had been just another ritual under the dark moon. They had a father, or a sperm donor more like. They'd figured out who he was before the night of the male sacrament—a ceremony that took place a year before the twins were to take their test.

Before he'd been offered, he'd been chosen by their mother. Before they mated, his body was laid before their circle while the coven conjured the gods to come down and possess his soul. Only after his voice had deepened and his eyes were no longer his own, did their priestess use his body to fill hers. For the magic to come full circle, however, their father (their seed bearer) had to be sacrificed.

As she stood before the lake, Dora's expression remained firm, neutral. She did not smile as she turned and looked at Malina. She did not speak. After all, there was nothing left to say. She'd already instructed her twin to appear to be in line with everything the Crone instructed while following the plan Dora had set up after hearing about Avalon. And somewhere in there, Malina had also been instructed *not to die*. Dora wasn't just being protective of her sister; her sister, to her, represented the free world. "Harm none," Betty had said before leaving their coven. Those words resonated with Dora. A dark witch born with a sparkling heart.

"Malina," spoke the Crone, "we now take her hands, but not with affection."

Malina's chin quivered.

Stop, Dora insisted.

Malina, whether she heard the command or not, inhaled a sharp breath and bit her lip. When their mother reached for Dora's hand, Malina followed suit.

There were no more words said as the three of them began to tread slowly into the lake. The lake that had already swallowed up the twins' father, and goddess knew who else.

The Crone had not risen to her status by slitting the throats of reptiles and bunnies. No, at every new recruit circle, where the new followers took their oaths, the Crone held goblets of human blood before her 'children.' The curtain between Forest Peak and the next world led directly into a place called New England. The human world; a place where witch hunters made up at least a good portion of the population. She would holler that these were the men and women who crucified her sisters and brothers while their blood would run down her chin.

Her coven thought her a hero.

The priestess savored the blood as it ran down her throat, and how she howled when it rained. She would often run out into the storm, covered in the blood of those she'd spelled to kill her kin so she could appear to be the champion who took down the 'hunters.' Nobody needed to know that it was her who pushed that first boulder down the mountain—who started the rumor to a group of men that the devil's mistresses were all around them. Her followers didn't need to know that they'd been forced from their homes in their own world because of her and her whispers to all that they were evil. Never mind the ones who were burned at the stakes or those whose heads were held under water for minutes on end —never mind the evil that was born from her false tongue. The truth was she needed all of their energies, and the only way to get them to follow her into Lorelei was if they had something to run from.

Yes, Dora knew many things about her mother. Unfortunately, the one thing she needed—that anyone needed to take her down—was buried. And until Dora, or Malina, could find the one soul who was armed with the right shovel, then all they could do was continue to be actors in their mother's play.

Dora's knees were now drenched in the same waterhole her and Malina could've at one time been found in, splashing one another in the face and giggling when their mother's back was turned. Except now, she was to die. That was the plan. She thought she'd have more to say, but the closer to drowning she got, the more she realized it suited her to keep her lips sealed.

"Any last words, Dora of Lantern's Edge?" asked the Crone.

That has a nice ring to it, the child thought. A little offkey as far as last thoughts go, but it was what raced through her mind.

Dora remained silent.

"Then mote it be," her mother said, using sacred words in an unholy manner. It was enough to anger the current flowing at the bottom of the lake.

Dora didn't turn and look at Malina one last time. She couldn't, and she wouldn't. The act might soften Malina, and she needed her sister to be strong. Instead, she walked the rest of the way into the water. There were no restraints, but that was only because they weren't needed. Not when their mother had a wand in her pocket. Dora had already been advised to drink the lake into her lungs, and if she didn't the Crone would force it.

The drop off was only about five feet ahead; she knew it well. As the water came up around her chest, she closed her eyes, filling her pink lungs with the satisfying influx of fresh forest air. And then, before the cowardice inside her stood front and center, she sealed her lips together and let her head sink under the water.

She managed to hold her breath for a long time. Two minutes passed as she tread about three feet under the water. There had been no sun seeping through the gray clouds that day, but still, she could see the light above her. It wasn't until the edges of her vision began to blur and she began to realize that this was going to be the end—that she was going to have to swallow the lake—that she looked down.

Now, that's bizarre, she thought.

For down into the depths of the lake, there was a light

much like what was offered above her. Very slowly, she began to let the air seep from her lungs, bubbles shooting to the lake's surface—reporting to her mother that her end was near.

Her body began to drift down to the bottom of the lake, and as it did the light grew. It wasn't bright—it was eerie. But Dora wasn't afraid. She hadn't been afraid of anything for a long time. Not since she'd decided to let Malina win.

As the neon green light continued to glow, her lungs began to burn, and just as her feet were pulled (because she *had* been pulled down, she realized) into the mud that made up the bottom of the waterhole, she found she could no longer hold her breath. Preparing for what would happen next, she let out the last of the oxygen she'd been holding and waited for the darkness that would follow as the lake entered her lungs.

But all that followed as she opened her mouth wide was a fresh batch of air.

Confused, breathing under water, staring out into the strange glow that was surrounding her, she held out an arm and spoke. "Hello?"

For a moment, only the sound of water moving around her filled her ears. That was until darkness shifted into the light. Dora's eyes grew wide, and her mouth hung open.

"I know you," she whispered.

Darkness spread out its arms, as if claiming this abandoned child.

"And I've been waiting for you, Dora of Lantern's Edge. You were right, that does have a nice ring to it, doesn't it?"

For reasons she couldn't explain, Dora smiled.

I I

Makayla

R ally had Danka blood. He was Danka's grandson. But was that really the worst of it? Layla had it too, but I could like *feel* her soul—she wasn't vengeful. Her parents had made sure she'd known love and she mourned that love. She wasn't evil. But Rally . . . he'd only exhibited ignorance and hate. *He'd been raised by Loral.* Could someone like that truly ever be anything but the product of their upbringing? One could argue that Toby was raised by Loral as well, but truly he wasn't. He'd had values instilled upon him from his parents. His mother had been Titania's keeper.

The worst of it all was that Rally had never been a baby so much as he'd been a spell ingredient. His *life* was an offering to the bad village . . . his life was as much his own as mine was. It was all I could do to see past the stars exploding all around me. I mean, I'd always known the elf was my enemy; I just hadn't realized how literal a statement that was. I was here to kill an infection, and he was here to leak a disease that had already been confiscated once. I couldn't help but think, as my head filled with all these new facts, of how Rally had acted the first time he'd met Cee-Cee. It was like he'd known her soul. He'd been attracted to it. At the time she'd thought him scurvy, but what would the unbound spirit walking around in her body say to him now if they came face to face?

I couldn't deliberate too far into that. It was important to keep our enemies in our thoughts. To be aware of where our opponents may possibly be lurking on the other side of this game board; that they may be strategizing a move that could take us out at any second. But if I let myself fall too far away from where I and my team stood, then I would lose track of my own footing, and in this game (other than Toby apparently) we weren't given a set number of lives to burn through before 'Game Over.'

All I wanted to do was dissolve back into the courtroom where the Great Beyond seemed to be waiting for me to take that plunge. But I couldn't. I hadn't come this far to just split when things got bad. As far as I could tell, things had always been bad. I just hadn't known about it.

Blythe's shift ended shortly after lunch, but she had to make a few phone calls and get the rest of her shifts covered before we could move towards our next destination. It was enough time for us to hit up some of the stores for supplies. I learned, rather quickly, that if it hadn't been for the pointy ears, magic wands, and wings, that this town could have belonged anywhere off the beaten track in the world I thought I'd been born into.

Here, cash registers were manned mostly by teenagers. Much of the population could be seen mulling around the sidewalks with phones in palms, and messenger bags at their sides as they headed off to work or study. There were bookstores, candle shops—apothecaries. Grocery stores. There was even a large town square complete with a working fountain.

"This place was intended to be a safe land for the humans," Layla explained as we perused a shop called Peak Chalet; a store packed with camping supplies and mountain climbing apparel. As she grabbed a thick bundle of rope and stuffed it into an impressive hiking pack, she clarified, "The town was founded around the same time the priestess began coming into her power."

The *priestess* had been brought up so many times that if it had been a drinking game I would have been properly tossed, but the blows weren't getting any less offensive. The face that popped up every time the leader of the bad village was named made me want to crawl into the ground and never come back up. I had to stop her from saying it any further.

"Does the priestess have a name—or did she?"

Layla looked at me like my skin was coming off. "Everyone has a name."

I was aware. Names had once meant a great deal to me.

A memory echoed inside my head, causing me to cringe. *Anastacia Montgomery is your name? Why that is—that is fabulous. I would kill for a name like that.*

Unaware that I'd sunk away into the past, Layla went on. "The Crone never disclosed her name to anyone; there were rumors that her followers knew of it, because she'd had to share herself with them as part of the oath ceremony, but even that is just speculation. Honestly, even if someone here did know it, it would be like pulling a dragon's tooth to get it out of them." She waited until I caught her eye. "These people who live here, they do so because it is safe. The energy is kind. They don't like to attract anything . . . unnatural."

I kept my gaze locked onto hers. "A name is a powerful thing."

"Yes, Makayla. It truly is."

I bit down over my lip, then took the extra rope she was handing me. As we walked on towards a selection of climbing shoes, she continued. "The witches of Lorelei founded this safe place for the humans, because as the priestess rose to power, more and more of the non-magical people began to go missing. It wasn't ever just humans though; Reefs had been disappearing for years before the cult grew popular. The truth was that no one was safe." She sized up my feet then reached for a pair of hiking shoes, tossing them into my arms along with some socks. "Lorelei has never been an evil place, but it doesn't take long for darkness to overshadow light, and as the coven in the deep end of the forest grew, the sun began to fade until it eventually just stopped showing face."

My left eye narrowed. "What about your people. The mer —they rule Lorelei, right?"

She nodded. "But the dark forest isn't their domain. I suppose if the curses are ever lifted, it may do everyone well to have a ruler for the land. It's just too far from the sea for the mer to keep tabs on it all the time, ya know."

"Right," I said. All I could see in the back of my mind were those rows of shark teeth staring back at me. They seemed like predators. "But do the mer, I mean, do they have the best interests of those who don't live in the water in mind?"

The mermaid squared her shoulders with mine. "They do. I realize they aren't perfect, and they could use a course on diversity, but they aren't ruthless. All they desire is a safe place for mer and land folk. My kind may appear savage, but their end goal is harmony."

I was chewing over her words, trying to decide if I believed her, when she nodded to a bench in the middle of the shoe section. "Try on the boots. We're going to need to get you some proper clothing also. That dress—"

"Isn't coming off."

Layla narrowed her eyes. "It's not practical."

"I don't care." It was a truly silly thing to cling to but, "It was a gift." I lifted the purple fabric of the dress. After everything I'd been through, it was still in amazing shape. Esmerelda really did use only the best fabric. I looked up at Layla. "It makes me feel like a queen."

She rolled her eyes. "Whatever."

"And I don't think these boots are going to work." I lowered them back to their display.

She continued to inspect me like I was growing fur, then scoffed. "You truly are a royal." She sighed, looked around, then pointed to a wall lined with footwear. "Come on, let's find something more suitable to your taste."

I shuffled behind her aligned gait; she was even the same height and build as the elf I despised. Since we'd left the coffee shop, Toby and I had had about a minute alone; it was long enough for him to whisper into my ear that we could trust her. Still, *Rally's sister*. What the actual—

"Hey," I said, coming to an abrupt stop before a rack of fashionable cross shoulder bags.

Layla sighed then returned to me. "What is it? We need to hurry, Makayla."

I reached out and touched the green fabric of one of the purses. "Alligator Lipstick."

Her brows furrowed. "What?"

My fingers were still pinching the material. It was made from plastic bottles. "It's mine."

"Uh, I don't think you'll need a—"

I shook my head. "No. I mean, it's my design. I picked this color because of the funny name." I looked over to find a confused expression coloring her face. "Here," I said, pulling at the zipper and revealing the logo on the inside pocket. "Sewn Back Together. It's my company . . . or it was." Back when I was just a human girl trying to break the glass ceiling. I couldn't help but feel proud that *my fashion line* had somehow found its way into other worlds. I dug out the face of Naomi Wood, her go to plastic game face, and dropped my hand down by my side. "Never mind." I glanced up at her. "So, let's go look at these shoes."

Layla just stood there for a moment before deviating her jaw. "Okay, this way then."

I followed behind her, but not before one last look at my old life.

"So," I said, receiving a pair of shoes that looked an awful lot like the black flats that were already on my feet. "What were you saying about this place? Something about how it was founded by humans?"

"Created by the witches for the humans. Try them on." She pointed at the shoes in my grasp.

"They don't look any different than what I already have."

She lowered her head to her shoulder and sighed. "The ones on your feet won't aid against the elements. These ones will."

"What? Are they, like, magicked or something?"

She raised her brows.

Right. Of course they were.

"Lorelei has seen a lot of destruction," Layla continued as I tried on the flats, and incidentally, they were oddly comfortable. As soon as I dipped my toes into them, they fitted around my feet on their own. Like a second skin. "Before the cursed coven began growing in the forest's heart, anyone with any magic born to them knew that to get too close to those trees meant that they might not get back home. None of the missing were ever found and fear kept others from searching too far into the forest. However, regardless of whether one was magical or not, many creatures weren't safe as the priestess rose to power and humans were near helpless."

"Why?" I asked with cinched brows. I knew the Bahidicaras sucked the marrow from the earth, taking the essence of every god and goddess, but so far, I hadn't been offered a lot more than that.

"It was rumored that the priestess grew powerful by drinking the blood of magic makers; that she designed her coven in such a way that her followers followed suit. Some say she was gathering as much magic into them as she could so when the time came, she could drain them and have all the magic for herself."

My jaw was hanging open. "Say what?"

Layla clicked her tongue as she raised a single brow. "At some point, blood draining wasn't enough. They moved on to souls—that's where our raw magic is stored after all. Anyone up against a coven, or a cult whose minds have been demolished and whose needs have become insatiable, is in danger. However, humans can't defend themselves in the way that magical creatures can, and though the priestess and her followers were always on the lookout for a more filling meal, they feasted heartily on whatever they could find."

"They actually fed upon souls . . ."

"Yeah," Layla said, nodding at the shoes on my feet in approval, before motioning for me to follow her further into the store where it became apparent that we weren't in Kansas anymore. The gear we were looking at, it wasn't for just hiking and camping. "After the threat died down a little this place began to grow. Everyone, regardless of *what* they were, saw this safe land as a place for equal opportunity. The space is limited. Not just anyone can get in through the borders, as you've seen for yourself."

All of that was pretty cool, but— "Shouldn't it be like that anyway. I mean, like everywhere."

Layla pulled at what looked like giant reigns. The tag said, "Durability tested, 100% Breath Proof." When she caught me giving the section we were in a hard stare, she explained, "Dragons. Riding them is a sport for those who do not know how to speak with them. But don't worry, the dragons like it. They think it's funny to watch non dragon dancers think they have a shot at staying seated on their scales."

Rigghhht.

"And why are we shopping in this part of the store?" Was I going to be riding a dragon?

"We have a long journey. We must be prepared for anything and everything."

Layla continued to pluck supplies like she was checking things off a weekly shopping list. I'd been compiling all this new information I'd learned into files in my head, but it just wasn't sorting.

"Exactly how were the Bahidicaras stopped the first time?"

Layla had backtracked and was reaching for a pair of shoes just like the ones I now wore on my feet. She sized up a couple of pairs then added them to her loot. "It's not confirmed—the exact resolution, that is. The most apparent story is that the priestess doubled her power by fusing with other members." Her gaze shot up to mine. "And before you ask, I don't know the specifics. I only know what others have speculated, and that is that she essentially grew insane from bonding her soul too many times, which then made her more susceptible to being pulled apart. It is believed that the majority of her power—or the souls of her followers—was pulled from the shell she was inhabiting and placed in a vessel; however, whoever was trying to end her reign failed to finish what they started."

"And how can you be sure of that?"

"That kind of evil leaves behind an energy. If the

Bahidicaras were truly completely gone, then we wouldn't still feel haunted. Even to this day, when the sun shines in Lorelei, it seems dull."

"Is that because this is where the priestess left her footprint?"

"Yes. And this is where you can find Lantern's Edge."

My attention flickered. "What?"

Layla started heading for the cash register. I could see Toby and Petal through the entrance as they waited for us to emerge from the shop. "The land is cursed of course. No one dares get too near it. It is where the meetings originated. The home of the priestess."

"I—uh—no. That's not right. I've been to Lantern's Edge. It's in Garlandia."

Layla narrowed her eyes as she turned to me after setting all the merchandise down on the counter. An elf wearing square-framed glasses raised his brows as he pretended not to listen to our conversation. "No, it's in Lorelei. Inside a clearing that lives in the dark wood. Forest Peak is what it's called." Then she added flippantly, "You're mistaken."

"No." She shot me an almost offended look, one that very much reminded me that she was related to Rally. "I was there. My friend, or at least she used to be my friend—" I hadn't mentioned her to anyone but Toby and Petal. But still, I knew . . . I just knew . . . A sharp pang ran through my chest and I shook my head. Cramming my eyes shut, I finished what I'd been trying to say. "My—Cee-Cee. She um, she made a deal with a witch to save one of our other friends, and because of that we ended up at this cottage and that's what it was called. Lantern's Edge."

"That's not—" Layla adjusted her stance, popping her hip out along with her jaw. "Unless it—"

"It was a memory," came the voice of my love. Toby had walked up behind us and was now laying a hand over my shoulder. As I looked up into his eyes, his pupils retracted just a little. "That explains why no one could ever find where Dora was rooted; the witch must've been using it as her habitat."

All I could fathom were a few blinks.

Layla, meanwhile, was staring at her feet in concentration. "Dora . . . that name sounds familiar, but I can't place it."

"She was regarded by the Garlandians as taboo," Toby explained. "She had a reputation bathed in secrecy. Makayla's friend sparked an interest in her though, and from what my queen has told me—"

A third voice broke into our small circle as the faery from the coffee shop jumped off a black and purple Vespa and burst in beside us. "You can't place the name, Layla, because the citizens of this world have tried to hush out every element from that circle of poisonous spiders." Giving me her full attention, Blythe added, "I am sorry, Makayla, but if your friend is in cohorts with Dora of Lantern's Edge than she is no longer who you think she is." Toby's hand moved from my shoulder to my arm. He pulled me in just as Blythe, slightly winded from the sound of it, stated the words that proceeded to rip my already tender heart into more pieces. "Dora is all that is left of the Bahidicaras; she went missing shortly after the cult left this land, but some have promised that they've seen her wearing a different skin. That in the right light, her white skin returns to brown and that Hecate herself can be seen looking through her eyes. She is, well, there's no sugar coating this—Dora of Lantern's Edge is the priestess's daughter." Bile rose from my throat as she added, "They call her the untouchable one."

Makayla

Blythe wasn't just any ordinary Reef; she was a survivor. She told us her tale as we made our way to her house, to the place we were to stay for the night. She still lived with family, which was the norm here. Many families lived all together to save from having to build more homes. The residents of this safe land were happy with their town and didn't want it growing much bigger than it already had.

She was 212 years old, though we were eerily similar in maturity. Then again, 200 years was kind of like a blink of an eye to the fey. She was raised by her aunt and uncle; they were one of the first fey families to live in this unnamed bit of magical land. That was all part of it, its anonymity—keeping it sheltered even from a label. The entrances moved daily, so if a resident left, they had to stay in contact with someone on the inside to be able to know where to find the pooka on duty.

Blythe's mother and father followed the cult that became known as the Bahidicaras. She knew all about everything, or at least all of it leading up to the point where her parents as she knew them began to transform.

Regarding how it all began, or ended, she'd said this, "I was so little that the memories are faded in parts, but there are some things you can't ever forget . . . no matter how young you were when it happened. No matter how hard you try."

Blythe was still telling her story an hour after we'd landed at her pad. Her uncle was at work; he was a chef at a local restaurant, but her aunt Phyllis was home, and she was extremely fond of feeding us. I'd already had a bowl of fruit and wasn't shy when the plate of cookies came around to where we were camped out in the living room, packing up gear. Also, she had a gray cat named Persephone who had landed on my stomach and wouldn't budge. Her emerald eyes kept diving into mine like she was reading my soul. It was freaky.

I'd never cared for cats, but I wasn't about to say that out loud.

"Phyllis and Dave had already gotten me out of there—my home, I mean," Blythe was saying. "The rumors had been flying around about what the cult in Forest Peak was really up to, and even though my parents had brushed off all of them as hearsay for years to anyone who confronted them about it, they couldn't explain why their bodies were beginning to change." She paused as her aunt, who had come in to refill our beverages like a flight attendant, reached for her shoulder and gave it a squeeze before heading back into the kitchen. The rooms were nearly adjoined; if the discussion wasn't so imperative, I would have been completely distracted by the feast Phyllis was cooking up in there. Were those meatballs I smelled?

I gazed across the living room rug, over the packing hands of Layla and Toby, and directly into Blythe's striking eyes. "What do you mean their bodies *changed*?"

"Cronies," Layla said. "That's what they came to be called. The magic they spun—the things they did . . ." Her voice drifted off as she shook her head.

Toby looked up at me. "Karma exists, my queen. Even in the magical worlds that you are just coming to know, there are restrictions. Gods save the one who meddles in the forbidden entrance."

I caught Blythe in a near smirk as I turned to face her.

"Does he always talk like that?" she asked.

"Yeah," I said, trying not to chuckle—laughter didn't seem appropriate, not while I was in the middle of processing all that I was. "My king has an old soul."

"Don't we all," Layla muttered.

Before anyone could say another word, Phyllis stuck her head in the living room, a sheer wing fluttering softly behind her back, as she looked to Toby and me. "Does Petal eat only vegetables?"

"She prefers carrots, but she would enjoy some of that sauce you're cooking the meat in," Toby answered.

"Of course," she replied, then returned to her kitchen.

"So . . . may I ask what happened to your parents?" I asked Blythe. My curiosity was boiling over. What was this memory that she couldn't get to wash out from her mind?

The Reef sighed, then leaned back in her chair, a large orange molasses cookie in one hand and her wand appearing in the other. As she spoke, she twirled the sparkling lavender wand around her fingers like it was a pencil. "They'd already become quite numb. The affection I'd once felt from them was completely gone. It didn't take very long after they made their oaths to the coven—that was pretty much the tipping point. Phyllis and Dave wouldn't let me stay with them once word reached them that my parents had officially taken to the cult. I was just a little Reef but old enough to know that they hadn't fought to keep me." Her gaze shot to the kitchen then back down at the cookie. "I wasn't allowed to see them alone and we didn't visit often. I didn't understand this back then, but I think my aunt and uncle were afraid my parents would . . ." She literally looked like she was going to choke on the words before she looked back up. "Eat me." Her wand disappeared into thin air.

I nearly coughed up my last bite of cookie. "What?" I choked out, covering my mouth with my elbow.

"Yeah, I know. But that's what the Cronies did," Blythe said matter-of-factly. "They weren't people, fey, witches, or elves anymore. They were disfigured *things*. Servants to an insane witch who was powered by something she decided only she could access. Her followers thought she could empower them in the same way—that she would bring them with her into the tunnel."

I managed to swallow the rest of the bite I'd been choking on. "What's the tunnel?"

I mean, did I really want to know?

Blythe waved a hand in front of her lap as though she was shooing away fluff. "To the priestess and her followers, it was *the* source of power. To everyone else in their right minds, it was and is a fantasy. It's said to be the link between all worlds and where the gods roam. If one is to find themselves there, they may own the tunnel. Or, in other words, they may harness the power of the gods. The priestess used it as a way to lure in her victims. Supposedly she'd touched it once upon a time—that was what she read from her script to any and all who would listen. She'd found the source of power that belongs only to the gods, and they'd chosen her to bring it to the Earth. She told her victims that as long as they made an oath to stay under her broomstick, that they too would be able to touch the tunnel, which she also referred to as light's end."

"What the—" I started. "They actually bought that crap? It's like cult junkie literature 101."

"It is," Layla said under her breath. "But to this day people eat that shit up like candy."

Blythe nodded towards Layla then took a bite from her cookie; after she'd swallowed it, she met my gaze again. "The last day I saw my parents, they didn't come to the door. We had to barge in and when we did, we found them hanging upside down from the beam in the ceiling. They were *sleeping* like that." She paused for effect. "Before they woke, one of my mom's wings fell from her backside to the floor. It, like, detached."

I couldn't help the gasp that left my lips.

Catching sight of my reaction, Blythe added, "To see a faery lose their wings—I mean, it doesn't even happen in death. And, well, that was essentially it." She motioned to the kitchen again, to where her aunt was. "Phyllis and Dave took me out of there pretty quickly after that. It was clear, my parents weren't themselves anymore. And then it was our turn to move on. As the humans say, we needed to get the hell out of dodge."

My voice but a whisper, I asked, "Do you know what happened to them? Your parents."

Blythe nibbled on the edge of her cookie then put it down on the plate next to her. "I imagine they faded into darkness with the rest of the rodents. There wasn't anything left of them from what I hear. You know, after they did what they did and slipped through this world into the next."

"Makayla doesn't know about any of that yet," Toby said, reaching for a crampon and giving Layla a quizzical look.

"In case we need to rock climb," she muttered, taking it from him and stuffing it into the main bag.

"Do you not use your magic?" he asked inquisitively.

She rolled her eyes. "Gods help me with these royals." Then centering her gaze over his, she said while openly mocking him, "Don't you ever prepare for the worst?"

Blythe hinged forward in her seat, balancing her elbows on her knees as she watched the two of them. "Are you two so sure that where we are going is the answer? It's not intact. And even if we did make it there in one piece, why should we assume that this is where the devil is headed?"

Layla shot her friend, or whatever Blythe was to her, a piercing look. "We follow the instructions of the keeper. You know how this works."

What?

I covered my mouth as a foul belch escaped my lips. I'd way overdone it, gobbling down the calories I hadn't been afforded over the past three days. I was actually starting to feel a little nauseous. Once I had everyone's attention, I used it to bring us back down a level. I may have been hailed as a prodigy in my old life and a savior in my next, but my head could still only handle so many details at a time. "Hang on— one excruciating thing at a time, *please*. Can we return to why my friend—" I unintentionally reached for my heart as it literally hurt just saying what I had to say out loud. "Can someone finish explaining to me what has happened to Cee-Cee."

I'd told them everything. Even about the bizarre moment just days ago in Garlandia when those strange witches had run up to us at Helene's old house and ranted on about some lost child, or something or other. The silence that had followed was more challenging than watching Helene murder Sabrina right in front of my eyes.

"Makayla Wood."

I matched my gaze with Layla's.

"You are too smart not to have put the pieces together," she said.

My jaw deviated to the front and back as I tried to remember my breathing . . . as I attempted to keep my wings from prematurely taking flight while indoors. Because yes, I was too smart. But not once had I allowed myself to think the actual words.

"It is said," Blythe said quietly, "that the Bahidicaras were put into a vessel and that is how they were contained. Another theory is that the priestess and all of the essence that came with her into Garlandia was moved to the ether. Whether that was the intention of she or he or they that performed this ritual, it was not the end all of the cult and its leader. The priestess's spirit lived on, along with whatever mass of energy she'd conjured in her following."

"What are you saying?" I whispered.

I knew what was coming. I just so badly wanted one of them to say *anything* else.

"Dora was only one of two," Blythe said. "There was a set of twins. It is rumored that one was weak while one was strong, and it was the weak one who the priestess wore as a suit when the time came to ditch her body and bind her power. And before you ask, she couldn't bind her intention with the strong one—I'm afraid there's no answers for that, other than it just couldn't be done." She paused and her chest lifted. "You've already been told that Dora was known to all as the untouchable one, but her sister Malina—since her spirit was taken with their mother's when the cult was demolished—she became known as the lost child." The room was so quiet, all that could be heard was the sound of sauce thickening over a burner. Even Phyllis had stopped moving around the kitchen. "Odds are, Makayla, that your friend was of interest to Dora because the witch from Lantern's Edge could smell it." She leaned even more forward in her seat. "Over the years someone has taken it upon themselves to rid the world of the Hecate bloodline, for it is only this blood that the priestess can merge her soul with." She shook her head. "No other vessel will work. From what I have heard, the bloodline is nearly extinct. Dora found interest in Cee-Cee not only because they shared the same blood, but because Cee-Cee had, inside her body, the spirit of someone who only knows destruction." She closed and reopened her eyes. "Cee-Cee is Malina, Makayla. And that personality that was uncovered when the witch from Lantern's Edge urged her to rip away her bindings, that was the priestess."

$\mathscr{K}$ 13 $\mathscr{K}$

Dora

The land they were roving over was known to all as Breya's Pass. To others, it was called a dead man's walk. Regardless of its label, it was the only route that existed between the Garlandian dark wood and the other surrounding lands. Dora had already instructed her passengers on this fierce and austere journey that those commonly referred to as the Easternly Witches would not be coming to the surface. Apparently, even *they* knew when to stay underground when something so unnatural graced their earth. But that didn't mean the winds were shying away. The world knew something terrible had arrived and it wasn't keeping quiet about it.

The clouds above the heads of Dora, Heime, Bally, and the girl were churning like ribbons of black licorice.

"Should we be wary?" Heime asked in a gruff voice, his

eyes squinting through the scarf he'd used to shield his rough skin from the elements.

Well aware that the girl could hear everything she was saying, even above the howling winds, Dora allowed her words to get carried away, "Even the highest power yields to consequence."

Suddenly, Dora came to an abrupt halt, causing the rest of her troops to do the same. As soon as their feet stopped moving the sky paused in its tracks and the gusts recoiled.

Heime stood shoulder to shoulder with Dora as he pulled down the gray fabric from around his face. "What has happened?"

"Nothing," answered Dora. "We've paused, so shall the world."

Behind them were Bally and the girl, who came to wrap around them from either side. Bally nearest his mentor and the girl standing but a foot from Dora.

"How much further?" asked the girl.

Dora pointed her cloaked arm up towards a mountain range in the distance. It was foreboding at best; its peaks as sharp as shark teeth and as dark as midnight. It did not snow on the Enclaves. The mountain wasn't like the others. It was a force more so than just a bit of earth carved by wind and water. The peak grew taller with every shadow it stole from its passersby. It was also a place that could be accessed from all worlds. Every world had an entrance to this despicable patch of land. That's what happens when a star dies on earth.

"As long as it takes us," said the witch. "Once we are there, we will take what we've come for then prepare for home."

Bally's voice was timid. "Home?"

Dora turned to look at the boy. "'Tis only home for some."

"What is it for the others," the girl asked, bending down onto one knee, and pressing her bare hand to the earth.

Dora, with her gaze still on Bally, retorted, "A return to the beginning."

The four remained in place for a few beats, peering out at their menacing destination and at the oddity of the weather frozen in place. At some point Dora's attention fell to the girl. She had her eyes closed and seemed to be concentrating.

"What are you doing?" Dora asked.

"Searching," she replied. Then shortly after added, "I'm hungry."

"You've just had some beets," Bally said, irritation licking the tail of his speech. "In fact, you ate part of my half as well."

"That's not what feeds me."

Heime looked questionably towards Dora, and then they all peered down as the girl who preferred to be called priestess lifted her hand from the sand only to punch a hole through it a second later. When she lifted her arm back up, it was to reveal a vole in her grasp. The small creature, a ninny at best, wiggled and squirmed as a foul grin began to form on the girl's face.

"I like my food fresh," she said, a tinny ring in her voice that made the guts of those who had to hear her sour. And then, with no further ado, she broke its neck and bit into it like a wild animal.

The ground they stood upon shook slightly as the girl sucked the blood from the small animal like a vampire jester who had been starved in a long tunnel for years on end. The clouds began to churn slowly, the wind began to whisper.

"This place doesn't want us here," Bally said very softly, a tear in his voice that had to have been bred from watching the face of a friend perform an unspeakable act.

"No," Dora stated, looking away from the unsightly thing happening at her side.

It was how it began . . . the draining of creatures. Her mother's memories were leaking back in.

"The *world* doesn't want us here," she clarified.

"Then perhaps we should go back," Bally said.

The girl dropped the vole to the ground and kicked dirt over it before wiping her mouth—her cherry red lips. "Not an option. Come, there's no time to waste."

The three of them stood in place as the girl began marching on, towards the Enclaves. Lightning struck the earth not so far ahead from where they made no move to follow.

Bally's broken heart could be heard in his voice as he directed his speech to anyone who might answer. "Why did she do that?"

Dora fixed her attention on the boy for a moment. "Why do people read about love, Bally?"

He turned and shot the witch a puzzled expression. "That's an odd thing to ask?"

Her gaze returned onto the back of she who was still marching forward into darkness. "Just answer, boy."

"I don't know—because it's a craving, I suppose. People like to experience it again and again. Especially if they haven't found it."

She blinked slowly. "Yes. We are drawn to that which we don't have. Some people crave bread because they only allow their bodies to take in protein, while others eat far too much sugar and may find themselves drawn to fresh vegetables. Something with a nice crisp crunch. When someone is without a spark of their own, they'll find a way to taste it . . . some might even discover a path that allows them to take the essence right out of a body. And sometimes the wrong body is taken, and the gods stain the earth with their anger."

Both Heime and Bally looked to the witch quizzically.

"You've been here before, haven't you, Dora?" Heime asked.

The witch clicked her tongue. "Perhaps," was all she said.

But in her head, the true story brought back visions of absolute horror and infinite destruction.

Neither Heime nor his associate chose to ask any further questions on the subject, for it was clear Dora would have rather drained her own vole than answer them.

They stood there for the count of ten before Dora signaled that they needed to get going. But before he took one more step towards the horror that inevitably stood before them, Bally pulled on Dora's cloak, forcing her to face him. "Is my friend still in there? Does she still exist?"

Dora very thoughtfully placed her hand over the boy's shoulder. "You wouldn't be here if she wasn't."

And then they were off, towards the Enclaves, past the cave that lingered in the sky for travelers who needed to avoid the Easternly Witches. Dora looked up at the hollowed structure as they passed, dipping her chin in a salute to the nearly transparent woman who shed tears down upon the travelers. When the girl wasn't looking, the witch kissed the tips of her fingers and sent an intention up to she who had lived on in torment.

You will be free soon, Breya. When this is all over, your ghost will be freed. She would make it so, for she had the power.

"Dora," said the boy.

The witch turned to give him her attention once more.

"I thought you were bad." When she gave him no reaction, his Adam's apple bobbed up and down like a lever. "But you aren't, are you?"

"Oh Bally," she said, giving the boy's shoulder a slight shake. "You've a good heart. A good spirit."

He stopped in his tracks, looking out in the distance as the girl continued to move ahead of them, then returned his attention to Dora. "How does this end?"

The witch sighed, then looked passed him to Heime. "'Tis wise to understand that when it comes to life, 'tis ill-advised to skip over chapters. The answers are always in the details, hidden in the script."

Bally's gaze moved from Dora's to nowhere in particular. "What's her name? That thing that's in Cee-Cee's body."

"Ah," said the witch, jerking her chin up and down before starting to move forward once more. "That is the question, isn't it? And I'm afraid that is something I wouldn't even have in my possession to give to you, even if I was in favor of skipping ahead."

Heime narrowed his eyes as the three of them moved forward in a single line. "Is it not essential to know what she is called?"

"Oh," Dora said, a throaty vibrato clinging to the edges of her speech. "Dearest friend, 'tis quite necessary. True evil cannot be disposed of properly unless one has figured out where it originated, and nothing comes forth as any sort of matter without a name."

"Makayla always doted over names," Bally muttered.

The comment was not lost on Dora. "There are no mistakes in this world, Bally. No coincidences."

Bally studied the witch for the beat of a short melody. "If we don't know her name, then how are we supposed to end this?"

"Again, young elf. 'Tis blasphemous to skip ahead."

They walked on in silence for almost a full minute before Dora shouted to the whole group, "Now then, my friends, it would be an advisable thing to let go of your apprehensions before we tread further towards the mount!" Both Heime and his apprentice gave the witch searching looks as she clarified, "It'll take from you your shadows before you ever have a chance to greet them for yourselves."

"And why is that a bad thing?" Bally asked.

"Awareness is a gift from the self. 'Tis grown from the residue of what grows around your heartbeats. 'Tis emotion—

fear. 'Tis healthy to own your trepidation—to rise from it, to face it. To have it taken from you before you learn to dance with it, is to steal away part of your soul. Do not allow that ground to take your shadows. Face them now, as we walk through hell, and then seal them up as we rise over the ashes of those who did not make it."

A ragged breath fell from Bally's lips as they moved on, but Dora held strong to her conviction that this boy would be fine. They all would. She didn't need to read ahead to know that. She'd already faced all her shadows, danced with her fears. She'd ascended as far up as she could go without leaving her body . . . she knew most everything about anything. She would not have brought this company if she didn't believe they could rally against what the Enclaves would try and get from them.

As for the priestess, her name would come. From there the seed that had grown into the most poisonous of plants would be permanently laid to rest. Expired. Exterminated. Extinct. And who was the one soul who had been created to get that name? Well, it *would* have to be someone who believed names meant a great deal to one's identity, now wouldn't it?

14

Makayla

The house was quiet and dark. Earlier that night, Phyllis had fed us all until our stomachs could handle no more, and to my utmost surprise, she'd ended the meal with the most beautiful and tastiest cake I'd ever had.

"Someone mentioned you've just earned eighteen rotations around the sun," Phyllis had said into my ear as she set down the cake. It was made of pears and cinnamon.

I'd turned to her just in time to catch her winking at Toby who was sitting next to me.

"What?" He'd shrugged, a slight grin on his face. "Do you think me ignorant of such a grand event?"

I'd simply bit down over my bottom lip and grinned. It might not have been the celebration I'd always envisioned— by any means—but it was all I needed and more. It was the first time in days I'd felt like my king was my king. Like he was present.

Dave, Blythe's uncle, had shown up just before we were all getting ready to retire. If it hadn't been for his wings and pointy ears, I would have thought he'd just gotten back from shooting some sort of celebrity chef show. He fit the bill, chef jacket and all.

For the briefest of moments, it was easy to imagine that I didn't have in my possession a sword forged by the gods; a weapon I was beginning to understand was meant for the heart of someone I loved very much. All I wanted to do was keep my eyes closed and take in the scent of this quaint three bed, two bath, split level home. Inside its walls were all anyone would ever need. Comfort, hot food, and love.

I didn't want to leave.

But I knew we couldn't stay and reveling in the comforts of this home seemed eerily similar to something I'd read once upon a time . . . a young adult book about some girl in a relationship with a guy who couldn't seem to love her back. She described the conflicting emotions she felt as she laid in his arms. Absorbing the euphoria of his touch while already fully aware of the impending fog setting in that represented their inevitable break up. This house and all it stood for was but a temporary thing. My life wasn't meant to be comfortable. If it was, I wouldn't have been born with such drive. Such purpose.

But sometimes even I had my breaking point.

Toby and I had been given the guest room while Layla bunked with Blythe. We were under strict orders from the mermaid to get as much sleep as we could because we needed to leave the next day, and once we left the safe land, we had to be hyper alert. The mer would be after Avalon's Sword, which meant they would be searching us out like we were carrying a nuclear bomb on our backs. Which it kind of was, if you thought about it. I mean, I'd been handed the one weapon that could kill a deity. Or a deity's offspring, which is the only way it had been able to splice open Avalon's heart and send her back home.

I'd been tucked into Toby's side, his arm around me. It was cozy. Still, I'd had way too much on my mind to sleep, and even though we'd been eating all day, my stomach had begun to growl as I laid in my king's arms. So, that's how I found myself in the kitchen in the middle of the night.

"Hey, what are you doing up?"

I paused from where I'd been perched on a stool in the kitchen, eating leftover birthday cake like it was cold pizza. The light went on and Layla strutted in; she was wearing a pair of boxer shorts and a tank top.

My tongue paused over the giant spoon I'd foraged for in one of the drawers. "I, uh—" I pulled the spoon away and swallowed some frosting. "I couldn't sleep."

"Yeah," she said, leaning against a wall while crossing her arms over her chest. "Me neither." She seemed to study me for a moment before saying, "Toby says you're a dragon dancer. Is that true?"

I bit off a chunk of cake that was stuck to the spoon. "I guess so."

I'd only used my weirdo dragon skills once, and that was to save my life against my Aunt Helene. To this day I have no idea how I'd done it.

Can you hear me?

I nearly dropped the spoon in my hand.

Layla's lips curled up at the ends. *Guess so.*

"What are you doing?" I questioned. "And how are you doing it?"

Her arms dropped down by her sides and she walked over to me, took the spoon out of my hand, and began digging into what was left of the cake. "Dragon dancers can talk to one another. Usually only if you've already spoken to a dragon. Guessing you already have."

"Sort of."

Her eyes widened as she swallowed her recent bite then set down the spoon. "You've got a lot of baggage, don't you?"

I just knew there was a long crease between my brows. "Why do you ask that?"

"Everyone knows who Makayla Wood is. The chatter started from your homeland into all of the worlds as soon as you reemerged into Garlandia." She raised her hand in the sky and used her finger to act like she was writing a headline. "Lost Erwain returns! And who is she? The most uptight, unfiery faery of all." She dropped her hand and centered her gaze over mine. "Except you're not uptight. In fact, you seem like you're more lost than ever."

"I—"

She shook her head. "You don't owe me anything."

I bit my lip and eventually nodded. It was a practice that I needed to get used to—not feeling like I had to respond to every single thing that was said to or about me.

"All right, well, I'm going to try and get some shut eye. You and I need to practice at some point, either before we go or along the way."

"Practice what?"

She pushed herself away from the kitchen island where the cake and I had been getting to know one another quite well. "Your dance. Trust me, Makayla, where we are going, there will be dragons. They don't look frightening to those of us who can speak with them, but you still need to understand the proper way of working with them."

"Yeah . . . okay."

She nodded once more then turned on her bony heels back towards the way she'd come.

"Hey."

She looked back at me over her shoulder.

"Don't you, like, need to be in the water sometimes?"

She grinned. "That's a myth. We can spend as much time on land or in the water as we like."

"Oh. That's pretty cool."

"Sure is," she said, before she disappeared from my sight.

I dug the spoon back into the cake and took another bite. In a matter of seconds, it had started to taste less sweet. As I pushed away from the counter, heat began to move up my neck, traveling north until it situated itself next to my eyes.

Stop it, Makayla! I shouted to myself. How was I ever supposed to slay a single thing if I couldn't stop crying? Without overthinking it, I jumped from the stool and fluttered over to the back door, not stopping to breathe until I was outside. Even then, I found myself doubling over while gripping the sides of my face. Thinking I was alone, I allowed my back muscles to shake as I gulped at the air around me. *Did I have baggage?* Of course I did—and by the loads! It was all just too much—too, *too* much. First Jeremy had been made into Bally, and then Cee-Cee was turned inside out, and now my king . . . I didn't even know how to circulate my thoughts around that one. I was just so—

"Miss Makayla, is that you? Why, are those tears?"

I jolted upright, turning to find that Petal had made herself comfortable under a large Maple tree. A tree just like we had in the human world. Oh, thank the goddess that it was just her. The old girl didn't have it in her to be judgmental. Ever so slowly, I began marching barefoot towards my Pegasus friend.

"Hey Petal," I said, using a knuckle to wipe at the moisture under my eye. "I just—I've never been this vulnerable. It's written all over me." I bent over with my face in my hands, then sobbed into them, "I have baggage!"

"Ahhh," cooed Petal, sighing as I curled into her chest, letting her head croon down over my shoulder. "You do know you wouldn't have signed on for this journey if you couldn't handle it."

I didn't speak for a whole five minutes. I just let Petal absorb my frustrations and anxieties. When I started to calm down, my thoughts transferred back to the last couple of days that Cee-Cee and I had together. The real Cee-Cee, before she did that unbinding spell. It was then that something returned to me. Something kind of big.

I looked up at Petal with large eyes. "Cee-Cee said just days ago that meeting me was for a reason. It was like she knew."

Petal cooed. "Somewhere, deep inside, she did know that. But Makayla, please understand that she is still your friend. Anastacia is the reincarnation of a soul once known as Malina, but Cee-Cee is very much her own person, and *this life was hers*. It was robbed from her just as she was robbed from you." She paused, nuzzling her nose into my open hand. "Does this make sense?"

It did, but— "It doesn't make it any less shitty."

We were quiet for a moment, staring up through the branches and leaves into the late-night sky. Were there more stars here?

As I watched the twinkling lights up above, my thoughts cycled back to the other reason for my recent unease. "He's different, Petal."

She didn't respond right away; she seemed to be taking pleasure in my playing with her ears. When she did speak, she stated her words very carefully.

"No one comes back to the same life twice."

A hitch grew in the back of my throat. Since I'd seen Rally's blade slice through the air, separating Toby's head from his body, I hadn't been able to get the image out of my head. Yes, my king had returned . . . the necklace he'd been wearing around his neck from the moment I'd met him had been gone. An insurance policy set in place because he knew his date with destiny was chasing him. He was solid, his tongue warm when it met mine. His touch sent shivers down my spine . . . but something wasn't right.

"Is he the same soul?" I asked, sniffling quietly.

"Yes, Makayla. He is the soul you are bound to."

"Then, um—" I couldn't get the shake from my voice. "Then what did you mean just now, when you said no one can return to the same life?"

"Just that."

"Please," I pleaded, my cheeks so hot I worried they would burn right off. "Elaborate."

Again, she took her time responding. Finally, she said, "You have heard of others who have left their bodies only to return, yes?"

"Of course." Who hadn't heard of near-death experiences? But Toby hadn't been near death—he'd been murdered. A spell had brought him back.

"They aren't ever the same because we aren't meant to see that far past the veil." Petal tilted her head and leaned back against the tree's trunk, letting me fall further against her. "The bodies we choose in these worlds, they cut us off from what exists out there, in the rest of the universe. If we remembered where we came from then we may not use this opportunity correctly."

"And what opportunity are you speaking of?" I questioned softly.

"The chance to learn, Makayla Wood. Soul ascension. Walking through dimensions, finding all that they have to offer—it is how we advance. 'Tis through our development that the light, and darkness, outside of these worlds grows."

I sucked in my top lip and bit down. After a very

thoughtful inhalation, I noted, "You sound like you remember what it's like on the other side."

She chuckled to herself, causing my body to bounce softly against her side. "I am merely a very old soul. Just as you are. The difference is I've spent a lot more time in this lifetime than you have. You shall live a long time, my queen, and one day you will be the wise one."

A slight smile found my lips. "I love that you believe in me, Petal."

Her fur danced across my cheek. "Why wouldn't I? You are someone who sees a wall before them and doesn't wait for a door that may not ever open to appear. You are not someone who tries to back track and find a way around it. No, Makayla, you are someone who learns how to fly and goes over the top of it."

I hiccupped and my heart beats choked. "What happens if my wings get clipped?"

"Oh," she said, sounding very much like a warm old lady offering me a platter of fresh cookies. "They will not be harmed, but if they ever were, I know you would pound your fists through those bricks until they were bloody, and you would smash your way through." She hugged me closer with her nose and my chest fluttered. "Failure isn't a word you have ever learned, and one you should continue to refuse."

I was relishing in the comfort of her heartbeats when I suddenly realized how heavy my eyelids had become. It had been one big adrenaline rush after another ever since I'd woken up wedded to my king. The world was getting blurry, which meant the day had more than expired. A reminder that for the rest of my days I would have to apply the drops Maude had made specifically for my eyes so that I could see. I would forever have Morcai venom in my veins. Poison.

I let myself fall asleep in Petal's care, but just before I

danced away from the world and into the all-encompassing dark void that cushioned us from these trivial lives we lived, I whispered, "Thank you for loving me."

"Forever and always, my queen. You have my sword."

And then I drifted.

15

Makayla

The sun was fierce that next morning as I was poked back into reality. Or not morning—it was far too bright for it to be early.

"Sup? Time to get moving, queenie."

I blinked and blinked but all I could see was the outline of a head.

"Blythe?" I asked, sitting up groggily, while reaching for the drops hanging from the chain around my neck. As I deposited them into each eye, Petal groaned as she, too, came back to life. "What time is it?"

The faery came into focus with each blink of my eyes. "Noon."

I nearly jumped out of my skin. "What? Why'd you let us sleep so late?"

The faery's right shoulder met her ear. "The swimmers

will be expecting us to have left early. Layla decided we should take off later so we could be the ones stalking them."

"The swimmers?" I asked, rubbing my eyes.

The voice that still made my stomach stir in all the right ways perked up and I looked out to find Toby staring out into the distance with his hands on his hips. "The mer."

"Oh . . . right," I said, carefully standing up. I'd slept like a rock against Petal, but my limbs and back felt like they needed to be pulled apart and reattached.

Layla and Blythe had traced out a potential route for us last night on a homemade map. We were still closer to the shore than anywhere, so poking our heads out from this safe land had to be done with caution. Layla knew the way her people thought—the way they tracked.

"The last thing they'll do," she'd said the night before, an arm on either side of the map her and Blythe had worked out, "is listen to reason. Their vision is tunnelized. All they care about is getting that sword back so that they can say they have it. They care not that it belongs to no one; that as soon as it has served its purpose it will return to where it came from."

That purpose being to slay the beast it had been made for. I couldn't think on what that meant, not yet. My heart was already sore. I'd liked things far better when it was only a beastly king who I'd chosen to confront. Loral was no longer the worst of our problems; he was but a symptom.

Layla assured us that the mer would be planted near the shore, along different forest points, and as close as they could get to Forest Peak. But unless we caught sight of one of them, which we hoped we wouldn't, we couldn't be exactly sure of their locations.

"Once we get over into the cursed lands, we should be clear of them," she'd said.

The cursed lands, apparently, were where the Bahidicaras

had begun. In the dark wood where Forest Peak had once been a beautiful place for witches, elves, fey, and humans to live. The land stretched out for miles, and everywhere the cult had stepped, the land had died.

With my vision back to crystal clear, I stood and cracked my back. However, when I straightened out, I nearly collapsed again—thankfully, Blythe was there to catch my fall. My arm tingled where she held it.

"Easy there," she said.

"Sorry," I said, shaking my head. My stomach growled for all to hear.

Toby made his way over to me. "We should have some food before we go. There may not be a lot of time to pause once we break into the outer world."

"Of course," Blythe said, giving me an odd look before turning for the kitchen, as if she wasn't sure I'd be okay. "Stay where you are, I'll bring out some stuff. Might as well enjoy the blue sky a little longer while we have it."

Petal had gone off to the apple orchards on the other side of the house. Once it was just the two of us, Toby wrapped his arms around me.

"Are you feeling okay, my queen?"

No. I was shaky, hungry, and had had a thin layer of sweat over my brow since we'd landed in this purple world. I couldn't seem to retain my balance and my veins seemed to be pumping twice the amount of blood they used to.

I couldn't look Toby in the eyes anymore. Not since I'd seen what I'd seen. Not since I'd watched him die.

But how could I tell him that?

"I'm fine," I lied. Because sometimes that's what the moment calls for.

Toby's mouth parted and his voice cracked. For the first time since Raton, I thought perhaps I was going to hear from *him*. The elfin boy who had bowed before me in that market where we'd first met, causing the Garlandians to chatter amongst themselves heatedly. The one who had cast spells around us in those forests of our homeland so that he could make me a secret stone and brush his lips against mine. My deepest love, who I had followed down into this life so that we could repair the relationship that had been broken during a different time. But in an instant, that Toby was gone—replaced again by this shell of the elf I'd married.

"Oh my goddess," said Blythe, carrying plates of food in her hands as she walked right past us and to the picnic table just a few feet away. She seemed completely unaware that she'd butchered the moment. "Phyllis cooked enough brunch for an army. Hope you bitches are hungry."

Toby looked at me while raising his brows. "Let's go take care of that growling stomach, shall we?"

"Yeah," I agreed, my voice a little shakier than I intended for it to be.

I had a seat across from Blythe. "Where's Layla?"

"Staring at that map still," she grunted, reaching for a raspberry pastry, and pouring herself some orange juice.

"I should go confer with her once more," Toby said, curling his fingers around his chin. "I'm unsure if popping out on the eastern edge is really the best strategy."

I shot him an irritated look and was about to object, because it would have been nice to share one last meal together before we were hunted again, but he was already three steps in towards the door.

"Let him go, queenie," Blythe whispered.

My attention shot to her just as Toby slipped inside the house.

"Excuse me?"

Her gaze froze over mine. "It is his job to keep you safe. That is all I mean."

I couldn't help the daggers that shot from my eyes. Her

assumptions were correct, I just wasn't in the mood to be protected. All I wanted was . . . well, I wasn't sure about that yet.

So obviously aware of the invisible objects I'd thrown her way, Blythe added, "He mentioned it last night—that he was Titania's keeper. That kind of means he's *your* keeper. It's his sole motivation to keep you safe. I just, you know, can like tell you're a little annoyed with him. But he's just doing what he's magically contracted to do, you know." When I didn't attempt to say anything back, she passed me a plate of sausages. "Eat up, there's no continental breakfast where we're going."

I held my stiff expression over hers for only a few seconds more; it would have been longer, but those sausages were going to make me drool if I didn't consume them sooner than later. Taking the offered plate, I added three links to my plate then reached for a raspberry tart of my own.

Deciding to change lanes, I asked, "So how do you and Layla know one another anyway? Like, how did she know to bring you in on our death march to the cursed lands?"

"It's not a death march," Blythe retorted, sliding some butter onto a bit of banana bread. "And we used to date."

My eyebrows shot up to the sky. As soon as she looked at me, she smirked.

"Didn't see that one coming, did you?"

"To be fair," I said, taking a very unladylike bite of both sausage and pastry, "I didn't see any of this coming. But I don't need to tell you that, right?" I shot her a look which caused her to grin. "I mean, doesn't everyone know who Makayla Wood is?" I added with heavy sarcasm.

She chuckled softly and sipped from her juice. "She ran away from the sea—Layla. That's when we met."

"When was that?" I asked.

The Reef faery sighed, and her eyes roamed to the left.

"Oh, shortly after they murdered her mother for having Danka's son as a mate. She knew her own life was on the line, so she swam away until she befriended Shell—"

"The dragon . . ." I whispered, my mouth so full a crumb fell as I spoke. My thoughts quickly deviated to the conversation Layla and I had had the night before.

"Yeah." She reached for a plate of fried eggs and put some on my plate before taking some for herself. "She was lucky she was born with the ability to dance with dragons. The beast saved her life." She took a huge bite of egg before going on. "It was one of the ways people or creatures used to get in here before we made a deal with the pookas. We hired a few dragons for transport. Shell was one of them."

"It's like the underground railroad," I mused between a bite of pastry and a sip of juice.

"Yeah, I suppose," Blythe agreed.

My eyes became slits. "You get the reference?"

"Yeah. Our education system covers all the worlds. Human history is just as important to us as any other. Every world has made mistakes and has risen above them—there's so much to learn out there, it's kinda crazy."

"That's so true . . ."

Blythe set her hands flat over the table and gave me her full attention. "Garlandia didn't always used to be like it is now. It used to be like it is here; in this safe land. There's no reason for it not to be that way again."

Something about the way she looked at me caused my stomach to stir and I had to look away. Perhaps it was too much—thinking about the future. What it could be . . . what it would inevitably turn into if I couldn't follow through.

As if she could read my thoughts, she said, "You're not alone, Makayla." My chest lifted as I felt her hand come over mine. I looked down at her light brown skin—it nearly matched Toby's. Light brown skin and lavender hair. And the way she looked at me—

"So, why did you and Layla break up?" I asked, pulling my hand gently away.

I could feel her gaze on me still, but whether she wanted to discuss her past relationship or not, she went with it. "Layla is . . . well, she's stubborn as shit, isn't she?" she chuckled.

I carefully looked up at her. She was adding some cream and sugar into—

"Wait, is that coffee?"

"Yeah," she retorted in a tone that suggested I was ignorant.

"You like coffee?"

"Um, didn't you, like, meet me at a coffee shop?"

"Yeah, but I thought faeries hated it." Except for this one, obviously.

A sharp canine came down over her bottom lip and she grinned. "It's not a Garlandian favorite from what I hear, but that doesn't mean every faery detests it." With her hand over the carafe, she asked, "Would you like some?"

My eyes nearly bugged out of my skull. "More than anything."

She shoved the carafe and an empty cup my way. As soon as the brown liquid was in the mug, I lifted it to my lips and inhaled deeply through my nose. It had been so long since I'd had a good cup of joe. I mean, sure, I'd had some time in the human world before returning to Garlandia, but Cee-Cee and Jeremy had been in charge of ordering the coffee and coffee, by their definition, translated to fraps. Right there, in that mug, that was what I truly lived for.

"You are so interesting," Blythe said with a laugh as soon as I had taken my first sip and my eyes had rolled back into the deep recesses of my mind.

"I've been told," I muttered. "So, what were you saying before I interrupted you? Something about Layla being stubborn."

"Oh yeah. Well, she knew if she returned to the mer that her life may be put in jeopardy, but she didn't care. She like needed them to know that just because someone is born with a certain blood that it doesn't mean they are destined to become a monster. She had already been raised to believe she wasn't good enough for them because she was half elf, and she knew that wasn't true because to this day she's the fastest swimmer they've got."

"So she went back on her own?" I asked, thoughtfully.

"About a year ago." She picked at her banana bread and stuck a small piece in her mouth. "We parted on good terms. I mean, what kind of an ass would I have been to hate her for wanting to prove herself to her circle? And we weren't meant to be, not forever. We were just kind of having fun."

"But you must've been close for her to know to bring us to you."

She locked eyes with me again. "I told her a lot. I guess she was really the first soul who I trusted enough to let my feelings out to."

I thought about my next words for a few beats before I said them. "Do you miss your parents?"

She inhaled a lengthy breath through her nose, then cupped her hands around her brew. "Yes and no. I wonder why they did it—gave themselves to that disgusting creature. But to be honest, I was so young, and Phyllis and Dave have always been so loving. They are my true parents."

"I know what that's like," I said, causing her to cock her head to the side. "I mean, not totally, but I know what it's like to be kind of like, adopted. How it is to wonder what life would have been like if certain events hadn't have happened."

Her mouth parted and she started to say something, but

just then Toby and Layla erupted from the house, the hilt of Avalon's sword perched in Toby's hand.

"Ready to go crush some curses, then?" Layla asked as they neared the picnic table.

"Weren't you going to teach me how to dragon dance, or whatever?" I asked.

Layla winked at me. *Later.*

I cocked my head to the side. *Fine*, I retorted.

"Nice," the mermaid said, nodding appreciatively my way.

Whatever, I'm good at things. I sent her a returning wink.

"Aren't you going to eat?" Blythe asked, looking at both Toby and Layla.

"Naw, all full from breakfast," Layla answered.

Toby pulled my bag back from his other hand and tossed it to me. "Fill it up with whatever you can. It'll save us a day or two of foraging."

"Ugh. More foraging," I sighed. "I hadn't thought of Petal as competitive until it was three of us and a berry bush. That Pegasus sure can eat."

Toby's hand had just landed on my shoulder when Blythe perked up. "She's a Pegasus?"

"Yes," Toby affirmed. "She was my father's. She brought me into Garlandia after my village burned down."

My attention was geared over how shocked Blythe seemed to be. I guess I was just as stunned the first time Petal's wings emerged. Apparently, though, there was more to it.

"How did you get away with that all of those years under your uncle's nose?"

Toby smirked. "How do *you* think? She's mystical. The old goat had no idea."

My gaze was moving back and forth between them. "What are you guys talking about?"

Layla centered her pointed eyes over mine and stated,

"Pegasi are of the ether. To entertain one of them in any world is extremely rare. To actually own one is nearly unheard of."

"It's also seen as a message," Blythe added.

By now I was leaning in over my plate so far that my hair had gotten stuck in egg. "What kind of message?"

"What else *would* it be?" Layla said with an added tone. "Wherever the Pegasus is, the gods be watching. From what we know of Loral, he wouldn't have been too keen on that," she said with a scoff.

"No," Toby stated stiffly. "Up until recently, he'd convinced himself *he* was a god."

"Where do you think the old boy is hiding these days, anyway?" Layla questioned.

"Did he get away?" Blythe asked, with a last-minute mouthful of yogurt. "We weren't sure what happened to him. News reached us of course, but we only heard that there was war."

"Oh, he got away," Toby grinned. "But he'll never last in the wild. My uncle was reared with a silver spoon and I'm on good authority that his status as 'untouchable' is waning."

"But you've got to get him back, right?" Blythe questioned, pointing a finger at me.

"How else will the crown move?"

"We'll get him back," Toby said, giving my shoulder a squeeze. "Makayla has been assigned to him, and from what I know of my queen, she isn't the type to lose a case."

"Yeah well," I said, a wave of nausea causing me to hunker down, "I haven't had a chance to—" Suddenly the world tipped over, bile rushed up my throat, and I leaned down just in time to heave up everything I'd just eaten.

"Damn that's a lot of wasted calories," Layla said dryly.

The world weighed in over my chest and I retched again. Once everything was out of my stomach, I immediately felt better. "Shit," I said, wiping my mouth with a napkin as Toby bent down to feel my head. "I hope we didn't get sick from that last batch of berries."

"No, I don't think it was that," Toby muttered, handing me some water.

"I think queenie's just a little stressed out," Blythe said with a gentle smile.

"Well considering we're off to kill her best frie—" Layla started but quickly stopped as soon as I stared bullets at her. "Uh, right—sorry."

"Dang, Lay," Blythe whisper shouted at her. "Do you have to be so cutting all the time?"

But as I rested by forehead in my hands and let Toby soothe me as he ran his hand over my back, I knew the mermaid was right. I'd handled plenty of stress over the course of my short life, but never had I been handed a sword and told that the end of its blade belonged in my best friend's heart.

Not that I'd ever had a best friend. Cee-Cee had been one of my firsts.

I leaned over the table and yakked again.

Poison. My body had poison in it.

Maude had said these drops were all I would need, but what if she was wrong? What if I was slowly dying from that Morcai bite?

Toby kept his hand on my back as I continued to puke my brains out. "It's okay, my queen, your strength will return," he whispered into my ears.

By the gods, I sure hope he wasn't just saying that to be nice. We couldn't afford for me to fall apart. Avalon's sword was in *my* keep. I couldn't fail. It wasn't an option.

16

Lantern's Edge

There is a phenomenon that most creatures and living beings aren't aware of. A slip of matter that exists between the divine and . . . well, everything else. The entrance isn't something that can be found via dirt or stone. Nor that of water. It can't even be discovered through one's mind. So how, one might ask, does one even find this opening between mortality and infinity? The answer: it's complicated.

Let us backtrack.

If, as some speculate, the madness we call creation was the effect of an explosion of light, then it could be completely plausible that the eruption caused a recoil in the form of pocketed darkness. A vibrational tunnel that served as the entrance place to the gods. If such a place existed, it wouldn't be a common place for one to find themselves, not even upon transitioning back into the ether. However, accidents happen. What if all one needed to experience such a place was for that individual to encounter both creation and death at the exact same moment? What if that is the secret to finding the tunnel? What if . . .

When Dora rose from the surface of the lake the day she was to be drowned, she rose from the waters in a beautiful velvety cloak. A gift. She'd also come out of that lake with a realization.

Soaked from head to toe and a burn in her chest that hadn't ever lived there before, she stepped back into Lantern's Edge and faced the woman who had birthed her along with her sister. In that burning heart of hers was a secret.

"No," the priestess cursed upon setting her gaze over Dora. "NO!"

Dora was only able to meet Malina's wide eyes for a fleeting second before the priestess jumped from the circle she'd been readying to open around her and her last remaining daughter. Their mother gripped the back of Dora's dripping wet hair and dragged her over the dusty floorboards until they were right back at the edge of that black hole she called a lake. She was so enraged that she didn't even take notice of the new garb hanging around her child's shoulders. Of how it was oddly dry.

"Now," she whispered haughtily into Dora's ear, "you return into that water hole and let it swallow you up. Do you hear me?"

Dora hadn't argued. She was still quite shaken from her experience in the lake. For all intents and purposes, she should have been dead. The last circumstance she ever could have imagined was what actually went down. So, she shuffled forward, all the while the woman (if one could still call her that) pushed Dora until her feet were enveloped by water once again. Before long Dora was down in the depths once more. No bright light this time, no odd experience with fate .

. . but still, air found her. And the shimmering, black cloak kept her warm.

Dora knew that the second she resurfaced, her mother would come undone. So, she waited. She sat into the pit of the lake that rested before Lantern's Edge, amongst the bones of all the other sacrifices the priestess had offered their deity over the years. If only Hecate had been humbled by the offerings, if only she'd been gracious. Then maybe Dora could just die. But that wasn't in the blueprints.

When the young girl felt that darkness had arrived overhead—that the stars had come into bloom—Dora finally got up from her cross-legged position and exited the water. As she walked up the stairs that led into Lantern's Edge, she hovered over that last step. *Should she just turn around?* She had nowhere to go, but if she kept moving forward, as she'd been instructed to do, how many more times would she have to count the seconds down in that grave that refused her?

The world has lost its music. You, Dora, are the last living instrument. You are victory.

She couldn't get that voice to stop echoing around her head. That frightening, yet maternal voice.

She crammed her eyes shut and balled up her fists. She'd never asked for this. All she'd wanted to do was save her sister —give her a chance to fight so that maybe she could find a way to live in this world. Find a way to use the light's end for what it was always intended.

The door swung open while her eyes were shut. This time, there was nothing but a heavy sigh to greet her. When she looked up, her mother was staring down at her with tired eyes. The priestess hadn't appeared this frazzled in a very long time. If ever.

"Why won't you die?"

Dora wrapped her cloaked arms around her soaking body and looked down at her feet. "I don't know," she lied.

Her mother waited for her to reenter the home, then let the door swing shut. With a sneer, she asked, "Where did you get that?"

Dora pulled the cloak tighter around her; it was so large that the bottom pooled around her feet.

"I found it."

The priestess all but growled. "I care not. I am done with this night. With this day."

"Where is Malina?" Dora asked softly, dripping lake water all over the floor. Her mother flopped onto the nearest chair while bringing a hand up to her forehead. "In bed. The work wouldn't take speed. And no wonder," she hissed, sneering at her daughter. "You are still breathing."

"I did try to die," Dora whispered. Another lie.

After several quiet moments, the priestess got up and shuffled away to her quarters, leaving Dora to stand there like an unwelcomed stray. Craning her head in the direction of her and her sister's bedroom, she padded over and silently entered.

Malina's chest was rising and lowering gently, but the reflection from the little bit of light on the other side of their room caught in her pupils. The young girl shot up as soon as she saw her twin. Dora lunged for her, holding out an arm, demanding that she stay in bed. She didn't, however, refrain from accepting an embrace.

"I thought you were forever gone," Malina muttered as she cried into her shoulder. "What has happened? Does mother know you've returned?"

Dora pulled away from her sister and looked deeper into her twin's eyes than she ever had. "Do not ever call her that."

She's not your mother.

Haunting words from the lake.

"Then what shall we call her?" Malina asked quietly, wiping at a tear.

Dora returned thoughtfully to that tunnel she'd peered into when she'd first landed at the bottom of the lake that day. She then licked her lips and pulled the cloak tighter around her; as she did, a wind roared from inside its folds, and she became dry and warm. "An unfortunate accident."

And that was one hundred percent the truth.

17

Dora

Dora, Bally, Heime, and the girl had made it through the storm. There hadn't been any place to find shelter or a place to rest, so they'd had no other choice than to brave the elements overnight. Each of them had been better acquainted with darkness than they'd ever cared to be. Just as dawn had broken, they'd found a grouping of rocks that served as a decent shelter and had taken the time to close their eyes. Dora kept watch as the three of them fell into their dreams, keeping a keen eye over the body housing the priestess's soul.

After waking from their dreams, their minds packed from all they'd seen—the heavy winds and sand in their faces and the lightning that had broken the marbled gray and black sky into billions of pieces—they were finally at the foothills of the Enclaves, staring up into nothing but gray for as far as the eyes could see.

"*This* is the mountain we are to climb?" Bally questioned.

"'Tis," Dora chirped.

"It doesn't look all that foreboding," Bally retorted. "I thought it was cursed or something."

"A nightmare isn't scary until you realize you can't get out," Dora stated with a firm jaw.

"I've always been told that it's not getting up into its peak that kills those who travel upon it," Heime stated in a gruff voice. "It's getting here and getting back."

The girl scoffed. "*We* had no trouble getting here."

Without removing her gaze from the stony foothills, Dora snapped. "Of course we didn't. Even the foulest of spirits know when they've been upstaged." Then, her gaze moving to Heime's, she added, "The mount may not kill those who climb it outright, but it will try its damnedest to drive them insane." She pulled at her cloak from where it rested around her neck. "We happen to be in a fortunate position. We won't be harmed, but you would all still do well to remain alert."

The girl looked like she'd just swallowed an egg whole. "What are you talking about?"

The witch's gaze moved in a straight line until it rested on that of the girl. She offered no more than a grin.

"You're. Up. To. Something."

Dora replied with an easy tone. "I'm a witch. I'm always up to something. Why must you always believe it has to do with you? You're really quite vain."

Dora noted as the girl inhaled deeply through her nose but said nothing. The *priestess* was determined to gain back her memories. She'd scrounged for more creatures to drain as they'd trudged over the sandy earth overnight, but anything with a beating heart was hard to come by the closer they'd gotten to the path that led to these foothills. Not that the animals would bring her what she was truly after. The act of drinking blood had returned to her, but why she'd ever done it in the first place was still lost on her.

However, the earth didn't need to remember. It shuddered with every step the girl took, fully aware of what was crossing over it. It wasn't near the effect the priestess had had over the grounds in her last body, but still, wherever the girl stepped, the ground darkened. If there *had* been life this far out in the desert, it would have fled or died in their wake.

Dora was well aware that the priestess was seething; repression coated her tongue like the animal blood she was consuming, but she could not prove that Dora was behind her lost memories. It had been Dora, after all, who had found Anastacia—who had invited her to Lantern's Edge—and who had given the girl the unbinding spell, which had unshackled the priestess from the prison Gloria had sent her into when the woman had realized who was inhabiting the body of her little girl.

Dora was only thankful that Gloria had been wise enough to realize that her bloodline was susceptible to this evil. That even though it had been years since the Bahidicaras had ruined Hecate's name, that the reincarnation of the priestess and her lost child was still a great possibility. And she was extremely fortunate that Gloria had also had the sense to realize that her little Cee-Cee, though sometimes gentle and kind, could in the time it took one to perform a finger snap, transform into a monster. Gloria had known that she had given birth to a body with two souls. And she knew how world-ending one of those souls could be if given the opportunity to reign.

This is what Dora had seen in the girl's tea leaves.

Dora observed as Bally turned and peered back in the direction from which they'd come. Though they were only at the entrance to the Enclaves, they'd already risen at least a thousand feet.

"Just our luck, the sky is blue back there and the storms have died down," Bally said haughtily.

Dora clenched her cloak around her throat and began to walk forward. "Haven't you heard a thing I've said, boy? *We* are the storm. *We* are the goblins who steal the babes from mothers' arms." She paused, using all her energy to pull herself up the side of the mountain. "The curses that feed from the travelers who come to stake their claim over these rocky hills aren't looking out their windows, for even the devil knows when he's been outmatched." She grunted as she took another giant step up. It wasn't widely traveled but there was somewhat of a trail to follow. "Come now. When you see a beast, pay it no mind. When you tire, sip from the remedy I provided, and when you hunger, nibble on your rations. Do not look behind you, do not look to the side. Keep your gaze straight ahead."

Dora continued up the side of the mountain, clinging to the rocky edge. Yes, she'd been here before, but back in that day there had been no mountain. No, that grew after her and her company left these grounds. Really, it was no more than a grave.

"How do you know so much about this place?" Bally asked as the witch huffed, pulling herself up the boulder.

Steadying herself, then placing a hand over her hip, she answered. "I know souls who know darkness; I've been told what to expect." Staring off into the distance, she added, "The last time I hovered over this ground, it was but a desert. The last time I was here, I watched the earth cry. In fact, I was here the day the mount began to grow by the hands of the gods."

"Seriously?" Bally scoffed. "How—I mean, what?"

The witch's gaze flitted to the girl. The priestess was busy scouring the grounds for signs of drainable life. She wasn't paying them any mind.

With her attention still geared over the girl, Dora stated carefully, "'Tis a long story." Then moving her gaze to her new elvish friend, she added, "I'll say this: when one is fueling themselves from the power of others, they tend to start small then slowly move on to bigger and tastier options." Her voice rose as she tempted fate, returning her gaze to settle over the girl. "When blood is not enough, there are souls, and when the souls within reach no longer curb the craving, 'tis time to move on to higher frequencies."

Bally waited for her to finish—to say more. But she didn't. "I don't understand."

Heime, who had been listening intently, took a step closer to the boulder Dora stood upon. "This is where it happened, isn't it?" he asked in revelation.

"'Tis," was all Dora said.

"Where what happened?" Bally asked.

Heime looked from Dora to the girl, then back to Dora. The witch gave a quick nod of her head, insinuating that it was okay to say it out loud. "The death of our bloodline, Bally."

Again, Dora nodded. "An excellent way to word that, my friend."

Bally's expression mimicked a blank sheet of paper. "I so don't get it."

Dora managed a half smile. "You will one day, Bally." And then she turned around and began evaluating their climb once more.

From the drawings she'd studied, she knew the beginning to be rough, the middle to be easy, and the summit to be deadly. She couldn't call on the dragons until they reached a certain height, for this mountain demanded travelers to pay their way to the top by getting at least halfway there on foot. At this point, she knew to just put one foot ahead of the other and to instruct her company to do the same. And for better or worse, the subject of what had happened to create this mountain drifted away, back to where it came from.

18

Makayla

The sun had grown tired by the time we were ready to go. Our aim had been to leave shortly after lunch, but when I couldn't stop yakking our plan got put on hold. Phyllis had given me something that tasted like a vanilla milkshake, and since I'd drank it, I'd felt a lot better.

"I've made some remedies for you," Phyllis added, as Toby and I stood near Petal, taking in the last of the beauty this place had to offer. Hopefully we'd have the chance to see it again. "Pill form," she added, holding out her hand, revealing a small bottle. "Take one whenever you feel a little woozy."

Woozy . . . what a mom thing to say. I missed my moms.

"Thanks," I said, receiving the meds then letting her pull me in for a tight hug.

"You'll do just fine, Makayla," she whispered into my ear. "And when this is all over, you come back here, do you hear me? You come back and have some more dinner with us."

My heart warmed as I pulled away to look her in the eyes. "Of course. Thank you for everything."

Her gaze veered in Toby's direction. "Keep her safe."

"'Tis my job," he answered coolly.

We were off shortly after that. Blythe, Layla, Toby, Petal, and I. Everyone, including Petal, was carrying supplies in a backpack. I'd crammed a little of what I could in the bag I'd been carrying from Garlandia into this world, but they'd all argued my load was heavy enough, for I still had Avalon's sword in my keep.

We said goodbye to Phyllis and Dave but as we marched away from their home and to the street, I felt their company still, and when I turned to look over my shoulders, they were following behind us. Soon, humans, witches, elves, and fey began to open their front doors and peek out. Shortly after that, they began following behind Phyllis and Dave. By the time we'd reached the town's square and had come to the place where we would cross out of the safe land, there were at least fifty citizens standing in the street.

"Well," Blythe said, the five of us taking a moment to look out into the crowd. "There's no pressure in that."

"Nope," Layla seconded.

"Peer support. Love. 'Tis the purest sort of magic," Petal added.

Toby's hand, which had been laced with mine, moved to my lower back where he proceeded to push me about an inch towards the crowd as he whispered in my ear. "They are waiting for you to say something, my queen."

I moved my eyes back towards him, then let my chin follow. "Maybe they'd prefer for you to do so."

He chuckled. "Since when have you ever been afraid to stand up and speak to a crowd?"

Okay, that was fair. And a good reminder. I'd been so

stuck in the quicksand of my mind I'd forgotten I was strong. Or that I had at least been that way at some point.

Toby was right. I needed to say something, and even more than that, I needed to quit wallowing in my own self-pity. Yes, I'd seen some unforgettable things—I'm sure there was more to come. I'd been poisoned. Technically, I was blind and would be at the mercy of my birth mother's remedy until it was time for me to return to the ether. I had no idea what was going on at the castle or where Loral was hiding out; I didn't have any clue where Dora or her new protégé were, and I had a flock of mer (were they a flock?) after our company and the sword that was rightfully put into *my* hands. But there wasn't time for grieving, for wondering . . . worrying. There was only time for strategy and to live our lives as we'd set out to do when we came to this planet and into these bodies.

I stepped forward, Toby's hand lifting away as I rolled my shoulders back. The crowd was completely silent, other than the sound of a baby Reef crying near the front row. His or her mother was holding the little swaddling, pulling the faery to her chest and bouncing him or her.

Slowly, my bag hanging across my body, over the purple dress given to me by Esmerelda Waukine, and the sword dangling from my other hip, I walked towards the people and creatures until I was stalking through them. I didn't stop until I was face to face with the baby's mother. The swaddling's chin had the smallest of seizures as it whined.

I held up my hands. "May I?"

The faery was very pale, and her pixie hair was light pink. Her sheer wings shimmered in the setting sun. She held my stare as a tear fell from her eye. "Of course, Miss Makayla," she said, a quiver to her voice as she handed over the baby faery.

I'd never held a baby before. In fact, the only time I'd ever really been around one was when our assistant, Rachel from Sewn Back Together, had one. She'd brought little Teddy into work to show him off and I watched him grow up a little. He was three last I saw him. I'd never volunteered to hold him or play with him. Unlike a lot of teenage girls, I wasn't keen to pick up small humans and play Pat-A-Cake or Peek-A-Boo. Paperwork, marketing details, and fashion design had always come way more naturally.

"What's her name?" I asked, grinning as she melted into my arms. Because I suddenly just knew she was a girl.

"Jackie."

I was very surprised at how natural it felt to hold little Jackie.

I ran a hand over her warm head and nestled my nose into her little pink peach fuzz. She smelled like love. In truth, I could've stayed there all day, holding that little miracle and absorbing the energy of new life . . . but that wasn't my job. So, instead, I did what they all were waiting for.

I pulled away from Jackie's mother just enough to let my wings—they were wider than the Reef's—have room to lift Jackie and me about five feet from the ground.

"Thank you all for being here," I said, using an effect I'd found from Maude's spell book to magnify my voice. "As most or all of you know, my life has changed quite a bit over the course of only a few months. I went from being a girl who thought she was a grown up into a faery who realized she'd forgotten what living was all about, into a wife and a royal." Juggling Jackie in my arms, I retrieved my wand and placed it in the swaddling's tight fist. Jackie beamed as my wand glowed with the iconic star and diamond at its tip. Per the usual, whenever new eyes laid upon it, there were many gasps and hoots and hollers. "I carry the ghost of Titania but even if I didn't, I would still be here." I held the child tightly against my chest with one hand, then pulled up the Sword of

Avalon with my other, raising it into the sky. The crowd went wild. "I once thought my life wasn't my own because of this destiny, but I am here to say this: my life is one hundred percent my own *and I choose this fate!* It is from my own decision that we go into the cursed woods and devour the beast who calls herself the Crone of Light's End! We will take her power and erase it from this world, along with any debris she's left behind!" I remained in that spot, levitating over their heads, closing my eyes and taking in all the praise this small world had to offer. I sheathed the sword, put out my wand, and left them with my final words. "When this is all over, I shall wear a crown on my head, but please don't ever think that separates me from you." A tear rolled down my cheek and landed on the swaddling's lips. She tasted it and began to laugh. "A land needs a ruler. It needs someone to keep things in line and in proper working order, but never does that land need a dictator. I plan to work with Garlandia, for Garlandia, and help other lands achieve the same balance. Everyone deserves the unity you all have achieved." My emotions were catching up with me and my voice was shaking. Very quickly I finished my speech. "I shall provide this or die trying."

The crowd was reeling as my feet touched back down, and I handed Jackie back over to her mother. "You have a perfect child," I said, cupping the little one's pink head one last time before readying to get back in line with my group.

"Queen Koehaias," the mother said, placing a brave hand over my forearm.

My attention fell back over her. It had been the first time I'd heard my full title said out loud by someone other than my king, and it made the world stop.

"Honeydew."

"I'm sorry," I said, with wet eyes and a confused look.

She jostled her head back and forth as her own eyes

glistened. "If your fey mother was here, she would have told you the same. It fills the petals of most flowers every morning. Sip on it, it will help."

"With what?"

Her arm dropped away, and she inhaled a sharp breath. "Oh, I'm so sorry—I thought you knew."

My brows began to furrow. "Knew what?"

"It's just that, um, well the symptoms begin earlier in fey than humans and I can tell you've lost your color. And well, you're starting to glow a little." Her voice was so soft that no one else but me could hear her. And then her gaze fell from the babe in her arms to my stomach. "The honeydew helps with the morning sickness."

$\maltese$ 19 $\maltese$

Makayla

Not a word. I hadn't spoken another word to *anyone* since we'd crossed through the safe land and back into the Lorelei woods.

Nobody had heard what the woman had said, what she'd insinuated, but I still felt like they were all walking on pins and needles. Like there was a sign over my head in pink neon and yellow flashing lights that read, WITH SWADDLING. Was that even the proper way for faeries to say it? Goddess, I was in so much trouble.

But no. That Reef had just been crazy. She was all strung up in baby fever; it was her life. She probably saw swaddlings everywhere, just like trash people saw trash everywhere. Right? For the love of intellectuals, I was making as much sense as a ninny snail.

"Oh god, oh god, oh god," I muttered, reaching for the nearest tree, using it to hold myself up.

"What's wrong?" Toby asked, jumping over a log to be my side. The others kept trekking on.

We'd been back out in the wood for less than twenty minutes. But even with the threat of the mer on our trail, I couldn't concentrate. I just needed a minute alone—to breathe. To *think*.

When I hadn't answered, my king rested a hand over my shoulder. "What did that faery say to you?"

Without looking at him—my eyes *crammed* shut—I muttered, "What makes you think it was her?"

"Because of the way you returned to our sides. You looked as though she'd just told you that your face was inside out."

"That would have been better."

His hand tightened over my shoulder. In an instant, the nausea from this morning was back. I let go of the tree and doubled over, dry heaving. There was nothing left.

The footsteps that had passed us by slowed and I could hear Layla grumbling something about my nerves getting annoying.

"I don't think it's nerves," Petal said.

Toby helped me lean against the tree. "I don't think it's nerves either."

I barely had the energy to do so, but still I frowned at him. "You *knew*, didn't you?" I thought back to his strange words the night we'd consummated our marriage. It was like he was inviting someone into our circle. Tears began to fall in pairs from my eyes. Like Titania and his mother, he just *knew* things. "You've known this whole time that *this* was going to happen! Toby, this can't be in the cards—"

His hands had come to wrap around mine. "It already is, Makayla."

"I'm only eighteen! You've turned me into a teen mom!"

"Makay—"

But I'd had enough. Ignoring the reactions of our group

from the announcement my tantrum had brought forth, I fought the urge to scream at the top of my lungs. My emotions were boiling over and I was so irritated by everything, and dare I say even irrational, that I just needed to be by myself. Somewhere, anywhere else. And so . . . I was.

I was surrounded by all the colors of my rainbow, and there were a lot of colors. My dust swirled around me like a cyclone as the world seemed to pinch at every square inch of my every being. I saw nothing and everything—dirt, sky—space. And then my feet found ground and my dust evaporated. At first, I thought I was being pulled back into the Great Beyond. Just another trial or heart to heart with Tanker, but this was definitely not that. It wasn't until I realized that some of my dust was still evaporating from around my feet that I had just POPPED for the first time in my entire life. But that wasn't what was getting my heartbeat racing—even more than it already had been from my most recent discovery. The real reason for my vital organ to be thumping as hard as it was, was because of where I'd POPPED into.

From what I knew, faeries could POP anywhere—from world to world—as long as they knew where they were going or had been there before. I wasn't surprised this was where I'd decided to come to be alone; it was in fact the place where I'd realized I was in love with Toby. It was our gazebo. The difference being that Peter Kiln's statue had been set free, as had Peter Kiln, but that didn't mean I was alone. No, not by a long shot.

As soon as I saw who I was sharing this space with, I hunkered down, hiding inside the gazebo. Still, the wooden slats didn't completely hide me, so I pulled out my wand and whispered the word to make myself sparse, or invisible. The act was just in time, for POPPING isn't known to be quiet.

My company stood. "Hello?"

I frowned. Not once since I had known this person, had he looked so unsure of himself. Nor had he looked as dead.

"The sun has fallen!" he bellowed. "Anyone out of doors is fair game!" A large pair of fangs slid from his mouth. In a slightly softer tone, he added, "And I've barely eaten anything since I became this . . ." His words trailed off.

I gulped silently. Rally. Not just my enemy but a *vampire*. Yes, even though I still had a crone and a vial king to take care of, this elf slash witch concoction had sliced the head off of my king, thus ranking him high above the others in order of individuals I needed to slay. We hadn't been sure before, whether he would make the change, but from the looks of it, he had. His skin was near the color of his half-sister's and his hair was longer, sticking to his face as though he hadn't washed it in the same amount of time he hadn't fed.

He walked around the gazebo, squinting as he dipped his gaze into it. I held my breath and remained as still as possible. He sniffed around a little but when he couldn't find anything, he crouched back down to the tree he'd been parked against when I'd arrived. When he hadn't moved for at least a minute or two, I carefully stood so I could spy on him. He appeared to be talking to someone, but for the life of me I couldn't see who.

"Neither Dankas nor Lanakes won. I ordered the war to end, locking the elves up in the dungeons. They're separated of course. I just—I—I was sick of blood filling my boots and the clashing of swords was giving me a headache."

I narrowed my eyes, peering out into the forest—looking for whoever he was talking to. But there didn't seem to be anybody. Other than a little yellowish butterfly fluttering around his head, he was alone.

"I've ordered the rest of the creatures back into their homes. Everyone is on house arrest regardless of their station. The order has appeased the Robes for now." He clenched his teeth then added, "The Robes believe I'm keeping the creatures locked up and set aside so their priestess will have food when she returns."

My heart beat out of my chest, and I nearly gave up my hiding spot by jumping as Rally, for no apparent reason other than for the sake of fury, screamed at the top of his lungs. Thank goodness a rabbit was spooked and ran across his vision, distracting him.

"Go on, then! Run off, you ninny!"

No way—were those tears in his eyes?

"I should eat you," he sobbed, before cradling his face in his hands. "I'm so hungry."

He continued to break apart right in front of me for at least five minutes. Finally, he wiped away the leakage with his arm. I hadn't really realized it up until that moment, that he wasn't dressed in Garlandian blue, but wrapped in a robe. But of course, Layla had already said it—he was born to lead the Robes of Lorelei. The thing was, unless I was mistaken, he looked incredibly miserable.

The butterfly continued to flutter around him. "I'm so sorry, where was I? Right, um, yes, of course—the, uh, the Robes have taken over the castle but it's only the threat they carry. They've no real power. I'm not sure what they've been doing all these years besides waiting for their priestess to arrive, but they can't even control those bloody dragons. It seems I'm the only one who can carry a tune when it comes to the Bathar twins. At least in the beasts I have someone to talk to . . . Sorry, drifted again."

Wait, was he talking to the butterfly? I thought only the fey could do that.

"Anyway, that's all I've got to share at this point. No real news otherwise. I've no idea where Toby and his bride have gotten off to. There are rumors that they entered Lorelei but no such proof. I shall be needing further instructions. Please do send further details my way as soon as you can. If you are where you say you are, I am to believe it may be sometime before I hear back, but please, *please* give me something." He paused, then added, "Anything would help at this point."

He made a gesture in the air and the butterfly faded from sight.

No way. He could communicate with the butterflies. What did that mean? Furthermore, who was he talking to? Loral? Presumably, for that was the only thing that made sense. I stood there for many more minutes, watching Rally suffer silently. Finally, he got up, rolled his shoulders back, and stalked off.

I wanted to follow him. More than that, I wanted to take the end of this sword and point it at his heart. Force him to explain everything I'd just heard. Except, not only would that be far too risky, but I could already hear the jingle jangle of bells nearby. It *was* getting darker, which meant the jesters were most likely out and ready to feed. Without overthinking it, I crammed my eyes shut and thought of the woods of Lorelei, of the last spot I'd been in. In the amount of time it took me to blink, my feet moved from the gazebo back into the dust tunnel and returned to the softened ground I'd been on in Lorelei. Except, it wasn't exactly where I'd been when I'd POPPED away.

Tanker had said that POPPING between worlds could spin the hands of a clock and sometimes the message of where you wanted to land could become slightly disturbed. I grimaced, for it was definitely later than it had been only moments ago, and I didn't recognize this bit of land. It was the woods, that much was clear, but it was darker than dark, and I was so very alone. Or at least that's what I thought.

My attention homed in over a small cottage in the near distance, to the lights on inside. I'd just started to put one foot in front of the other, silently marching over the pine needles that carpeted the ground, when I felt a hand cup my shoulder.

"Gotcha."

My chest constricted and my body stiffened. That touch, it wasn't friendly.

I didn't need to turn around to know what had happened. I could smell the ocean on this person's hand. Though it wasn't a person. Not at all. I'd stupidly run away from my group and now I'd been captured by a mer. Suddenly, finding myself pregnant wasn't the worst of my problems.

20

Dora

The beginning of the ascent truly was the most difficult, and at only about an hour into the climb, Dora heard Bally mutter to Heime, "Why are we here again? I feel like all we're doing is accompanying the two of them on the worst hike in the world. If we aren't needed—"

"Oh," Dora said loud enough for him to hear. "You're needed. Even with the strongest of wills, two would never be able to travel away from this place with what we're about to retrieve."

The witch could hear Bally gulp behind her. "And *what* exactly are we retrieving?"

Dora gripped a knob-like structure in the rock and pulled herself up to the next landing. "You'd do yourself a favor to stop questioning why we're here and focus your energy on your whereabouts." Jumping the tracks, she stated, "The ghosts of those who did not make it away from this place are vengeful. They are also intelligent." Bally became extremely silent behind her as she repeated what she'd said just a few beats prior. "Discard wandering thoughts and focus on your steps. Do not peer in any direction other than directly ahead."

The young elf did not bring up the subject again. Dora had been in and out of Bally's head enough during this journey to realize that he was smarter than he appeared. Like his faery friend, he wanted answers more than anything, but the more he was around the face of his other best friend, the more he was realizing that Cee-Cee was held down by a disease with but one cure.

You are part of that cure, my boy, she'd tried to whisper into his mind. Whether or not he heard her, she couldn't fully know, for he never showed her that he had. Dora, like the woman who birthed her, could dive in and out of other's heads—she could whisper thoughts and images into those around her, even if they weren't dragon dancers. The difference was, her mother used it as a weapon; whereas she was simply tapping in for the sake of the greater good. Dora felt a bit of tension melt after Bally quieted down and focused his energy on making it up the mountain's side.

From there, up, up, up they went. Dora, Bally, Heime, and capping the back of their small train—the body of Anastacia Montgomery. Dora knew that the girl was aware that something great was atop this mountain . . . something she may have worked very hard to attain in her past life. Even the girl couldn't be sure of what she would see until they reached the very top of this monstrous highland. And even *she* couldn't say whether they would make it back down and out from this place, not with what she knew, deep down—buried under whatever nonsense Dora had used to muffle her memories— she *needed back* to rise into the crone she had once been.

Dora was wise enough to keep one ear tuned into the workings of the girl's mind, and as they traveled, she heard a voice that caused even her to stumble slightly over a small rock. Dora hadn't been blessed with very much time with Anastacia before she'd handed her that unbinding spell. Still, she'd spent two days with Cee-Cee and hers was a voice she'd have known anywhere.

Yo! You're not going to get away with this, you nasty, evil—

The girl's foot slipped from the rock she was climbing and she fell backwards. If she'd fallen just a little harder, all the air would have been knocked from her chest.

"Oi!" Heime called out, causing the two before him to halt. "Hang on!" He turned and looked down at the girl. "Are you alright?"

It was obvious to Dora why the girl appeared to have a pain in her skull that was incapacitating to say the least. In fact, the witch had to quiet the excitement in her chest as she heard the priestess scream into her mind, *GO AWAY!* She was trying to rid her head of the other soul that went with that body. It was interfering with her concentration. According to Dora, things couldn't be going better.

When the girl's outburst was followed by a moment of silence, she craned her head up at the male elf. "I'm fine." She started to hobble to her feet. From the awkward dance she did getting there, it was probable that her ankle was tender. "On second thought," she stated haughtily, "I may need some healing. It seems I've twisted my joints."

"I'm afraid that's a hard no!" Dora shouted from where her and Bally stood a few feet up on the jagged rocks. "To use any enchantments during this section of the climb would wake the dead and you don't want that—I promise!"

Dora remained in the girl's head as Heime took a step down and held out his hand for the girl. After cursing under her breath, the priestess reached up and took the leathery hand, letting him pull her up.

You should say thank you, said the voice of Cee-Cee.

The girl flinched, and Dora, still leading the pack, grinned.

"Are you sure you're going to be able to walk?" Heime asked the girl, his right brow arching towards the darkening sky.

"Yes," the girl chirped. "Just a little bit of dirt in my shoes." *And in my head,* she thought. "I'll shake it out before this journey is through."

Heime dipped his chin forward sharply then turned around and began climbing once more. As the girl followed, choking back painful grunts from her already swelling appendage, she worked on blocking out the sound of that vile, bubbly voice. But Cee-Cee, as she'd been named in this life, was just as much a part of that body as she was.

You have no idea what you're up against. This world WILL NOT allow you to turn it against itself again. There are forces out there readying to ensure your demise.

"SHUT UP!"

All three of the bodies in front of her turned around, staring down into the twisted lunacy that had become the girl's face. She looked up at them and told them to keep moving, then spat on the ground.

Dora turned back to face the rocky path, that grin pasted back on her face. There would be no lemon here to air out the 'riff raff' and no living creatures to suck at their marrow. The priestess was stuck with two elves and a witch—a witch who had been extremely careful to make sure that she'd only allowed so much of the priestess's memories to leak out. Just enough that the head of the beast could be secured by a collar, and attached to that collar was a leash, which had been set firmly in Dora's hands from the moment she'd handed Anastacia that unbinding spell.

21

Makayla

My breaths were ragged as they moved in and out of my nose. I'd crammed my eyes shut along with my fists. I knew the mer was male from his voice, though I was pretty sure there would be no accounting for chivalry in this manner. Trying to keep my breathing at an even pace, I cautiously brought my left hand across my stomach so that I might grip the hilt of Avalon's sword, but just as I was about to make contact, the mer reacted.

"Don't even think about it."

My chest sunk and my shoulders rolled forward. I was screwed.

"Hands up."

I reluctantly began to do as I was told, slowly turning to face the mer. His black hair was shaved on the sides with a mohawk spanning his whole head. His skin was greenish blue, and his teeth were just as shark-like as all the others. The way he was grinning at me made me want to wretch, but for the first time all day I wasn't nauseas. He had a spear aimed right where life was purring inside me.

"Where's your posse?" he asked. "More specifically, where's Layla?"

"I don't know," I answered with a quick shake of my head.

"Lies!"

"No—seriously. I—I lost them."

He was just in the process of narrowing his eyes and taking a step closer—that blasted spear so close to cutting the fine fabric of my purple dress when—SNAP.

I froze and the world moved in slow motion as I watched his body fold in half. A second later a white flash moved around him, and he was completely gone.

I didn't move for the next few seconds—I couldn't. My feet were, like, rooted to the ground. When the shock began to wear off just a smidge, I slowly backed one foot up, then the other—my eyes still wider than ever and my jaw parted—until I heard yet another voice. Softer this time. Older, wiser, and more feminine.

"Oi! Whatchu doin' out there? Get yerself inside now, ye hear! Ain't no place for a lost Erwain this time a night!"

With my hands still raised, I turned back around to face the cottage I'd seen when I'd first POPPED into the forest. Standing by the door was an older woman with gray locs and a crow on her shoulder. After she yelled at me to hurry up and get inside for the second time, she turned to the crow and told him to 'git.' Obediently, the crow did as it was told, transforming into a bright ball of light before disappearing.

"Come now," she said, waving me in. "Faster now!"

I started jogging the best I could with the sword at my side.

"Get ye in here. Sandy will do 'er best to keep the rest of them off track but ye can't just POP and not expect the whole damn forest ta hear ye." She rolled her eyes as she said it and pulled me into the cottage as soon as I was close enough.

Per my usual, I had all the questions.

"Was that—Sandy, was she a—"

"Pooka. Yes." She closed the wooden door and secured it, then brushed past me to where a kettle was steaming over the stove. She fetched two mugs hanging from pegs over the stove and filled them, then brought them over to a bar set between the kitchen and dining room.

"Have a seat, then." The way she panted as she talked reminded me of Cajun Cathy. Actually, the way she looked also brought me back to the kitchen witch.

I remained planted, quietly taking in my surroundings while trying to decide whether to trust the strange witch in the woods who had, *I think*, just killed a guy.

"Come now, warm up." She jumped up on a bar stool and patted the seat next to her. "I'm not gonna bite. I'm on yer side." When I still didn't make a move to join her or speak, she sighed. "Whatdaya need? An oath?" She paused, then geared her eyes to the ceiling as she pulled up a witch's wand. "I, Dorothy of Lorelei, daughter of Artemis, pledge myself and honor to—" Her gaze fell to my shoulders. "What are ye calling yourself these days?"

I stuttered instead of speaking. "Uh—well—technically— I mean. You can just call me Makayla."

Her pinpointed stare remained over me for a moment as if she was ensuring I was done blabbering all over myself. "Just fine then. I pledge my loyalty to Makayla." She set down her wand and took a sip from her tea. "What now?" she asked. "De ye need me to dance for ye?"

I let my posture relax and slowly neared her. The tea smelled awesome, and I didn't even really like tea. "No," I finally said. "That's not necessary." I pulled out the stool and slowly had a seat. I wanted so badly to let down my guard for a second, but I was wary. Dorothy, presumably, kept her eyes on me as I lifted the steaming mug to my nose and gave it a sniff. My mouth immediately watered.

"Ginger and mango. 'Tis my favorite." She took another sip then set down her mug. "Ye can drink it; poisoning or druggin' ye would go against my oath, and I really would not like to be a spider."

"Is that what would happen to you?" I asked with a crossed brow.

"Perhaps. I'd rather not to be findin' out, if ye know what I mean."

"Right." I slurped some tea into my mouth. "Oh my god," I said, sinking down into the stool and wrapping my hands fully around the mug. "This is the best thing *ever*."

"'Tis a nice concoction." She plucked her wand back into her hand and shot it out at a cabinet, which then opened and sent a package of cookies flying at our station.

"OREOs?" I questioned. Had I accidentally POPPED into the human world?

"The local grocery gits stuff from all over. Gotta love these dang cookies, right?"

"Uh, yeah," I said, gingerly taking one, then another. And another.

"Take as many as ye like," she added, biting one in half then letting her shoulders droop down to the sides.

I took a smaller bite, another sip from the wonderful tea, then squared my shoulders with hers. "Did you kill that guy?"

"The swimmer?"

"Yeah."

"Of course. Did ye not want me to?" she raised a brow.

"No—I mean, yeah, I guess. It was just, sort of, like . . . wicked. The way he snapped in half." It was upsetting just thinking about it. But he was probably going to kill me, so. . .

"He would've speared ye like a fish, then proudly had ye for dinner with his keep."

If everyone knew my story and what I was here for, then, "Why are the mer so dead against seeing reason? All they care about is this damn sword. They won't take the time to listen to me about why I even have it."

"The swimmers get kinda fixated on things. They really are good rulers, but they have their quirks, now don't they. Got kinda hung up on Avalon. They miss her. The heaviness of it all and what happened here all those years ago . . . they've started to lose sight. Part of the curse that awful witch left behind, I suppose." She paused, then frowned. "What had ye POPPING into the wood, *alone*, in the first place?"

I swallowed the cookie in my mouth then washed it down with a bit of tea. "It's a long story. Believe it or not, I'd never POPPED before. It just sort of happened while I was out with my group. We'd just gotten on with our journey before I got sucked away."

She peered at me in disbelief. God, she really did look like Cathy. As if reading my mind, she said, "Ye see her in me, don't ye?"

I turned my chin to the side. "Excuse me?"

"Castonia. She was my cousin. As was Aeslin."

"No way," I muttered, reaching for a fourth OREO.

She held her gaze over mine for a long minute before grasping her wand and pointing at the counter. Before our eyes, a movie clip appeared. "'Tis a memory," she said as it unfolded.

It looked like any old black and white footage. Four witch children were running around a clearing in a forest. In the background was a cottage, a bit bigger than this one, and there were three little Reef faeries playing with the children. There wasn't any sound, but we could see them laughing and holding hands—the young fey playing keep away with a witches' broom.

"That's Castonia and Aeslin," Dorothy said, licking her third finger then pointing to the two little girls. "And that's me, the youngest. That was my brother—Leroy." I noted how her eyes dimmed just a little as she said his name.

"Who were the fey?" I asked.

"Ruby, Rory, and Rubert. They were neighbors."

Just then an adult Reef walked up and took the broom from one of the mini Reefs, handing it to Castonia, who stuck out her tongue at the boy faery and rode up and away. The memory faded, but not before the adult faery turned to face whoever was taking the memory and waved. Something caught my eye.

"That necklace," I said, pointing at it as the moving picture disappeared. "It's just like Toby's!" Dorothy gave me a queer look. When she didn't say anything, I said, "Or at least it looks very similar to what he had on before—" I stopped. I couldn't say it.

"Before what?"

Her gaze was firm.

I set down the cookie in my hand and dusted the crumbs away. "Um, nothing." I shook my head as though I was ridding my red locks of sand. "So, you have a brother?" Anything to move on.

Dorothy didn't seem as quick to follow as I'd hoped. What I'd said had caught her by surprise. Thankfully, she began to take strides to where I was on the other side of that conversation. "I did." She kept her attention over me as she sipped from her mug. "Leroy fell in line with the wrong crowd, I'm sorry to say."

A hand came up to cover my lips. "He didn't go to *her*, did he?"

"I'm afraid so." Her words were heavy. "He became a

Cronie. Castonia and Aeslin went there, to Forest Peak, to Lantern's Edge. They went to try and bring him home, but the Cronies weren't there the day they were let in."

"Let in?"

"Yes. Followers were made only upon visitation days." She huffed a little. "The Crone eventually inlaid barriers around Forest Peak, so no one apart from her followers could get in or out. It was obvious she didn't want spying eyes to catch on to what she was doing, though some still got close enough to grasp that whatever she was up to wasn't anything desirable. Leroy had always been after something apart from our practice; in hindsight we should've kept better tabs on 'im. Our family had a tendency to keep to ourselves, for no other reason than we enjoyed our unique camaraderie; but Leroy was very outgoing—vibrant. He'd always been out to discover something *more*."

Another cookie had found its way into my mouth. I chewed around it as I said, "Doesn't sound like the kind of individual to join a cult."

"Ah, but to the contrary. The Crone didn't rise to the status she achieved by only comin' across as malicious. She held meet and greets an' offered cookies an' punch. Dressed her twins up in frilly dresses. Hid her dark side. Sent telepathic messages to her visitors so softly that they didn't even know they were being hypnotized. She welcomed her guests with open arms and ensured she sparked the sort of curiosity each one was after. Leroy followed the cookie crumbs all the way to the altar."

It was all starting to connect. Aeslin and Cajun Cathy went to the meet and greet to look for their cousin . . . "And that's when they figured out how sick and twisted the cult was," I muttered.

"What's that?" Dorothy questioned.

I snapped my wandering gaze back up to hers. "My

grandfather met your cousin—Castonia—when they left this world for Garlandia. She filled him in on what she knew."

Dorothy nodded. "We knew better than to wait for Leroy to come home. Not only did Aeslin and Castonia see first-hand that something terrible was brewing in that cursed wood, but I found 'im one day a few years after that. He was wanderin' around the wood, close to home. At first, I thought he was a monster—some sort of *creature*. It wasn't until he looked at me and I saw his eyes." She took a deep breath and wiped at some moisture in the corner of her eye. "That *thing*, with its gray skin an' veins protrudin'. Elongated limbs an' hooked spine—" She sobbed. "That hideous monster, diggin' its nose into the dirt, seeking rodents, I suppose, scamperin' around the tree like a rabid squirrel, graspin' at birds. It was our Leroy . . . he, or it, was lookin' for somethin' to feed upon. And when I spoke his name, his head twitched to the side, and he began comin' at me on all fours."

"He was going to try and eat you," I whispered.

She wiped at her eyes again as she nodded. "I stood there, in place, until he was but three feet away—it wasn't even a mouth anymore but a gapin' hole that formed into a circle, like he was preppin' to suck the soul from my body. I ejected from that spot and returned to my mother's side. Told 'er what I saw. Cried into 'er bosom for hours."

"I'm so, *so* sorry." I couldn't imagine seeing someone I loved like that—then again, I sort of had. Cee-Cee wasn't hideous looking, but that soul who had usurped her body was just as monstrous as Dorothy had described her brother to have been. I started to say something more, but a yawn interrupted. I covered my mouth and tried to shake it off, but Dorothy was already standing.

"I've not got a ton a space, but ye can rest yer eyes over on that sofa for a bit if ye like. If I were you, I'd get as much rest as I could while ye can. Yer group should be here soon."

I sat up straighter as I sniffed. "My group? You mean—but how would they know where I'm at?"

She was pulling at an old, crocheted afghan, laying it next to a pillow. She winked as she replied, "I called to them. Not all of us witches be bad."

"How did you—" I began, but just as quickly shook my question away. It didn't matter how she'd signaled to my friends and husband as to where I was, the point was she had. Furthermore, that old brown couch of hers was looking pretty comfortable and my eyes were rather heavy.

I took one more sip from my tea then moved to the living room, curling up in the space provided. "Thank you," I said as she dimmed the light. "For helping me."

I was already half asleep when I felt her warm hand over mine. Her touch was like feeling the trunk of a tree; her age and intelligence seemed to travel from her energy into my soul. As I drifted away, her words fell over me like snowflakes.

"Rest child and know this: darkness will always be, just as light will always be. The truly enlightened ones know that to find one's truth, they must stand in the shadows. 'Tis the gray that tells the truth and to avoid the gray is to live a plastic life —one that is prone to damage and bad for the environment. Ye are fierce; no longer a lost Erwain, but a found queen. Yer world is but one component of a massive project seeded by energies far and near, but that doesn't mean 'tis any less valuable. Any less worthy of being saved. A diamond in the wreckage still sparkles, still brings joy to those who find it, and 'tis joy that adds to light. Shine bright, faery queen, let yer sparkle reign.

"When pain finds ye, let it in. Do not run. Stand in the gray. The light will return. Now sleep, faery queen. Dream of butterfly wings and sparkly hair, fer she'll be here before ye know it."

I was out before she finished her prayer or spell talk or

whatever. My snores filled every part of that cottage, but that didn't mean I didn't hear what she said. That I didn't tuck every last word away.

The gray . . .

Meet me in the gray.

Makayla

It was still dark out when I woke. As I stirred and began to come back to life, I recognized my king's voice. I was just about to sit up and rub the sleep from eyes, when I stilled, shrinking back down into the sofa. Dorothy was saying something to him . . . and it wasn't anything to be found in shallow waters.

"She knows, Tobias. Maybe not on the surface, but she knows somewhere down deep in that ancient soul a 'ers."

Silence. Then, "Are you positive?"

"As sure as the mud on my boots."

Again, silence so cutting I could feel it in my bones.

"What shall I do?" asked my king.

"Nothing to do. But fer the sake of the life in 'er body, let it follow ye with grace. She's already got the world of the fey over 'er shoulders."

I got the sense they had turned and laid their eyes over me. I had to remind myself to breathe.

"She's been going elsewhere," Toby said. "One minute she's there with us and the next her soul is gone. I believe she's found some place to escape. I'm not sure it's a healthy outlet."

"But this was the first time she's POPPED?"

"Yes," Toby answered.

Again, their gaze was heavy over my body.

"Oi be the turmoil of the keeper, and Titania be not that of a regular faery." I felt their gazes lift and turn in the other direction. "She is strong of will, that Makayla. She will hammer on. Do what ye need to do to finish burying this curse over our land, but do not keep that faery in the dark, fer she has already been hidden away fer far too long."

"Yes ma'am," Toby answered very softly.

I remained still for only a moment more before acting as though I was just waking. I yawned and stretched my arms and legs as far out as I could, pretending to just notice that my king was in the room with us.

"Toby!" I exclaimed, shoving the blanket from over my stomach and fluttering over to where he was standing near the door by Dorothy's side. Doing my best impression of surprise, I threw my arms around his neck and said, "I thought I'd lost you guys forever! Where are the others?"

Toby took a minute to return my embrace, holding onto me for a few seconds longer than normal, then pulled the door we were next to wide open. Outside, Blythe, Layla, and Petal were standing there, waiting. The way they were posed made them look like an album cover from the 90s. In Blythe and Layla's hands—OREOs.

"By the dragons, queenie, don't do that again," Blythe said.

"Yes, that was quite irritating," Petal said, chomping on

some fresh hay. She had a bucket under her nose filled with hay and apples. "And frightening."

"I'm sorry," I offered, pulling my arms back from around Toby's neck. "I didn't mean to leave you guys. I—" I stopped cold. I'd been in and out of so many worlds so quickly and had been encompassed by so many emotions that I'd completely forgotten what I'd seen back at that gazebo. I'd forgotten about Rally. I turned from the three oddities waiting out of doors, to Toby. "I POPPED back into Garlandia . . . back to our gazebo. You'll never guess who I saw." And then I proceeded to tell them about what I'd heard, straight from the vampire's mouth.

Once I was done, Dorothy—who had heard every single word—hinged forward on the balls of her feet. "'Tis an odd thing, for anyone other than a faery to commune with the butterflies." She held her stiff expression for a bit longer, lost in thought it seemed. "However, ye said he is of the undead?"

"Yes," I answered.

"Then he was reborn," Layla said from where she stood with the rest of our company on the other side of the door.

"What?" I questioned.

Blythe gave her the same inquisitive look I was offering her.

Petal finished her bite of apple then looked my way, revisiting a line she'd already rehearsed. "No one comes back to the same life twice."

I turned from her to Layla, to Blythe, then finally to Toby. "I don't understand. Has he been given special powers or something?"

"He already has special powers," my king answered. "If he's learned telepathy with nature, then that can only mean one thing."

"And what's that?" I pushed.

Toby started to answer, but Layla beat him to it. Leaning

in towards me, she said, "Savannah lurked around him his whole life the same way Titiania has been reaching around corners to get you to see her. It's a sort of ancient kind of magic, not letting go . . . using one's soul to cling to another to finish an interrupted destiny." She paused, her gaze steering fiercely into mine. "His heart stopped then began to beat again. When he died, so did the connection between him and his mother's soul."

"I don't understand—what are you saying?" I pleaded impatiently.

"I think what the mer lady is trying to say," Dorothy said, "is that this Rally figure has been given free will fer the first time."

"Which means it is up to him whether he decides to fight or surrender," Toby added. We all looked to him as he contemplated his next words. "I've known him my whole life; he can be wicked and foul, but the fact remains that up until those last moments, he was never anything to me but a brother." He looked up, matching his gaze with mine. "He has the ability to see reason, though it is still in him to perform as a predator, and I'm afraid we'll not know who we're dealing with until the time comes."

"Great," I said as I heaved a sigh. One hand cupping my stomach, I muttered, "I hate surprises."

"Well then," Blythe said, "you're for sure gonna hate where we're headed."

‹❁ 23 ❁›

Lantern's Edge

ays turned to weeks and months; as time moved on, it
sped up. Years passed. Forest Peak had become
cursed, though the Cronies didn't see it that way. The foul
creatures were the only other life in this part of the forest,
though it could be argued that they had no life left. Not even
the insects had chosen to stay.

If Dora and Malina had been given a normal life, they'd
have been the age to experience courtships with whoever
their hearts were drawn to. They'd be discovering where their
talents laid and perhaps readying to open an apothecary shop
—that had been a dream of Malina's once upon a time. But as
it was, this was not the imagery that showed up after their
cups were drained of lavender and chamomile.

The priestess had long since been forced to come to terms
with the fact that Dora wasn't going anywhere. Of course,
she'd tried other routes when she'd realized drowning wasn't

in the cards. She'd done it all. Poisons, knife wounds, strangulation—but not even her bare hands could remove her daughter's soul from her body. The truth was unbelievably firm: Dora was untouchable. Even worse, that's what they'd all been calling her.

The cult that had been named the Bahidicaras kept to itself, but that didn't mean there weren't spies now and again. Great weavers of magic that were able to scamper along the borders of Forest Peak and gain enough information to share it with this world and the others. It had gone round and round the mill—the priestess was insane and one of her daughters was untouchable. One Reef who had gotten in and out without being seen (or eaten) had stated that he'd witnessed the untouchable daughter being set on fire, only to walk away from the burned ruins with a mild cough; around her shoulders, a sparkling black cape. An elf and witch pairing, had said they'd seen the daughter struck by lightning. She'd gone away after the incident with little more than running a few fingers through her frazzled hair.

The rumors were all true.

As far as the priestess was concerned, after realizing Dora couldn't be harmed, her next move seemed obvious—she ought to kill Malina and merge her own power with Dora's. It was this daughter who she'd always thought would come out stronger anyway. It was Dora's power that made her salivate. But when she'd set down her intention inside her conjured circle she'd been met with sparks of fury. The portal she spoke through, the same portal she'd been using since her youth, had but one answer for her: Malina had come forth as the champion and that was that. And she could only use the spell to bond herself with one witch. If that worked, only then could she move on to the others.

So, it was Malina or no one. There were no more twins and the portal had already stated that there would be no more offerings in trade for the intention they'd chosen to act upon. But no matter, the Crone held firm to her mission. She'd convinced her followers that she'd traded words with those at light's end, and that they'd confirmed that the ritual could still work. Even with the untouchable one refusing to die.

The Crone's true talent laid in improvisation. All she knew for certain was that she needed to bind herself to a magic maker to move forward, to gain more power, and until she did, her and her Cronies would remain stagnant. So, like any decent cult leader, she stood firm with her convictions. That was all one must do, she decided—that and come forth with something big to look forward to. One day she announced that the key to unlocking the roadblock they'd been up against all these years was simple: take out Pontus's daughter—Avalon. Once that was complete, so could be the ritual she'd been preparing for all this time.

The issue was Pontus's daughter wasn't coming to them as they'd so thought she would. The Crone had even gone so far as to personally invite the daughter of the sea; she was now old enough to journey forth on her own after all. But still, nothing.

Drastic times called for drastic measures. The Crone did the unthinkable.

Lanake. A game piece that had been carved with great care then set down into their playground by the direct hands of the gods. A light so bright that even the most despicable of creatures bowed before it.

This was the Crone's next play, and if this didn't get the ball rolling, nothing would.

It did not take long to figure out how to summon the one she sought, and the place for which they were to meet was written in the Devil's handwriting in a book of twisted fates. A desert that roamed in the center of all worlds, a place that had no home. It was where Danka had thrown Lanake's bride just to see his brother weep.

The Crone and her daughters, followed by the Cronies, entered the desert. She'd summoned Lanake by requesting his service. She wept to him, feigning a disturbance within her heart. "I've gone too far in one direction, oh dearest one," she'd said to him. His torment was that he saw the good in everyone—believed he could turn even the foulest of souls to the light.

But even he wasn't prepared for what the Crone had become.

When the moment came, the Crone didn't think twice. She took his light into her own hands and drained it like it was a chilled glass of lemonade, sharing bits of it with her salivating Cronies. When it was over, she grinned at her company, ignoring the ground as it began to shake.

"I suppose now, the souls of mankind just will not do. Now that we've tasted that, my lovelies, we will require *more*."

They'd already begun drinking from the earth—feeding from the gods. But now, now that they'd tasted the finest light on earth, they were left with a hunger that reached into the core of their planet.

Dora cringed through the whole ordeal. Her mother was nothing more than an addict and these *things* that clung to her were just smaller versions. Sucked in by her fantasies, then left with a craving that wouldn't leave until their souls were laid to rest.

However, what was done was done. Lanake was no more. A mountain began to rise from the grave of one of the greatest light bearers to have graced the earth; a physical stain placed there by the gods to remind everyone that taboos do exist.

The priestess didn't even notice; she took her company and moved back through the worlds until they stood upon the grounds of Forest Peak. They didn't have to wait long after that; the day they'd all been waiting for came to them like the last leaf falling to the autumn ground.

They'd heard the cries that echoed all the way to their forest compound—the cries from all over the worlds. A great light had been put out and in the most horrific of ways. Yes, the outbursts and outrage from all sorts of creatures reverberated to where the Crone stood, but it was the anger of one soul in particular that caused her to grin the widest. One of three tears who had been shed on the earth from the gods around the same time her girls had been born. And why three? 'Tis a perfect number, that's why. The Crone only knew of two of the three, but of course she was most concerned with the offering who she knew had been sent to Lorelei. The one who had been biding her time, waiting for when the gods would tell her to move.

"Avalon," the Crone said in a near whisper as she stood apart from her following, her white robes rippling against the enraged winds. "'Tis about time."

And so it was.

The cult's ending began on a day with a sunless sky. The Cronies, these followers she'd spent years attaining—they hung upside down from every tree on the property. They slept like bats; their toenails long and curly, growing from elongated toes. Their bones gnarly, a side effect of churning magic to unnatural rhythms. That chosen day, they fell from their hibernations and landed on the grounds only to slither up to the steps of Lantern's Edge like snakes.

The Crone's daughters stood behind her, as always. If they'd had the wits to tell them apart, the Cronies may have noted that one daughter always looked out at them with fear in her eyes while the other stood tall but did so with heavy heartbeats. For better or worse though, the Cronies lacked even the slightest bit of intelligence. They'd sacrificed all they were to their priestess and now they existed only as vessels.

The Crone lifted a chalice she'd made from the bones of hundreds of sacrifices. Her own limbs had become only slightly exaggerated, her back only a little hunched. The Cronies served as a cushion, it lessened the blow to her own appearance, but no one can work that kind of twisted craft without taking on a bit of its reflection.

Malina and Dora, as beautiful as the Crone had once been, stood behind their mother as the priestess lifted the bone chalice to meet the rafters above their porch. "'Tis the time we've been seeking, my children." She loosened a hand from around one side of the cup and held her palm out before her, as if she was feeling the particles in the air. "The air is electric." Her eyes caressed the hundred or so beings who were scattered upon her lawn. The fey had lost their wings years ago and the elves were nothing more than moving skeletons. The witches were like giant cockroaches. Still, these were all hers, and soon they would all be one. "Today we take it upon ourselves to find the daughter they call Avalon. If we must, we shall part the sea and walk on the earth that has never seen sky. But, my lovelies, I don't believe that will be necessary, for salt is in the air."

The lawn erupted with chatter as the Cronies did their best to cheer, though to any passerby it might've sounded like the dead waking . . . insects swarming.

The Crone laid her eyes against the bits of hips, metatarsals, ribs, and femurs that made up her cup. "Finally, our union may be complete." She lowered her gaze to the lawn. To the same place these travelers had once come to inquire about a new coven. Promises of eternal command, a higher dominance than any god or goddess could ever achieve, handed out like fliers. "I am the Crone of Light's

End, and no entity may demand anything from me nor my family ever again!"

The Cronies answered their leader by crawling towards one another, coming into the formation of a circle until it became like a tunnel.

Dora's chest lifted as she quietly turned to look at her twin. Malina did not return her gaze, nor did she attempt to close off the terror emanating from every angle of her body. Years Dora had spent, training her sister, trying to refine the importance of a game face. Still, there were just some stories that couldn't be rewritten. And the fact remained, though their souls had bonded in the womb, they came from two very different places. Dora's soul held certain vibrations that Malina's never would. She couldn't fault her sister for that. It was just the way things were.

Finally, as lightning struck from a churning cloud just above the Cronies' heads, Malina turned and faced her twin. Two words were all she dared to mouth in Dora's direction. "Save me."

Dora turned back to face the Cronies' display of affection for their rotten leader only after affording her twin a terse nod. Keeping her thoughts tucked into that fold she'd been handed that day in the lake, the day she'd been sent to die, she let them flow quietly where her mother wouldn't hear them.

I will live a thousand restless years if that's what it takes, my Malina. But yes, I will save you.

Before they left the porch, Dora quietly went back inside and gathered the three glass jars she'd collected and attached them to her belt. They'd appeared to her only days ago. A bonus, thrown to her from the unseen players that watched from above . . . from below. From all angles. Either way, it was a gift. "So mote it be," she whispered. Then she put on her cloak and walked out the door.

24

Dora

This far up the mountain the air should have come passing with a chill, but the Enclaves weren't just any regular land formations. The mountains were created long ago from an eruption of irregular magic. It was heat, not frigid temperatures, that found the four of them the further into the sky they traveled, an unpleasant slow burn. Once they came to a stopping point, Dora built them a fire.

"Why are the flames blue?" Dora heard Bally whisper to Heime as she steered towards the edge of the cliff they'd come to rest upon. It was the furthest they would be able to climb without transport.

"The flames are magicked," the girl declared. She picked up a wandering spider and popped it into her mouth like a Skittle. Chewing the life out of it, she added, "It's giving off cold instead of heat, to keep us from melting into the ground like tar."

Dora needn't turn around to know that Bally was giving his old friend, or the face of his old friend, a curious stare.

She'll need you, Dora thought. *Don't dislodge her from your will just yet, young elf.*

This time, the witch of Lantern's Edge did turn around, just in time to catch Bally's gaze meet hers. She grinned before spinning back to where her attention had been laid just before. He'd heard her.

"Are you so sure the transport will be arriving this very night?" Heime asked in a gruff voice. He was munching on a bit of jerky he'd brought for him and his apprentice. Bally hadn't had much to eat since they'd begun this journey, but Dora couldn't blame him. Watching someone you love dissolve into dark magic is truly a terrible thing on the intestines.

"'Tis a sure thing," Dora replied.

Seemingly unphased about how long they might be waiting for what was to come next, the girl spoke aloud for anyone who might have an answer for her. "Does anyone have any news regarding Loral? Is he still in hiding?"

"I expect so," Heime muttered, biting off another chunk of his jerky with his back teeth.

"I wouldn't worry about him, Anastacia," Dora answered, purposefully using the name the priestess detested. "His time will come when it is time for his time to come."

She felt the girl's frown in her belly.

"Will he not prove useful once we get the vessel?"

Ah yes, thought Dora, *always about the vessel.* The rotted-out soul in that body had a memory made of Swiss cheese thanks to Dora's eloquent spell work, but if there was one thing that couldn't be kept from her, it was the vessel. She'd been circling around this subject the whole day long. And by all means, they needed it. But it was near annoying, the emphasis the girl put on it now that she'd remembered it existed.

"Sebastian is working on shared magic, and I have it on good authority that it is dwindling," Dora stated, her cloak flapping in the warm wind. "His life was one of those unfortunate ones, twisted and reformed by an illness that grew from the ground and up around his ankles like vines. There was a storm in that boy even before he became a man; he became Loral to silence the raging wind he couldn't get to keep from hollering into his lobes. As soon as his magic is gone, the howling will return. He will be useless."

For a moment, all that could be heard was the cold fire spitting ice sparks and the blistering breeze that gusted continuously over and through the ridge. Then Bally spoke.

"How do you know that?"

Everyone turned to the elf, even Dora.

When she didn't answer right away, he added with a slight tremble in his voice, "I mean—how do you know so much about the king?"

Dora's eyes were piercing Bally's, but before she could utter a word, the priestess answered for her. "She's not going to tell you that," she said with a sinister chuckle. "The witch keeps all the tasty stuff locked up in that vault of hers. Believe me, I've been trying to get in there since the day I arrived."

Dora moved her attention to fit snugly over the girl. "Have you, now?" Of course she had. This wasn't news. "Well then, everyone has secrets they would like to keep." Removing her gaze from the girl and transferring it back to Bally, she stated firmly, "When the time is right, I shall tell you. I promise you that."

"When the time is right," the girl muttered to herself. Then, lifting the two jagged pieces of coal that served as her eyes, she stared at the witch. "You know, at some point we're all going to get sick of you deciding when that time shall come."

Dora's attention splintered off. Just as she prepped to toss *the priestess* a retort, an eruption startled the cozy circle around the frozen flames. Dora didn't have to turn around to know who it was who had caused a large gust of wind to surge into their shelter.

"You rang, Dora?"

Those around the blue flames only heard a giant bellowing roar.

As Bally, Heime, and the priestess stood, the witch slowly turned to face her old friend. "Hello again," she answered. The dragon levitated across from where the four of them stood; its ginormous wings flapping and sending hotter and hotter air into their faces.

"A dragon?" Bally questioned, clearly in awe. "*That* is our transport?"

Dora turned a cheek towards her traveling companions. "How else did you suppose we were going to get to the tippy top? 'Tis why most travelers fail at this point. Not many know the choreography that is needed to move on."

Dora returned to the dragon and began to speak to her; it had been a long time since she'd conversed with any beast. As she explained their reason for traveling to the peak, two words flew into her mind.

Dragon dancer.

She stilled. And for a moment she almost turned to face the girl. But no—the last thing she desired was for that detestable soul to catch any semblance of hesitancy residing anywhere in her person. If she faced the girl, the transparency would show in her expression. It would be readable to the one who Dora had once called mother, that she had heard her speak to her telepathically. That she knew the girl was growing stronger. At this point—this close to the end—the last thing she wanted to do was throw water or sunshine on that which was struggling to grow.

"Come," Dora hollered back at her company. She dared not look their way as she waved them forward. "Rosaline will not wait on us forever."

"Rosaline," Bally repeated as he came to stand next to Dora, his eyes so very wide as he took in his first ever dragon.

"Yes," Dora answered.

"The beast looks familiar," the girl said, coming to the other side of Dora as Heime pulled up next to his apprentice.

The dragon growled to everyone but Dora.

"Come on then," the witch said, leaning forward and taking hold of Rosaline's neck. The dragon moved in and Dora reached for Bally's hand, placing it next to hers on the red scales. "'Tis just like mounting a horse, just a bit thicker of a saddle." She bounced her head from shoulder to shoulder. "And there's no saddle."

The elf boy trembled only slightly as he did as he was told. He was so much braver than he'd been when he was a boy; Dora could read his soul like a book and Jeremy never would have jumped onto a dragon. Not even for all the money in the world.

After Heime followed suit, Dora turned to the girl. "'Tis your turn."

The girl's eyes narrowed, and a firm and hasty grin shot over her face before fading instantly away. *I know you can hear me.*

Dora didn't flinch.

"What are you waiting for?"

Acknowledgment.

Still, Dora said not a word. Her expression remained simple, and if anything, annoyed.

Finally, the girl sighed before flinging herself up. Once she was aboard the dragon, the three of them inched back so Dora could take the front.

"Make it a smooth ride, will you?" Dora asked of Rosaline. "These fools know not the beat of your heart. They have no music to follow."

The dragon listened and did as she was told. As they began to ascend the mountainside, Rosaline howled to Dora, "*She* is dangerous."

"I am aware," the witch answered.

"I am surprised she cannot hear me."

"'Tis one of her greatest frustrations. For all her conjuring she could never speak to someone like yourself. Had to have others do it for her."

"Shall I just burn her up now?" Rosaline asked, fire erupting from her mouth.

"No," Dora answered, peeking backwards to find her crew giving her speculative looks. Anastacia appeared particularly distrustful. "'Tis not the body we must burn. 'Tis the soul."

"Ahhh," sighed the dragon. "I now understand why you've come."

Dora bellowed back to the dragon in a language only the two of them could understand then turned back around to face her apprentice. She grinned at her in the same way the girl had just glared at her. Then, blocking her thoughts—keeping them locked up in that vault of hers—she wondered silently to herself whether the girl was trying to communicate with anyone else.

❧ 25 ❧

Makayla

Dorothy demanded we stay the rest of the night, spitting out curses about how someone in my condition shouldn't be trying to outrun a school of hunters.

"They'll be smellin' it on ye," she said, after she'd forced Layla and Blythe to come into the cottage. "Surprised they didn't use it against ye when ye were first captured." She tried to bring Petal in as well, even though I wasn't sure how she'd fit, but the Pegasus was stubborn as an ass. Dorothy made a point to say as much, and for the first time I saw a glimpse of Petal turning bitter. "Ah now, ye cool down," she'd said to Petal before shutting the front door on her narrowed eyes. "Now, about ye, Miss Makayla. Ye need to get some sleep. When ye wake, I'll have somethin' for ye to take away that scent."

"Can everyone smell it on me?" I questioned, as Toby took my hand and began leading me back to the couch I'd been resting on before they found me. "My queen, I believe even the gods can scent that babe growing in your stomach."

In typical Makayla Wood fashion, I'd been the last to know about this very life-altering situation happening in my own body.

In any case, we did as was requested by our host and rested. Me against my king, Blythe on the chair next to us, and Layla—well, the mermaid didn't sleep much. When we woke that next morning, her and Dorothy were hunched over the kitchen table, pointing to different sections of what appeared to be a map.

Toby and I rose, letting Blythe snore away in her chair. As we neared Dorothy and Layla, it became clear as to what they were up to.

"If the soldier who accosted Makayla was planted here," Layla said, pointing at a place on the map that denoted Dorothy's cottage, "then I can only imagine the next two would be planted here and here."

Toby and I snuck up and aligned ourselves on either side of the witch and the mermaid. What we were looking at was super strategic. Without looking up at us, Layla acknowledged our presence by explaining, "It is how we attack in the sea. We move forward in formation, but far enough apart that our enemies don't see us coming. I can't be sure, but I imagine they are spread out this way, like a—"

"Manatee," I finished for her.

She glanced up at me. "Yes. This is how they will travel, together as one, yet far apart."

She was just beginning to point to another section of the map when there was a thud outside; whatever it was, it shook the walls of the cottage.

"What was that?" I asked, my gaze shooting from one wall to the other. But even though I was preparing for something wicked, the rest of my party were wearing nothing but mischievous and excited expressions.

"I believe our guest is here," Dorothy said, automatically nearing the door.

Layla followed the witch with a bounce in her step just as Toby squeezed my hand and Blythe popped up out of her chair.

"Our guest?" I questioned.

Layla grinned as Dorothy opened the door. As soon as she did, I heard it—a strange melody unlike anything I'd ever heard before.

"Oh cute!" Blythe said through a yawn, automatically fluttering over towards the opened door. "How old is he—or she? I can never tell what gender they are."

"He's a boy," Layla said with a smile. His name's Kurt. I asked Shell to send him—she's not too far away."

Toby grinned at me. "Are you ready to dance, my queen?"

"What's going on?" I asked, pulling away from Toby and following the others until I was peering out into the sunshine, where between the woods there stood the smallest dragon I'd ever seen. And by small, I mean this little guy was probably about eighteen feet tall. "Oh my god," I said, a hand coming to cover my mouth. The dragon hiccupped then quickly began looking over his shoulder, then after another moment, began to cry. "Oh no," I said, creeping up between Layla and Blythe to get closer. "What's wrong with him?"

Layla didn't hesitate; as she moved towards him, she spoke back to me. "He's but a toddler—not used to being alone yet. His mother's near but considering your condition, I thought it would be good to start small."

I followed close behind her as she spoke to the tiny beast.

"It's okay, Kurt. Mama's close. I just wanted to say hello to you, and my friend here would also love the chance to sing by your side."

"Sing . . ." I whispered. But the closer I got to the scaldron, the less weary I was. And the music, like, *ran* through my veins. "Hi," I said to the creature as I gently lifted my hand up towards his belly. For reasons I couldn't explain, when he moved, I knew which way he'd turn, and how to comfort him with my own movements.

"You see," said Layla, in tune to the steps I was taking with the young dragon, "it's as simple as following the current. His energy knows yours and yours knows his."

"This is wild," I murmured, my hand feeling his body. It was warm . . . and soft. "How come I didn't feel this way while you were riding Shell?"

"Because normally your skills develop overtime." She smirked as she finished her speech. "However, we didn't have the luxury of letting you figure things out. I rewired you while you were sleeping. You're welcome."

Wait— "You what?"

"Don't worry, I got Toby's permission," she said, while she rubbed at Kurt's tummy; he slowly folded towards the ground until he was rolling on his back.

"Oh, well then—" I started sarcastically, while leaning down to pat Kurt's side.

"Look Makayla, time is not on our side. We all needed you to know how to dance in case a scenario finds us where you'll need the skill to survive."

"Okay . . . I get it, I guess. But how were you able to speed up the process?"

She pulled out a wand. "I'm half elf, so I get one. Just used it to access the code you were born with but hadn't accessed yet."

I stared bullets into her. "I'm not a computer."

"Meh," she said lightly. "Brains are kind of like computers."

I was struggling to figure out something to reply with

when a soft, furry wing, scooped me up and set me back down onto Kurt's back. I actually heard the scaldron giggle as I reached for his hide and held on as he began to flutter up into the air.

"Don't go above the trees, Kurt!" Layla hollered up at us. "We're trying to keep our heads down right now!"

"Okie dokie," the voice of a child answered back.

"You can talk!" I exclaimed, holding tight to the dragon's back—but really, I didn't need to be. My body automatically knew when to duck with him or when to lean forwards, or backwards. No matter what, I wasn't going to fall.

"Kurt getting smarter," the little beastie said over his shoulder.

We only rode around for another minute or so. Eventually there was a squawk coming from the clouds and Kurt chirped back. I knew in my heart of hearts that his mama was impatient to get her dragon heart back. Once I was back on solid ground, my own wings raised above my ears, I bowed slightly to the scaldron.

"Thanks for the ride, Kurt."

"You welcome pretty faery," he said back, then shot up into the sky.

When I turned around, it was to find everyone staring at me.

"That . . . was the coolest thing I've ever experienced," I stated, walking towards them.

Blythe raised her brows. "Only someone who was raised human would say that after being handed a sword forged by the gods."

My head fell to my shoulder as I said the only words left in my head. "But so were the dragons."

Dorothy was kind enough to let us stay a bit longer. We took turns cleaning up in her washroom and eating the rest of her cookies. If I made it through this alive, I was going to have to set her up with an unlimited OREO subscription.

Eventually we were back to where we'd been just before Kurt had made his entrance: planning our strategy. The lot of us were gathered around the table—Layla's spine was curved over the map she and Dorothy had been scouring, with Toby nearly pasted to her.

"Any chance your people might serve us in a new, unique formation?" My king asked, his arms gently crossed over his chest.

Layla's gaze rose and landed firmly over his. "It's possible. This is the most commonly used one and the mer are somewhat predictable. However, we must still be prepared."

As they conversed over the other possibilities of how the mer might be tracking us, my attention drifted and fell to the part of the map that was labeled Forest Peak. I pointed a finger down at what appeared to be the entrance to the cursed land. "How far is this from where we're at? I gather the land may be more spread out than what's illustrated here, but this looks quite close."

"It's only about two miles from here," Dorothy started. "But—"

The energy became stiff. When I turned to my left, Blythe was tucked into my side.

"I believe what our host was about to say is that the land is jacked. And that," the faery said, gripping my hand with hers, "is why I'm here, queenie." She waited until I looked up at her. "I'm the only one who's ever tried to make it back to the beginning."

"To the beginning . . ." The words barely left my lips.

Her hand was soft over mine and my stomach stirred as she squeezed it. "I guess I wanted to say good-bye to my parents." She pulled her hand away and drew a line on the map with her finger, starting back from the safe land we'd come from and into the section that read 'Cursed Earth,' as well as 'Forest Peak.' "It was kind of like trekking on to find a grave, you know. I thought if I could speak to the land that they last walked upon as themselves I could find some closure."

I released my teeth from where they were holding my lip hostage. "Did you make it there?"

"Not quite," she said, raising her eyes to meet Layla's. The mermaid held her stare for only a second before looking away. "But not because I didn't believe I wouldn't make it. I'm too stubborn to give up."

"Then what stopped you?" I asked.

Her chest lifted, and her wings spread out—the wing closest to me curled just a tiny bit around my own butterfly extension. "Sometimes we just get to a point where we know that what we're doing isn't working. I knew risking my life just to pay homage to a couple of cult junkies wasn't going to make me feel better."

"Then what did you decide would?"

She looked me dead in the eyes. "Scraping out the heart of she who destroyed my family and stomping it into oblivion."

She continued to stare into my eyes as though they could offer a glimpse into a nearby galaxy.

"So," I stated in a near whisper. "That is why you're *really* here."

A slight grin colored in along the delicate lines of her face. "You may have been chosen to walk with Avalon's blade, but if it's okay with you, I'd like to be right there the second that sword pierces the Crone's wicked little heart."

And there it was again . . . the unbearable fact, that to take down one of the worst souls ever known to creatures of all shapes and sizes, I was going to have to slay my best friend.

Good luck, faery scum.

My wings rose directly above my head and my heart stopped. Everyone paused their conversations to look at me.

"Makayla?" Toby questioned, worry lining every edge of his beautiful face.

She could live . . . But if you kill me then I'll ensure Cee-Cee's soul dies right along with mine.

A slow, burning sizzle coursed through my veins.

"Yo, queenie? You okay?" Blythe asked, reaching for my hand again.

Toby was instantly at my side, reaching for my face. "Makayla? Are you still here? Have you gone away again?"

I opened my mouth to respond but no words came out. *That voice.* I knew that voice. Cee-Cee's but *so not* Cee-Cee's. Could it be?

"Makayla?" Toby continued to hammer out.

"Layla," I whispered as if in a trance. "Did you do anything else to my mind?"

"No," the mermaid replied gravely.

"What do you mean," Blythe was asking Toby, "when you say, have you gone away again? *Where has she been going?*"

I continued to stand there, nearly locked up, as Toby tried to explain what he couldn't understand. "She's been traveling . . . in her mind. Ever since we got to this world."

Layla leaned in over the table. "You mean like daydreaming?"

Toby shook his head. "No, more than that I'm afraid."

The voice wasn't speaking to me anymore, and though it took some effort, I shook myself back into the present. "I wasn't wandering away, I promise. It's just—"

Suddenly, a hiss erupted from Dorothy's lips. "The

Crone," she said, in the most despicable manner known to mankind.

I matched her hardened eyes and nodded. "Yes."

The table we stood around was suddenly filled with chatter as everyone spoke at once, but Dorothy quickly demanded that our attention find her speech and hers alone.

"The Crone is gaining strength. Telepathy was once a weapon she favored, but unlike you two" —she glanced at both Layla and I— "she was no dragon dancer. She was workin' on tabooed magic and the darkness allowed her into other's minds." She reached across the table and gripped my forearm. "Do not speak back—'tis fuel. Keep yer thoughts quiet. 'Tis not a sure thing that she can read them but be wise and keep yer arrangements hidden just in case."

I heard every word she was saying, but still I had to know — "How did you know she was talking to me? Could you hear her?"

"Oi," said the witch. "I felt it." She made a fist and pounded her heart. "Right here. She's the disease who killed my brother, and somethin' with roots that wicked . . ." She shook her head. "'Tis palpable."

"What am I supposed to do? She's—She's found a way into my mind."

Dorothy looked at me with a set of iron eyes. "'Tis both simple and impossible. Don't be lettin' her back in."

We all stood there quietly for a few beats, letting our host's words sink in. All I'd been doing ever since I found out about my wings was trying to keep an open heart. Now, it seemed, I needed to lock myself back up and throw away the key. Or the better option—simply tread carefully.

Layla looked to Toby. "We must be going."

My king nodded. Regardless of this horrifying new detail —that the Crone had figured out how to get into my head— we weren't at this cabin on extended leave. We needed to be on the path towards our destination; the only way to ensure the Crone stopped growing in her power was to take her out, and it wasn't going to happen as long as we were sitting around here eating cookies.

Layla broke away first, packing a few more supplies given to us from our gracious host. Toby placed his lips against my cheek then took off to be with Petal. I was about to go freshen up, throw some water on my face, when Blythe reached for my arm.

"Hey."

I turned and looked at her.

"What spell are you using?"

I furrowed my brows. "What?"

She rolled her eyes. "To check out, queenie. You're using magic to distract yourself. Shit like that can be kinda hazardous, and since all we're all in this thing together, it'd be kinda nice to know what you're dealing with."

A slow breath left my chest as it caved, and without overthinking it, I reached behind me for where I'd left my bag the night before. I brought out Maude's spell book and opened it to *The Great Beyond*, laying my finger over the title.

"Here. I've been going here."

Blythe's lashes fluttered as she looked from the spell back up to me. "Dang, Makayla, this is some heavy shit." Again, she reached for my arm, squeezing it. "This isn't an escape—this is—"

"Permanent. Yeah, I know."

Careful to keep my voice low, so as not to announce to everyone what I'd been going through and where my thoughts had been drifting, I explained everything to her. From Rally's blade crossing Toby's neck to crossing worlds, to the heavy fog that had settled in my guts and then crossed over into all parts of my soul like a cancer.

Words I hadn't yet said out loud fell from my lips, "I don't think Toby's real."

When I looked back up at my new faery friend, her eyes filled in with moisture and my heart ripped in half. If I was reading her reaction correctly, then she didn't have anything positive to offer. Was Toby truly just some form of a ghost? It took all of two seconds for two waterfalls to come streaming from my eyes.

"Hey," Blythe said softly, bringing her arms around me and letting me fall apart. "You know what this is—it's stress, queenie. You literally have the world on your shoulders, a babe in your belly, and a group of self-centered misfit fantasy characters to help guide you." She chuckled as she said that last part.

"You're not telling me what I need to hear." I shook in her arms. "Just tell me Toby's real! Tell me that I'm losing my shit and that's all!"

She pulled herself away then touched her forehead to mine. "You need to calm down." She waited until my watery eyes matched her gaze. "How about this, I've got an idea."

Tears were streaming down my cheeks and my nose was running like a hose. She pulled out her wand and used it to dry my face (it was just like mine—minus the star and diamond—and it glowed a beautiful lavender color). "Get out your wand."

"Why?" I sniffled.

"Just do it, queenie."

I shook my head as if it was a silly request and used the back of my hand to wipe my nose, but still did as she'd demanded.

She pulled away and held out her wand towards me. "Now, put the end of yours to mine."

I frowned slightly. "Why?"

Her free hand found her hip. "Just do it."

It was my turn to roll my eyes. But still, I did as I was told. As soon as our wands touched, they began to blink, sharing colors. Blue, purple, and lavender.

"What are we doing?" I asked.

"Sharing our strengths and weaknesses," Blythe affirmed. "It's ancient magic. If one of us gets wary, the other will know and come to the aid of whoever is feeling weak. Either physically or mentally. It's really rad fey magic, not all creatures can—oh my god—"

She stopped talking as soon as the wands went from flashing shared colors to something else. I'd never seen it before, but then again, I'd never been a party to this sort of magic. I thought what was happening was just part of the spell. As I watched the wands fill with an eerie translucent glitter, glowing and bright, I was just about to state out loud how beautiful it was, when Layla walked towards us and stopped cold.

I didn't even realize she was there until Blythe's head turned very slowly in her direction and the mermaid said in a very murky voice, "What the actual fuck, Blythe?"

The Reef's mouth had fallen wide open, and in an instant, she pulled her wand from mine and started shaking her head. "I—I didn't—I mean—I guess I sort of knew, but I mean, she's already wi—"

"Apparently that doesn't matter," Layla said with words so bitter my tongue soured. And then she marched away.

Blythe cursed, pocketed her wand, then whispered a hasty "sorry queenie" in my direction before running after Layla.

I was left there with only myself and my wand. No one else had seen what had happened—not that I was very clear on exactly what had ensued. But still, something *had* happened. Something big. And even though there was still sadness and little tendrils of depression clinging to my sides, I couldn't help but notice that I felt a little lighter. For the first time in *a while*, that little light shining from somewhere deep inside—it was back. I was a little stronger, a little less queasy, and a lot more like myself.

Knowing I couldn't stay rooted in that spot forever, I put away my wand and gathered my things. I had an urge to send a message back to the Crone squatting in my best friend's body, but Dorothy had said that would be unwise and I had a feeling I should listen. So, I kept my thoughts to myself, threw my bag over my shoulder, reached for Avalon's sword, rolled my shoulders back, and marched outside to meet my team of misfit fantasy characters. To be fair, if I'd been able to hand pick the crew for this life-threatening voyage, I wouldn't have changed a thing. As I walked up beside him, Toby took my hand in his. I'm not sure if it was the charm Blythe had just used or what, but this time his flesh felt solid against mine. His heartbeat, my heartbeat.

"Now then," he said, "that's the grin I've been missing."

I knew where we were going was dark, but this was the best I'd felt in a long time. I wasn't even stressing about the seed in my belly. I wasn't nauseous. I was read to move on. To fly, climb, hack, or ride to the top. I was a dragon dancer, dammit. And once there, I would deal with what had to be done. No matter what.

26

Lantern's Edge

Their feet were bare as they trekked across the land. The priestess making up the head, Malina and Dora taking the shoulder positions, and behind them, a following made of detestable Cronies.

"Is the land cracking?" Malina whispered to her sister.

"'Tis doing more than that," Dora answered.

Only the untouchable one had noticed as they walked away from Lantern's Edge how the earth had shaken. How the land had torn apart as though the core of the earth had bellowed, as if the clay, dirt, and roots had all become enraged.

On they went, curses filling the land, until they finally made it to the edge of Forest Peak. For years the priestess had been laying down spells, barriers to keep her people in and the enemies out. If anyone dared get too close, the whispers would find them. Terrible voices, screeching cries of children—begging them to turn from the ground and make their way in any other direction, for if they didn't the cries would escalate, the torture.

As they neared said obstacles, the priestess lifted her palms to the sky and undid the bindings over the earth. For the first time, Dora felt a release. Still, she knew it was a temporary thing. The shackles may have been lifted for the first time in her and Malina's lives, but that didn't mean they weren't still tethered to that awful crone. Or that her sister wasn't about to be used as a demonic battery. Even if she could run, she wouldn't. Dora hadn't come this far just to leave Malina to her mother's devices, and she still didn't have what she needed to end the Crone's reign. All she could hope for was that Avalon did.

The second the Crone laid her foot over the forest outside of their territory, there was another crack. Any woodland creature within earshot fled, and though Dora couldn't see her mother's face, she could feel her grin surface; it caused Dora's guts to turn.

"Ah," said the Crone. By now her voice held an unnatural echo. Every time she spoke, the eardrums of those in her path thrummed excessively. "You've finally taken it upon yourself to come to us. How valiant."

Malina looked to her sister and whispered very quietly, "To whom does she speak?"

Dora was squinting through the surrounding brush, looking for the culprit. "I know not, I'm afraid." Though she had her suspicions.

"Come on, then," stated the Crone. "Be out with it! We've not got all day!"

Behind them the Cronies were growing anxious. Swarming together like a pile of rabid cockroaches. Just hearing their limbs rub together, the chatter of their gums and teeth—it sickened Dora to the end of the world.

Apparently, the Crone had had enough as well. Pausing from her task, she turned and faced her following, then bellowed unto them, "QUIET!"

The forest immediately became silent.

She nodded her head, her black eyes lowering and finding themselves in Dora's for only a mere second. Though it was a fleeting moment, Dora used it to slide into her mother's mind. Normally, the Crone was more than skilled at keeping up her defenses, but Dora had a feeling that if she could see into the beginning—find the soul who started all this so long ago—maybe she could turn this around without everything getting even hairier than it already was. *All she needed was her name.*

Alas, it wasn't in the cards, not in that fine second. Instead, the Crone grinned even more and let three words slip into her daughter's mind.

Nice try, witch.

Dora's teeth clenched together as her mother turned and faced the woods once more.

"Come out, come out, wherever you are!" the Crone yelled.

This time, she didn't have to ask twice.

The birds had even ceased to chirp as the Crone and her following inched over the grounds. They could hear sticks and pinecones crunching before the person they were seeking walked out from behind a tree.

There was a slow tremor in the Crone's voice—a bitter excitement—as she spoke the name of she who they'd thought they would have to part the sea to find. The name poured from her mouth in three syllables, as if the Crone was tasting and savoring it. "Av—a—lon."

The daughter of the sea appeared wrapped in a garb made of seaweed, and as she came to stand across from the Crone, she stabbed the ground with her sword. As soon as she made her appearance, Malina gasped and inched closer to her sister, tangling her fingers into Dora's.

"'Tis her," she whispered.

"Oi," replied Dora.

This wasn't the way Dora had seen this happening. For years she'd been trying to plot a way to get into Avalon's head —sending her messages telepathically. Warning her, pleading with her . . . They needed help. They needed her sword. At least, Dora supposed, she thought they needed it. It was said that the weapon could take out deities and her mother had been drinking the sort of raw energy that is sourced directly from the gods. But never once, no matter how hard Dora willed her messages to find Avalon, had she heard back from her. Not a single word. Dora had been left downtrodden and confused. She'd come to second guess every truth she'd ever seen and heard, every whisper of confidence she'd gained from the bottom of that lake.

Finally, the mermaid answered the Crone. "Aye," was all she said, her voice deep and rich.

"So stupid," the Crone said, her speech slithering out from her tongue. "To come alone, all this way. So stupid."

"I've no fear in my heart."

The Crone twitched her head to the side. "Do you think this will save you?"

"I wasn't put on this earth to live forever, *priestess*."

"I don't go by that title any longer. You may call me—"

"I know what they call you," Avalon stated dryly. "But to settle over a title like that one, you must first own the tunnel." She narrowed her eyes and shook her head. "I'm afraid that you haven't quite earned the right to Light's End."

"Blasphemy!" the Crone cried out. "I've given years to the Light's End! I've earned the right to wield its power!"

"You've earned something, all right. Just not that."

The Cronies could no longer stand it. They were

extensions of their leader. What she felt, they exhibited. As soon as one began to crow, all the others followed suit. Malina leeched onto Dora and the two—now young women—stood together as the Cronies began to scamper towards their precious Crone, lunging for Avalon as the Crone held them back with her intention.

"If they get to her, they'll eat her whole," Malina whispered heatedly.

"Her light is more than they can handle," Dora said calmly. "They may be unable to contain themselves, but there is only one way the daughter of the sea can die." Malina looked to her sister, searching for the answer. "'Tis by the sword she carries. The only weapon that can take down a god, or in this case, the daughter of one."

The Cronies were surrounding them all. The Crone had them under her control, softening their impulses to hammer forward and lunge for the tasty treat that had entered this part of the wood. *Clickity clack, clickity clack* went their bones as they stalked around the daughter of the sea. *Tickety tik, tickety tak* went their jaws. There were so many of them that they wrapped around the Crone and her daughters, along with Avalon and her sword, three times. It was a moving circle; these giant insects chirping like cicadas.

Paying her followers no mind, the Crone taunted Avalon. "I bet you taste like a fish."

Avalon hadn't shown even the slightest bit of hesitance, and when next she spoke, she remained strong of voice and stature. "You and your sad creatures can drain me all you like. It won't kill me."

"I don't want your soul," retorted the Crone. "I've grown full and I'm ready for my final ascension."

"And how exactly do you plan on doing that?" Avalon asked, her tongue coated in disdain. Before the Crone could answer, she added, "You seek the power of the gods—correct? That's what all this is about." She waved her free hand in the direction of the Cronies. When the Crone said nothing in return, she lifted her chin and continued with her speech. "You bit off more than you can chew. You know it, I know it, and *she* knows it."

All the air left Dora's chest as Avalon's ocean blue eyes fell over *her* golden irises. As soon as the Crone followed the sea daughter's gaze, Dora cursed.

Dora had spent years playing her part, ensuring she didn't rest for even a single second—for that is when the Crone would have tried to get into her mind. Now was not the time to show any sort of emotion. Especially surprise.

The Crone removed her glare from over the stain that was her daughter and returned it to Avalon. "Speak not to her. She is but a spec, an unneeded appendage."

"I wasn't speaking to her," Avalon said, her tone mocking she who stood apart from her. "I was but taking a moment to point out the obvious. But since we're here—" She laid her eyes over Dora's once more. "'Tis a pleasure to meet you in the flesh, Dora."

And then Avalon did the unthinkable. She winked in Dora's direction. The action sounded just like a coin being deposited into a metal container.

She heard me, Dora thought. *All those times I didn't think she did . . . but she heard me after all.*

It was more than the Crone could bear. Already Dora had taken so much from her. She'd stood far too straight all her life. She'd foiled her rituals, refused to die, and now she was usurping *this moment*—this moment of which the Crone had been salivating over for days on end. It was enough!

The Crone nearly broke in half as a wail that could be heard into the ether shook all the corners of all the worlds. It was a scream so harrowing that even the Cronies paused from their skippering and scampering. The whole land became quiet. Until it didn't.

Just like the quiet before the storm, the madness inside the Crone began to form itself into a cyclone. She twisted and curled and twisted and curled—the wind waking around her and beginning to howl—until she rose to a new height right before Avalon's eyes. When she'd risen to at least double her stature—the wind picking up steadily—she pointed a gnarly finger down at the daughter of the sea and instructed her Cronies to feed.

The events that took place after the Crone made her demands happened so quickly that no matter how many times Dora would attempt to replay the scene in her mind in the years that laid before her, she would never be able to see it coming. What Avalon did next, that is.

As promised, the Cronies pounced on Avalon. Tendrils of her light could be seen escaping from the mass feeding, for they were sucking from her soul so rabidly that pieces of it were getting tossed into the air like blood splattering from a vampire's feast. But somewhere between the attack and the moment when the Cronies had had their fill and backed away, the sword had disappeared from Avalon's grasp. The sword that meant the world to the Crone. For she had it on good authority that the sword wasn't only the one weapon that could kill a god or their offspring, but the one blade that could pierce *her* heart and forever end her reign. Once she had that tool, the world was wide open. The earth was hers.

Imagine her surprise when she turned to face her daughters only to find that the sword of Avalon was set stiffly in Dora's grasp.

"How did you get that?" the Crone demanded, her voice like thunder.

But even though she'd been nearly sucked dry, Avalon

wasn't dead, and the daughter of the sea seemed to take pleasure in informing the Crone that she'd given it to her.

The Crone, still towering over everyone, looked from the squashed bug that was Avalon to her daughter and back. "Is it true?" she bellowed. Dora stood as still as a statue; the sword heavy in her arms. When she didn't offer a reaction, the Crone repeated herself. "SPEAK CHILD! Did this sea witch gift you with the sword?"

Dora stared at the blade. It had just appeared in her hands. One moment it wasn't there and the next it was.

"Yes Crone," Dora finally stated.

The Crone returned her cutting stare to Avalon. "The meaning of this?"

Avalon simply lifted her chin and said, "I want her to do it."

"WHY?"

"Does it matter, priestess? Once I'm dead, I'm dead. I'll be out of your way."

The leader of the Bahidicaras stalled. If one didn't know better, they may have accused her of being stumped. "'Tis a trick," she muttered, her words echoing against the trees of the forest like pin balls. *'Tis a trick, 'tis a trick, 'tis a trick . . .*

Avalon, completely depleted of energy, spoke as clearly as she could. "What do I have to gain? The sword is out of my reach. I am already dead."

The Crone swayed in the now blistering wind like a miniature twister. Her previous words were still bouncing around the trees and circling round her head. It was an insane thought, to believe this wasn't some sort of game the child was playing with her. But then, right on point, Avalon used her last key to turn the lock inside the Crone's chest.

"You're too powerful, Crone. I cannot fight you."

Lies, Dora thought, though she was ever so careful to keep that truth inside her vault. She'd learned from a very young age that the vault was needed. Still, Avalon's speech was what the Crone needed to hear. And of course, Dora and Malina's mother was a true narcissist; Avalon's last words worked.

The Crone spent less than a minute savoring Avalon's dialogue as if it were poetry, before turning to her untouchable daughter. "Do it."

Dora's first reaction was to shake her head. But that only got her surrounded by a group of her mother's Cronies who then carried her to Avalon and set her before the girl. The Crone repeated her command. Dora only stared down at Avalon. She knew they were the same age. Perhaps they even shared a birthday.

Don't make me do this, Dora stated telepathically.

She wasn't caught off guard when Avalon answered her. She'd expected as much.

Look into my eyes. Never falter. One, two, three. One for distraction, two for war, and three for victory. You know where you lie. You know your number. Now, pierce my heart, send me home, then follow the scent of the blade. She blinked three times. *You'll know what to do next.* Her gaze fell to the glass bottles hanging from Dora's belt. Lots of things came in threes. Mother, Maiden, Crone. Tears of the gods. *The sword will be in safe keeping until you find her name.*

A ragged breath left Dora's lips and she crammed her eyes shut so she wouldn't accidentally let her attention veer towards her mother.

Avalon continued to send pieces of light into her vault. *It's far from over, Dora of Lantern's Edge. But that doesn't mean you can't stow them someplace safe in the meantime.*

Dora stood there for a long moment, the furious winds chafing against her cheeks. Against the scars put there by her mother. Stow their souls away until the moment was right . . . at least the glass containers were beginning to make more sense now.

"WHAT ARE YOU WAITING FOR!" the Crone roared.

Do it now. Or do it never, Avalon said into her mind.

Dora bit down over her lip and raised the sword. Before she let it fall, she whispered, "I'm sorry." Then only for Avalon, she said, *May you return to light and love.*

And then she brought the blade down into the heart of Pontus's daughter.

As soon as it was done, the Cronies screeched, and pitter pattered into madness. The Crone held up her hands to the heavens as lightning sprang from her fingertips. She was so drunk on power that she didn't notice the tear that fell from Dora's eyes to the patch of land that was left where Avalon's body had been—now taken back to where she'd been sent from. The Crone never saw how the small bit of land where the tear had landed turned from black to green. But the Crone *did* take note, as her gaze lowered and her body began to wind down to its normal size, as the sword disappeared into thin air.

"No," she said, the wind finally beginning to settle. "NO!" She began to circle the ground where Avalon had been struck from this earth. Her panic was palpable, and her creatures were stirring. "NO, NO, NO!"

She wrapped her long fingers around Dora's neck and squeezed with the strength of a thousand men. "Where did it go? Where is the sword!"

Dora could feel the pain, the lack of air. But she could also hear Avalon whispering in her ear. *It now lays in two's hands. March the bad village into the land of the fey. Proceed with your plan, Dora. The sword will find thee.*

Finally, when she couldn't take it any longer, Dora used her strength to push her mother away. As she choked on the air reentering her lungs, she spoke the words that would haunt her every day of her future life. "Garlandia." She wrapped her hands around her neck and lunged for more air. "The sword has found Garlandia."

The Crone stood from where she'd hunkered down to peer into her daughter's eyes. The group of Cronies gathered closer to her and her daughters. She raised her fist in the air as if it had been her vote, her idea. "'Tis time to travel the worlds, children! 'Tis time to GROW!"

Malina dropped down before her twin and rubbed Dora's back. "What has happened? Is that truly where it's gone?"

Dora looked into Malina's innocent eyes, but before she could send her any messages, their mother pointed a finger at the girl. The weak one, but still *the one*.

"'Tis time, Malina," the Crone said, as though she was simply pulling down star shine to make her child glow. "Come now, give me your hand."

Malina's chin trembled as she did as she was told. The Cronies moved into formation; robotic *things* coded to know when it was time for something great. And Dora stayed where she was, forced to watch as her mother dug stakes into the ground, culminating the spell of a lifetime. The Crone had been waiting, *oh how she'd been waiting*—waiting for the time to come when she could finally merge her power with she who held the dragon's breath. For in that breath, after she'd taken on the power of two witches and joined forces with the souls from her Cronies, she would use the breath to rip away her earthly restrictions. She'd find ascension.

Or at least that was her plan.

The truth was, Dora hadn't come out of that lake all those years ago just to watch her sister get consumed by their terrible mother. No, not at all. Even if it was already written that her sister was to be sacrificed . . . it wasn't something she was willing to let happen.

She gripped one of the vials around her belt as she

watched the madness unfold, the preparations for the one spell they'd all been waiting for.

Malina.

Her sister turned her cheek towards her from where the Crone was situating her.

Remember what I taught you. Just before she begins her work, reach for it—my power. We'll trade, just like we practiced. We'll trade souls.

Over the years Dora had been scheming. She'd figured out that she wasn't only capable of exchanging or taking on another witch's power. She'd successfully traded souls with her sister three times now. All she had to do was do it one more time. And it had to work, for Dora knew more than anything that Malina wasn't strong enough to pull that Crone down into the dirt. No, the only one powerful enough to do that was Dora herself.

Malina? Dora questioned again. *Can you hear me?*

But as the time came for the conjuring to commence, Malina's eyes saddened and looked away. Dora, who had started to fall to her knees, heard but one line before the Crone began chanting.

You're not the only one who loves. I'm sorry, sister, but I cannot let you ingest this poison. I'll find you in the ether.

And then the fog rolled in.

27

Makayla

Cee-Cee, Jeremy, and I stopped watching *Grey's Anatomy* after the second season. We already knew what was going to happen in the future episodes because every hot mess of a plot twist was littered all over social media the second each one happened.

"Everyone just gonna die," Cee-Cee had said after we'd finished the last episode of season two. "Can't we just leave it like *this*? We know who she's reaching for, and we know he gonna reach back."

Jeremy had been lying on his stomach, his face propped in his hands. "I really don't like to end something before it's over."

They'd both looked to me as the tie breaker. I thought about it for less than ten seconds. I turned off the television and threw the remote at the couch. "I'd like to leave it right here. That way, we can believe what we want to believe." And

I believed that Meredith and McDreamy would be together forever.

Together eternally. That had been the idea when Toby and I stitched ourselves back together. It was still bizarre to believe that our souls had known one another for zillions of years. It was kind of like we were soul mates. Meant to drift along and find one another as we journeyed far and near, wherever our souls were directed through space and time. I wouldn't ever mention it to him, but I'd heard Toby whisper into my ears the night before, when he thought I was fast asleep, "I'll always be with you, my queen. Connected are we, in sync always."

I wanted his words to comfort me . . . why didn't they?

In the blink of an eye our lives had changed. *Grey's Anatomy* was a distant memory, as were my two best friends. I had no idea how Jeremy was doing as Bally, or where Dora and her apprentice had gotten off to. From the start, Toby had made it clear that we were to only think about *our* journey. *Our* destination. If our paths crossed with those we knew in the past, then we'd worry about that when the moment came.

I was still strong from whatever charm Blythe had worked between the two of us. I only hoped she hadn't somehow given me *all* her strength, because ever since we'd done that weird wand thing, she'd appeared unsettled. And Layla refused to look either of us in the eyes.

It was Toby's voice that shook me back into the present. "We'll most likely be separated once we enter the cursed lands."

I shot my king an estranged look. The four of us and Petal had been padding through these woods for hours, stopping only once or twice to pause and listen for the mer and to nibble on our rations. Hungry didn't even come close to describing how I felt *all the time*. I had a feeling that even if we weren't exhausting countless calories by hiking through this world, I'd still be famished. The goddess may have chosen nine months, the same as humans, but pregnancy was different in fey. Every symptom surfaced earlier, and this little faery that I was growing was ever so demanding.

"What do you mean?" I asked of Toby's strange and abrupt observance of fate.

He pointed in the direction we were headed, northwest. "Forest Peak is right up ahead. The land is broken."

Blythe, who had been silent for much of the day's journey, spoke up from where she and Layla were in sync, about ten feet from Toby and I. "The Crone set down spells all over the land she thought of as hers. Magic, especially dark magic, rots if not cared for. This isn't going to be just your ordinary nature hike. We *will* be pulled apart. We *will* be tested."

I didn't like the sound of that.

"But *you do* know what to expect, right?" I asked Blythe. "I mean, you've done this before."

She shook her head softly, her gaze still set directly ahead of her. "That means nothing. All I can be sure of is that we will be coming up against some serious shit, but magic is like lightning—it doesn't strike the same place twice."

"And it evolves," Layla added. "It grows and twists and turns." She sighed. "We'll not know what we're up against until we're face to face with it."

I cupped my hand protectively around my belly. The act was noted by my king.

"Don't worry," he whispered into my ear. "She'll be fine. I promise you."

I arched a brow as I looked his way. "She?"

The right side of his lips lifted. "I might have it on good authority."

Over on her side of the group, Layla scoffed. "Damn pompous royalty, they always have it on *good authority*."

For the first time in hours, every single one of us broke into a laugh. And not just any laugh, but the kind that brings light to the darkness. And it was a good thing too, for just then we curbed the top of the hill we'd been hiking—my new shoes making each step effortless—and found ourselves staring out into madness.

The humor left us as we stared out into oblivion. For that's what it was. The land wasn't just broken—it was in pieces. Chunks of earth floating in the air as if they were their own planets. Giant bits of forest, singular trees. A random pinecone. Dirt levitating in the air like frozen confetti. It went on for as far as the eye could see.

"What—how are we supposed to—how is this possible?" It was all I could manage to get out.

Toby, myself, Petal, Blythe, and Layla. The five of us stood on the last of the solid earth and stared out into obscurity.

"It's as if she ran her claws over the earth," Petal observed. "If she couldn't have it, then no one could."

My head moved ever so slowly towards Blythe. "Can this be put back together?"

She moved her attention to meet mine. When our eyes met, something knocked against my heart. "They say you carry Titania's ghost." I nodded. "Then I guess we'll just see."

"What's that supposed to mean?" I asked.

Toby patted my shoulder then took it upon himself to be the first to walk towards the destruction that laid before us. "'Tis the creation at your fingertips, Makayla. She's betting on you to recreate what's been shredded and left to die."

My jaw unhinged as I looked from my king's backside as he trudged forward, to where Blythe's gaze was still locked firmly onto mine. We began marching forward, towards the broken land. Petal came by Toby's side and my king jumped to her back—her wings carrying the two of them from one edge of the fragmented forest to the next clump of dirt.

Blythe took a hold of Layla and flew her over to meet them. I swallowed any lingering doubt and followed suit. But as soon as I crossed over into the Crone's world, something happened. Something so cutting that I barely made it to where my misfit army was waiting for me on a bit of land with a damaged tree for its only company.

All four of them lunged towards me as I fell, hard, to the ground.

"Makayla!" Blythe and Toby yelled together as three pairs of hands and Petal's nose reached for me.

"What's happened?" Layla asked, worried. "What's wrong with her wings!"

My butterfly appendages were vibrating.

"I don't know," Toby stated, clearly confused.

I begged my body to let me raise my head, but there was a storm going on in there and it made my skull ever so heavy. At first, it had come to me as a screech, like the wail of a demon whose heart had just been punctured. Then came the breathing—as if this evil entity was reaching for its last and final breath. But then it came up for air and when it did, it spoke directly to me. It was a voice so abysmal I'd have been just fine never hearing it twice.

She can't hold me down forever, Makayla Wood.

"Makayla," Blythe whispered into my ear. "Queenie . . ."

"It's her." It was all I could fathom through my heaving chest—through the madness infiltrating every cell in my brain.

You're in MY house now, faery. I was willing to let you go—I thought you were Loral's problem and his alone. But things have changed. I know now what you carry. I REMEMBER EVERYTHING.

Even though the echo of *her* voice was still ping-ponging against my skull, my head eventually cleared. After three long breaths I let my people help me up, only to double over and throw up everything I'd manage to eat that day.

Once they got me to standing and whatever had happened had passed, Toby took me by the shoulders and asked, "What just happened?"

I wiped a hand across my mouth, trying not to focus on the terrible taste coating my tongue. "The priestess knows we're here. I—" I stumbled a little, but Blythe grabbed onto me and between her and my king, I managed to remain standing. "I think when she came back to—when Cee-Cee did that unbinding spell—she didn't remember everything. But something's happened. She knows who she is now." I licked my dry lips and looked out into the wasteland that seemed to go on forever and ever. "And for the first time, she now understands that I am a threat." I gulped. "That I am *the* threat."

$$\text{❧}\quad 28 \quad \text{❧}$$

Dora

The heat from the mountainside was unforgiving. Their entire party was slicked down with perspiration. Well, everyone except Dora. Her cloak kept her cool.

Rosaline had dropped them at 'the tower.' It wasn't an actual tower of course, but to anyone who knew the Enclaves, this is what the summit was called.

"Oi!" Heime hollered to his apprentice as they began the final ascent on foot. "Don't touch the mountain side, you'll burn your fingers and I've not packed salve!"

Dora's attention shot to where the young elf had been prepped to run his hand down the side of the rock. "'Tis steaming, boy! Have you not eyes?"

Bally turned to face Heime first, then the witch. "I—I was just curious."

The girl with the face of his best friend grinned as she strutted past him. "Curiosity killed the cat."

The boy sneered at her as she strolled past, and Dora couldn't help but dive into his thoughts to hear what he was thinking.

Then how do we make you into a feline with a hankering for snooping.

The witch chuckled to herself before stalking up to the boy and linking her arm with his. She ignored his hesitance and dragged him along. "How are you doing, Bally?"

He scoffed. "*How am I doing?* Well, I've been taken from the only world I knew existed and turned into an elf. I don't know if I'll ever see my family again, and I don't think I care. I worry that that makes me kind of a bad person. My best friend is evil as shit and my other best friend is—well, I don't even know where Makayla is."

Dora dipped her chin then looked up at the twisting, gray sky. "For starters, your identity in the world you came from was erased the second you became Bally. Your family will never remember you unless you very much want them to. Second, you're not a bad person. If you don't care whether you see your family again, then it is surely for good reason. Third, your best friend—Anastacia—"

"Cee-Cee."

Dora looked to the boy.

"She prefers to be called Cee-Cee," he added, looking down at his feet as they walked on.

"Right. Cee-Cee isn't the one who, as you so eloquently stated, is *evil as shit*. In fact, Cee-Cee is the kind of soul, who in her past life, liked to make clothes for rabbits and top hats for snakes. She wasn't allowed to be a child, but she still found a way around it. She might not have been as powerful a witch as some, but a fine witch she still was. As for Makayla —" If Bally had looked into the witch's eyes, he would have seen a sparkle. "That Erwain was never lost and she never will be."

The two continued to walk on, taking thoughtful steps up towards that winding summit. Heime behind them and the girl—anxious—was several feet ahead. The air should have been thin, but it was thick.

"Tell me more," Bally said, gesturing with his chin to Cee-Cee, or the priestess. "What she was like when you knew her."

Dora showed her teeth when next she spoke. "She wanted to run an apothecary shop when she got older. We knew it would never happen, but she still talked of it often. She would scribble down odd combinations for the soaps she would carry in a small leather journal she made." The witch sighed. "We weren't allowed toys or anything for enjoyment. But regardless of where our gifts came from, we were skilled at all sorts of crafts. She taught herself how to make paper then bound it together. She had pages full of business plans. I used to call her a schemer." Dora chuckled as she said it.

Suddenly Bally stopped, which in turn caused Dora to come to a halt. He pulled his arm from hers and squared his shoulders until the two were facing one another. Heime walked past the two of them as Bally asked the witch, "Who was she to you?"

Up ahead the girl had turned a corner, disappearing. But she'd only been gone a second or two before she came running back around the bend. Pointing a finger back towards the way she'd just come, she hollered at the three of them, "There's a door! It's carved into the mountain!"

"And?" Dora yelled back as if the girl was daft.

The priestess's arms opened wide. "What are we to do next?"

Dora nearly rolled her eyes. "What we came here to do—knock!"

The girl stared at the witch with uncertainty, then allowed

her gaze to flit back and forth before turning back towards the door.

"Does the one in waiting behind that door know we're coming?" Heime asked, as he stalled by their sides.

Dora ran her thumb over her bottom lip then started stalking off in the direction of the door. "I suspect she has her suspicions," she said over her shoulder. "She's hid herself well over the years, but no descendant of Hecate is safe from the hunt."

Heime and Bally ran up along her side, keeping step.

"Aren't you a descendant of the dark witch?" Bally asked. Then almost as if he was embarrassed by being so forward, he explained, "That's what I've heard, anyway."

Dora, wearing a smug grin, retorted, "One is safe from the hunt if they aren't being hunted."

"But—wait. How come you're safe?"

"Oi," said Heime in an exasperated tone. "Don't you get it, boy? *She's* the huntress."

Bally, who had been trying desperately to keep pace with the swift moving legs of Heime and the witch, came to a halt. Only after they'd gotten nearly to the spot where the priestess had come running back to announce she'd found a door, did the two turn back around to see the wide-eyed elf standing still on the mountain built from nightmares.

"You've hunted down your own kind?" he asked, innocence radiating from all parts of him.

Dora simply stood there, facing him. "T'was the only way."

"The only way for what?" Bally questioned.

"To ensure that there would be no body for my mother to be reborn into, and if there was that there would only be but a couple to choose from."

"Your mother," the boy said, repeating her words. Then

cocking his head to the side, he answered his own question. "So that means Cee-Cee is—"

Dora felt for the soul inhabiting Cee-Cee's body. She wasn't far from them, but her attention was saturated over that door she was haughtily knocking her fist against. Only when she was sure it was safe to do so, she lifted her chin and sent the words straight into Bally's mind. *Her name was Malina. And she was my twin.*

Bally stood there, frozen and in shock, for what to him must have been several minutes, but in reality it was but the time it would take one to click their tongue three times. Heime was the first to notice as the girl began venturing back their way, and as he did, he motioned for his apprentice to come be by their sides.

"What is it?" Dora asked gruffly as the girl took long strides to meet them.

"No one is answering the door. You better not have brought us all this way just for—"

"You may want to adjust your tone," Dora warned. With her gaze sharpened, she added, "And of course there is no answer. Why would someone who ran through worlds to escape the soul of one, willingly open the door for that very soul?"

The girl frowned. "You told me to knock."

"Yes," Dora echoed, beginning to stalk around the bend to where that wooden door had been placed against the mountain side.

The girl, along with Bally and Heime, were stalking up the steep bend, their toes on the heels of each other.

"Why'd you have me do that then? For a laugh?" Her tone was void of any humor.

"'Tis a door," Dora stated matter-of-factly. "You asked what to do. I told you."

The girl grunted as Dora stood before the same door and

lifted her arm, preparing for her fist to meet the wood. "You are very frustrating, Dora of Lantern's Edge."

"Yes," Dora affirmed, her lips in a firm line.

She turned her head to the door then proceeded to knock. As she did, the discontent from the mountain spread through each of them like a cursed tremor. It was displeased that these travelers hadn't given to its foundation their terrors of the night—their dread. It could sense the greatness of the witch whose feet pounded against its rocky exterior and it knew better than to attempt any marrow sucking from the bones of the travelers. Still, it hissed—now and again it even shuddered.

The two elves and the two descendants of Hecate stood in line next to the door. For several minutes it didn't open. Dora never did knock again—she knew better. The witch inside this tower knew they were there. She would open that door when she was good and ready.

At some point, Dora groaned and slouched down until she was sitting on the mountain edge, her back to the door. Her glamour and her magic kept her face young, but her bones still ground and ached like someone who had aged more than two hundred rotations around the sun.

She could sense the confusion from her friends, Bally and Heime, and the anxiety from the priestess, but she said not a word as she continued to pull out a clove cigarette and began to smoke it.

"*What* are you doing?" the priestess spat out.

Dora held out the smoking clove and gave it an appraisal. "This? Oi, I quit several years ago, but oh how I've missed it. I figure there's no better time to start again then towards the end."

The girl scoffed. "Towards the end of what?"

But Dora never did get the chance to answer, for it was then that the door crept open from the other side. The witch took a hefty drag from the clove then let the smoke exit through her nostrils as she stood and faced the woman they'd come to see. The woman they'd come to take.

The vessel.

Brown eyes stared out from a light brown face. Her braided hair spun on top of her head. She'd only opened the door a crack, enough to see who was standing there, though Dora was brutally aware that she already knew.

Gloria mouthed two words. "The untouchable."

And then the unthinkable.

Dora heard and felt it as the priestess sunk in her ship. Her crow seared through Dora's mind, so violent it almost shook open her vault. The witch turned to face the girl only to see a softer set of eyes looking out to the woman crouched behind the wooden door.

"Mama . . ."

The door opened and the woman took a hesitant step towards her daughter. Only Dora could hear what came next, for Gloria's voice seemed stuck in her head.

Cee-Cee.

Makayla

I t was far too quiet. Too silent. You don't realize how common it is to hear the sounds of nature—even in the city—until they're gone. There were no insects, no birds. No breeze. But there was some*thing.* A sort of crackling. Like ice breaking.

And it was all around us.

We each stood on different grounds, facing one another. Toby and Petal on a chunk of earth with nothing on it but dead grass. Blythe stood upon a boulder which was floating like a lost planet. Layla had found a piece of broken land with a puddle and was sticking her hands in it; as soon as she did, scales ran up her arm, the blue and green colors a stark contrast to the lifeless imagery that was our background. And I was next to a broken tree on a bit of land that wasn't quite floating straight. Some of these fragmented sections of terrain hung in the air as if their axis were tilted.

We faced one another from our separate grounds. We knew what we were here for and what we needed to do. But getting there wasn't the issue; we had wings and magic, we would survive these elements, as harried as they were. What we weren't thrilled about and what was keeping us grounded on our separate pieces of earth was the *tone*.

"It's a medley," Blythe announced from where she stood tall on her boulder. She looked like a faery warrior as she held up her hand and rubbed her finger and thumb together as if she could feel the air. "The Crone left something behind when she marched out of this forest; no one can recreate this sort of pain."

"'Tis the screams and lost emotions of her followers," Petal stated. "They became buried in this ground when they took their oaths. When the land cracked, it freed their emotions—but until the rest of their souls are set free, this part of them is stuck here. In this graveyard."

"Yes," Blythe said softly, releasing her grip over the air and dropping her arm down by her side.

It was these caged emotions that made taking even one step forward excruciating. You didn't just hear begging, pleading—*please, release me from these harrowed grounds! Undo the magic! Sew me back up, I beg of you!* No, it wasn't just the voices. It was the way they reached into you; the way they sunk their fists (their many fists) through your ribcage and into your guts. It turned everything bleak. Any feelings of love or light were stuck somewhere on an endless highway that existed some place very far away.

And here I'd thought I was just starting to feel better.

Layla stood, her piercing gaze landing on me first. "Any more word, Makayla?" The scales that had been growing along her arms began to fade away.

I shook my head. "*She's* here though." I centered my gaze. "And she's not leaving."

The priestess, or the Crone, was awakened. Her ghost was wrapped around my shoulders, snooping, peaking. Readying to pull out my heart and lick it like a lollipop. And *oh*, how she was hungry. Her appetite was growing by the second. Souls—she needed all the souls.

"Wherever they are—" Dora and Cee-Cee, "—they've found the vessel." The vessel that contained what was left of the souls who followed the priestess into their own light's end. I was still piecing together all these bits of tattered prose, but from what I could gather, the vessel contained the power that the priestess would need to fully rise again. I squinted my eyes as I looked out towards the way we'd come. We'd been trekking over this shattered forest for only about an hour, but we could still see the uncursed land we'd crossed to get here. It was distant, but it was there. "I can't tell exactly where they are, but it is gray and hot."

The Crone may have had gotten her memory back, but she was flitting back and forth between my head and wherever she'd been spelled down into, like a moth trapped in a glass jar. She was reckless enough that I could catch glimpses of where she was—of what she was forced to see through the viewfinder she was stuck behind. I'd seen Dora's eyes as they peered into the pit that was keeping the Crone imprisoned.

"They aren't far," Blythe stated, her back stiffening. "The Enclaves are but a slip between any world and that dead stretch of land."

"What are you talking about?" I questioned.

"You said it yourself," Blythe answered. "It's gray and hot."

"She speaks of the place where Lanake took his last breath." Toby stated, and as he did, my heart cracked and sputtered like this forest floor had done once upon a time. "We never finished that discussion. The one where we began to explain what happened to Lanake."

My gaze was alive, drifting—dancing, between every pair of eyes that surrounded me. "*Okay*. So out with it then. What happened?"

Layla sighed. "It was always the priestess's intention to get her hands on Avalon's sword. She'd heard the rumors—that the gods had sent down their offspring the second they'd caught wind of what she was up to. They were prepared for her even before her cult was fully formed. Avalon was the age we send our maids to mate by the time the priestess had her killed."

Blythe cut in, picking up where Layla left off. "The mer were wise to the priestess's motives. Avalon could take care of herself, seeing as she was a deity's actual offspring, but they kept her heavily guarded. Still, the priestess sent many messages their way, inviting their kind to come see for themselves what they were up to in Forest Peak. She claimed" —Blythe rolled her eyes— "that she and her followers were doing the work of the gods. That they had spoken directly to her, and that Pontus desired for her and his daughter to come together."

"It was a sham, of course," Layla said, slipping back into the narrative. "The priestess was so delusional that she thought everyone would just stop what they were doing and do as she had requested. When they didn't, she geared up to do her worst. She lured Lanake to where his bride had been cursed to live on as a ghost."

I was readying to form some sort of inquiry, but before I could, Blythe jumped back in.

"Breya, that was Lanake's wife before Danka ended her heart's beat and dumped her tortured soul into a place that no one dares go unless they've no other choice." Out of the corner of my eye I noted as Petal and Toby shared a look on the floating land they both stood upon. Blythe continued. "They say Lanake knew the second he saw the priestess that his life was over. That he had the power to leave but he chose to stay."

The words fell from my mouth. "Why didn't he run?"

"Because he was lovesick," Blythe answered. Her eyes softened as she stared back at me. "He'd lived long enough without his mate; he was ready to return to the ether. And he had faith that Breya's curse would be lifted, and that she would be able to join him sooner than later."

"So what—he just let that evil piece of shit kill him?" I asked, horrified.

"No," Layla stated. "He underestimated what the priestess was capable of. Doing her worst didn't involve killing him. She drained him of everything he had. She took his soul." My jaw unhinged, and she didn't stop to wait for it to come back together. "That one act was enough to shake all the worlds, and it was enough to cause Avalon to slip away from her guards and find her way into Forest Peak. Alone."

There was a moment of silence—and when I say that, I mean it was a moment of the eeriest silence known to any person, place, or thing. "And that's when the priestess took out Avalon," I guessed aloud.

"'Tis," said Petal. "As for the gray and hot, the Enclaves were placed there by the gods after Lanake's death. A grave marker, but also a gesture to those who dare venture towards that place to turn around. It's nearly an impossible mountain to climb, and a journey that will lead most straight into Hades."

"The Enclaves?" I shook my head as I looked to Toby. "Why would they be there?"

"Because." Toby stated, causing me to swing my attention towards him. "Breya herself told Petal and I that a Hecate witch came to her years ago, asking where she could hide, and the ghost sent her directly to that mountain."

"What?" I asked.

Layla spoke next. "A Hecate witch?"

Toby nodded while Petal whinnied.

"Makayla." I gave my attention to Blythe. "That witch had to have been your friend's mother."

"Her name is Gloria," Toby stated in my direction. "And she walked away from the soul she loved the most so that she could save the world." His mouth tightened as he said, with a crack in voice, "Cee-Cee's mother took what had been born into her daughter, the vessel so to speak, then hid it away; in doing so, she had to hide herself away."

My heart was beating too fast. My palms were more than sweaty. "She hid inside of a grave?"

Blythe spoke without pause. "If you gave birth to the reincarnation of the foulest entity known to all creature-kind, wouldn't you want to find the last place on earth anyone would expect you to hide?"

"But why did she leave?" I asked. "She tied up the priestess's soul and tucked it so far deep inside Cee-Cee's body that Cee-Cee didn't even remember it existed. So why would she escape?"

No one answered. I just stood there in the quiet, all their narratives and half explanations spinning around in my head —all that information separating into individual files. And then something surfaced.

"Dora."

Blythe tipped her chin up at me. "What about her?"

"You called her untouchable." I tapped my foot against the cursed ground. "Everyone in Garlandia knows her to be one of the most powerful witches in the forest . . . They fear her." I moved my gaze from one misfit to another. "If she wanted to summon her mother's soul and bring it back from where it was buried, then don't you think she would have done it all the way?"

"I don't understand," Blythe stated.

"What are you trying to say, Makayla?" Toby asked.

"Only that it seems to me that the priestess I met inside the body of my best friend didn't really remember everything . . . like she knew she was something to be frightened of, but she couldn't have told you why. And now it seems she's been sent into lockdown all over again." I looked down at my feet, at the magicked shoes that fit around them effortlessly, then looked back up at my company. "What if all Dora wants is all any of us wants—for this to end? And with all her intelligence, maybe she's already figured it out. Like how to end this without tragedy. I know the chances are slim, but what if Cee-Cee doesn't have to die?"

My words bounced around each and every one of their shoulders. Petal raised her brows while Toby's eyes seemed to widen. Layla remained expressionless and Blythe—well, Blythe was frowning.

"Regardless of Dora's intentions," said the Reef, "she's leading the priestess back to where it all started. The Crone may have been existing on an artificial power she conjured out of despicable methods, but she is still fierce. She's not going to remain as a sunken ship for long and she's incapable of going down without a fight." When I did nothing more than stare at the faery from across our floating pieces of land, she added, "You and I may have wings, queenie, and human children are taught to believe in us through storybooks, but don't get things twisted up. There will be no happily ever after." And then, so carefully did her eyes sink into mine that I lost my breath. "At least one of us will die, that is if we aren't already dead."

"Hey!" Layla shouted, causing us all to look her way. She had her hand over her eyes like a visor, but as soon as we gave her our attention, she dropped it and pointed it towards the way we'd just come. "Check it out!"

"Check what out?" Blythe questioned.

"The land," Layla chirped. When all we offered her were bare looks, she rolled her eyes, shook her head, and stated in an exasperated voice, "Roots people! Some of the land we've crossed is growing roots!"

With furrowed brows and parted lips, Blythe, Toby, Petal, and I followed Layla's gaze. It took each of us a moment, but at least for me, once I saw it, I couldn't unsee it. The land was suturing itself back together.

Finally, Petal stated almost too quietly for us to hear, "'Tis creation."

"What?" I asked stupidly, looking to Toby and the Pegasus. Her wings were laid out by her sides. The most elegant things I'd ever seen.

"It's you, Makayla," Toby said, locking his gaze with mine. "The spell left behind by the Crone is getting erased wherever you've laid your feet to rest."

I looked from him to every other creature floating around me, then down to where I stood. Very carefully, I lifted my foot. As sure as the red color of my sparkly hair, the burnt remains of the native grass were turning green. A slow breath fell from my lips as I let my foot rest back down to the ground. With every step I took towards the broken tree I stood apart from, I documented how the deadish ground seemed to sigh. I hadn't paid attention to it before, but it *was* coming back to life.

I sensed all their eyes on me as I placed a hand against the broken tree. At first, it appeared as if nothing had happened, but the longer I stood there, I recognized that same sort of sigh coming from the tree's corpse. When I lifted my hand away from the blackened bark, a pine needle began to sprout from a branch.

When I looked back up at the others, I found Blythe grinning. "Girl, you got serious talent."

I crouched down to the ground, fresh sprigs of bright

green grass popping up all around me. Then, cupping some of the soil into my hand, I muttered only to myself, "If one of us may surely die or already be dead, then this is the least I can do to keep the world from completely turning on its side. I will breathe life back into this castle."

And then the world began to shake.

❦   30   ❧

Lantern's Edge

D usk had fallen whilst between the worlds. This land smelled fresh, like sweet grass mixed with dew and honey. The world of the faeries—this was how Dora had always known it to be. How it had been branded between the other worlds. But when one is as gutted as Dora, after having been forced to watch the epic devastation that she'd been made to watch—even the dew had lost its sweetness.

The shuffle and scuttle of creatures swarming to the ritual circle consumed Dora. She'd grown up watching them transform. Most of these excrements no longer had things even remotely close to feet. Their magic had soured their soul and once it was done disassembling what was left of their thoughts, it moved into their bones. Not even their fat cells had been spared. The infection they'd bought into had destroyed them from the inside out.

As they trekked over this new land in the kingdom known

as Garlandia, Dora found herself having to put up blinders so as not to pay them much attention. The foulness of the Cronies was near debilitating now. The ground they walked over was already turning black. How long before it cracked like Forest Peak? Somewhere, deep inside the recesses of her mind where her vault had been built, she listened to her thoughts: *do not dilly dally. This must end NOW.*

Dora slipped her hand beside the wand resting in the pocket of her bunchy skirt just as Malina, or the body of her twin, docked from their old world into this one. She wasted no time nearing Dora, a scowl fitted upon her face as she ran a set of once brown, now paled fingers over her forehead.

"'Tis humid here."

It was the first time her sister had spoken to her since the ritual in their old world. Dora had to keep reminding herself that it wasn't her sister though. Malina was still in there, just buried.

Dora's plan hadn't worked. Years of plotting, of instruction, and when the moment came, Malina refused to do as she'd been told. Through everything they'd been through, all she'd had to do was—there was no point in rehearsing the what ifs. It was over and done. When the moment had come, Malina had simply looked to Dora and shook her head. She thought she was being valiant, taking the punch all herself, but it wasn't brave. It was, in fact, the most reckless decision Malina had ever made.

Now what? Dora had thought, as she'd watched their mother take all that was left of what was good in the world. *Oh Hecate, what am I to do now?* They'd come from one world into the next and she still hadn't heard a peep from her goddess. All she could do was keep moving forward and that included keeping up the banter with the most despicable creature on earth.

"'Tis very humid," Dora stated. Then, using the name her

mother would be expecting her to use when addressing this likeness, she added with a bitter tongue, "Welcome to the forest, Malina."

Finally, after all these years the Crone had gotten her way. After waiting so very long for the perfect moment, it had finally come. She'd taken the winning twin (the one who'd arrived from the dream with dragon's breath) and taken the body and all the power that came with it for herself. Yes, this horrible creature who had been gaining her power all these years by drinking the magic of others finally had what she needed. The body of a magic maker. Sure, it wasn't as powerful as she'd hoped for, but it would still do.

As for that perfect moment, even one as destructive and reckless as the Crone knew that a moment was everything—every magic maker did. One only spun magic when the sparkle was present. Every sort of magic had its own sort of flickering response to allow the spinner of elements to know when the time was right. Luckily for Dora—a witch with the strength of a thousand witches—she had a handle on this. *She'd* ensured the moment hadn't been right for many years, and if she'd had her way, the moment would never have come. Alas, the Crone wasn't giving up and she never would. As soon as Dora had set her gaze over those glass jars—jars that had appeared from nowhere but reflected the eyes of the one who had spoken to her down in that lake—she'd known the moment needed to come, and that it needed to come soon.

With their feet firmly rooted on Garlandian ground, Dora watched as the Crone lifted Malina's nose into the air. The Crone wouldn't ever admit that she knew she wasn't as strong as Dora, but still, she *knew* it. Down to her bare, wicked bones, she knew it and she couldn't run from it.

Still, the wicked had a show to run. Mocking Dora's last words, she stated in an unfriendly manner, "*Welcome to the forest.*" She scoffed. "*We* are of the forest. This is not the same." She sniffed then almost immediately broke out into a bout of coughs. "It's suffocating."

It's pure, Dora thought. And then she took a deep, satisfying drink from this new world.

"And *what* is that?" the Crone asked, turning her ear into the direction of the sound of music.

"Flutes," Dora stated. There'd been a time when music had played in the Lorelei woods also. That time had expired.

"Well, they are just awful," the Crone drawled as she lifted a waif-like arm into the space next to her thin and wiry body. The second the twisted magic had finished, and their mother had stepped fully into Malina's body, the shell sunk in on itself. All her sister's curves had been taken—her color, flushed. She wasn't in the same condition as the Cronies, but she didn't look quite human either.

"Come then," the Crone said, waving Dora along as she walked barefoot over the luscious green grass, not paying any attention to it as it wilted and died under her flesh. "Let us finish what we've started."

Dora was careful to shield the thought that caressed her mind. *What YOU started, you mean.*

A few months before Dora was sent to the lake to die, the young girl had stumbled upon her mother's Book of Shadows, but unlike most witch's diaries, it didn't open with a happy crack that sent notions of cloves and rosemary wafting into its visitor's nostrils. No, it had groaned and though it did open, it was as if the book itself had tried to will its bindings shut. And what it smelled of—oh! It was terrible. Like decomposition, death, and suffering.

Yes, suffering had a smell.

Dora's fingers had blackened the moment she'd set them against the pages, and it had taken several spells and weeks of magic to get the stain from her skin. She'd told her mother that she'd gotten too close to a woodpecker and that was why she'd had to wear bandages and gloves over her hands for so very long.

Still, she'd gotten into the book. Not many others would have been able to do so without agonizing more so than she had. And that was the point, wasn't it? The Crone grew from the suffering of others. Her Cronies were proof of that. All their goodness had been taken and what was left of them fueled her game. It was just so sick. As were the spells Dora had laid her eyes on that very day she'd gotten into the Crone's book of spells. Yet, she had a destiny, and if it was to be achieved, she had to ravage through hell to find where the devil slept.

Or in this case, where a singular wand waited to be found.

A wand full of magical blueprints. It had been enough to get started. However, the ending was upon them, and all Dora could think on was that the main ingredient needed to end this fight was still missing. Avalon's last words floated through her mind. *One, two, three. One for distraction, two for war, and three for victory. You know where you lie. You know your number.*

She wanted to believe she knew her number, but the truth was that she was hesitant. How was she supposed to end this without a name? And if war came before victory, then where was this day headed?

Dora's head continued to spin as she followed behind the wispy train of Malina's garb. The head priestess moved over the warm and fertile forest floor to where the Cronies existed only for her. A circle of grey limbs shrouded in torn clothing. Blood-sucking insects.

"Welcome to Garlandia, my lovelies."

Though they were still, the scampering that Dora had learned to associate with them still seemed to radiate around the circle they'd created. The click of a tongue here, a snap of one's finger there—the sick sound of wet lungs trying to fulfil the need their bodies (or what was left of them) still clung to.

Malina stood tall in the circle. "The time has come. All that you've done for me and all that you've sacrificed—it has all been for this moment."

She raised her hands into the air as if she were connecting with some lost god or goddess. But the truth was, there was no mystical hand to touch—not for her.

"It is HERE!" Her voice erupted and croaked, as if the power surging through her was causing her motor skills to waver, and her Cronies began to salivate as their bones chattered.

Meanwhile, Dora stood silently just inside the circle. Off to the side, or her designated place in her life as the Crone's daughter; it had been her place since the very beginning. Since she failed to do the one job she'd been given. To die.

Malina's spine curved as she lowered her head. "Jealousy. That is what those who have come to take us down were formed from. Fear. We found the break at the light's end, a sliver of sparkling magic that the gods falsely believed was theirs and theirs alone." She stood straighter as she shot a pointed finger up into the air. "They were wrong!" The Cronies copied her by shooting up whatever limb or jagged fingernail they had left. There were many grunts and squeals as they did so. "We've already taken one of their daughters and we won't hesitate to take another!" Again, there was the prattling of excited feedback. Avalon was no more. And then Malina—no, Dora couldn't call her that any longer. At least not in her thoughts. Then the Crone pounced. "I ask of you now, my lovelies, to hold out before you the chalice you were given when you pledged your allegiance to the cause."

Without hesitation, each Cronie did as they were told. In each of their grips (some tighter than others, and some barely able to hold on) was a small silver and bronze chalice. The steel the Crone had used to create them had been rumored to have been handled by underworlders.

This is what they'd been bred for, this very moment. Innocent creatures, brainwashed to believe they were taking part in something revolutionary. Heading off into nothing more than a fictional tale spun by someone who needed to use their bodies and souls to get what she wanted. A fictional and hellish fairy tale ending where they would rule as one.

No one had ever dared to question the validity of what this crone, this head priestess, was preaching. Perhaps it was because most of the Cronies had never been all that well equipped to handle what life threw at them. Or maybe it was as simple as an addiction. The Crone had not only rounded up those without stars in their eyes; she'd offered them a taste of what she was asking them to find. Of what she'd asked them to eat. And then she'd given them artificial stars to look at.

"Now, let us repeat the words we've learned to stand upon together as one."

Dora's lips remained sealed tight as the Cronies began to recite the spell they had been taught. The same magic that was to be used to put one twin's magic into the other. If they'd paid any attention to their leader, they would have noted that her lips were barely moving and as far as a spell leaving her mouth, there was none. Still, the Cronies continued to chant until the enchantment started to take effect.

The first two went at the same time. Their throats shoved forward as if by an invisible hand upon their backside, and from their heart center a glowing ball of light and dark—moving together like the fireball that is the sun. The occurrence drifted to the goblets of the first two Cronies, and as soon as it dropped into the chalices, each mutilated being fell dead to the ground. Seconds after each one died, their bodies went up in flames until all that was left was burnt grass.

The Crone sauntered over to the closest goblet; it hung in the air as if it was perched over an invisible table. Without any semblance of hesitation, she reached for the cup and drank it dry. She paused only long enough to savor the consumption and to lick her lips, before heading directly over to accept her next drink.

She went on like that as one by one the Cronies—these members of the Bahidicaras—fell like bags of rocks, then went up in flames. It was so unnatural, Dora thought, to have these tainted bones fall to such luscious ground then destroy it. It just seemed infectious, and not in a good way.

Dora didn't move, not an inch, as her mother dressed in sheep's clothing drank from the last cup—nothing left of the hundred or so followers the once priestess had gained over so long a time. Once she was done, the Crone faced her daughter. Dora remained in character; she couldn't afford even one small tick of her lips.

"Let them try and stop me now," was all the Crone said.

How could that many souls even fit inside one body, Dora thought with a shudder.

"Malina," Dora began. The witch before her seemed bigger, though she was still rail thin. Her white robes were flowing around her like an aura.

"Yes?" the Crone asked after Dora had offered no more explanation as to why she'd gotten her attention.

Dora swallowed then stated with as much confidence as she could muster, "Do you think it wise to enter the kingdom as you are. We know nothing of this land; the sword we seek may find us first."

The Crone stood tall. "I'm not worried." She held out her hands; they were glowing. "Do you see this? I have the power of a god."

Dora bit her tongue.

"Bottling some of it up may be wise. That way if something does happen, there is a backup."

The Crone stood like a celebrity who had earned their poise through the showering of fame and adoration from their fans; and in one respect, she *had* earned it. She'd consumed the 'gifts' of her followers. She hadn't killed them, at least not out right. They'd done that to themselves in their race to satisfy the needs of their high priestess.

One word escaped her thin lips. "Backup?"

Dora didn't dare move even to breathe. Her hand was still gripped tightly around the hilt of her wand. "Yes. Wasn't that something you always used to preach. Treat your magic as if it were a dog; don't expect it to hang around without a leash."

The sound of a stick breaking traveled from the depths of the forest to where the two of them had faced off. They took turns looking around their shoulders.

"'Tis nothing," Dora said. They needed to get this show on the road, and she didn't have time for distractions. There was enough power surging through the Crone—through Malina's altered likeness—to shine light across the ocean and back; it had caused the Crone to slow down for the moment, but it wouldn't be long before the witch figured out how to move freely with it. "It was but a pinecone falling from a tree, I suppose."

The Crone squinted out into the thick woods. "I suppose," she repeated. Behind her voice there was the echoing of all the souls she'd consumed. She'd *become* the Bahidicaras. So many souls—too, too many—circulating through that single body. She was a vessel.

Dora took four carefully thought-out steps in the direction of her sister's body. Once she was but a foot away from her, she pulled out her wand.

It was all Dora could do to remain in charge of her bowels as a thrumming noise sounded from the orbs that had used to be Malina's eyes. Something with that much power—that much unnatural energy—it could potentially be enough to kill even her. And then the Crone grinned.

"We are in this together, are we not?" Her tone was skeptical.

Dora forced a gentle breath into her lungs then slowly let it out.

"I was under the impression that the Light's End had room for only one," Dora answered.

The Crone's head tilted slightly. "Oh, dearest Dora . . . what are you doing?"

She knew. She knew this whole time that Dora would try to stop her. And of course she did. What was Dora thinking? This monster who stood before her hadn't trusted her for a second, not ever. Luckily, Dora had prepared for this.

In one second, her wand was out.

"What do you think you're doing?" the Crone questioned.

Dora's posture wavered for only a second as a tear squeezed out from the corner of her eye. A memory manifesting of two little girls holding hands as they stared up at the sun.

Two innocent lives meant to go to war.

With the wand pointed at the Crone's heart, she began to chant a spell from a language lost on its people long ago. At the root of all it encompassed was a message, *come home*.

Once Dora began to unfurl the spell, the Crone, *this all-powerful leech*, could do nothing. Paralyzed by her daughter's magic, the evil temptress she'd spent so much of her life becoming began to fade away. The vision of a hungry model, eyes struck by terror, was all that stood in her place.

The procedure took less than thirty seconds, but it felt like lifetimes to Dora. The wand in her hand became incredibly hot and it was all she could do *not* to scream. She still wasn't sure how far they were from the residents of

Garlandia, but just before the last of the Crone's essence was captured, a howl the likes from any bloodcurdling nightmare screeched from the Crone's mouth into Dora's wand, and it could have very well woken the children who play in the center of the earth.

Finally, it was done. With the disease captured, the Crone fell to her knees before face-planting into the ground. To any observer, it would have appeared as though the operation was an easy one. That taking down the head priestess of the cult known to all as the Bahidicaras had been as easy as slicing through fresh baked bread. But that was not the case. An observer would not know the power that Dora had, nor would they understand the plotting she had gone through to end the war her mother had started.

With shaking hands, Dora held steady to the wand as she unfastened the first glass vial. Once it was in her grasp, she attempted to control her chest's erratic behavior as she tipped the end of the wand into the bottle as if she were pouring honey into a small jar. Yellow light poured from one vessel into the other until the glass was full. Very carefully she tapped the end of the wand and capped the bottle, setting it on the ground before reaching for the next. She had just moved to the last one when out of nowhere, footsteps clearing the forest floor interrupted her. They were followed almost immediately by a demanding voice.

"Oi there! What is all this?"

The last glass bottle fell from Dora's hand, and she cursed. The jar shattered and its contents immediately dispensed into the air.

"NO!" Dora gasped heatedly under her breath, reaching for the energy that was shifting from this realm into wherever it was off to next.

There was no time to reflect on what this could mean, for the elf who had come upon her was now in her circle. He held out an ivory wand and took one more step in her direction. He was clothed in a pale blue cape and wore white leather boots. If Dora hadn't been so upset, and more than flustered by the interruption, she may have noted the conflicting vibes he carried with him—arrogance and defeat. When she didn't answer the elf, his gaze began to travel south, to where the grass had blackened from the Cronies' deaths.

He struck his wand further out and blurted, "Speak now, witch! What is this that discolors my land? You should know witches are on thin ice these days. We want nothing to do with what has been transpiring between the worlds."

Of course, what her mother had started had brought suspicion over the shoulders of any witch. It was all a cycle of negativity—a way for the ugly powers that be to lower the vibrations. But then—what had that elf just said? Dora's next words were but a whisper. "*Your* land?"

Without falter, he replied, "I live in the castle that rules this land, so yes, this earth is mine."

She guessed at the truth. "But you are not the king."

The elf's eyes narrowed into slits and his mouth became a firm straight line. That was enough of an answer for her.

She lifted the wand in her hand as she stood, mindful of the bottles still resting by her feet. "I have with me the remains of the evil most refer to as the Bahidicaras. I don't think, *sir*, that you want to disturb me any further."

His reaction was not what she'd been prepared for.

The stiffness in his gait relaxed, as did his eyes. His lips parted and his ivory wand fell to his side. "You speak the truth?"

She gestured to all the scattered goblets over the darkened ground then pointed her wand in the direction of her sister's body. "What else would you call this?"

The elf very quickly let go of his pretense as the realization of what was before him settled in. "Th—This is no lie." He sidestepped a dead piece of land and stepped over an empty chalice. As his jaw trembled, he lifted both his wand and gaze back up to Dora. "What happened to them?"

"Mass suicide." She waited a beat before adding, "The leader took their souls and I took the leader." She clicked her tongue. "But she's not dead. Her soul, along with all the others, is being . . . held." She still didn't have what she required to completely end the Crone's life.

The elf's eyes couldn't have grown any wider. "Who are you?"

Dora stilled, digging into her thoughts, into her very beginning and her once possible ending to find the answer to that question. Alas, she took too long. As she was reeling, the elf crossed one leg over the other and lost his balance, falling towards the dead body of her sister. To keep his flesh from colliding with the dead, he shifted and came crashing down over the glass bottles containing the worst evil any world could ever imagine.

From there, it all happened in slow motion. A wail escaped Dora's parted mouth and her hands fell as her knees buckled—trying as she might to reach for the vials. The elf fell too quickly, his elbow knocking down the first of the vials, before they knocked into each other like dominoes. Glass shattered and yellow liquid seeped up into the air before exploding into several particles and flying away into wherever things of this nature went—off to join the rest of the souls that had already escaped. The magic would keep the souls bound together, and now that the entirety of the vessel was into the ether . . . the Bahidicaras would have a chance at reincarnating, or simply put, revival.

Dora fell to her knees, her hands reaching for the broken vials. "NO!" she screeched, so visibly crushed that it was painful to watch.

"I—I'm so very sorry," said the elf, very carefully coming

back up to his knees, grappling through the blades of grass to find his wand. It was clear that he could see he'd botched something very important. When Dora didn't answer him, nor give any indication that she was breathing, he said, "What was it?"

She picked up a piece of glass and studied it as if she was searching for a lost ingredient. "It was them. It was her. It was . . ." She dropped the glass. "It was the end of our imprisonment." And this glass hadn't been any ordinary glass. It had come to her from the other world. Now what was she supposed to do?

The elf scooted closer to her, then waited until she rested her gaze over his. "That was all that was left of them?"

Her answer hitched a ride on her next exhale. "Yes."

She dropped the bit of glass in her hand and was about to scream when the unimaginable happened. The broken pieces of the jars started to vibrate until the chunks separated into crystal sand. From there, the particles danced close together until there were three piles of sparkling embers; and then they grew back into themselves. Into three glass containers. As new as the day she'd found them.

"Wh—What has just happened?" asked the elf, his expression one of terror.

Dora stated quite plainly and truthfully, "I am not sure." She leaned forward and touched the top of one of the jars. *'Tis a second chance,* she thought. *This isn't over. Not yet.*

Somewhere in her mind, Dora was putting the pieces together. Avalon had said it herself: there had been a distraction, now there would be war, and then there could be victory.

The elf was now sitting up, his gaze wandering from the jars back to Dora. "How did you manage to get a hold of such an evil cult. Are you a hunter?"

I might be now, Dora thought.

"I'm but a witch, sir."

He scoffed. "You are a very strong witch. To take down the Bahidicaras . . ." He shook his head in disbelief. "Even the gods struggled to do such a thing. Even their children."

"I wasn't taking them down. I was only pausing the game." She watched as the elf let her words sink in. "But now . . . now I know not what I'm to do."

The elf gingerly laid a hand over hers. The stimulation of another person touching her was enough to cause her to still. It had been a very long time since she'd felt the contact of another. "You are the most powerful witch I've ever met. You, dearest crone, have just—well—" As he said his next words a gray cloud seemed to fall over his shoulders. "You've just made it so my brother and his queen can rest their souls at night."

And why is that a bad thing? She thought.

Dora found herself in the elf's eyes—and all too soon in his heart. And his heart was broken.

As the elf continued to speak, his tone stiffened, and he lifted his hand from hers. "Now the world can go back to spinning in the direction of progress. My brother will crown his *faery* and they will display their love as if it is a trophy . . ." It seemed such positive prose, but the way he spoke—Dora could tell that this elf wasn't pleased. "What will Titania do with her cousin's sword now? Hang it on the wall? Stare at it as she labors half breeds through her loins."

So Titania does have the sword . . . and the sword will remain until it has slayed what it was brought here for. Dora's thoughts circled round and round. *He's ignorant, this one. Broken. Quite possibly prejudice from whatever has sliced his heart into quarters.*

"Sebastian."

The elf looked up into Dora's eyes. "I did not tell you my name."

And that was when the idea came for her.

She sat up straighter, gripping her wand. "You didn't need to." That part was true. "What if I told you that I was willing to make a deal with you. I'll help you but only if you agree to help me." Her thoughts skimmed around yet another issue. "And you must leave the witches be. *I* will deal with *them* myself."

He narrowed his left eye. "Go on."

"Have you ever heard of the Crone of Light's End?"

He narrowed his vision. "This was what the priestess of the Bahidicaras called herself, was it not?"

"Yes. But you should know, the power she took from light's end was false." That part was also true. "'Tis why I was able to take her down. She was never truly part of what she called the tunnel. But I happen to know the real Crone of Light's End, so well in fact that some might identify me as one of her workers." Dora allowed her gaze to fall, and with a set of electric green eyes that hadn't been there before, she set her sights on the elf. "I've an offer for you, Sebastian."

The elf wrinkled his forehead. "What's wrong with your eyes?"

A sly grin appeared on her face. "They belong to the light's end." If a witch was good at anything, it was improv. Using her tongue as an instrument, she designed an offer the elf couldn't refuse. "It's called an exchange of services. You spread the word of the Crone's existence—whisper into your company's ears that Dora of Lantern's Edge has some sort of affiliation with this crone—and I will ensure that you get everything you think you want."

As Dora waited for the elf to react, she took a deep breath. Her mother was out there, as was Malina and the rest of the souls, swirling and twirling towards the ether, searching for a new body to take. Their souls were bewitched with the magic the Crone had infused into them. Their lives unfinished. They would need a body created from the Hecate bloodline, and though their lineage had decreased in numbers over the years, there were still plenty of vessels. Dora was going to need to remedy that.

The elf appeared skeptical. "I *can't* have everything I want. That much has already been made clear."

Dora skimmed through his heartbeats once more. No, he couldn't have all that he wanted. But still, she could use him. She needed to be feared—to be left alone. Because what laid before her was nearly impossible. She was going to have to find every last Hecate line in existence and essentially wait until the last one or two remained, then watch as her mother was reborn into new skin. This elf could help her. He was broken—she could use that to her advantage.

"What if I told you that once we were through, you wouldn't care about anything anymore." A cramp found her side as soon as she said it. It was a rookie mistake, the offer, and though she was no rookie, she was under a great deal of stress.

Sebastian's tongue ran along the back of his teeth before licking his lips. "I'd say . . . well, I'd say tell me more."

Of all the wrongs Dora had done over the course of her life to make things right, this was the one wrong she'd regret until the day she died. But still, she put herself in character and very carefully stood. As she did, she let her eyes grow to an even brighter neon green. "The Crone of Light's End calls upon only a few. 'Tis how I was able to get this far in ending the Bahidicaras. I am but a host for her greatness; she communicates through me." Dora had spent years watching her mother con people out of their lives; she knew exactly what to do. As much as she detested the act, she needed to remain in contact with this elf, for he was her link to that sword. And she would need that sword, for she wasn't going to be able to rest until it was in the heart of her mother's next incarnation. "The Crone of Light's End is the all powerful. And she has chosen you, Sebastian. Will you accept?"

He was still crossed in more than one way. "Why would she be interested in me?"

Dora's eyes glowed brighter and her voice echoed as her mother's had at the end of her life. "She sees something in you, Sebastian. She sees a great ruler. But her services aren't free. You should know that."

He looked up at her, taking several minutes to stand up and answer. "What must I do in return?"

The Crone had killed the Cronies, but as history had shown, there would inevitably be followers left behind. Witches and the like seeking to reform what was lost. And those creatures would be after that sword. Who knew if the sword could even be taken by anyone but a child of a deity; regardless, she needed to make sure it was safe until she needed it, and even if she found the perfect hiding spot in this forest, it was a burden she feared she didn't have time for.

Dora answered Sebastian. "The time shall come when the bad village will try to reform. I do not care what role you play in their games, but I do have one requirement."

"And what might that be?" he asked hesitantly.

"Titania's sword—'tis not to leave the castle. I care not how you ensure its safety, just as long as it stays put."

Three breaths left the elf's mouth before he asked, "The sword is glued to the faery's body. How do you suppose I get it from her?"

For a fleeting moment Dora wondered if she could just bail out on all of this. Titania was the daughter of Gaia. She'd been sent to wash away the mess the Crone had created. But again, Dora knew deep down that even the gods were in over their heads. The Crone had spied something during the beginning of all this—something she hadn't ever been meant to see. It had infected her . . . caused her soul to spoil. Black mold was *very* difficult to get rid of and just as hard to keep from spreading. The gods were all powerful, but it was never in their destiny to end this.

It was always in Dora's hands.

Titania was a warrior but even though she carried the weapon that could end what was left of the Bahidicaras—she would never be able to find Dora's mother. Only one with Hecate blood would be able to sniff out *that* mass of energy. And if that evil rose again, it would be near impossible to stop twice.

The words were out of Dora's mouth before she could take them back or regret them. "I care not how you do it. Just make sure the sword stays in the castle."

Sebastian was skeptical for another excruciating moment or two. "Fine. What is it that you need from me then?"

Dora blinked. She'd done nothing but invent excuses and or diversions from the moment she was born. She bent down and picked up one of the glass bottles. "Your love, Sebastian. I shall require it."

He looked mortified.

She squinted at him. "There will be no more pain. No more jealousy. Your biggest hinderance will be dissolved."

She sank into his heartbeats as he thought over her words; she even skimmed the pictures floating around his mind. She saw the face of who it was who had wrecked his heart.

A low gurgle emerged from his lips. "Fine." He held up his wand. "I agree."

Dora smiled then held up her wand, crossing it with his. A magical handshake.

"You will no longer know me as this," Dora said, as she lowered her wand. "I will be needing to alter my appearance. No one must know who I have been affiliated with."

The elf nodded.

"We will communicate only via scry, and you will refer to me as the Crone of Light's End."

Again, he nodded.

When all was said and done, Sebastian walked away believing his love was contained in that small glass vial. And yes, Dora had taken it; but it wasn't in that vial. It was locked away inside the elf. The key—simple. All he had to do was remember the way his heart had used to beat before she covered it in magic—magic she'd leant to him. Magic that one might even call untouchable.

She didn't dwell on what she'd done. His love would return. He might act out a little for a few years, but it would come back.

At least that's what she'd thought.

The problem with improvisation is that it is often hasty. She'd pulled upon the last heartbeat she'd heard from the elf's chest, and in that beat was music unlike anyone should ever want to hear. Extreme bitterness and jealousy. Scorn. A melody that only someone who had creation at their fingertips would ever be able to change.

🦋 31 🦋

Dora

Gloria was in a solemn state when they arrived. What she'd taken on—hundreds of Cronie souls—had altered her sanity. She had good times and bad; she'd learned to make sure her nails were cut extremely short for the bad times, still scars littered every inch of her skin. Inside her tower there were chains bolted to the wall, as if a werewolf had been living there. One couldn't house that many souls in just one body without lunacy as a side effect. Dora wondered, after seeing Gloria, if she'd just let her mother go on instead of trying to end her on that fateful day, if the insanity would have simply dragged her down to her grave. But she hadn't thought on it very long before recognizing that her mother *could* have fought off the negative eccentricities, for her mother had no conscience, nor had she much, if any, humanity left.

Gloria, however, was a moral soul. Pure. So good in fact

that she'd sacrificed her life to save the rest of the world. It was the reason she did not fight the motley crew who stood on her doorstep when Dora announced they would all be leaving the Enclaves together.

It was all going according to plan. And why had Dora thought it would go any other way? Neither Dora nor Malina had ever known a mother's love in that life they'd shared together. But Cee-Cee *had* known. The second the girl and Gloria looked into one another's eyes, Dora could see that so very plainly. It had been enough to drive Cee-Cee to the top of the pyramid, shrinking the priestess back down into the pit of despair where she'd spent most of her life. And that was just fine. Cee-Cee was strong enough to hold her down now, and when the moment came, they would still be able to pull her back to the surface. Back up for one more sip of air before cutting her throat.

Yes, they'd been lucky that Gloria was having a 'good day.' Dora had been prepared for the worst. The witch left her tower willingly, but she wasn't right in the head. She couldn't speak; in fact, she hadn't been able to for years. The only way any of them were able to communicate with her was through her touch. Palm to palm, forehead to forehead. This was how she was able to tell her daughter she loved her still and to tell both Anastacia and Dora exactly what happened and what led her to the tower.

And how she came to be in that tower was a story worthy of being told. A story that Gloria shared with every one of them on that mountain as they waited for the dragons Dora had summoned to come and fetch them.

It all began with a spark of life and a second heartbeat.

By the time it happened, Gloria had no family left of her

own. But before all the witches she'd ever known had returned to the ether, she *had* been warned about the blood that ran in her veins. About the curse the Hecate bloodline carried.

"You will be hunted as will any offspring you have. Either by the caped one or by *the priestess*." Words spun and delivered to her from a very young age by the grandmother who raised her.

Gloria had been a product of a reckless mother who never had any intentions of keeping her. It was her grandmother who came to the hospital to get her shortly after her mother sped off after childbirth. Her grandmother named her and raised her. She passed down all the warnings that had been passed down to her, and then she did what she'd done for her daughter before her daughter ran away. She shielded Gloria in magic that made her bloodline transparent. The magic *did* work but there were disadvantages.

It hindered creativity for one. And what is a witch without inspiration? Gloria never once met the woman who had birthed her, and by the time she was seven years of age, she knew she never would. It was a grim day when she found her grandmother weeping over their dining room table.

"What's wrong, Gram?" she'd asked.

Her grandmother was a thick woman with an even wider heart. She was proof that not every witch born with Hecate blood was driven towards the darkness.

The old woman had just looked at her granddaughter with bloodshot eyes soaked in saltwater and pressed the tissue in her hand to her overly large heart. "Oh, dear Gloria, it's but a mother's pain. Oh, dearest child, just a mother's pain."

Gloria might have been young but the magic she owned granted her an enormous amount of empathy. "She's gone, isn't she, Gram?"

The old woman's lips sputtered as she nodded her head,

her eyes closing over the tears pouring down her cheeks. Gloria dove into her grandmother's bosom and let the old woman hold her tight.

After several moments, Gloria asked in a small voice, "Was it the hunter?"

"Could've been," her grandmother answered through a sob. Though Gloria's mother most likely left her body due to yet another curse.

Like most witches, Gloria was an avid dreamer, and in her dreams, she often saw a woman with a face like hers sleeping with a needle in her arm—her face sunken and emaciated.

"Mom's okay," she used to tell her gram because she knew the woman worried. "I saw her last night. She fell asleep taking her medicine."

Gloria never understood why this good news seemed to set her grandmother's heartbeats into a quick and hasty dance. Either way, that solemn day the world lost another Hecate witch.

Gloria, with her grandmother's magic strewn around her shoulders like a knitted garb, grew into a happy young woman. However, sometimes things just aren't meant to be. Eventually, her magic began to deepen—her dreams began to lead her into another world, under a dark pass and to a mountain that grew into the sky. She began to recreate what she saw. Her fingers covered in charcoal; her cheeks marked with what looked like ash. The more she drew, the heavier her magic became, and the more rooted her magic became the lighter she felt.

"I found a place, Gram—a place I can fly to!" she said one day when her grandmother had come to visit.

Gloria was twenty-eight and had landed a job as a paralegal. One of the lawyers in her office had asked her out three times already, but as soon as the day was done, she couldn't wait to get home and draw her dreams onto canvas.

Her apartment was littered with portraits of dragons, a mountain draped in nightmares, and a sky to match.

"Gloria," her grandmother had said with a mighty gasp. Her arthritis had gotten so bad she hadn't been to the city to visit her granddaughter in so very long (another side effect of the protection spell was that she couldn't heal herself freely as witches often tend to do). As soon as she set her eyes on what Gloria had been designing, she knew. She knew her granddaughter had been found. Not by the huntress but by someone else. Someone way more deadly.

And that it was too late.

"What's wrong, Gram?" Gloria had asked.

Gloria was and always had been so beautiful. Long braided hair, that as a child she'd often used bleach on it so that she could add strips of green. Nowadays she had to be more professional, so she left her hair black and painted her eyes in emerald eyeshadow. The color was supposed to be a lucky one . . . however, the way her grandmother was looking at her denoted that she was anything but.

"The Enclaves," the old woman stated gravely.

Gloria had jutted out her chin. "What are you talking about?"

Her grandmother's eyes were too wide, taking in the fifty or so drawings hanging around the small apartment. "This is nowhere for a girl to travel . . . even in her dreams. Fate is pulling at you." And then, before Gloria could question her further, her grandmother turned and placed all her intention over her. "You've let the protection I gave to you slip away. You're hers now."

"What—Gram? What are you talking about?"

"The bad village," stated her grandmother. The old woman had lost at least an inch over the years and her bones hurt constantly. But it was now obvious that none of that mattered.

She inhaled and when she exhaled, she stood taller. She let go of the protection over her soul; as soon as she did, her pain went away.

Unsure of what her grandmother had just done, Gloria observed as the old woman began to glow. "Gram, what did you just—"

"Let us sit, Gloria," her gram stated, holding out a now steady hand toward the small dining room table just feet away from where they stood. "The clock is already ticking."

Gloria's dreams were exceptional—always had been. A star that shines that bright can never be covered up. Her grandmother knew from the start that shielding her from the hunt would be nearly impossible. It was only a matter of time before she would be found. This was the reason why she'd infused the magic with something she'd failed to do with her daughter: instruction.

"The priestess has found you," her grandmother stated with her warm hand over hers. Gloria followed her grandmother's hand as she lifted it from over hers and pointed to the nearest compilation of the Enclave mountains. "There is but one place in any world that you will be safe. Your dreams have already begun telling you about it and in time they will lead you there."

Gloria's face was long. Her glow, frozen. "Gram, what are you saying? How can you know—"

"She's found you, Gloria. It was only a matter of time. Just like your mother, my protection couldn't work over you forever."

Gloria immediately shook her head. "I am nothing like my mother! I've worked hard to get to where I'm at and—"

"That's not what I meant, child."

Gloria's mouth remained open as her Gram's eyes hardened. The wrinkles around the woman's great round orbs were no longer there. "You've removed your protection."

"There's no need for it any longer," said the old woman. "We've been found."

She then explained that she'd created insurance. The Hecate line was near extinct, which meant that the priestess would be on high alert. She needed a body to finish what she started and something as foul as that entity wouldn't just walk away without a proper fight.

"I ensured that if you were ever found so would be a place where you could hide."

Gloria had started shaking her head again, this time she couldn't stop the movement even if she tried. "No! I never removed my protection. Why would I allow the priestess to find me? I—"

"You didn't remove it, child, as much as it came off of you like a Band-Aid on wet skin." The old woman pursed her lips together before going on, then reached up and cupped her granddaughter's face with her hand. "Not even the most skilled magician can stop fate."

Gloria relished in her grandmother's touch, closing her eyes, and letting her cheek roll against the old woman's skin. But she couldn't hide in the palm of her Gram's hand forever.

She pulled away and sat up straighter in her chair. "What are we to do then?" She gestured to all the portraits she'd been working on so feverishly. "What am I to do? Drop everything and go live in this strange world?"

To her utter surprise, her grandmother shook her head. "No. You are to do nothing. Let time pass—live your life. When the time comes, you'll know what to do."

She waited for more, for any further explanations. But that wasn't in the cards, at least not for that day. Or month. Or year.

Her Gram left her apartment that day and as she did, she did so with a kiss on her granddaughter's cheek. She touched

Gloria's heart. "She can't have this. No one can. Be sure to tell that to your daughter when the time comes."

"Wait!" Gloria shouted as her gram began to walk towards the car waiting for her. "What does that mean?"

The woman just smiled warmly. "I'm late meeting an old friend. Be brave, my beautiful girl."

And then she was off. It was the last time Gloria saw her grandmother. Fate. It was fate that was her gram's old friend.

With no other options, Gloria went on with her life. She pulled down all the pictures she'd drawn and burned them. She accepted the invitation to go out on a date with the hunky lawyer from her office when he asked her a fourth time. Five dates later and she was in love. Three years later and she was married, moved into a gorgeous house in the suburbs and holding a positive pregnancy test.

The baby was born. A little girl. Two brown eyes.

A second heartbeat.

A second soul.

It wasn't anything her mundane husband could hear or see . . . but she knew the second that babe was in her arms what she had in the body of her daughter. A vessel.

That many souls were bound to drive anyone mad. Anyone but that foul priestess.

Cee-Cee was three when Gloria did the first binding meant to bury every bit of evil residing in that little body. But the priestess was too strong. She kept seeping back through. Gloria had been told the story of the bad village from start to finish. She knew where the priestess had gotten her strength, and she knew that to bury that soul and keep her down, she was going to have to remove the baggage. The problem was, she didn't have in her possession the tools needed to capture what was swirling around inside her daughter's body.

So she did the only thing she could.

When Cee-Cee was seven she performed the binding

once more, but this time she took that churning mass of unfed energy into herself. She ingested all of it—all of *them*. She became the vessel. The foulest part was still left in her daughter's body, but without her 'village,' the priestess was much easier to bind.

For the first year, nothing really changed—other than Gloria felt like she truly had her daughter all to herself. She knew it was the one they called the lost child, but Cee-Cee truly was her own person. This was a new life for her, and the spell Gloria had used to bury the priestess removed any memories from that horrid nightmare that poor soul had endured when her name had been Malina.

It was after that first year that things began to change for Gloria. The symptoms of housing over a hundred lost souls first arrived in the form of headaches. Shortly after that came the ticks, the weight loss, then eventually her mood began to shift. By year three her outbursts were uncontrollable.

Her daughter was ten when she made her final decision. Her husband was smart, so she had to be smarter. Her symptoms suggested mental illness, but she couldn't and wouldn't feign suicide. Through it all, she didn't want her daughter or husband believing she had given up. Not to mention, she couldn't risk getting put in a cage somewhere. That wouldn't help. No, what she needed to do was get away. Far away.

In dreams it would come, the answer. That was what her Gram had said.

And so she made note of her dreams, of where they would lead her, and on a day where she had enough control to aim her wand, she dropped images into the minds of those closest to her. She inserted portraits of illness into her loved ones.

All the while remembering what her Gram had said.

She laid the pieces of her story into the minds of her daughter and husband. The cancer was eating away her mind.

It wasn't a complete lie.

Gram had said the only way to end the priestess was to separate her from the power, then impale her host's heart with Avalon's sword while calling out her name.

Gloria had taken the vessel.

She knew not where the sword was, nor what the priestess had been called at birth.

The host would have to be killed.

The host was her daughter.

It would have been enough to drive a mother mad even without the insanity she'd gained by ingesting the Bahidicaras. She decided she'd already sacrificed too much. If a sword was going to drive into her daughter's chest, it was going to be by the hands of somebody else, and that same soul was going to have to climb through hell to get Gloria.

Gloria left her family. She slipped between the worlds in the way her Gram had shown her when she was just a little girl, and she marched towards a sky that threatened any traveler to turn back the way they'd come. When her mind brought her down, a ghost saved her. And when the collaboration of souls once known as Cronies settled down again, she returned on her path towards the Enclaves. Just as the ghost named Breya had said, the summit provided. A door waited for her and in that door, a warm cave furnished with sleeping quarters and a place to write.

Her mind was too scattered to read and being the vessel also meant she could hardly ever keep her mind sorted onto one thing for more than thirty seconds at a time. Which was also why it took her the better of seven years to write the letter she so badly wanted to. Words she knew she would never be able to say if and when she got the chance to repeat them. But the point was that she did get them written, and she had just finished blowing on the red goop she'd stamped on the provided envelope when she heard the knock on the door.

She'd never wondered who left the stack of paper, ink and quill, and envelopes.

She never knew, but she had her suspicions.

Gram.

Gloria's story had been told, and now Dora had in her keep the letter the witch had worked so tirelessly to write. *Ensure it gets to her*, Gloria had inferred with a touch of her hand as she handed it to the caped witch.

"Aye," Dora replied. And she would.

Before long, the dragons arrived. Three in total. One for Dora and the vessel. One for Cee-Cee and Bally, and one for Heime. The dragons had been given instruction to treat the non-dancers with care. The dragons didn't hesitate to do as they were told, for even the beasts knew this mission meant one of two things: the end of something world ending, or the beginning of the end of the world.

"To the old world!" Dora had exclaimed once they'd jumped on the backs of three different dragons. Though to Bally, Cee-Cee, Gloria, and Heime, all it sounded like was a series of growls.

Dora let a grin surface over her face as they brushed through gray clouds that in a split second turned to violet. The vessel had her arms around her waist as if they were riding a Harley rather than a dragon who was nearly half the size of a football field.

The wind became full of saltwater as it brushed against their faces and somewhere in the distance Dora could feel the earth trembling in her bones. She was going home.

$$\text{❦} \quad 3\,2 \quad \text{❦}$$

Makayla

We were too far in to turn around, yet still so far away from where we were headed. Blythe said Lantern's Edge—the real one—was several miles into Forest Peak.

Everywhere I set foot the ground began to heal itself. Everything I touched returned to green or brown, or whatever color nature had intended for it to be. I carried creation with me wherever I went . . . even in my belly. I felt sort of untouchable, except I knew I wasn't. I could be killed just as easily as the next faery, except now this story wasn't just about me. There was something actually growing in me. Some*one*. If I died, so would they. I already knew I couldn't let that happen.

"Hey."

I looked up to find Blythe looking down at where I'd had a seat on the ground. She rested her hand over my shoulder and shrunk down until she was sitting by my side. One would think that we could just use our wings to fly over the destruction that was left by the priestess and her followers, but it wasn't that easy. The magic had rotted and the only way to our destination was through this maze; it looked more like an asteroid field than a forest. The supplies Layla had gotten for us at that shop were making a lot more sense now.

"What's up?" I asked, stringing together some ninny flowers I'd picked.

I'd been resting on this piece of land long enough that it had rejoined the ground it had initially separated from, and flowers were beginning to pop up all around me.

"Whatcha doin'? Making yourself a crown, queenie," she said with a smirk.

I shrugged a single shoulder. "I guess."

"Hey," she said again, squeezing my arm. I squinted one eye in her direction. "You good?"

I remained in her eyes for long enough to realize I was staring, then shook my head as I looked away, focusing in on three giant mushrooms levitating between where we sat and a floating tree.

"I think that maybe we should do that thing again. You know, that spell or charm or whatever that we did at Dorothy's cabin."

When she didn't answer right away, I turned to find her looking at me speculatively with her mouth slightly a jar. "Um, I don't think we can, Makayla. It's kind of a one-time thing, you know." She must have seen my spirit shrink, because next thing I knew she was moving her hand to where my knee rested under the fabric of my purple dress. "You've been doing great, why do you think you need a boost?"

My mouth opened and a wonky cackle escaped. "Oh, I don't know. Maybe because of this." I dropped the crown made of flowers into my lap and framed my stomach with my hands. "And the fact that none of this was ever part of my plan."

She chuckled. "I'm sorry to tell you but nobody's life ever really is, and even if things work out like they're supposed to on paper, shit still finds a way to hit the fan."

"Easy for you to say. You're not getting ready to become a teen mom. This shouldn't have happened to me—" I wiped at an annoying tear running down my cheek. "Being a mom was definitely not on my to do list. Like ever. I mean, Toby and I are practically kids and—" I ended up sobbing through the last of what I had to say. "I'm scared I'm not going to be good at this! I'm already a crappy daughter; how am I supposed to manage one of my own?"

"Hey," she said, rocking my knee and forcing me to give her my attention. "Don't be talking trash about my new best friend." She framed my face with her hands and forced me to look at her. "I hate to remind you, queenie, but you're royalty now."

"What's that have to do with this," I muttered, my tears squished between her hands and my cheeks.

"Duh," she said with an eye roll. "You're not going to suck as a mother, but even if you do, you've got people to help you now. Like *tons* of people."

For a moment, I did something very uncharacteristic for Makayla Wood. I listened. Like really opened my ears and let what she was saying sink in. Not that it was all in her words—it was in her touch. I could *feel* her intention.

She was so genuine, so kind, so not full of shit. And surrounding all of that like an aura was something else. I thought back to the way our wands had glowed when we held them together. How strong I'd felt afterwards—like I'd been rewired.

"Hey," I said. She dropped her hands away and lifted her

chin, waiting. "What *was* that spell we did back at Dorothy's, anyway?"

Her jaw moved up and down as her beautiful eyes dimmed. "It—It was just—"

But before she could finish, Toby and Layla landed next to us, flung over Petal's back like a couple of rock stars.

"Oi!" Toby hollered as he hopped down to meet me on the ground. There was a level of excitement in my king that I hadn't seen practically ever.

"What's gotten into you?" I asked him, noting that Layla looked just as over the top as he did when she came sliding down Petal's side.

Toby's arm raised in the direction of the mushrooms and was about to say something—his chest heaving—as Layla ran over and pointed at the oversized red and white fungus.

"Portals!" she exclaimed, dancing up and down on her toes.

And here I never thought I'd see a mermaid jumping around on land like a fish out of water.

I looked from her to Toby, who was nodding like a young kid when asked if he wanted a puppy, and then to Blythe who incidentally looked anything but excited.

"They are mushrooms," I stated, clearly befuddled. "Large ones, but still—"

"No," Blythe said, her tone flatlined. "Those numb skulls are correct. They *are* portals."

My brows rose to meet the gray sky.

"Then you know of them?" Toby asked, practically panting.

"Yes, they were here last time, just not as big."

"Why didn't you ever mention them!" Layla questioned. "This could change everything."

"They are volatile, Lay," Blythe stated firmly, causing both Toby and Layla to come down from whatever artificial high they'd conjured. "They grew from rotting magic—who knows where they'll lead."

Everyone grew quiet, gazes flitting from one another back to the large mushrooms I'd simply assumed had just learned to float in space like the rest of all these things.

"How do you know they are portals and not just a ginormous species of Amanita muscaria?" I surprised myself by knowing the name of that particular mushroom; but then again, I had files in my head that I'd never taken a lot of time to go through, including riff raff from Biology classes I'd been forced to take to earn my degree.

"Because that's what those mushrooms *are*," Layla said, "and they are HUGE!" Again, she jumped up and down as if she couldn't contain herself.

I turned to find Blythe shaking her head just as Toby jumped up from my side to join Layla. The two of them were like little children who couldn't wait to get on the next rollercoaster ride.

"I'm telling you guys, it's a bad idea," Blythe repeated.

"Wait." Everyone paused to look at me. "If they really are portals, then where do they lead?"

Petal, who had been quietly sauntering over to inspect the shrooms, finally spoke. "'Tis different for everyone."

"It takes you on a journey inside your own mind!" exclaimed Layla. Truly, up until now I hadn't been sure the mermaid knew how to smile at all.

"It could spring us out on the other side of this mess!" Toby added.

"It *could*," Blythe agreed gingerly. "Or it could embed us even deeper into this spiderweb. It would be reckless to find out."

"You mean, it would be reckless for *you*," Toby stated, his eyes centering over the Reef.

And then he did something I never would have ever

expected from him. I mean, sure, I'd really only known Toby for a very short time. What we'd done, getting married and knocked up so quickly, *that* could be seen as reckless—but to us it simply felt right. Other than that, Tobias Koehaias had always been so rigidly put together. Attentive to detail, controlled. Not someone to look someone else in the eyes with what could only be described as a dancing fire in their chest, then jump up onto one of those toad stools and—

"Oh my god!" I shot up, plastering my hands over my mouth. "Where'd he go?"

The second he'd stepped both feet onto the mushroom, he'd disappeared.

"I don't know," Layla said, her hands pumping by her sides, "but I wanna find out."

"Layla, don't you even—" Blythe started, jumping up to be by my side.

But the mermaid had already made her decision, and just before she climbed up to the same mushroom, she turned and set a pair of stiff eyes over my new faery friend. "How many chances do we actually get to come across something like this?"

Blythe shook her head once more. "It's not worth it. This is not the place to experiment."

"Why's it even matter to you?" Layla questioned, looking from Blythe, to me, then back to Blythe. Blythe seemed to be searching for what to say back when Layla grinned and stepped up onto the same mushroom that had taken Toby. "That's right. You've got nothing to say, because there isn't anything you *can* say. How about from here on out, we just worry about ourselves, all right. This one here" —she pointed to the next mushroom in the row of three— "this one's just for me."

And then she jumped onto the next shroom like it was a miniature trampoline, and just like Toby had, disappeared.

"Shit," Blythe cursed, bringing her hand up to cover her lips.

I began to cross the land over to where Petal was sniffing out the three portals from a safe distance. "Where did they go? Are they going to come back?"

"I believe," said the Pegasus, "they have gone into their own respectable rooms of instruction." She looked to Blythe. "I believe these are safe."

Her lips still covered by her fingertips, Blythe used her sheer wings to be closer to Petal's side in the blink of an eye. "How can you be sure?"

"I can't, 'tis but a feeling."

Meanwhile, neither of them noted as I began to creep up on that first mushroom, very tenderly touching the top of it. When nothing happened, I carefully climbed to the top and looked to the other two floating shrooms.

"Miss Makayla," Petal said in a near exasperated tone. "This is not a good idea—not in your condition."

Blythe, suddenly aware of what I was up to, began having a near panic attack. "Get down! What the actual—"

"Why isn't it taking me away?" I asked calmly. It wasn't that I had no anxiety, it was just that all the sudden I didn't care. The second I touched the top of this shroom, all apprehension seemed to drift away. Like I saw the emotion for what it was now—a reaction. If I didn't let it cloud my vision, then I could simply move forward rationally.

"You touched it, didn't you?" Blythe asked. "You touched the damn mushroom."

"Why hasn't it taken me away yet?" I asked for the second time.

"'Tis the poison," Petal stated. "It's already gotten into her."

Blythe loosed a heavy breath, then stepped closer to me, holding up a hand for me to take. "Toby and Layla are still with those two mushrooms, so you can't use them right now. Just take my hand and let's get you down."

But it was my turn to shake my head. "No." I stepped from this shroom to the next, then looked to the third.

"Makayla, please!"

I stared down into Blythe's pressing eyes. "I'm sorry, but I feel like I need to do this."

"NO!" Blythe yelled, then continued to plead as she fluttered by my side, holding out her hand. "The poison has gotten into you already, that's all this is. It's coercing you to follow the path, but this magic is—"

"I've never been wild. The craziest thing I ever did before these wings reappeared was get hot pink Post-its instead of yellow. If we make it out of this place in one piece, I'll be expected to be a mother and a leader. I may never have this opportunity again. My king is not irrational. If he took this plunge without a second's hesitation, then why should I stutter before doing the same?"

"She's going to do it," Petal stated quietly. "We might as well just let her."

"Makayla."

I turned to Blythe. Her face was but inches from mine. "Please."

I looked down to her open palm, then back up to her eyes. "Do you know what a keeper's necklace is?"

She narrowed her eyes and furrowed her brows. "Why would you ask me that?"

"Because Toby was wearing one before I saw Layla's half-brother slice off his head, and when next I saw my king—*alive*—the necklace was gone."

Blythe made a sound in the back of her throat, like she had the words I needed but let them go before they could find me. Next to her, Petal had dropped her gaze to the ground and was looking the other way.

"Okay," I said, nodding as I did so. "You see, here's the thing. My whole life people let me live with secrets. I didn't know who I was or what I was. I've learned that if I want to know something, it won't suit me to wait around for someone to hand me a shovel. I'm better off digging through the soil with my own two hands."

"Mak—"

But her pleas were lost on me as I let my wings lift me from one shroom to the last, and as I fell through that third poisonous mushroom, Blythe gripped my arm and came through the wormhole with me.

Makayla

"Wait—what?"

This is not where I thought I'd go. I mean, it's not like I knew where a very large poisonous mushroom portal was going to take me but being *back here* was not what I'd bargained for.

This time I was sitting at the defense table inside the courtroom containing the great beyond. At first glance, no one was with me, but it took only about a second or two for that to change. In the time it took for me to grip the table and start to turn around, the door behind where the judge was to sit opened, and through it came—NO WAY.

"How—what? I don't understand—"

"Oh, stop that," Helene chirped, lifting the dark judge's robe she wore and taking a seat. Goddess, was it me or did she look significantly *good* up there? She could totally have pulled off this position while she'd been alive . . . that is, if she hadn't been a murderer and all that.

"How are you here?" I questioned when I could finally get my words to come out right.

She lifted her arms out to the side, her dark wings standing up behind her back. "This is your party, Makayla. How about you start asking yourself that question."

"Right," I whispered.

"But we don't have all day, so if you wouldn't mind telling the court who you'd like to call upon first to take the stand."

"What?"

She narrowed her eyes. I'd forgotten how distinct her features were. "You've chosen to defend yourself. Now please, call upon your first witness."

My chest sunk in on itself. "Who do I need to defend myself to?"

She posed the answer as if it couldn't be any plainer. "Yourself."

"Myself? But that's not why I came here."

"Then why did you come here, niece?"

"I—" My throat offered no more than a crack. "I wanted answers. I—"

"My god, absolutely nothing has changed," she said, her sharp gaze flitting to the orange lighting before falling back down over my shoulders. "You are going to be searching for answers until the day you die. It's just who you are. Unfortunately, this spell is finite. My role is to judge you and I've been informed that you are here on behalf of yourself because at this exact moment, you are wary of your position in life."

I met her hard stare. "I jumped on a poisonous mushroom because all the other cool kids were doing it. That's all."

Before she could answer, the back door opened and Naomi Wood walked down the aisle, winked at me, then took the stand. In typical Naomi fashion, she didn't sugar coat her speech.

"Sorry baby, but that's not the truth and you know it."

"Mom," I whispered. *Was she really here?*

Helene scoffed. "Oh goodie, my least favorite human."

My mom turned and offered Helene one of her famous plastic smiles. "So nice to see you again, Helene. So sorry to hear about your unfortunate situation. Tell me, can you still hear everything down in that tree where your statue sits, or is it like an endless sleep?"

Helene chose not to answer, instead she sneered at my mother before moving her pointed chin in my direction. "Let's get on with this, shall we, Makayla."

I hesitated for only a second before standing up. I was still wearing the purple dress and slip-on terrain shoes. I was happy for that; I was way more comfortable this way than in a suit.

Okay, I'm supposed to be defending myself. If this was real, what would I ask my witness?

Very slowly, I lifted my gaze to meet the same eyes who had made a point to never look down at me, but to look at me straight on. I rolled back my shoulders before speaking. "Mrs. Wood, how well do you know me?"

"Well enough to understand that this isn't the first time you've gone through this amount of emotional pain. It's simply the first time you've gone through it without blinders on."

"Please explain," I stated firmly.

Naomi sighed. "You never fit in with the human world. It was one reason you chose a professional path at such a young age. You created the life you lived so you would remain at a constant swift pace; you didn't give yourself time to worry about why you didn't *feel right* in the world you were living. You looked away from friendships or romantic love. You told yourself you didn't have time to deal with those things, but in reality, you knew that somewhere—lurking inside you—there were answers. And those answers had the possibility of taking down the tower you'd spent every last second of your life building."

My next breath was stuck somewhere between my lungs and my throat. Still, I hammered on. "Why do you think I need to defend myself to myself right now?"

Her face softened and her eyes twinkled. "You don't believe you're strong enough to do what needs to happen next."

"Please clarify," Helene snipped.

For once I was thankful for her rudeness. The agonizing truth of the matter was that I wasn't sure which circumstance my mom was speaking about. I had more than one thing looming before me, more than one thing I was going to have to deal with.

"You're worried you'll not be a good mother."

And that was all it took. My face grew hotter than a fresh mud pie straight from the oven, and as I stood there, facing the woman who had raised me as her own, I began to cry.

I wasn't even thinking on my next words or about what could possibly happen next when someone else entered the courtroom. This time, it was my other mom. My birth mom. Before she walked up to the stand, where she and Naomi smiled at one another before Naomi stood and Maude took her seat, she paused next to where I was standing and ran her thumb under my left eye.

Looking down at the sparkly tear, she said, "If only magic could mend our hearts as well as it can make our gardens grow."

Naomi moved to sit in the jury box as Maude took her seat. Meanwhile, Helene didn't hesitate to remind us that she was still there.

"This is all so very touching but let me remind you that our little Lala" —she sneered as she said my name— "is in the middle of a hallucinogenic trip. Our time is unmeasured and could end any moment." She moved her attention wholly onto me. "Please address your next witness."

"Right," I muttered, drying my wet cheeks with my hands. "Mom, or um Maude." Her cheeks definitely colored when I called her mom; she seemed to glow from the inside out. "We're here because I don't believe in myself. Something I think you might understand." Her brows softened. "The only reason I say that is because I found this place through your spell book. The Great Beyond was *your* spell."

"Yes," was all she said.

"Do you mind explaining to the court why you wrote this spell in the first place?"

She bit her lip and looked down into her hands. When she peered back up at me, she was smiling. "I don't think it's a secret to everyone that those of us who lived in the Garlandian forest had to go through some things. It was no woodland stroll. But even before the damnation cursed us, *our* lives weren't ever easy." She didn't look at her sister, but I knew that's who she meant when she said 'our.'

I, however, dared to look at Helene. I wasn't surprised to find her attention geared at Maude, her lips pursed.

"Your grandmother," Maude stated to me, "our mother—" She shot her sister a sincere look. "She was taken from us far too early, and it was her statue that marked the old Garlandia from the new. The days following her leave were some of the darkest I've ever experienced." Her eyelashes fluttered like a hummingbird's wings. "Other than you having to leave Tanker and I, that is."

Of course, I thought to myself, a hand gently finding my stomach.

"Music suddenly became played less frequently in the

forest and though the sun continued to shine, it had a cutting quality to it—like its rays were sent through Loral's fierce and unfeeling eyes. Our father became more and more distant with every passing day until that one fateful moment when he told us that we were leaving."

Though I was still standing erect, my chin lifted, I found myself leaning into her story. This was the part I hadn't ever heard—at least not directly from her lips.

"Helene and I were brought from the home we'd always known straight into a foreign land." *Raton.* "Our father said it was necessary; that we were to be the bravest of our kind. But I didn't want to go—I didn't want to be there. I'd already met Tanker and fallen in love; no matter what my father said, I just knew that this faery was my mate." She looked away as she let the rest of her words fall from her mouth. "It was written in our wands."

Helene cleared her throat. "Makayla, if you wouldn't mind, please keep your witness on track."

My lips twisted to the side as I let my attention shoot to my aunt's. "I'm sorry, do you have somewhere more pressing to be?"

She only stared back at me, her eyelids falling halfway over her eyes.

Whatever.

"Maude." I waited for her to look back at me. When she didn't right away, I said, "Mom." Her gaze met mine. "Can we please return to why you wrote this spell?"

She sighed, but eventually did as I asked. "I missed your father terribly, but Allender was blinded by hatred and ironically, he was much like you in that he chose to be a work horse so he wouldn't have time to acknowledge his pain and suffering. It wasn't long before he was known to all as the leader of the rebels; he made me feel like a terrible faery for having what he called a droopy attitude. For having saggy wings all the time."

"So you designed a way to escape," I guessed.

"Yes."

Out of curiosity— "Where did *you* go?"

Helene inhaled audibly through her nose. "Makayla, please don't drift from the subject."

I shot her an angry look. "This is my damn trip and I want to know."

My aunt's gaze narrowed over mine, but she didn't object.

I turned my shoulders back so they were squared off with my birth mother's. "Please, I'd like to know."

Maude blinked once, twice, then three times. "I came here."

My heart skipped a beat. "I'm sorry—what?"

I thought this was a vision of my own making. It only made sense since becoming a lawyer had once been my one and only dream.

Maude set her hands over the armrests of her chair and looked around the courtroom. "I thought it was the oddest place. I hadn't been to the human world all that often. Helene and I used to sneak into it when we were little fey, but in truth, I didn't start exploring it all that much until I met my little friend over there, which was many years later." She smiled over to where Naomi was sitting, listening. "But still, this is where I turned up." She placed her hands in her lap and roped them together, giving me her full attention. "Now keep in mind that Anthony and his bride had already been killed, and Helene, Father, and I had been in Raton for several years. Tanker and I still communicated, but it was only via magic. I'd drawn up a spell that would take me away from everything I knew—that could dissolve my pain. Imagine my surprise when I arrived into this strange room only to find myself standing directly where you are right now, daughter."

A soft breath left my lips. "Were you here to defend yourself as well?"

"Sort of." She licked her lips, her wings rising slightly behind her shoulders before slipping back down. "I waited in that spot for several minutes before my judge arrived. May I allow you to guess who that judge was?"

My eyes flitted back and forth, then to my mother (who seemed relaxed as if she already knew the answer), then to Helene (who was quite the opposite—hinged forward in her seat as if she wanted to know just as badly as me).

"I have no idea."

What she said next nearly caused me to stumble forward, however the shoes I was in made that a near impossible thing.

"Titania."

The room was so quiet that one could have heard the fizzle of magic stirring inside one's wand.

"Excuse me?" I stated.

Maude dipped her chin and blinked her eyes. "I've never told a single soul about this; not even your father. It had been *years* since our mother was taken, since Anthony and Titania were murdered. The world was wrecked. But there she stood, the faery queen, as real as I'd last seen her once upon a Farmer's Market.

"She moved with the air of a queen as she had a seat right where Helene sits now. She laced her fingers together and told me to have a seat. I did." Maude chuckled. "I mean, of course I did. She then asked me what I was doing in this place, at which point I answered her with a question of my own. I asked her if she was real. *Of course I am*, she said. And then she restated her initial inquiry."

"What did you tell her?" I asked as if I was in a trance.

"I told her the truth. The world wasn't special anymore. We weren't allowed to love because our king had lost all his ability to do so. And even if I was allowed to be with the one faery I wanted to be with—even if my father had given me permission to do that—there were rumors that the king had cut off reproduction of the Erwain race.

"I sobbed to the faery queen, dispensing all of the details that had been crawling up and down my spine like Zappyweed infection. When I was done, I looked up to find that even though my face was the color of a tomato and my wings were soggy, that her expression was still as firm as it had been when she walked into this place. She had been listening, but it was as if she was without an ounce of empathy. And then she spoke.

"She said, 'You came here to die.'"

My heart nearly broke.

"I answered her. 'Yes.' She then said to me, 'You will not die today, Maude Voss of the Erwain descent. Instead, you will leave this court room with your head held high. You will leave Raton and build a home with your chosen mate. From there, one day, you will have a child.'" Maude's eyes grew as she told her story. "I shook my head at the faery queen. 'It's not in the cards,' I said to her. But she was firm. Tis in the cards. Your child has already chosen you.'

"I remember distinctly that I shook my head at her. This *was* Titania, no doubt about it, but what she was saying was ludicrous. Still, she held firm. 'Your child has chosen you and I have chosen your child.'"

The courtroom was quiet as Maude continued to look down at me from her perch.

"Are you telling me," I said, "that you knew this whole time that I'd been slated to save the world you loved so dearly."

Her lashes fluttered as her gaze met her lap. "Yes." She

looked up, trading glances between Naomi and me. "I left this room all those years ago with the vision of what my daughter would look like." She licked her lips and sniffed. "You see, Titania didn't just tell me what was fated to happen —she showed me a glimpse of the faery you would become."

I bit down over my bottom lip and my eyes began to glisten in the same manner as Maude's already were. As she pounded on with her testimony, the tears waiting in the wings freed themselves.

"Now, daughter of mine, I shall do the same for you." She pulled out her wand and as she began to spin magic before our eyes, she continued with her speech. "These words I once heard from the mouth of a queen, I shall now repeat to you: You will leave this room. You will be brave. Heartache will find you but so will unconditional love. You will do what you have to do to let *her* survive." The glitter pouring from her wand began to form into a picture and as those blurry colors began to become clean, firm lines, I began to see the face of someone I already loved. Someone with sparkly hair and my king's eyes.

My right hand met my trembling lips as my left reached for the table next to me so I could steady myself from falling. Maude turned and looked to the likeness her wand had conjured, and though I could tell she was trying to keep from weeping, she still managed to finish what she'd been saying in a level tone. "When all you have is taken, you will still love her. When it feels like she's no longer yours, she still will be. Romance comes and goes but she will be your blood and dust forever."

My eyes had crammed shut so tightly and my tears were so hot, I had to wonder if the poison from the Morcai that lived in my veins was reproducing. But once I was able to return my breath to its normal rhythm and clear away the copious amount of tears my body had made, I was able to take one final look at the vision of my daughter that Maude had conjured. And yes! This was my daughter. She was me, she was Toby—she was us.

A second later, the vision was gone, and Maude's attention was geared stiffly over mine. "I came here to hide, Lala, because I felt as if the world had gone and turned against me. I'd decided I didn't have a choice, but here's the thing, one always has a choice. Sometimes it doesn't feel that way but there is always a door lurking somewhere—an exit or opening to reveal a new circumstance. I chose to believe Titania. I left this courtroom then promptly turned away from Raton and what was left of my family. I married Tanker and my father disowned me. Tank and I built a happy life—we found a way to make our neighbors laugh again, to smile. And then many years later, we had you."

"And you never told anybody about this place?" I questioned, even though she'd already stated she hadn't.

She shook her head. "I've always known who you are— who you came here to be. As you'll soon discover though, letting go of what you love the most is near damning. Even when you know it is how the story was always meant to be told.

"You brought me to the stand because you needed someone to remind you that you are strong. That you are someone to believe in. Well, Lala, I believed in you before you were born. I believed in you that fateful night I walked into your nursery to find you giggling—your back completely bare of its wings. I believed in you as I watched you grow up through that glass window of your bedroom, as you grew into the most defiant little faery I'd ever seen. And I believe in you now. Not only that you'll end this war, but that you'll be ready for the next one. And finally, I believe that you'll be the best mother there has ever been and that if your own little Lala ever finds herself here, that you'll be able to do as I have today. That you'll be able to make her believe in herself again, because they may have tried to knock us down, but we fey are built upon fierce magic and no one can take away that kind of love. Absolutely no one."

The courtroom became silent again, but only for about the count of ten. Then, out of nowhere, the ceiling began to leak. Sparkles fell like snowflakes; it was almost like a calming effect—that was until the walls began to crack. Light pouring in from those cracks like the sun itself was trying to bust through the concrete.

"What's happening?" I asked, my voice unsteady.

All of the sudden, my moms were standing near the door, hand in hand. "We love you, Lala," they said together.

"You've got this baby," said Naomi.

"Tanker and I will find you soon," added Maude.

I blinked and they were gone.

"Wait!" I held out my hand towards the door where they'd been rooted.

"It's too late," Helene said, standing. Her robes straightening out as well as her wings. "They've gone. Our time is also up."

My gaze hit the floor as my palms came up to catch the falling sparkles. "No, no, no, no—NO! I'm not ready to leave! I haven't—"

"You haven't *what*, Makayla?" my aunt asked me.

I stopped panicking and stared her dead in the eyes.

"You—You look calm."

Helene had always held herself like a ballerina—astute. She'd carried herself as though she was on a never-ending agenda, which apparently she was. But still, the sky was literally falling.

"I am," she replied.

The room we were standing in was literally breaking into

pieces, and— "You're a statue! You were killed! And you don't look fazed one bit!"

"Yes," she said matter-of-factly. "I deserved it. I lost myself. Why do you think I'm here?"

The sparkles were coming down harder and fiercer, making it near impossible to see Helene from where she stood only but a few paces away. "I—I have no idea."

"Don't you see, Makayla? I chose the opposite of my sister. I have my father's temper. I did *not* choose bravery. I chose revenge. As you and I both know, it did not work out well for me. You may not believe this, but I have the utmost respect for you, niece, and I desire for you to do better than I ever did."

"You were going to kill me," I whispered.

The light shining in through the walls was blinding, but still I saw her smile. "And you stopped me." She grinned larger than life. "I was able to kill two hundred faeries without hardly breaking a sweat, but you—you I could not kill." Her voice rose as the court room crumbled—as the floor broke away and nothing but bright light held me in place. "You have a fiery heart, a magnificent brain, and skill unlike any other." She parted her arms and lifted her chin. "You never needed this escape, Makayla! You don't know how to be weak! NOW FLY AWAY!"

My mouth opened wide as I tried to find the words to say back, but it was too late. Helene was lost in the explosion of light, and as the Great Beyond imploded I was sent spiraling through some sort of corridor. Both light and dark flashed before my eyes as I reached for anything to hold onto—to keep me from twisting through whatever wormhole this was. Until finally there was something to grasp. Or some*one*.

"Here!" I heard someone shout. "Grab hold! Come on, queenie, we don't have all day!"

It was a hand that I saw first, through the dust or stars or whatever this was that I was speeding through. And then a shoulder and a pair of iridescent wings. And then she was there—Blythe.

I took her hand and she pulled me into her chest. I don't remember much after that other than floating in darkness. I passed in and out of consciousness—coming around briefly to find that we were on a giant leaf, floating down a black current, and the sky was as dark as the water.

"It's okay," Blythe said over and over again. "It's going to be okay, Makayla. I've got you now. We've got each other."

I heard myself asking where we were, my voice muffled and my vision waning in and out, but I couldn't keep my head up. What she said before I fell away into unconsciousness though was something I wouldn't ever forget. It didn't make a lot of sense, but I knew it was key.

"We've found ourselves in some sort of . . . tunnel."

☙ 34 ☙

Dora

For Dora of Lantern's Edge, home had always been more of a feeling or a person she missed than anything else. Yes, one could argue that her physical home had a place in her heart, for it was in the memory of Lantern's Edge that she spent the majority of the years she had after her mother and sister (and all those other poor Cronie souls) were washed away into the ether. But the truth was, it was but a cottage. An easy way to conjure a place to rest her bones. And it kept her grounded. Living in the memory of Lantern's Edge was a constant reminder that she would never rest again until what she'd set out to do was finished.

Dora led her pack through the purple clouds and around the forest that belonged to the inhabitants of Lorelei. She suspected that Makayla Wood and her troop would be venturing from the sand into the forest and from there into the cursed lands of Forest Peak.

They ought to be finding some interesting veils to uncover by now, the witch thought as Gloria remained as a large potato sack behind her. She'd had to spell the poor thing into paralysis. It wasn't something she enjoyed doing but as soon as the souls inside Gloria's body became aware that they were back home, closer than ever to the compound of Light's End, the vessel became erratic. Losing oneself whilst riding a dragon isn't a practice that leads one to glory. It is a way to die.

"Oi!" Heime hollered from where he rode behind Dora and Gloria. The witch turned her cheek to him. "Not that I've been here before, but from what you've said, it seems you're taking us on a roundabout!"

"I am!" Dora yelled back to him, using a spell so everyone could hear her clearly. "It would not benefit anyone if we were to meet up with the others amidst that cracked world! We must find them where it ends!"

Dora waited for someone—anyone—to say anything else, but no one did. At least not out loud. The witch peered back to find Bally and Cee-Cee having their hair windblown. Cee-Cee still had a halo of cotton candy around her face; the look suited her.

Rosaline's smooth voice flowed through Dora's mind like caramel. *Are you ready, old friend?*

For just a moment, Dora closed her eyes and let the wind swim around her face. Her neck. She did feel alive up here in the sky. Only a few short minutes and they would be to their destination.

I don't know if anyone can ever be ready for what must happen.

But you will prevail, whispered the dragon telepathically into the witch's head.

No matter what happens, someone will lose. 'Tis the way of the world.

Again, the dragon whispered, a bit softer this time. *But you will prevail.*

Dora wanted to grin, because it feels very nice when others believe in you, but the smile wouldn't come. *For the sake of the worlds, I hope you're right,* she whispered back.

Dora searched through the clouds they soared through for the ground below. They were so far up that it was near impossible to see a thing on land or water, but still, she searched. Her mind was quiet as she did this. That was, until it wasn't.

Dora searched for the soul of Makayla Wood. *Where oh where had the faery gone? Where oh where were her wings?* Dora's spine straightened as a vision appeared somewhere in the deep recesses of her mind, and her breath slowed as she took it all in.

Rosaline spoke over the witch's daydreams. *We'll be making our descent sooner than later. Do you suppose we'll have beat them to the dirt?*

Dora's pupils grew wide then small. After several moments, she replied. *Oh yes, we will be the first to arrive. It seems our company has been redirected temporarily.*

Is everything okay? Rosaline asked.

And though joy was something her heart still ached for, Dora did finally let loose the smallest of sparkles. *More than. I think Ms. Wood has found the gray.*

‏ 35 ‏

Makayla

My eyes had been fluttering between open and closed,
like a newborn baby finding its place in the world for
the very first time. I couldn't say how long I'd been between
consciousness and wherever else I was, but when I was able
to finally keep my vision focused—and after I'd deposited
Maude's remedy into each of my eyes—I assessed that we
were nowhere near the place we'd come from before we'd
taken that world-bending leap through the mushroom.

I believe these things were called lazy rivers. I'd never
floated on one, but I'd seen pictures of them on the internet.
One of our interns from Sewn Back Together had completed
an entire marketing campaign with photos of families using
our bags while hiking, shopping, and at amusement parks. For
some reason that picture of the 'perfect family' in their raft,
floating down that man-made river of sparkling blue jewels—
their heads back in laughter as one of our bags rested in the

mother's lap (we had a waterproof bag)—stayed with me. Perhaps it was that piece of me inside, that spark of Lala, that clung to that moment. The part of me that wanted the rest of my soul to wake up, to put down my binders—and blinders— and change out of the suit I was wearing and into shorts. To throw my hair back into a ponytail and head out into the sun to let loose. Perhaps it was her who couldn't let that photograph go. Because Lala is the piece of me who understands that there is more to life than work. These wings belong to Lala because Lala is the one who never forgot how to fly in the first place.

"Hey queenie, you're back."

Blythe's voice was as gentle as the calming sounds of nature encompassing us as we traveled over a steady current in this oddly beautiful stream, surrounded by one of the thickest forests I'd ever seen. We were enveloped by chirping birds, twigs falling to a blanketed forest floor, and dragonflies so large they could've been prehistoric.

"Where are we?" I asked, sitting up. Our raft was a giant leaf, curled up at the edges so that it appeared like a green canoe. "Wait," I started, before Blythe could even contemplate an answer to my question. "Are we—"

"Tiny," she said with a smirk. "Yes."

"Oh my god."

We weren't on a giant leaf; we were on a regular one, and the forest looked so big and thick because we were the size of grasshoppers. Before I had a chance to stop them, my wings began fluttering behind my back, much like they did when they'd first reappeared to me.

"Oh no," I muttered. "It's happening—I'm going to have an anxiety attack!" I'd just left that courtroom, and now I was going to be pulled right back in because I couldn't ever seem to keep my heartbeats from pouring out of my chest! But just as my breath started to shorten and my body started to lift from the makeshift boat, Blythe leaned forward and rested a hand over my knee.

"Relax, Makayla."

My chest immediately settled, and a full breath entered my lungs. My wings began to lower from where they'd been raised above my shoulders. When she removed her hand, I missed it.

"Cool. Just keep breathing, it's all okay."

After two steady inhalations, I asked, "Where are we? Are we real?"

She snickered. "We're real. As for where we are, I don't really know. I reached for you just as you dove into that portal so technically this is both of our trips mixed together. I'm guessing that court room scene was all you, and once it broke apart you rebounded to me."

Her explanation flitted around my head, searching for neatly labeled files to fit itself into, but there were no such files. "You saw the courtroom?" I hesitated. "You knew that's what it was called?"

"Yeah, I told you, we studied that stuff in school. Your political system not excluded. We studied as many systems as we could—from all the worlds. It pays to know what works and what doesn't."

I hinged forward because I *had* to know. "Out of curiosity, how does your hidden world handle things?" Because they were doing *something* right. "Are there courtrooms, or like, is there a jail?"

She shook her head. "We keep things simple. Three strikes you're out."

I waited for more. When there wasn't any, I said, "Seriously?"

She nodded. "We don't have a jail. There's a three-tiered system: If you break the rules, you get tossed out of the safe land for a day. You do it again, same thing. You do it three times, you get tossed out and can't ever return. It's simple and it works. Nobody's ever been kicked out because nobody who lives there wants to leave. But we have had kids grow up and decide they'd like to explore the rest of the world or worlds, and in that case, they may return whenever they want."

"How do you know they won't leak the information about your little utopia and attract the wrong sort?"

"We don't, but we haven't ever had an issue. As you saw when you first entered, you really must know all the details to get in, and even then, those damn pookas are nearly impossible to catch."

"Huh," I mused.

It was so simple that it didn't seem possible, but somehow it was. As my mind opened new shelves for these interesting files to sit upon, I returned to our present situation.

"So, we're still tripping?" I mean, that's what all of this was, right? I stumbled over a very large poisonous mushroom and then entered a very long dream.

"Yep. When your weird little escape spell cracked and blew up, you were sent to where I was because we came through the portal together."

"When my spell cracked?" It was then I realized two things: one that Blythe really had been able to see *everything* that had just happened to me, and two—"The spell actually blew up . . . Does that mean I can't ever return there . . . to the Great Beyond?"

Her left brow raised. "Why would you want to?"

"I—I don't." I didn't. I don't think. "I just—how was it able to dissolve?"

She scoffed. "Girlfriend, that thing didn't dissolve, it exploded like a dying star. But to answer your question, I think it was because you knew, deep down, that you didn't need it anymore." She bounced her little pixie head from shoulder to shoulder. "These portals are kind of like therapy for a lot of souls. You don't really go through one unless there's stuff you want to deal with, unless you're looking to lighten your load. You dig?"

Do I what? She must've read my confusion.

She inched forward so that our knees were touching. As we floated over the current of what must've been only a small creek, we passed a ladybug, who from our angle, looked to be about the size of a small building. "The Great Beyond was a coping mechanism for you, one that had the potential to be extremely unhealthy and even dangerous. It's no wonder you went straight there, because the mushroom knew it was what you needed to deal with first."

Okay, that made sense, but—"How were you able to see everything? Didn't you say you were right here?"

She blinked a few times before her hands found my knees again. "It wasn't like this when I first got here." Her gaze lifted then roamed from bank to bank, from earth to sky. "At first, I was just floating in darkness, then scenes began to blow up around me like they were playing on little tube televisions. One of them was your courtroom drama—and by the way, who was that judge? She was ridiculously fabulous. Fierce, ya know."

I scratched the skin over my left eye. "Uh yeah. Totally fierce, that was my Aunt Helene. She's no longer living. She sort of tried to kill me."

"No shit?"

"No shit," I snickered, then went ahead to give her a CliffsNotes version of what had ensued when I'd first gotten my wings back.

"Dang girl, no wonder you dove into the Great Beyond. You really have been through it all."

"Yeah," I agreed, before letting my words drift.

When I looked up it was to find Blythe studying me. Her soothing touch was starting to feel a little too intimate. The air around us was growing heavier. She must have sensed it too, for a second later she pulled away.

Without addressing the extra sparkle hanging around our floating leaf, she said, "So yeah, I saw your little dream . . . And I saw Layla spearing off with that dick mer leader, and I also watched Toby staring at a waterfall."

My head fell to my shoulder. "My king . . . I wonder what was on the other side of the waterfall."

Blythe bit her lip. "I don't know," she said softly. "Anyway, you popped up in my weird little leaf here soon after your series was cancelled. We floated in darkness for a while, but it didn't take long for the scenery to start appearing." She looked around peacefully. "It's actually kind of nice here."

"And where is here exactly? Do we know?"

She returned her attention to mine, then shook her head softly. "I think maybe it's the in between."

I let the words linger over my tongue for a moment before stating them aloud. "The in between?"

"Yeah." She grinned. "Witches like to refer to it as the gray. It's like this place where our souls can come to recharge. To reevaluate our missions." She pressed her lips together as she continued to look at me like I was an outfit she was seeing through a glass wall. An outfit she wanted to try on but wasn't sure if she should. "I don't want to you confuse you, Makayla." Her gaze lowered to her lap. "I can't imagine how baffling this all is for you. Like even before you were thrown into this mission, you were still adjusting to having a goddamn butterfly on your back. I just—" She turned her cheek to me and closed her eyes.

This time, I placed my hands on *her* knees. I wasn't sure what it was about this place, but as soon as I did that—as soon as she turned her gaze to fall deeply back into mine—everything slowed. The current, the slight wind rustling through the giant trees like a large transparent hand . . . our chests as they rose and fell. For once, I didn't think about what I was going to do next. At least in that moment, there were no files in my head. No worries about what would happen after I did what I didn't just want to do but had wanted to do from the first time I saw Blythe's face.

I didn't just lean in, she met me. Our noses touched, and in the reflection of her lavender eyes I saw my king. I saw what she saw as he stood facing a waterfall, one arm reaching through it. Whatever he was doing, wherever he was, he seemed content.

And then the oddest thing happened. He turned to look at me. There was no sadness to be found anywhere on him, and in fact he smiled. "My blessing, my queen," was all he said, his voice echoing into my ears.

What occured next was the easiest thing I've ever done.

The first time it happened, I'd been stuck on the what ifs. What if it doesn't go right? What if it doesn't feel right? What if I do it wrong?

The first time it happened, Toby kissed me.

This time, I kissed her.

It was the drug trip; it had to be. It was warm and light. A sunset. Soft colors bleeding together, hazy. Natural.

As we kissed, nothing mattered. The Sword of Avalon ceased to weigh me down, the idea of using it against the very first friend I ever had—it all drifted away. Not like so far that I couldn't see it; I mean, it was there, I just wasn't worried about it. With my lips against hers, all I knew was that things would manage to get done, and from there we would go on living.

At some point the kiss ended. We pulled away at exactly the same time. Still, I wasn't worried. I didn't feel bad.

I didn't feel bad about not feeling bad.

But, as is often the case, dreams do end. We couldn't stay in the gray forever, and even if we could have, the priestess who had coined herself as the Crone of Light's End never would have allowed it. Portal or no, we were still on her turf.

My lashes were fluttering and my chest was just beginning to fill. I was hoping I wouldn't have be the first to say something—when it happened.

"Shit," Blythe whispered. By the way her gaze had rolled to the edge of the creek and up, I knew something damaging had found us.

"What is it?" I asked, turning around to see what had darkened the cotton candy that was lining her aura into a burnt sugary brown. "No," I muttered. Even though I'd met the priestess, I'd never seen her previous likeness. Somehow, though, I knew as soon as I looked into those dark eyes that this is who had found us. She was dressed in a blood red skirt that pooled around her feet and the top half of her body was covered in a tight, lacy blouse with a pattern that moved around like snakes slithering around bushes. Shooting my attention back to Blythe, the ecstasy we'd just conjured slipping back into the ether, I whispered heatedly, "She found us."

With Blythe's attention still wholly over that beastly soul, she retorted, "Of course she did; she's one hundred percent evil. That sort of wicked is capable of almost anything." Her eyes moved to mine and she mouthed two quick words. *Fly away.*

I didn't hesitate, and neither did she. In one fleeting heartbeat, she held out her hand which I gladly took, we raised our wings, and without a second's thought, we began to lift from our sanctuary and flap away from that awful vision of a monster on the hill.

But Blythe was right. That kind of wicked is capable of more than anyone cares to admit. We'd only gotten as far as the first tree trunk in our path when we felt it. Something had stopped us in our tracks, causing us to bounce against it and fall *hard* to the earth. The wind was knocked from my chest, and I struggled to sit up. As I did, I could see that Blythe was in the same boat. Still, we crawled to one another, reaching for the other's touch. But just as our hands came together, the force field that had stopped us from escaping lit up. Bright neon green lines crisscrossed right in front of our eyes, making an impenetrable mesh. I'd just opened my mouth to cry out when I was silenced by the swishing of a blood red skirt.

She walked up to us—the crone. She was the same size as we were, and she stood straight as an arrow with her hands coupled together. "Well, well, well. Looks like I got myself a couple of fireflies." Her pinched face grew sharper. "You know what I used to like to do with fireflies when I was but a girl?" When neither of us answered, she said, "I used to pinch them between my fingers, feel the life inside of them slowly die. And then, just before their souls went out, I would rub the glow against my hands." She moved in closer, her smile turning into a sneer. "I liked the way their dying light glowed against my skin."

My mind was blank as the two of us stared at the priestess. The magic of whatever portal or poison the shroom we'd dove into had offered seemed to be dissipating. For anxiety was returning full throttle.

"This isn't real," I whispered to myself again and again.

"Oh," came the cutting voice of that awful crone. "Silly lost Erwain, lucky for me, 'tis real as that endearing little kiss you just shared with she who is not your king."

36

Dora

They didn't land in the asteroid field that served as the remains of Lantern's Edge. No, the dragons dropped them off in a little corner of the woods where only a thicket of trees separated them from Forest Peak.

The patch of land they stood upon wasn't broken, but everything around them was.

"What is this place?" Cee-Cee asked.

Goddess it was good to hear her voice again.

"Mother's cabin," Dora stated.

She'd managed to get Gloria from Rosaline's back without disturbing the sleep she'd fallen into. The witch was still spelled into paralysis, but Dora hated to see such an innocent life tortured by what lived inside her. It wasn't Gloria's fault she'd been born with Hecate blood. It wasn't her fault that she'd been good enough of a soul to sacrifice her life so that others could live.

Bally had come up by Cee-Cee's side and the two were now holding hands. Heime was stalking around their small bit of land—surrounded by floating mayhem—like he was some sort of inspector.

"Mother?" asked Cee-Cee.

"Yes," Dora answered the girl. She roped her hands together under her cloak. "This is where she was born. Her father, my grandfather, wasn't a good man." The witch's eyes squinted so tightly together that they nearly closed. "The rumors stated that my grandmother was a harlot. That she often left her child and husband's side to meet men and drink their rum. The banter was all nonsense of course. Her husband was no magician, and though no one really knew the family that well that lived in this small cabin, it was said that Miranda—that was my grandmother's name—that she was a witch."

"Wait," Cee-Cee stated. "Are you saying that the Crone isn't a full-blooded witch?"

Dimples grew in the pale-faced likeness Dora had been wearing so long that she sometimes forgot her true skin was the color of the girl's. She raised a single finger in the air and said with a bit of flare, "Aha. Finally, we may start to string together the origins of a curse. Magic sometimes skips a generation. And though my grandmother had veins full of magic, the Crone was never born a witch at all."

With her tongue coated in the kind of victory that comes when one knows a winning play is about to ensue, Dora looked around at her gathered heroes. Every single one of them was watching her with interest.

"Go on," she said, holding out an arm to the small cabin. "Go in, walk around. Though there isn't much room to do so, I suspect you'll still find at least one very interesting discovery." She blinked two or three times, observing how each and every one of them stared at her as though they weren't sure she was the 'good witch' they'd been thinking she might have been. "'Tisn't a trap," she said with a grin that said otherwise.

Not a single one of them moved a muscle.

Dora pressed her lips together as she inhaled deeply through her nose. "Fine," she said, retrieving a log from where it was stacked with many others against the side of the cottage with the flick of her wand. After she had a seat, she recovered three others and set them before each person in her company. "Well then, have yourselves a seat," she stated. When they remained standing, she sighed. "'Tis story time. Come now."

When they finally did as they'd been asked, though it seemed to take several minutes, Dora laid her wand across her lap, then tended to her glass bottles, ensuring they were still hanging from the belt around her waist. When all was finally settled, she looked up at her small assembly.

"T'was many years ago. I was but a little girl. My sister Malina and I were just getting old enough to know that we were different from other kids. For at that time Forest Peak hadn't yet been labeled as cursed land, though it was on its way to being so. The families who saw our mother for what she was and what she was trying to do hadn't all left yet, so we still had non-coven kids to play with, even though we weren't supposed to." She grinned as she said, "But even our mother couldn't keep eyes on the two of us every second of the day.

"We were six years of age, just on the brink of seven, when we first found this place. We'd been playing hide and seek with some other children in the forest. Some were of the coven, and some weren't. Malina found this place and was the first to enter, but she was still caught up in the game. She didn't find anything peculiar about the cabin. I, however, had been born with a scent for things. Like a dog, I could smell wrongdoings from a mile away." She was speculative for a moment as Heime, Bally, and Cee-Cee watched her. "I guess that's why I sent us in this direction that fateful day. I was too young to understand it, but I was pulled to this place. I was the one who led the group of children into these woods, and I was the one who said that they should all close their eyes while my sister and I hid first. And when Malina spotted the old cabin and said it was the perfect hiding spot, I was the one whose shoulders relaxed once I laid my gaze upon it."

Bally leaned in just slightly. "What did you smell?"

Dora pierced his gaze with her own. "We'll get to that, I promise. For now, I think it would be best to let you experience it for yourselves." Dora licked her finger and placed it in the air. "I do believe we have some time to spare and though I tell a good story, I paint an even better portrait." She turned her attention to them just in time to see all their spines stiffen. "Do not worry, you are friends, not foe. Relax. Be still. And be free."

Then, before a single one of them could blink or attempt to stand, Dora reached for the cape around her shoulders and flung it up in the air like a parachute. As it floated down, it grew so that it could envelop every single one of them, and as it fell around all their shoulders, she began to say, "T'was an overcast day. The wind was still and the grasshoppers were quiet. I think maybe that was why I was able to hear them so easily for the first time—the whispers . . ."

The land was warm and prickly under the twins' bare feet as they made their way swiftly over the forest floor. Butterflies kissed their shoulders and the sound of children near and far tickled the senses of any passerby, though there weren't many out and about at this end of the forest. It was rumored to be haunted, as most places that sit between the worlds often are. So, naturally children flocked to where the trees were almost unnaturally high, and the sunlight was thinner. It was a fine place to play their games.

"Look Dora! Through the cedars—'tis a cabin!"

Dora's gaze locked on the small cottage. "'Tis more of a shack," she said thoughtfully, treading just behind Malina's footsteps.

"Do you think anyone lives in there?" she said over her shoulder as she picked up her pace and ran for the quaint dwelling.

Dora's pace was more of a pensive one, her nose lifted in the air as she drank in the scent that had been infiltrating every aspect of her dreams for nights on end. Driven was she, to find out the reason why this place had been calling her. But she'd been born cautious.

"Let us just see if there is anybody home," Malina shouted back at Dora as she skipped forward.

Dora said nothing as her sister ran up the gravel path to the front door. The young witch did, however, reach into the pocket of her sundress and grip the hilt of her wand. Did she think anyone was home? No, but still, her sister was frivolous and innocent. In fact, Malina still hadn't put together that witches had a tendency to walk in the other direction when their mother entered the local apothecary. She *had* figured out that love wasn't something the priestess offered, but even that had been a hard lesson for Malina to learn. She'd only just stopped trying to hug their mother's legs when insecurity found her. Dora had now trained her to come into *her* arms rather than have to watch her twin sister go through the emotional torment their mother offered in place of solace.

Dora planted herself about eight feet away from the door —the peculiar scent that had gotten her attention all the way back at Lantern's Edge was nearly suffocating. *What is that?*

she questioned to herself. Every kind of magic had a scent—she'd learned that from a very young age. White magic smelled of rosemary, cinnamon, and cloves. Life. Gray magic introduced a more earthy smell, like charcoal and ash. Dark magic (the kind Malina and her were subjected to more often than not) smelled of sweet rot. Though, through her own manipulations, she'd taught herself to spin any sort of magic without ill intention, and when she was able to pull that off, the smell of honeyed garbage turned into something else. Not sour or offensive. Simply put, it smelled of the whole world.

"'Tis your respect for the craft," a witch in passing had said to her not that long ago. "You are a great witch, Dora. You could come with me. I can take you away from all of this."

The witch in passing had been one of her mother's 'guests.' Just another wanderer who had wanted to see for herself what that newish coven was doing so far out into Forest Peak. But just as she would find herself doing as the years went by, Dora had resisted the opportunity to flee. She might've had a young face, but her soul was ancient, and she knew more than she liked to admit that there were shackles around her and her sister's ankles. It's just that no one else seemed to see them.

"I don't think anyone is home," Malina said as she turned to face her twin. "What shall we do?"

"See if the door opens," Dora replied.

Malina nodded then did as she was asked. Without much force, she was able to get it open—however the creak it made was loud enough to shake the dead, and the smell that wafted out and into Dora's nostrils was enough to cause her to pass out. Dora toppled a little from the light headedness as soon as Malina swung open that door but quickly gathered herself back together. She rolled her pointed shoulders back then took careful steps until she was so close to the door's opening that she could no longer stand it. Whatever had invited her here was causing her brain to feel as though it was being crowded by her skull closing in on itself.

"Dora!" Malina shouted, reaching for her sister as she fell to her knees. "Are you okay?"

Dora couldn't answer at first. Her small fists had come up to her eyes before moving to either side of her head—as if she could undo the pressure inside of it. After many torturous seconds, she moved her gaze to meet Malina's and tried her best to give a fitting answer.

"I'm so foolish. I forgot to eat my lunch." She let Malina help her back to standing but was careful not to let go of her twin, for that stench was nearly debilitating. And for whatever reason, her sister was immune.

"That is a falsity, Dora, and you know it. I saw you eat with my own two eyes."

"No, you saw what I wanted you to see," she lied. "I've been giving my rations to Squeakers most days." Squeakers was the mouse that lived in their room. It was an unusual pet for a pair of small girls, but he was theirs regardless of what the world thought.

Malina curled her bottom lip up and out in a way she didn't dare ever do in front of their mother—at least not anymore. "Don't you dare try to shield my eyesight with your magic, Dora. We are one and the same, remember. You and I are in this together. Forever."

Dora used her waning strength to match her sister's gaze, and as she lifted her chin, she nodded slightly. "Yes Malina. You are right. We are in this together. I dare not lie to you ever again."

A promise she would do her best to keep, that was if it was a fitting promise to adhere by. From a young age, Dora understood that sometimes you had to do as you had to do— because there was often only one way to survive.

"Okay, well, come in then. I daresay no one lives here—'tis quite bare."

With her sister's help, Dora hobbled into the cabin. It was sparse, there was but a wooden table and a cot without a mattress. Dust and dirt layered every findable surface, but as far as any dead animal or dead anything, there wasn't any. The smell was left over from something quite terrible, but nothing that one could wrap their hands around.

"I don't know if this is a good idea," Dora muttered. Her sister had led her to the one chair that stood next to the table. As she had a seat, she looked around the cottage. "There's not really many places to hide. If the others find this place, all they must do is come inside."

"True," Malina said, her gaze roaming from wall to wall. It was just this one room, or at least that's how it looked to the naked eye.

'Tis not true . . . Dora thought. Her vision had already sunken to the floorboards. The spot under her foot was loose and the more she worked it, the more she realized this was where the smell was coming from.

"How about," Dora stated very slowly, "you head out into the woods and find a spot to hide, and I'll remain in here. The rules clearly state that they must find us both for their team to win."

Malina scrunched up her little nose. "When have there ever been rules?"

"Always," Dora said confidently, though she was already going against the promise she'd made to her sister about lying.

After a doleful moment, Malina nodded then proceeded to put her hand on the wooden door. "Fine. You know how to find me if I pick too good of a spot."

"Yes," Malina answered with a forced grin. They'd linked their wands the second they'd been given them. From that moment they'd always been able to track one another with ease.

"'Tis a good idea." Malina grinned. "It's like a strategy."

Dora did all she could to keep a neutral expression. They'd recently learned the word from eavesdropping in on one of their mother's coven meetings. What the priestess had been preaching had gone right over Malina's youthful head, but no matter how she'd tried, Dora hadn't been able to get it out of hers.

Strategy, as it pertained to the coven, meant world domination. Power akin to the highest powers available. Even someone as small as Dora understood that her mother represented something very terrible.

Malina exited the cabin and Dora waited only a few short minutes before coming down to those dusty floorboards and yanking the loose board away. The smell was even more alarming, but that wasn't what caused her eyes to come to the size of two full moons. As soon as she looked down into the gap, a small hand found her lips and she gasped.

Ever since she could remember, her and Malina had been taught how improper it was to lay hands over another magic wielder's wand. But what if the owner was no longer alive? No one seemed to live in this cabin, and even if they did—what harm could it do just to hold this particular find for even just a second or two.

Though her thoughts were warning her to move forward with caution, Dora's hand had a mind of its own. It reached inside that hollow and grasped that wand—so dark that it looked like it had been created from charcoal—and held it vertically before her eyes.

That was it. That was all it needed to share its story with her. All it had ever needed was someone's touch. Or maybe, as Dora would concern the workings of her mind with over her future years, maybe it was looking for just *the right* touch. Either way, she'd gotten what she came for. Answers.

Were they terrible? Oh yes. More than terrible. They were wicked. Licked by the tongue of demons. And in any case, more than any child should ever bear witness to. But Dora was thankful to have found them, for she'd already suspected her place in this world was so much more than their mother had told them. She wasn't an ingredient. She was—well, one thing at a time.

❦

"Wait. That's it?" Bally stated, his eyes narrowed at the witch.

"Yeah, what the hell?" Cee-Cee demanded. "You didn't even tell us the best part."

Dora smirked at the three pairs of eyes staring at her from their logs.

"I thought you might want to see things for yourselves."

Heime, Bally, and Cee-Cee took turns looking from one to the other, but it wasn't from them that the next words were spoken.

In a voice shrouded with thorns and ruin, Gloria finally spoke from where she was still curled up on the ground. "It's still in there. I can hear it speaking."

"Hear what?" Cee-Cee questioned with an arched brow.

"The wand," Gloria said, just before offering to the space around them the loudest and most cruel of bloodcurdling screams.

37

Makayla

We were Hansel and Gretel, stolen into strange woods with a wicked witch who wanted to eat us. Except there was no candy . . . which would have made things so much better. My stomach was queasy. I'd tried to reach into my satchel for the pills Blythe's mom had given me, but the priestess had quickly put an end to that—aiming her wand at my head like a gun.

Meanwhile, we were still stuck in this strange force field net, holding onto one another like a couple of scared kittens who had been hunted by the cruelest wolf in the forest. Not that it was currently on my mind, considering we had way worse things to worry about, but the kiss didn't matter. I'd already decided that it could one hundred percent be explained by the drug trip we were experiencing. Because that's what this was. I mean, right? None of this was even happening.

"'Tis happening, faery," the priestess said, the words slithering out from her mouth like three separate snakes.

The world started to spin a little, my stomach growing increasingly sour. "Get out of my mind!"

The evil crone grinned.

"Stop it," Blythe whispered heatedly to me. "Don't let her see you getting worked up. It fuels her."

I nodded too quickly. "Right . . . you're right—"

I hinged forward and for the zillionth time since this little faery began to nest in my body, I puked.

The priestess hissed. "Stop it."

I looked up at her, my eyes heavy and yuck dripping from my lips. "Like I can help it."

The last I saw of her was a frown as I bent over and began yakking all over again. It was so forceful that I worried I would throw up my little swaddling. Was that even a thing?

Was I truly worried I'd lose her?

I was. For the first time, I really was.

"It's okay, queenie," Blythe said, rubbing my back.

I wiped at my mouth as I said, "How is she even here? I thought the priestess was locked into Cee-Cee's body?"

"She is," Blythe said with a bitter tongue. She raised her gaze to meet the evil sorceress as she said, "But she left pieces of herself in this land. So technically this is really her."

My eyes wanted to close—I was so tired. Still, I was about to retort when we heard someone shout.

"Makayla!"

All three of us snapped our heads up at attention. Who had called out my name?

"Blythe!"

Blythe and I turned to face one another with wide eyes. "Who is that?" I asked heatedly. "Who's calling to us?"

"I told you," Blythe said, running a smooth hand over my

red locks, now wind-blown and harried. "We're fine. I think we're getting pulled out of here."

"But you said this was real—" I lunged forward again, heaving up yellow bile.

As the priestess began to flay about around our imprisonment, raising her hands to the sky in agitation, Blythe continued to soothe me. "It is real. You and I—our souls are here. Together. But we're still working through the magic of the—"

It was her turn to yak.

"Makayla!"

"Blythe, wake UP!"

This time, the voices were clearer. Toby's and Layla's. And as Blythe lifted her head back up, gulping for air, the world we were in began to shake.

The priestess lost her balance and fell to the ground, rolling down the hill until she gathered herself and began crawling back up towards us on her elbows, pointing her wand at us as she struggled to maintain.

"You'll not get far!" she screeched at us. "Do you hear me —I'm always near!"

Blythe took me by the shoulders, forcing me to look her in the eyes. "It's the poison. The more we throw up, the more it fades. Keep yakking!"

It took me less than the blink of an eye to do as I'd been told. There wasn't much left, but my stomach was still all tied in knots, and it wasn't hard to lean over and let it all go.

Layla and Toby's voice grew louder with every bout of sickness we let loose. The world we were in grew shakier. The court room of the Great Beyond had literally exploded and this forest we'd wandered into was working its way to breaking apart as well.

At some point, I looked over to find Blythe fading in and

out, like static on an old television overlapping the picture. White noise was all around us.

Through jagged breaths, my faery pal tried to push me. "Keep going, Makayla. We're almost out of here."

I did as she said. When next I looked up after heaving a whole lot of nothing, it was to find the land turning to darkness. The priestess was still aiming her wand at my head —a mere eight feet away or so—and she was still in a crawling position. That was until she realized she was floating amidst pure nothingness. Just before she fell, her eyes narrowed over mine and she hissed out her final warning, "I'm not going anywhere."

And then she was gone.

I looked to my side. Blythe wasn't there.

And then neither was I.

❦

When we came to, we were not in the same place we'd been when we jumped through the mushroom portals. I was in Toby's arms and when I was able to gain the strength to look for her, I found Blythe being pulled up by a very worried Layla.

"Shit. Where the hell did you guys go?" the mermaid was asking as she pulled Blythe in for a snug embrace.

Blythe rubbed at her forehead as she let her head hang over Layla's shoulder. "Queenie had some shit to sort out." Her eyes met mine and stayed put for just long enough for me to understand—our kiss would remain our little secret.

Though my face was in Toby's hands, and he was pulling my forehead to his, I still managed to nod her way. *Thank you,* I thought, hoping my words would reach her.

Immediately my body shifted to melt in Toby's arms. "How long were we out?" I asked him.

Petal, who had been observing us all from the side, answered in place of my king. "At least five more hours than the other two. At least you were all dropped in the same place. As it was, I might as well have been herding ninny cats trying to find you all."

I took a second to gauge where we were. There was an enormous crack between us and the hillside that floated across from where we were. Gently pulling free of my king's embrace, I neared the edge of the floating land we were on. There was a stream here that had since stopped flowing; a still brook on a jinxed plot of land. I made a visor out of my hand as I looked up at the jagged hillside, its edges meant to lock directly into the edge of where I stood. The stream was on pause on that land as well . . . just waiting until it could be reunited.

Petal clomped up beside me, as did Toby, Blythe, and Layla.

"We've not been able to get to the next landscape," Petal said. "'Tis not a friendly place for wings."

My head very slowly met my right shoulder and my wand appeared in my hand. I closed my eyes for a moment, picturing Helene's face. I don't know why I still put her on a pedestal, and I literally just had in my head, for as a judge she'd loomed over everyone. She'd taken the wrong path while she'd been alive, but that didn't mean she wasn't super intelligent, or as Blythe had coined her—fierce. Either way, it wasn't the ghostly queen I'd clung to my entire life that aided me in my next decision. It was in the spirit of a faery who didn't worry about consequence; a faery who did whatever she needed to do to get what she wanted.

My wand lit up, the star encased in a diamond glowing brighter than ever, and I closed my eyes. I had the gift of creation. Essentially, I could do whatever I wanted. If I'd learned anything from all those visits into the Great Beyond, it was simply that.

My hand began to shake as I concentrated on what I wanted to happen. Gravitational forces started to pull my wand in every direction—as if this world itself was trying to get the magical tool out of my hand. But my wand was part of me and if this land was going to absorb it, then it was going to take all of me.

That's exactly what I plan to do . . .

"Shut up," I muttered to the terrible crone who wouldn't stay out of my mind—carefully though, as not to disturb my concentration.

The priestess wasn't going anywhere. She was in my head, under my feet, above us—she was everywhere and anywhere, and she would be until the sword I carried pierced the body of her host.

Behind me, my group was both mystified and troubled.

"What is she doing?" Layla was whispering heatedly.

"I'm not sure," Blythe answered, "but if I had to guess—"

"She's fixing it," Toby said, his voice as clear as crystal waters.

My concentration unwavering, I kept my eyes crammed shut, my lips pressed firmly together. I didn't know if there was a spell for what I was attempting to do, but I'd always been more of a leader than a follower and that meant that I needed to write the words for others to speak rather than the other way around.

The curses in this land were stringent, unwilling to move —but I had something it hadn't been exposed to before: the will to end it. "I'm not afraid of you," I said more into my head than to the world around us. "You can't take us down."

Something tried with all it's might to pull the wand from my hand, but I just gritted my teeth—picturing the two creeks coming back together. It had taken a hallucination for me to understand something very important. This was real; what I'd experienced during that trip was also real; but similarly, it was all an illusion. All one had to do to become the master of their universe was figure out how to make one and one add up to two. Luckily, I'd always been pretty good at math.

"This water WILL flow!" I said through a tight jaw, and then just like that, the force pulling on my wand lost its grip and a wail ran through my head so fiercely that I had to wonder if it left tracks.

I didn't let my eyes reopen. Not right away. Instead, I saw it happen in my head—I watched as the hill floating above us came down to meet our bit of land, as it shook like a giant beast until the rough edges began to merge, as they locked together. My team was quiet, breathing heavily behind me— the exception being Petal whinnying in excitement. The ground shook as it had when Blythe and I had been held together under the priestess's net. It shook and it shook, and it bellowed.

Until it didn't.

My eyes were still closed. It was the wind breathing against my cheeks that first told me it had worked, for in this land of curses there was no wind. Not until now.

My chest lifted and for the first time in a while I felt the weight of Avalon's Sword pulling on my belt. I lowered my wand until my arm was resting by my side then let my eyes flutter back open. I was looking at a hillside, and to my right was a trickling brook. It was no longer still.

Toby walked up so that we were shoulder to shoulder. To my left, Petal did the same. Blythe and Layla came to meet Toby's side. We each just stared at the hill for a few seconds, taking in creation—watching as sprigs of blackened grass returned to green. It wasn't until a bird flew over our heads, another sign that things were coming back to life, that anyone spoke.

"What now?" Layla asked gravely.

No one moved their attention to anywhere other than straight ahead.

"I think we walk," was all I said.

And so we did. One foot and one hoof at a time, the five of us stalked up that hillside until we reached the top. Only once did I dare to look back as we did so, and what I saw was amazing. It wasn't perfect, for the curses buried in this dirt were rooted and wicked, but it was *something*. Pieces of earth, rocks, broken trees —roots, were beginning to stitch themselves back together. And it wasn't just where my feet had been. It was everywhere.

I smiled before turning around. The five of us took that final step together. None of us sure what we'd see once we got to the top. I'd simply assumed it would just be more of what we'd already gone through; we'd packed enough supplies to climb an unclimbable mountain. But, as is life, this place was completely unpredictable.

We rose to the top and as we did, mine and Blythe's wings rose over our heads. Petal and Layla gasped, and Toby was still as stone.

"Well then," Petal stated, "it appears we've arrived."

No one spoke again for a minute or two. My head was churning as if it was full of insects, and I suspected everyone else's was too.

We still had to come down from this hill and there was a decent sized lake between the land at the bottom and where the cottage stood, but still I could see quite clearly that it didn't look like the cottage I was used to. My spell had stitched the land back together, but the curses left behind by the priestess and her cult hadn't protected the wood and stone holding together the real Lantern's Edge. The sign out front was falling apart as was the roof. The front door was hanging crookedly from its hinges.

Other than that, it was familiar.

"What now?" Blythe questioned, from where we stood all in a row.

"I think," Toby stated, "we will soon find out."

And then, from somewhere in the far southwest, a scream came bellowing out to meet us. A scream of someone in pain —someone who just wanted the end to come.

Another hiss rang through my head and then a slow release as though the priestess was letting her hair down.

My vessel is near.

38

Dora

The witch from Lantern's Edge knew it was but a short hike back to the place she'd once called home. Or at least the place she'd rested at night and had been fed (when the Crone saw fit to let her ingredients fill their stomachs). But it wasn't the trek that would prove to be time consuming. It was dealing with the vessel. Dora's traveling companions had yet to know what was about to happen. As far as they were concerned, Gloria would be coming with them.

"Why did we let the dragons go?" Cee-Cee asked, as all four of them stood around the poor woman with too many souls bound to her. "We could have just strapped her on top one of them and road in like we did to get here."

"Yes," Dora agreed. "Unfortunately, the dragons don't care to get too close to the cursed grounds. No one does. We were lucky that the beasts had the heart to bring us this near to Lantern's Edge."

Dora allowed her gaze to rest over the shoulders of the girl. For once, that's all she was. An innocent child; a soul who had already been dealt an unfair hand at life once (perhaps more than once, for Dora couldn't speak to *all* Malina's—or Cee-Cee's previous lives). True, the burden of the priestess still lived on inside that body, but Cee-Cee had overpowered her and forced her back down into the pit of darkness that Gloria had willed her into so long ago.

The girl caught Dora looking at her and sneered. "What?"

The edge of Dora's lips twitched. "I was just wondering, have you heard from her?"

Cee-Cee's expression fell flat. She knew who the witch meant. "No. It's been pretty quiet in my head. She feels distant."

Dora nodded. "She's using her energy elsewhere. Typical."

Heime had been chewing on his lip while staring down at Gloria's passed out body. They'd had to spell her into such a state for the screaming and screeching was enough to make an infant's skull crack. "Without the dragons, how are we to move her? Or will we be taking a chance and leaving her in these woods."

Bally's brows rose. "We can't leave her!" Then, almost automatically, his attention moved to Dora. "Or can we?"

Dora wasn't one to hesitate, but she was careful how she worded her answer. "To end the Bahidicaras, we need all the villagers."

There was a moment of silence as they all seemed to reflect over what this meant. Dora hadn't spoken about what was going to happen once they reached Lantern's Edge, or once they got to this point. But she had a feeling she hadn't needed to.

The girl knew.

Heime knew.

Bally didn't.

Dora and the young elf had so much in common. If only she would be around after this blew over . . . she would love to nurture him in the way he'd always needed to be nurtured. To be a mother.

She would have liked that very much.

"Gloria growing into an old woman was never in the cards, Bally." All three of her companions looked up at her. She offered a warm smile, specifically to her little elfin friend. Bally didn't move a muscle. He was kind, not stupid. "Now then, I suppose we should be on with it," Dora stated. They had a schedule to keep after all.

She was just messing with the jars around her belt, confirming that they were all in order, when Cee-Cee stated the obvious. "Okay but—seriously, yo. What are we supposed to do with her?"

The girl's expression was hard, it was an affect she'd worked hard to achieve . . . to keep in place. But even through all the armor she wore, anyone within close range could see the quiver in Cee-Cee's chin as she gestured to where her mother slept over the desolate ground.

Dora sighed, then reached for the girl's hand and held it tightly in her own. "I wanted you to have as much time with her as time allowed, unfortunately the clock has grown tired." As she held the girl's hand, she removed her glamour. Her skin darkened and her scars returned, along with a smattering of freckles that laid across her nose.

The girl gasped.

"See now, we aren't all that different, you and I."

Cee-Cee was only about an inch shorter than Dora, and as she looked up into the witch's golden eyes, she lifted a hand up to meet the scars on her cheek.

"*She* did this to you," she whispered.

"Yes," Dora affirmed. "And the person you were, once upon a time, healed it for me."

A look of understanding seeped across the girl's face, and then something happened that nearly broke Dora's ancient heart into pieces. A tear fell from Cee-Cee's eye, down her cheek, and lingered by her chin. Just as it was about to fall to the ground, Dora held out a hand and caught it. As it evaporated into her brownish palm, she whispered, "Aye, for she is still, at the heart of all things, a magic maker."

Cee-Cee's brows turned down just slightly in the middle, but she chose to leave the comment hanging in the air. Dora didn't care if her words confused her. Dora knew in her heart what she meant, and that was that regardless of whatever life this soul lived, she was always going to be a descendant of Hecate and she would always have magic at her disposal. These eyes Dora was looking into didn't belong to her sister anymore. They were positioned into a new body with a new life; and if she was given the chance, her powers would grow and become more refined. She could rebuild the Hecate name in a positive light and grow their ancient magic to what it was and had always stood for. If all was fair in love and war, those eyes would see a new day.

Dora couldn't be sure they would. But she *was* sure that she would die trying.

Ever so slowly, the glamour Dora used began to return and as it did, she took a hesitant step to the side. "I am sorry you couldn't have more time with her, but as you can see, every second that she lives is torture." As the witch spoke, she pulled out her wand and began to unbuckle the jars from her belt. Laying them down next to her feet, she opened the first. She then knelt next to Gloria and set her wand against her head. "Once she's free, she'll be weak, but you'll be able to say good-bye."

Immediately, the girl fell to her knees next to the witch, placing her hand over Dora's now paled skin. "Do you have to do this?"

With the sincerest of apologies, she nodded. "I'm afraid so." Then, before the girl could try and stop her, she said, "'Tis either this or let the village have the opportunity to live on." Then, in a graver tone, she added, "'Tis either this or impale her chest with the Sword of Avalon. At least this way, she feels nothing, and she has the chance to hold her child in her arms one last time and feel your heart beat next to her own without burden."

That first tear that Dora collected was nothing compared to what came next. As white, gold, and greenish light began to flow from Gloria's body into one single stream that easily entered Dora's wand, and as she emptied the first batch into that first glass jar, she noted the sniffling that was coming from the girl. When she emptied the second batch, Bally came to sit beside his friend—his hands around her shoulders. And when it was all over, that third jar full of glowing Cronie souls, Anastacia Montgomery fell into Bally's arms. Her body shaking, her chest heaving.

Dora stood out of the way, securing the jars back around her waist. "'Tis because you love," she said, a small quiver to her lips. "That is why it hurts. But I must stress this, 'tis better to love and endure this sort of pain than to never have loved at all."

Cee-Cee pulled away from Bally just enough to wipe at her nose and look up at the witch. Dora had a feeling that before all this, before the girl had known what she was or that she'd lived down the street from a lost Erwain her entire life, Cee-Cee may have cocked her eye at the witch and said something snarky. But as it was, the girl had aged many years in the span of only a few days. She'd been robbed of her body only to get it back so that she could look into the eyes of the mother who she'd thought dead.

She was no longer a child. Not a girl. She was a magical woman ready to take on whatever laid before her.

And then Gloria's eyes opened.

It was clear, being the vessel for that long had taken its toll on the Hecate witch. She looked older as she sat up— even the hair closer to her head began to turn gray. Still, she had eyes but for two souls.

She looked to Dora first. "Thank you," she said, so candidly that even the wicked may have felt an erratic heartbeat in their chest. Then she turned to her daughter, immediately opening her hands to her as if they were a blooming flower. "Anastacia." Her breath shook in her lungs as her daughter crumbled into her chest. Her hands wrinkled as she patted Cee-Cee's back. "Do you know why I gave you that name?"

"No," the girl whispered.

A tear slid down Gloria's withering cheek and she sighed. "It means resurrection."

Though the two were shaking in each other's arms, Gloria still managed to pull away so that she could look into her daughter's eyes. "You are strong, baby. You've been reborn, and you don't do that if you don't think you can finish what you set out to do the first time."

Cee-Cee continued to purse her quivering lips tightly together, her face having a small seizure. Finally, she unlocked one of her hands from around her mother only so she could wipe at her eyes, before tightening her grip over Gloria's shoulder once more.

"I guess she was right along," stated the girl.

Gloria licked her cracking lips; she was dying. In seconds, she would be gone. It was the curse of having consumed so much dark magic for so very long. "Who was right, baby?" she whispered.

Cee-Cee shook her head and chuckled. "Kayla. That crazy faery knew it all along. Names are more important than we'll ever know."

Gloria nodded, her own lips pursed so very tight. Her gaze dipped to what had been slid into the belt around her daughter's waist. A wand. *The* wand. "Then you know. When the time comes, hand it over to she who needs it. It's locked in there, like a key. It's the only way to turn the lock. The only way to end this."

Dora, Bally, and Heime stood apart from the two as Gloria's light began to dim from her eyes. It was almost as if they could hear it, her heart slowing. The organ was tired, and it was ready for slumber.

Gloria died in her daughter's arms. There is no need to draw out the pain, for it could've colored the largest canvas along the largest wall. And living in that moment wasn't what Cee-Cee wanted. No, the girl wasn't one to dwell, she was one to get even. A trait that she'd perhaps added to her repertoire after spending her previous life in the shadow of the Crone. Cee-Cee wasn't obedient any longer and she wasn't about to stand apart from the army that had gathered to end the disease that followed her into her current body like a parasite.

So she held her mother, *like she was the mother*, and when she was ready, she set her down into the earth—leaving her with quiet words that were meant only for Gloria to hear. When she stood, she faced her company and looked to Dora.

"Lead us, witch. Lead us to Lantern's Edge."

"Yes," Dora said, the glass jars glowing as they hung from her belt.

And with that, the four of them—two witches and two elves—made their way to the end, and as she marched on, just behind

Dora, Cee-Cee kept her hand on the hilt of the wand they'd found inside that miniature cabin, her mind cycling through the images she'd seen when she'd first taken the tool into her hand.

It wasn't just an ordinary wand. It was the truth, and besides the Sword of Avalon, it was the only other thing that could end the Crone of Light's End.

$\mathbf{\$ \quad 39 \quad \$}$

Makayla

Our magical team of misfits had dispersed carefully around the property. We made sure to stay in sight of each other as we roamed around the lake to where Lantern's Edge stood—or tried to stay standing more like. It reminded me of those cabins you see when you're driving down an old rural highway. Pieces of the past left to rot and decompose. Once we got to the porch, we could see through a missing panel in the door right into the house and then through the other side. I figured the only reason it was in as good of shape as it was, was because the curse had kept it from completely bailing from this world.

It had been an hour or two since we'd arrived. At least that's what it felt like; nobody had a watch (or a cell phone), and the sun was buried by the gray clouds that wouldn't be clearing out until I did what I had to do. The time had managed to scrape by, other than of course my brief encounter with the unexplainable . . .

I'd been off behind the remains of Lantern's Edge, readying to dip a toe into the creek that was now nothing more than a trickle of water. That's when it came to me.

The butterfly.

Listen for the butterflies . . . That was something that had been engrained in me from the time my wings had found me again. When I saw it, a light lit up inside me. Up until this point, the only interaction I'd had with any of my parents since my wedding had been through hallucinations. As soon as I saw those small yellow wings flutter towards me, I stilled. I may have even blushed.

Toby and Petal had been near, but far enough away to miss the butterfly's welcome, and Layla and Blythe were inside the cabin. Fighting. Or a lover's quarrel. We all acted like we didn't know what was going on between the two of them, but we all knew. There had been no mention of them being back together, but from what I'd been told, their parting hadn't been because of anything other than logistics. Layla had wanted to be with the sea. Blythe had wings. That was all there was to it. Toby, Petal, and I pretended not to hear Layla's terse speech to the faery as, "I guess our love will just have to wait for another lifetime," came shooting out from one of the broken windows.

Regardless, no one noticed the winged messenger, or as I slipped my foot from where it was about to dip into the nearly still water and set it back on the earth. I placed my hand in the air—the tips of my fingers lingering before the beautiful—

Rasha.

My head tilted back as my eyes remained over the tiny creature.

It's her name.

The voice was much like the one I'd heard when my grandfather's butterfly had found Cee-Cee and I at 13 Ambiguous Fox. Grainy and squeaky. Fuzzy. But I wasn't speaking to the butterfly, was I? No, someone had sent her to me. Someone . . .

Rumors have made it into the land that the new faery queen to-be may be housing a young swaddling.

My heart picked up its pace. My first thought as the butterfly —as Rasha—fluttered before my nose, was that this was Tanker and Maude sending me a butterfly to scold me for getting knocked up. And what a silly thought that was! But still.

However, the butterfly's next words caught me off guard.

Makayla Wood, this is not the only rumor. There are also insinuations that before you were blessed by the goddess with future life, that you were bit . . . that you've been terminally poisoned. If this is all true, then you should know: your swaddling may be born fanged.

This place had been set to quiet for years, but with my ability to walk over the land and automatically allot creation *everywhere*, the sounds of nature had been picking up. That was until now.

I could hear nothing but the sound of blood pumping in my ears.

It isn't something that has ever happened, at least out loud. There are no texts to read about what you may experience with your new life. No versions of what you must follow. However, WE will accept her. We will teach her. We may even crown her. What I ask of you now, Makayla Wood, is whether you will do so as well?

If your child is what some may allude to as a curse—an abomination—will you assume her to be a burden, or will you love her as she is? I am aware that you've got quite a bit on your plate at this time, but I do require an answer. You see, I cannot possibly hinge forward in one direction or the other without your reply.

It is a necessary thing, you see. I must know. Which direction do you love?

The butterfly lingered, fluttering before me. Its message had been sent and now it was waiting for my reply.

Which direction do you love?

It was such a peculiar question, and still I was stuck over who sent this. Right away I thought of L. The vampire jester who had angled his followers to join our side. This was the way he spoke. But L was dead; I'd watched one of the Robes of Lorelei score his heart with my own two eyes. My thoughts then immediately jutted to Firefox. Just before I'd been torn from Garlandia, he'd sworn himself to me. But this didn't sound like him. Not at all.

I was stuck. Torn. Not to mention terrified.

I'd hardly had time to ingest the idea of becoming a mom at all, let alone add into the equation that I truly did have Morcai venom permanently in my system. Of course this would be something that would or could affect my swaddling.

And then another stray thought popped up. *How did the sender know my child was to be a girl?*

Whoever this was, they were cunning, and my intuition was screaming at me that my answer to their question was going to be life-altering. Whoever this was, was asking me whether I was going to be an ally or an enemy. And how was I to know which was the better option?

As I stood there pondering, the wind shifted. The clouds that had been starting to disperse just enough to catch sight of a yellow sun, once more began closing in over our heads. It immediately became darker. Regardless of the hour, it was quickly beginning to look more like night. I turned briefly from the butterfly to find Toby staring back at me. He then pointed an arm out to the west. Upon catching sight of the four figures—so tiny in the distance—a wave of nausea ran over me. They were too far away to make out their faces, but I already knew who two of them were. Dora and Cee-Cee (or at least Cee-Cee's body). I had no idea who I would see when I next looked into my friend's eyes.

The sword hanging from my side vibrated just enough to let me know that who it was here for was near, and when I glanced down at it, it was softly glowing. A new occurrence. Blythe and Layla stepped out from Lantern's Edge. They stood side by side, staring out into the distance.

The time had come.

My attention quickly snapped back to the butterfly named Rasha and I gulped. It was a good thing, just then, that my mind worked as quickly as a computer.

"I don't know who you are," I whispered to it, "but I assure you that no child of mine—no matter who or what they are—will ever be considered a burden. I may not have planned this, but it's just one thing out of a million other things that I never accounted for. That doesn't mean I won't absolutely love her. And if she has fangs then I'll learn how to show her how to use them." Blythe had fangs after all. It wasn't completely unusual in these worlds.

I paused, assessing the positions of my company. They were all slowly making their way to where I stood. I needed to wrap this up.

"If I survive this, if any of us do, this child will be a new beginning for not just me, but the rest of the world. All I can do is hope that you, whoever you are, agree."

Thunder clapped above our heads and the land shook as if it had been angered. My crew was closer than ever, and our opposing council was slowly coming into focus. It was Dora and Cee-Cee—but who were—oh my god! It was Jeremy and that elf Heime. What in the world?

I had to get ready; I needed to focus. I had to get rid of the butterfly.

Sounding like my king, I stated clearly to Rasha, "The end is upon us. If and when we make it back to our land, I do hope to meet you, whoever you are. All I can hope for is a peaceful introduction. May the gods be with us."

I centered my gaze over Rasha's black beady eyes. "Go," I said. I could've sworn she nodded before flitting through a transparent curtain and back to whoever sent her.

"What was that?" Toby asked, as he and Petal rushed up by my side. Blythe and Layla stepped up just behind my other shoulder. Everyone's gaze was locked on what was coming for us.

"Nothing," I lied.

"'Tis Dora of Lantern's Edge," Petal noted of our incoming company.

Blythe squinted then shook her head. "No. Dora wasn't pale of skin. That's not—"

But just then, the wind seemed to push our opposing council forward and they grew close enough that we could witness as Dora's appearance shifted from the one I'd always known to another. Her skin darkened and her blonde locks became a thick mass of dark auburn hair.

The four of them stalked closer to us and as they did, my hand fell to find the hilt of Avalon's Sword. My heart was racing, my stomach was sour, and the world wouldn't stop spinning. I did want this over with. I wanted to get rid of this nuisance then move on to slay Loral, but then again—to take down the worst of the world I would have to cut into the flesh of the innocent.

No matter how I looked at it, it wasn't fair.

Finally, the moment came. The four of them faced the five of us. We stood maybe twenty feet apart, but still I could make out the scars on Dora's face—the freckles smattered across her nose. Jeremy Love (I couldn't just then quite allow myself to call him Bally), Cee-Cee (or maybe the priestess), Heime, and Dora—they were all looking at us the same way we were peering at them. Firm mouths and hesitant eyes.

Just as I was contemplating who might make that first move, my hand tightening around the sword's handle, Dora stated plainly, "They say come as you are, so here I am." She took a step forward and held out her hands, looking to the sky, the earth . . . everywhere. "Well, Crone, here I am. I've no reason to hide behind a mask any longer." The wind howled in response.

Dora turned to Cee-Cee and held out her hand. Cee-Cee willingly pulled a nearly black wand from her side and handed it to the witch, who then immediately began walking towards us.

My company cinched together, our shoulders all in a snug

line. Petal loosed a whinny. But nobody pulled out a weapon or a wand, not right away.

"Let us wait and see what she is up to," Toby whispered as she got closer.

And then she was before me, holding the wand out as if it were an offering. "What are you waiting for, Makayla? 'Tis answers you've sought from the moment you were born. Well, here they are."

I looked down at the wand in her grasp. It looked burned. I met her eyes for but a second before a slow breath left my lips and I threw caution to the ever-churning wind and picked it up.

❧ 40 ❧

Makayla

J ustice. That's what I worked for all my life. Not because it seemed like a prestigious career, but because I grew up noting every single chink in the chain that our government either hadn't worked out or chose to ignore.

I wanted to do more, not just for our country but for the world. Yes, I lost myself somewhere along the way (quite literally, I might add), but even though I somewhat lost myself to the Harvard emblem that was now more of a fantasy to me than the worlds I'd been inside of, I'd regained my initial reason for wanting to become a lawyer. Normally, when I would assume the daydreams of *Ms. Wood, please address the court,* I would be working for the defense of someone who had been wrongly accused. Now, I was the prosecutor. And oh my goddess did I have one hell of case to make against maybe one of the wickedest criminals known to any world, on any planet.

When I first gripped the wand, I was taken by how heavy it was—not in weight, but if there was such a thing as *feeling* the density of an emotion or a memory . . . Actually, there was such a thing, because the wand weighed more than any object that size or nature should have. I'd held it for only long enough to properly stare down at it, then back up at the witch who'd handed it to me before I was taken again. Taken away this time, into a place that made even the darkest, dankest tree basement feel like a sanctuary. What I saw and heard; it was a tale. And unfortunately for them, there *were* faeries.

⁂

Straight from the witch's cauldron, 'tis an origin tale . . .
Only the one with the right shine shall inherit the last word.
—Miranda

As soon as she was born, the killdeer came. Earl shot it with his arrow and ate it for dinner. It was a mother. Have you ever heard a baby bird cry? I have. I went hungry that night.

I wouldn't have shot a bird like that, but I'd never been entitled to an opinion of my own. I was told from a young age that my life didn't matter. I was no more my own person than the sheep my father raised before the wolf came into our land.

My mama was called a whore. She was called this because my father told any neighbors we might've had that this was so, when in fact my father killed my mama when I was young, then buried her behind the house. He had fair skin while her's was painted darker. Where we lived, in the sticks, there weren't a lot of people who looked like her or I, and the ones I did see never raised their eyes from the dirt. Mama told me once before she left me forever that we had it better than most . . . apparently there were levels in hell. I sure didn't want to descend any further to find out what it looked like at the bottom.

Once my mama was gone, I felt like a stain. Years later, and with a lonely heart, I went back to the spot where my father buried her and took a bone from her arm. I thought it would be nice to have part of her with me.

"Ya best na' star' act'in all strange like yer ma', naw ya hear," my father said the day Earl came to get me from what was left of our house. Or shack, more like.

Earl Pecking was a man who lived closer to a town in a large white house with four fine pillars on the front porch. His folks used to sit on rocking chairs they'd used the trees on their property to craft. This part of the land didn't know a lot of kind faces. The Peckings were kind.

Their son was not.

My father sold me to Earl . . . sold me. Like a sheep. By the time my father did that, Earl's parents were no longer alive. No one knew how they died—they just weren't there one day. If I had to guess, their bones were buried behind that big white house . . . hearts impaled, or skulls broken.

All my father saw in Earl was a man with a big white house. The ignorant fool was so sure he would be filling his empty pockets with gold in no time. Too bad that big old house burned down the day after Earl took the life of the killdeer.

Earl moved us to a plot of untouched land in the woods that the locals steered clear of because it was rumored to have been haunted, and he built us the smallest cabin I'd ever seen. I hadn't spoken nearly a single word since the day my mama was knocked to the ground by my father's hand . . . since the day her head was caved in. When Earl led us into this part of the wood, I kept my lips sealed, but there was something quite different about this land. It sparkled in a way the world didn't have a habit of doing. Earl didn't seem to notice.

My babe was about three months old the day I realized the

sparkle could talk. Earl had beat me so bad the day before that my eyes were nearly swollen shut, and as I rocked my daughter against my chest—sitting under the puffy white clouds above us—I chewed on my fingernail until it tore away from my finger. Blood began to trickle freely. I didn't pay it any mind.

My babe eventually fell asleep, and I was able to get her to feed, for she wouldn't ever latch while she was awake. It was then that I finally listened to the sparkle. There was a code in that glitter and though I didn't know a lot of things, I understood it. I listened as it told me how to spirit walk; how to leave my body.

That day, while my babe suckled in her dreams, I stood apart from the two of us, and as soon as I did, my destiny found me.

"'Tis life feeding from death," said an ominous voice.

When I flipped around, I saw a woman wearing the moon as a hat. When next she spoke, her voice echoed and her likeness vibrated, tricking my eyes to see multiple versions of the woman.

When I had no words to return, the woman stated, "Did you not realize, Miranda, that one always has the choice as to whether they live or die? This man doesn't have to kill you."

It had been so long since I'd spoken that when I chose to do so, it was like learning to talk for the first time. I stuttered as I said, "I-It isn't u-up to m-me."

"Oh?" Her voice was so drawn out that it sounded like it was coming from the other side of a long tunnel. "'Tis only what you've been taught. And child, you've been taught wrong." We stared at one another for a second, before her attention returned to where my body sat on the other side of the sparkle. "'Tis the folly of a man . . . jealously. He cannot create life, cannot feel it in his womb. He tears down what he fears may be above him before she has the chance to see that she is powerful." Her eyes landed on me with a thud. "Do you understand, Miranda?"

"I think so," I whispered.

The woman chuckled, causing the land to vibrate. "You're going to have to do better than that."

The longer I stood in the sparkle, the more I began to see myself as part of it. The trees began to fade, and darkness grew around us. It hugged my shoulders in a way that felt familiar.

"I f- feel my m-mother," I stated, looking around to find that the world I knew was both right there and yet so far away.

The woman licked her finger then stuck it in the air as if she was feeling for the direction of the wind. "I'm not surprised. Everyone experiences this place differently, though not many have the opportunity to come."

My zombie eyes moved to her. "Why h-have you ch-chosen me?"

"'Tis simple."

She sliced through the air with her arm then pointed down to the ground. The image of me and my babe reappeared. Except my babe was no longer sleeping and she was no longer latched. But she was feeding.

"What is she doing?" I asked of my daughter. She had my bleeding finger in her mouth, and she was sucking on it.

"'Tis one reason why I'm here, Miranda. I like to check up on those who've inherited my magic. Sometimes it skips a generation. Sometimes it skips five."

I looked from my likeness back to her. "I don't understand."

"Your mother was like you. She was unaware of the strength she carried, but your father could sense it. He took it upon himself to end it before she could find it. Your husband is no different. You'll soon return here, but without the option to go back." She lifted her head high. "Seems to be quite a waste if you ask me. I don't bless just anyone."

Speaking was getting easier. "Your speech is puzzling."

"But for how long?"

I frowned. Was she assuming to only speak in riddles?

She grinned. "You took the bone of your mother."

"Yes," I admitted.

"What once was taboo will now be your survival. Create life from death—turn the bone of your mother into your wand."

"A wand?"

She grinned. "You didn't eat the killdeer, that's another reason I came."

I bit at my lip.

"Oh, and Miranda," she said, lowering her voice so low my ears thrummed. "Be warned, she suckles at your blood because she was born without the ability to see the sparkle. If she drinks too much, she will gain an unnatural gift."

I blinked several times but could still not absorb her message. "Please do simplify your words."

"The tunnel is not hers. I've handed it to you, Miranda. One day I'll hand it to another. To someone else worthy of my blessings."

Darkness began to fade and once more grass filled in under the soles of my feet and trees began to stand around us like a choir.

"The world looks different when it sparkles," I observed.

"'Tis because you're a witch, Miranda. You can see into the world you belong. 'Tis not the land your body rests on. 'Tis Lorelei. Take your babe and go."

"Lorelei . . ." I'd never heard of such a place. "Is it outside of New England?"

"'Tis old," she stated simply. "'Tis waiting for you."

After that the sparkle began to intensify, and before I knew it, I was sinking away from the woman and her tunnel and back into my body. But as I became one with my flesh, the glitter remained and I heard her whisper, "Follow the sound of wings fluttering."

I kept the experience tucked neatly in the back of my head—afraid that if Earl saw it he would end my life before I had a chance to discover Lorelei. Then, remembering the warning, I pulled my finger from my daughter's mouth. She immediately began to scream and howl. It took less than five minutes for Earl to appear. He held an axe above my head and promised to use it on the both of us if I didn't quiet her down.

I had no choice. I bled for her.

It would have been wiser to let him kill us.

Shortly after that episode, I began to search for Lorelei. With my mother's bone in my pocket, I took my babe and walked into the sparkle. The more familiar I became with it, the more I understood how it spoke. It was like the river—it had currents, and it wasn't long before I heard what I'd been sent to hear—wings flapping.

At first, I thought it was an angel slipping from one plane of existence into another, but as I got closer, following the sound of flapping wings, I couldn't believe my eyes.

My memories of my grandmother were very few and far between, but before she returned to what my mother called the ether, she told me tales of otherworlders. She called them faeries. "If you ever catch sight of one, Miranda—follow it," she'd instructed. I did not hesitate. As soon as I saw those purple eyes and cherry lips that twisted into a mischievous grin, I did as my grandmother had said.

My sleeping babe to my chest, her tummy full of fresh blood, I sauntered through the curtains that no one else in my world seemed to have eyes for, then followed the nearly transparent wings as my guide fluttered over the long grasses. Before long, her wings began beating faster and I lost sight of her. I cursed as she danced away from my sight.

Glancing over my shoulder, I tried to memorize what the woods looked like, for before me was open land. I desired nothing more than to search out this place that could be my new home, but I still needed to know that I could find my way back if so needed.

I wandered for what felt like a lifetime, though the sun had not moved terribly far from where it took its daily route in the sky. I wandered until I came to a medium-sized cabin with a lake out front. Unsure of what to do next, but curious as a cat against the outer side of a glass window, I approached the porch and hesitantly climbed the steps. No one came to the door. Not when I stood there, dumbly, and not when I knocked. Not even when I flung the door open.

It was abandoned.

Not a scrap of evidence to suggest that any soul of any kind lived there.

But there was a black shimmery cape slung over a single wooden chair. When I touched it, I somehow knew that it was mine.

That was the day that I moved in.

✺

Two years passed. I hadn't intended to stay that long without checking back on the old world. I could have cared less about Earl, for the more I was away, the more the witch inside me grew. I realized I didn't have to pretend any longer that I had a taste for poison. Not to mention this place felt more and more like home the moment I found some wood scraps and made a sign. Lantern's Edge .. . for even when darkness seems eminent, there is still always that spark of light. A lantern at the edge of the world to help you find your way.

My babe was growing like a weed. I'd managed to ween her from my blood as much as possible. But no matter how many fish I caught, or game—her tummy fat and full—she would still pull at my finger and beg for me to open a vessel. I did my best to mind the warning I'd been given: ". . . she suckles at your blood because she was born without the ability to see the sparkle. If she drinks too much, she will gain an unnatural gift." She wasn't a witch, at least not in the way I was. But oh! how she wailed when she didn't get her way, and oh how she smiled at me when she did.

A mother is nothing more than putty when she sees her child smile.

I should have paid attention to the way her eyes crinkled as she fed—how a different sort of sparkle lined the irises of her eyes. But I didn't. Not until it was too late.

My daughter had just fed from me the day I saw the wings flutter again; the same wings that I'd followed from the old world into this one. This time, the faery didn't run off.

"*Why hello, young mistress,*" *she said with a coy smile.* "*It's been some time since I last saw you. I see you've settled in.*"

"*Who are you?*" *I asked, my eyes wide in awe. I'd never seen such a spectacular creature.*

"*Aventurine. What do they call you?*"

"*Miranda, and this is—*"

"*Oh no,*" *the faery said, framing the sides of her face with her hands. Before I could finish what I'd started, she came over to me and lifted my finger. Black and blue from how many times I'd let the blood flow.* "*What have you done, Miranda the witch?*"

My shoulders rolled forward in an almost forgotten way. "*A fish,*" *I lied.* "*Clumsy of me, really.*"

"*A fish?*"

She questioned my truth.

"*I was preparing to kill it after catching it for dinner and it got a hold of me.*"

Aventurine's smile slowly faded away and her gaze fell to where my daughter was playing on the ground with my mother's bone. I'd held it in the flames of our fire until it turned black the first night we made this our home, then I carved it until it resembled something useful.

"*'Tis your wand?*" *Aventurine asked, pointing down to where my child was using it to shoot green sparks into the air.*

"*Yes,*" *I answered, folding my hands together in front of my stomach.*

The faery bent down and laid a hand over my child's head. My daughter looked up at her and licked her lips. I bit my own lip in anticipation—willing her not to try and bite at our guest.

When next Aventurine looked up at me, she had formed a plastic smile onto her face. "*She's not inherited your magic, has she?*"

"*I—*" *How did she know that?* "*No.*"

Aventurine stood apart from my babe then stood so close to me I could smell the sweetness on her breath. "*Dearest Miranda, tell me you are not letting this child drink from your magic. 'Tis taboo.*"

I'd never been a good liar. I didn't even try. A slow breath left my overly filled chest.

"Oh no," the faery said, clearly exasperated. She reached for my hands and bundled them into hers. Shaking her head at me, she stated very clearly, "Miranda, you mustn't do this any longer. Do you understand?"

My gaze roamed from the faery's eyes down to where my babe had dropped the wand and was now counting her toes. "She's harmless. I assure you."

"Right now."

I met Aventurine's eyes once more. It was my turn to flash an ingenuine smile. "What's brought you to this neck of the woods today, Aventurine?"

Her entire expression was the reverse of what it had been when she'd first arrived. Even as she spoke, she seemed to be slowly backing away. "I'd heard the rumors that someone had moved into this place. I remembered you from so long ago; one doesn't often forget when someone follows them from one world into the next."

Inside, my guts were churning. The faery wasn't just trying to leave—there was fear in her eyes. In attempt to reverse this, I held out a hand. "Please, don't go yet. It's been so long since I've spoken to anyone." My chin lowered. "Especially someone who doesn't wish me ill will."

The fey stopped in her tracks, her wings lowering from where they'd been slowly reaching for the sky. "Please," she said, reaching forward and taking my hand. "Heed my warning."

My eyes heavy in hers, I whispered, "You're not the first to warn me. I just, it's not that I want to continue, it's that she screeches terribly when I don't."

"Oh now, sweet witch, 'tis not a fanciful thing, having to watch your child ache. But if you don't stop, you'll be sorry. Fey aren't keen on making promises, but this is one promise I can safely make."

I looked down at my feet. "And what if I can't stop. What if she doesn't let me?"

It was quiet until I looked back up. I could have sworn that darkness was whirling behind me in the reflection of Aventurine's eyes.

"Then you shall call on me and I will help you." She then pulled out a sparkling wand from thin air. "Get your wand."

I did as I was told, then faced her again.

"Tip to tip," she instructed. Again, I followed her lead. She then proceeded to mutter a few words that didn't make sense to me, and after that a ball of light moved through her wand into mine. "You now have my number," she said with a slight grin. "Call me whenever you need a friend."

I pulled my tool down and laid it across the palm of my hand. "How does it work?"

"Just say my name," she repeated simply. "The magic will do the rest."

"And if I do not call?"

"Then I shall check up on you in two more years," she said with a wider grin this time. Her wings began to flutter, and she started to back away.

I kissed the tips of my fingers before waving good-bye. "I'm so glad to have met you, Aventurine. I hope to see more of you and your people."

"Then why not explore!" she shouted as she got further away. "'Tis more to this world than Forest Peak. You should dance through the brush until you find the shore. Lorelei is quite lovely all times of the year."

"Lorelei . . ." The word danced over my tongue. "I thought this was Lorelei."

The faery grew dimples. "'Tis just the beginning."

And it was. It was my new beginning. Too bad it was going to have to end.

Seasons didn't change very much in Forest Peak. Most days it was warm and sunny, but now and again the wind would blow and if we were lucky, we got to catch a few snowflakes on our tongues. But if I had to call it, I would say we were in a forever summer.

Most days were spent gathering firewood and fish. Now and again, I hunted. Aventurine had been the only other someone I'd seen, and I was awfully curious about what else this world had to offer. I just wished the seasons would've changed more—that the lake had frozen over. If it had, we wouldn't have been down at its edge that fateful morning, for it was the time of year that in the old world would have been considered Winter.

My babe was for the most part obedient. I'd been diligent about keeping my magic to myself, for I had now been warned twice of what my bloodletting could do. That day, my child was rolling around on the sand that ran around the lake, playing with stones while I threw out the line to try and catch fish.

The day before I'd taught myself to swim, then shortly after had taken my babe into the water and listened to her squeal in delight as her toes danced in the soft currents. She naturally took to moving her arms and legs in the right directions, but she was still just a babe, and I knew better than to let her get too close to the water without having me within arm's reach.

That particular day, however, we had been a little hungrier than normal. It was another reason I needed to explore this world; I was worried we'd caught the majority of the fish in this lake. They were growing harder to come by. We'd been sustaining on moss and berries. We needed some meat. That's why I was concentrating so hard on catching a fish that day that it escaped me when my little one slipped her toes into the lake, cooed, then began crawling until she was all the way in. It wasn't until I heard the yelp that I turned to see air bubbles over the spot she'd just sunk.

The line dropped from my hands, and I lunged for my babe. The water was dark, but the sun was fierce, and I was able to catch sight of her. I dove into the water until I could feel her pudgy little arms.

They were limp. I pulled her into my chest then swam to shore. As I laid her down into the sand her lips were already turning blue. It had taken no time at all for her to ingest the lake.

"NO!" I bellowed.

Unsure of what to do, I gently shook her shoulders, then pumped her chest. When nothing happened, I picked her up and laid her against me—patting her back ferociously. But there was nothing.

Curses filled the air around us as I began to sob, placing my babe back down into the sand and pumping her chest. When still nothing happened, I pulled out my wand and held it to the sky, shouting the name of my faery friend.

A ball of light shot out of the tool and moved at light speed towards the trees in the distance. I sat there for a moment, rocking over my heels, biting my lip. I bit it so hard that it broke the skin, a bead of blood trickling down my chin.

I wiped at it then stared down at my finger.

What I did next was an act of desperation. My whole life, I'd been taught that I was nobody. That my existence was both a disappointment and unneeded. Creating life was the one thing I'd done right—the one thing no one could take away from me.

I couldn't let her go. Even if help came, at this rate it would be too late.

My finger shaking, I placed it in my babe's mouth. Her tongue was cold and lifeless as the blood on my finger felt at it. But then it happened—her little lips wrapped around my finger, and she sucked.

From that moment, I didn't hesitate. I pulled a knife from my side and slit my wrist open, laying it next to my child's mouth. As it trickled in, she drank, and the more she drank the more color filled in around her cheeks. Finally, she opened her eyes.

By the time Aventurine appeared by our side's minutes later, my child was sitting up, sucking from my limb like it was sweet nectar.

"Miranda, no," Aventurine said with a gasp.

My gaze slowly lifted to meet hers. "She was dying . . . I had no other choice."

The faery fell to her knees and gently pulled my child away from my arm. My daughter was giggling, and as Aventurine pulled her in to have a good look at her, the faery forced a playful smile. "Hello there," she sang, looking into the child's eyes. I noted how my babe's pupils rose and fell as she did. "Miranda, you should heal that," the faery said, referring to the gash on my arm.

"I'm not sure how," I muttered. My child had taken a lot of my blood. I was weak.

Aventurine held out her wand and without saying a word, pointed it at my arm. Within seconds, my skin was sutured. Only a slight pink line to denote there had ever been a gash.

"It's time you learn some things." Her gaze was still settled into my daughter's. "For starters, we're going to have to fix this."

"Fix what?" I questioned.

"You gave her magic during a time where her soul was in limbo. She saw something—" She was peering into her eyes like they were doors into an otherwise locked galaxy. "I'm seeing some sort of tunnel . . ."

"The tunnel! Yes, I've been there. The woman who saved me, who told me to find this land—she told me it was mine."

Aventurine's gaze moved so slowly towards mine that I almost expected the earth to shake. "You've been given the tunnel?" Then, before I could answer, she added, "You're a daughter of Hecate?"

"I—I never learned the woman's name."

"Not a woman. A goddess."

I hesitated. "Wh-What?"

A weighted sigh escaped the faery's perfect lips. "Oh dear, Miranda. I was not aware you came from such power." My child still within her grasp, she stated heatedly, "We must remove the magic from her; and if worse comes to worse, we must hide your magic so that she can get to it no more."

I thought for a second that she must be joking. I had only just earned my magic; I didn't want to hide it away. And even if it came to that— "How would we even do such a thing?"

Without pause, she went on to instruct me. "First, you must make your wand untouchable by others. 'Tis your tool and yours alone. No one should be able to access it. After that, remove your child's magic, and be thorough for even the smallest twinkle left next to her heart could sour her. If she is still exhibiting signs that she is demanding of your magic, you must shelter your own sparkle. And do not fret, you only need to hide it away until she grows old enough to forget about it."

With a heavy heart, I nodded. And from there, with Aventurine's guidance, I removed my magic from my daughter's heart. It went into my wand where it would eventually flow back into me.

Things were fine after that for quite some time. My daughter began to age, and we even welcomed a few more visitors. Aventurine visited often and began to bring more fey and other witches along with her. It was a merry time. I learned a lot from my neighbors and before I knew it, I was starting to become very tuned in with my powers. If I ever had to see Earl or my father again, I wouldn't have to raise a finger to let them feel the wrath I felt towards them.

My little girl was six when the milk turned sour.

The day had finally come. We were to trek through the brush and forest into Lorelei. Aventurine was to be our guide. I'd worked continuously for days on end to ensure we were prepared for the journey. We had plenty of jerky and berries to get us by. I was inside packing up the last of the rations when I heard it—the shriek.

I didn't hesitate, I came running out of the house, down the porch stairs—and that's when I saw it. My precious baby lifted her mouth from the pile of flesh and wings that laid dead on the ground. Blood ran down my child's chin.

"I can't yet see it."

I just stood there, struck down by numbness.

My voice shook as I took two gentle steps towards her. "Baby, what have you done?"

"You won't let me use your magic anymore, so I had to try and use hers."

I stepped in even closer, looking away as soon as Aventurine's lifeless face came into view. Her eyes were frozen on the sky above her.

"I want to go to the tunnel again."

"The tunnel," I whispered.

"I saw it when I died that day. But then you took it away from me. I want it back."

Though I'd never made it to the Lorelei shore, I knew in that moment what it felt like to have a wave crash over me.

From there, I did what I had to do. You see, a killdeer represents defending your loved ones. It also opens our eyes to new paths. I didn't eat the killdeer and the goddess gave me a special gift. I wasn't going to let her down, nor was I going to sacrifice my daughter.

I kissed Aventurine's forehead then sent her to the lake. After that I waited until my child was sleeping contentedly—for our trip was going to have to be delayed. Once she was out, I removed the magic from her as Aventurine had shown me to do all those years ago. And then I removed all of mine. When all was said and done, I placed my wand somewhere far from where we'd made our home. Earl was no longer living in the small cabin. No one was. I figured the hiding spot would be a fine one; the cabin was after all between worlds. Only those with the sight for it, would be able to enter.

Now comes the important part. If you're listening to my story, then this means my magic knew you needed to hear it. It also means I failed, for the only reason anyone would need to know what happened at Lantern's Edge, would be if I accidentally left any spark of Hecate in my daughter. 'Tis unnatural to her heartbeats and goddess knows what she's capable of. For she bit into that faery's neck as if she was a lion.

Aventurine told me one more thing the day I brought my child back to life at the lake's edge. She said when a soul whose energy does not match that of a great magnetic pull (the likes of which can be found in THE TUNNEL) then that soul can rewire itself in a very unbecoming way. Its vibrations can go awry and essentially cause it to become terminally unstable.

The soul becomes a different entity.

I never for one second wanted to believe my daughter had been transformed into something so foul and demented that the only way to send her so far into the void that she would never be able to come back was to instruct her to do so.

When a soul becomes what my precious child became, it binds its identity so deep inside itself that no one can ever find it. People look at it and either cannot remember who this soul is, or they begin to start calling it by another name. Aventurine warned me of this. I should have done something when she started referring to my child as Polly.

I never would have named my daughter that. Even when that's all I saw when I looked at her. But for some reason, I decided to just go with it.

If you've found this wand and you're hearing my speech, then I was unable to do what I set out to do when I returned to Lantern's Edge. I was going to walk my child to Lorelei and find someone who could help us. Who could take the lich and give me back my little girl. Because she was all I had left. She is all I have left.

There are some things a mother doesn't forget. The way her babe first looks at her after coming into the world . . . that first smile . . . the way her baby smells after she's been cleaned. How soft that new hair is on her head.

And the reason for why you named her what you did.

My life wasn't good before I knew my child. In hindsight, it wasn't good after (not if you can hear me), but at least we had a shot. Polly is a happy name. It's nice but I never would've picked it. Neither would have Earl.

I needed something that wouldn't fade away, and that's the meaning of her true name.

If you are listening, then know this—you have my blessing. I am sorry for my failures, but I will never be sorry for trying to bring back my child. No mother would live on a single day knowing that she hadn't tried all she could to save the love of her life.

And so, with no further ado, my distant traveler, I shall tell you her name.

'Tis—

❧

I came back to with a stiff neck and the wand shimmering back into a dull black stick. Or bone. The wand was made from bone.

"Well then," Dora asked. Her new likeness was still throwing me for a loop. "Did you hear the name?"

I gulped.

"Yes," I whispered.

"Good." She turned and nodded back to her company. "Then let's get this show on the road."

"Wait," I sputtered. "Wh—What's a Lich?"

Cee-Cee and Jeremy stood still as stone, but everyone else gasped.

Dora centered her now golden irises over my shoulders. Peeling her lips apart, she said, "In the case of the woman who birthed me, 'tis an entity who grows into their power by usurping the magic of others. In rare cases, the lich may rise to the power of a god. And like a demon, there is only one way to end its reign."

"By impaling its chest with a mystical blade while saying its name," I whispered.

"Yes," was all that Dora said.

❧ 41 ☙

Makayla

The wand had long since fallen from my hand into the grass. Because of the power I carried at my fingertips, flowers bloomed—root systems discovered old land and returned to where they'd once belonged. Still, I felt more discombobulated than ever.

"How did you know what she was?" I asked Dora, not even trying to cover up my accusing tone.

"Aye," said the witch. "I found the wand when I was but a child."

My face was taking it upon itself to move into odd expressions. My eyes cramming themselves shut of their own accord, my lips pursing. Blood simmered through my veins.

Dora took her time looking everyone present in the eye before stating clearly. "This is a case of a perfectly normal soul who incarnated into a body and then became exposed to vibrations that changed the make-up of its soul. My mother was born mundane. She was first exposed to magic in a way no ordinary person should be, but pile on a near death experience with an even heavier dose of raw magic—her soul transformed. 'Tis the reason she was so obsessed with gaining control. 'Tis the nature of a lich to do so. Her soul was no longer human when it was taken from her body; it was monstrous, and there are rules against certain vibrations returning to new life. Her soul was aware she would never be able to reincarnate without the attachment of someone who could, thus why she was so adamant about merging her power with someone else. It wasn't just to gain power; it was to ensure that she had a ticket back into this world if anyone dared tried to separate her from it."

Heime was staring down at where I'd let the wand fall to the ground. "Isn't a lich but a demon?"

"There are differences," stated Dora, "but many similarities. Demons cannot reincarnate which is why they possess people. The Crone, in essence, used possession when she created the coven of Light's End. Those poor souls never had a chance."

Never had there been a truer statement. That was how a cult worked after all; the leader got into the skin of their people and then had their way with them.

"Well, let's get on it with it then," Blythe spit out, taking a step forward. "Let's kill the bitch."

"Yes, let's," Layla added dryly. "Where is the cunning Crone anyway?"

"In here."

Dora moved out of the way just as Toby's hand cupped my arm.

Heime took a step to the side and Cee-Cee stepped forward. Her hand was still tied to Jeremy's. "She's in here," she repeated.

My chin quivered as Toby very slowly took his free hand and placed it on my lower back. The way Cee-Cee was looking at me, it was almost apologetic. Before I could overthink things, I blurted out, "Why do you look sorry—this isn't your fault."

Cee-Cee shook her head and her eyes watered. "I don't know, Kayla."

I gritted my teeth as I turned my head towards Dora. By now I had learned that all Dora had ever wanted was to end this, but still I *hated* her. "Why couldn't you just have told us the truth from the beginning?"

"Because we were and are working with a grenade."

"So you made sure that the pin was pulled, and then" —I pointed to Cee-Cee— "you stuffed the pin back in?" I scrunched up my face. "Why did you even come at her with that unbinding spell if you were just going to push the Crone away again?"

"I was the one who shoved her back down."

I flinched in Cee-Cee's direction. I had a lot to say. All of which was aimed at Dora. So without further ado, I let my friend's comment evaporate then adjusted my gaze to fit back into the witch's golden irises.

"Why did we even have to go through all of this?" Shaking my head and throwing my hands up in the air—ignoring Toby's hand clutching me tighter, I continued to rattle on. "Why did we even have to come here at all! I mean, we were all there together on Garlandian soil—I had the sword then just as I do now! Why all the theatrics?"

It was clear that I was coming undone, but I could've cared less. Every inch and hair on my body was shaking, my voice was unsteady, and the world was buzzing. To hell with all of it.

Almost annoyingly composed, Dora clasped her hands together and said, "The priestess had to be awakened; 'tis why

I gave your friend the unbinding spell. I was careful to ensure she didn't remember everything, but eventually she still uncovered her truths. Next, we had to get the vessel, so that is why my company and I had to travel away, and then we had to get the wand—"

"The wand!" By now I was starting to sound a bit eccentric. "You had already listened to what it had to say— you *knew* her name this entire time!"

She was shaking her head. "I'm afraid I did not."

"What?" I asked, cocking a brow to the sky.

"She didn't," Cee-Cee said. "And neither did I when I held it. Anyone with magic can hold that wand and hear Miranda's story, but only the one with magic and the tool to take her down, would ever be able to hear the priestess's name."

Quiet. It was irritably quiet.

"As for the rest," Dora explained. "It started on these grounds; therefore, this is where it must end. This is where things must be put to rest."

I had more to say—so much more, but suddenly it became very clear that we weren't the only ones here any longer. The clouds had already been bothered, for they'd started churning above our heads as soon as this other group walked the land, but now the wind was picking up. Howling, like it had already been through many wars and didn't want to participate for the hundredth time.

"She's here," Layla whispered.

"Correction," Dora stated, looking up at the twisting cyclone directly above us. "She's *been* here. She's simply tired of being stowed away."

"Hang on," I spit out. "What happened to Miranda? Sure, she left the wand for us to find, but she never had the chance to say what—"

"I killed her."

Dora moved out of the way and the body that belonged to

my friend stepped an inch closer to where I stood. Except Cee-Cee wasn't there anymore, at least not anywhere on the surface. I noted as Dora nodded to Jeremy, who then flicked his chin back at her before stepping in line with Heime. They were up to something, but the priestess didn't care. She had eyes only for me.

Blythe, Layla, Petal, and Toby began inching around me as the priestess slithered closer. Out of the corner of my eye, I thought I saw Dora whisper into Blythe's ear, but that wasn't where my attention needed to be. I had a snake to track.

"My mother," said the priestess with a sour tongue, "had the nerve to tuck her magic away, thinking that would stop me from being who I am."

"She was trying to save you," I snapped. "She loved you, as a mother should love a child."

The foul spirit narrowed Cee-Cee's eyes into slits. "Will you love your child if she turns out to be a monster?" Her nostrils flared. I hated that she'd been inside my head—that she knew my thoughts. "Will you, Makayla Wood?"

"Koehaias," I hissed.

She cocked her head to the side. "Still?"

Toby tightened his hold over me and whispered in my ear. "She's trying to dig her claws into you, my queen. Do not let her. She'll taunt you until you spear the chest belonging to your friend."

Steam exiting my nostrils, my wings more rigid than I'd ever felt them to be, I shot back at him, "Isn't that what I'm here to do."

Green lightning struck the ground feet from where Dora stood, causing my attention to waver over to where the witch was standing. It was then that I realized that Heime, Blythe, and Layla were each standing around us with a glowing glass jar in each of their hands.

"What's going on?" the priestess asked heatedly.

"Sorry, Mother," Dora said, though her gaze was anywhere but on Cee-Cee. "I know you had a plan, but I have a different one. Do not worry, Avalon's distraction and Titania's war were not for nothing. I will still reign victorious."

"Oh? And what plan are you alluding to?" asked the priestess.

Dora's gaze roamed around until it met the lich. "I wasn't talking to you."

"Then what *mother* are you referring to exactly?" questioned the priestess with a scoff. When next she spoke, her voice bellowed in a way no earthly persons should. "I'm the one who birthed you!"

"You did birth me, but you were never my mother. The second you slit your mother's throat and ate her heart, the gods were alerted. When you turned up the volume on your scheming, so did they. They sent down their children, but a child of a god is incarnated just as any other soul." Dora walked over the restructured land. "I didn't know who I was. Not until the day you tried to drown me in that lake. That's when she came to me and told me what I was brought here to do."

"Oh?" the priestess mocked. "And who exactly do you lay claim to be? If you're not my daughter, then who do you and Malina belong to?"

"Malina was just an innocent bystander. All she ever wanted was to live her life. Her only crime was falling into the wrong body. I, however, was sent here by my true mother. Hecate. And even if she's not her true daughter, Malina belongs to Hecate as well. You have never been a mother. Not for one second. You gave up the opportunity to know love a long time ago."

Lightning struck above us, thunder clapped, and just as it started to rain bullets, Dora lifted a wand into the air and shouted, "NOW!"

I stood frozen in Toby's arms as Heime, Layla, and to my utter horror—Blythe—sucked down the glowing light inside each of the vials in their hands.

Makayla

Cyclones dropped from the sky like the gods themselves were throwing punches, and lightning struck with the rhythm of a strobe light. Toby was still clutching my arms, Petal kicking her front hooves up repeatedly, as one by one the glass jars in the hands of our sorted company disappeared. Heime, Layla, and Blythe's throats glowed as whatever was inside of those vials was ingested.

"What did they just drink?" I said into Toby's ear.

"The remains of the bad village," answered my king.

My jaw unhinged and ticked as I tried to make sense of why they all would have done that. There wasn't time to think. Especially not when Cee-Cee's eyes had begun to glow as if she'd swallowed nuclear waste. The pink I'd given to her hair once upon a time began to bleed back to black and she held out her arms as if she was collecting all the elements from all corners of the world.

One by one, Blythe, Layla, and Heime fell to their knees —reaching for their throats. I gripped Toby's arm. "What's happening to them!"

By now the unthinkable had happened. The sky had fallen upon us. A cyclone, half the size of a football field, had come down around us. It sounded like a train moving in a continuous pattern. It didn't push us; it didn't pull us. It simply hugged an unescapable boundary.

An angry woman's voice billowed from Cee-Cee's lips. "Fools!"

Dora, who had been unusually calm through this entire venture, simply looked to the creature who had birthed her. "Perhaps," was the one word to run away from her lips.

"Did you really think I couldn't smell it on you this whole time? Your true identity? That blonde hair and those blue eyes could never have covered—"

"Yes, actually. I know I had you fooled, for if you'd remembered who you were early on, you could have balanced the planet over your finger." Dora's head met her shoulder. "Let's not pretend any longer."

A low growl vibrated out from under the priestess and as it grew, the ground shook—still the cyclone stayed wrapped around us. Heime had his hand around his throat, wiggling around the ground like a worm, when suddenly his eyes went blank and he started crawling towards the priestess.

"Yes," she affirmed, though a growl still seemed to be exuding from her presence. Like it was a recording coming out from her pores. "Come to me, my lovelies."

It was then that I realized Blythe and Layla were mimicking the elf. Army crawling to their master. They'd been possessed by the bad village.

"No," I whispered. I turned to my king. "What did Dora do?"

But Toby didn't answer, instead, he just kept clinging to me. Protecting me.

"Toby!" I yelled through the restless energy spiking through this wind tunnel. "Answer me!" Tears of rage were starting to pop up at the corners of my eyes and my expression was twisting. Still . . . he remained stiff.

And then the words that had been readying to tip over from the moment we traveled into this world slipped out of my mind and into the open. *He's not really there. He's been showing me and everyone else what we need to see and feel. But he's not . . . really . . . there.*

I held onto his mannequin arm and screeched at the top of my lungs. I didn't care that this was what we'd been leading up to this entire time, that *this* was the moment of no return. I just wanted out. And so I crammed my eyes shut and began to let my dust whirl from my toes, to the bottoms of my feet, up my legs, through my body—until—

"You chose to do this."

My transition came to a screeching halt. My second ever POPPING experience ended before it even really lifted off into space. Static ran through my veins when next I opened my eyes.

This is how it all started. The vision of a ghostly queen. Her presence not so much haunting but pressing. Like she was nudging me every step of the way—showing me how to roll back my shoulders, lift my chin, and one day how to spread my wings and—

"Fly."

I turned, though the cyclone continued to churn, and the priestess howled as if she was growing stronger, I squared my shoulders with Titania. Other than the glow coming off her skin, she was completely whole. Wings and all.

It was elementary and completely mundane, but I was weak, and it was all I had to offer. "What?"

Next to her, another figure appeared. A young woman, clothed in seaweed. Somehow, I just knew she was—
"Avalon."

"We're here," said Titania, "to remind you."

There was a tremble to my voice. "Of what?"

This time Avalon spoke. "That you found us. After so many years, it was *your* spirit that finally found *us*. Who showed enough strength and will to end this nightmare."

My chest was moving erratically and if I'd been grounded enough to have even an ounce of bodily awareness, I would have tasted the bile coming up my throat for the zillionth time in days. But the adrenaline my body was producing was enough to distract me. Except there was still that one thing that I'd been trying to run from this whole time. And not even the cyclone or two ghostly queens could tear me away from it.

"He's gone."

Titania and Avalon simply kept their gaze firmly over mine.

"That's not true," Avalon whispered, pointing across the way.

And sure enough, there was Toby, standing next to Jeremy, whispering into his elongated ear.

I jostled my head softly. "He's not really there."

Titania placed a glowing hand over my shoulder. "Every life offers something unique. Your soul has already known love. It has known destruction. This life is for glory."

A tear ran down my cheek into my lips until I tasted the sparkle. "No . . . why would I write a story for myself without love?"

"You chose the crown. You chose the weight of its symbolism. You chose to be great."

"You chose sacrifice," Avalon echoed. "It does not mean you'll never love again."

"You are great because of the love in your heart," Titania added.

My mind was reeling, the action was spreading just mere steps away from where I stood. Dora was calmly watching as our friends roamed around the priestess, reaching for her like they wanted to be inside her. Their teeth were chattering—they moved like spiders crawling around a web. And then there was Jeremy Love, walking steadily towards the priestess.

Titania and Avalon walked away from my side, taking opposing positions. Toby was between them, and as I stood there with my jaw still shaking, and my hand clasping not the hilt of Avalon's Sword, but the blade—the three of them began to form a circle around the rest of us. They were chanting something in a language I'd never heard, and then a whisper only for me to hear.

Fly.

I looked down to find my hand dripping blood. I'd gripped the blade too tight again and my blood was sinking into the silver and bronze. The sword was trying to tell me what I needed to do.

"Fly?" I questioned. My stitching had become so loose that one could almost see my light coming through the cracks. "Why do you keep telling me to fly?"

Fly away? Fly up? What did this bloody thing want from me?

Meanwhile, Dora was in the midst of facing off with the priestess. Her hands were out before her as though she was reaching for something. The closer she got to the lich, the more they began to glow.

As her toes danced over the grounds, her words rang out and danced around the priestess's head. "Dear Crone, you failed to ever mention what the dragon's breath was for."

The priestess, whose eyes had continued to burn like

green fire, looked straight across at the witch growing nearer. "Dragon's breath." The two words echoed.

"The test," Dora chirped. "Only the stronger of the twins, the one who could communicate with the beasts, could attain the breath you so dearly wanted for yourself."

"Who ever said I wanted it?" the priestess questioned with a click of her tongue.

"You wouldn't have gone to such lengths if you didn't need it. You could have conjured any other sort of game for us to play. To show you who had the gift you so grossly salivated over."

Cee-Cee's head ticked. "You don't know what you're talking about."

Dora grinned. "Oh, but I do."

Jeremy was now so close to pure evil that he could have reached out and touched it. Meanwhile, Titania, Avalon, and Toby were still stalking around us. And the fated sword attached to me was still telling me to fly.

Dora hammered on. "From the moment you accessed the tunnel, all you could think about was getting back in. Because the tunnel is the entrance to the land of the gods. But it also has a safety key, doesn't it?" the witch asked condescendingly. "Even if you could collect enough hearts and souls—enough magic—you still wouldn't be allowed in. But aha! You thought of something that had to work, for dragons were brought here by the gods, therefore their breath would have to be the key to getting out of that tunnel and into their world." Dora paused, now face to face, nose to nose with the soul of the damned. "What were you planning to do then, I wonder? Did you really think you could disarm every single god and goddess, then take the reins for yourself?" When the priestess did nothing more than snarl, Dora grinned. "I suppose all that blood-letting did make you mad. You see,

Lantern's Edge was meant to shine light on those who had been raised by darkness. The tunnel, which you interpreted as Light's End actually leads to the brightest light there is ever, in any world, in any galaxy." Dora then removed the cloak from around her shoulders and handed it to Jeremy before bravely gripping the hands belonging to Anastacia Montgomery. The priestess looked down but didn't react, at least not right away. "You were never the Crone of Light's End, you were but an unfortunate product of a witch who only ever wanted to believe that darkness could be reversed. And though it can in some cases, you were never going to let go of what you saw and of the power you felt when you saw it." And then, without looking at anyone, Dora shouted at the top of her lungs, "NOW!"

My heart was already racing but just then it started fluttering into a muddled pace. I wanted to throw up again, but there wasn't time. My legs were buckling, and the sword was getting too heavy. Jeremy looked at me with a set of extra wide eyes, "Now Makayla! Fly!"

Fly.

Fly where? What was I supposed to do?

Panicked, I watched as Dora began reciting a spell. As she did, the priestess began to shriek, trying to pull her hands away from where Dora had them tied down with her own. Heime, Blythe, and Layla had frozen from where they had been looking up to the priestess like they were baby birds waiting to be fed, and now light was beginning to seep from their throats up into the air that existed between witch and lich.

Toby passed behind me as he, Avalon, and Titania continued to march in a circle just inside of the cyclone. "Fly, my queen," he whispered.

Then, as if on cue, everyone who still had a voice—other than the priestess of course—began chanting the unbearable word. *Fly, fly, fly.*

My head was spinning, and my tongue felt swollen in my mouth as my gaze rested over Toby's. "I love you," I whispered. Still chanting, he blinked, and though it was but a feeling—I could have sworn his voice danced through my head. *I love you too, my queen.*

Jeremy called my name and when I turned to him, he had urgency in his eyes. "NOW, MAKAYLA! FLY!"

I was operating on improv. No one had given me any special training. Ever since my wings had returned to me, the advice had been "search within." Every. Single. Time.

Now there was instruction, but it was vague, and it didn't make any sense. Still, I wiped the blood from my hand and whispered a spell to heal the cut. When the flesh was united, I gripped Avalon's Sword and let my wings pull me from the ground.

I centered myself over the main event. Dora had stopped chanting and Heime, Blythe, and Layla were lying still on the ground—their eyes closed. The contents of what they had swallowed was now thick in the air between Dora and the priestess. For one fleeting moment, the witch of Lantern's Edge, Hecate's own daughter, craned her neck up and stared me dead in the eyes. "You have my cousin's creation at your fingertips and my other cousin's blade. Use both, and don't forget to say her name."

Before my next heart's beat, she returned her gaze to the priestess, closed her eyes, and then—then all the light and darkness went into her. Cee-Cee's body fell back into Jeremy's arms just as Dora's body bent backwards in the most unnatural way. Her mouth opened and the most heart wrenching wail escaped. When she reopened her eyes, she was looking straight at me. The green fire was back.

"NOW!" Bally screamed.

I shook my head, my wings fluttering so erratically that I

was worried they would spin me out into the cyclone. But then I caught sight of Titania. She was looking at me and she was nodding.

I'd chosen this. Not the other way around.

I wrote this for myself. *My soul wanted this.*

A slow hiss began to emanate from down below and then it happened.

Through most of this ordeal, I'd spent more energy escaping my reality than sitting with it. But I do recall wondering when I might first meet the soul that thought me worthy enough to bind herself with me. The spirit of someone who thought me great enough to want me to love her. To choose me to be her mother.

It was so slight that I couldn't believe I felt it, but then it happened again, and I knew this time for sure that the moment I'd been so curious about had finally come. My lips quivered and I chanced a quick glance at Toby. Whether he was real or not, I had to assume that part of him was still here. "Her wings just fluttered for the first time," I said. And though it was slight, in between chants, he smiled.

That was it—all I needed. I'd hand-picked this life and I'd chosen the form of someone who followed through. Who was capable of achieving the impossible. Yes, my mental health had been on thin ice ever since leaving Garlandia, but my guard was back up and I was ready to strike.

Jeremy was busy laying Cee-Cee's body on the ground and pulling the others towards her when I yanked the Sword of Avalon from my belt and held it high over all our heads. "Crone!" I yelled, and the green eyes shot up to meet mine. I saw it in my head, what Dora had meant for me to do. There was no time to waste, for the power churning in that witch's body was far too great. So without pause, I flew down and pasted my hand against her forehead. Even though her skin was on fire, ice still grew from my palm. She bellowed like a great beast whose sides had just been impaled, but still I did not waver.

"Look at me!" I screamed through the churning winds. The cyclone had grown darker, the gray almost black. The green fire shot bullets into my skull. Then like a priest with butterfly wings, I pounded my words into her skull just before impaling her chest with Avalon's blade, "May you finally find your peace, Amantha."

There was a crackle—like the worlds had been listening and had just let out a screech. And then Jeremy Love threw Dora's cape into the sky and stood back to watch as the cyclone lifted over our heads for the first time since it had wrapped itself around us. The cloak separated into so many particles that it just looked like black sparkles dancing in the wind—and then it became one with the cyclone. What was left of the beast who had once called herself the Crone of Light's End, glanced up at the sky just in time to watch the sparkling cyclone fall over her shoulders. A black, shimmering tunnel pounding against the earth's surface until all that was left was . . . nothing.

The world froze as if someone had hit pause on the remote. Everything around us, around the blade now stuck in her chest—the cyclone, the chanting, the marching, the storm—it all stopped.

My heartbeat was heavy in my ears. My blood flowing from me to my child. The fire in Amantha's eyes went out, and her shoulders and spine curved as if she'd just got socked in the guts. She had no more words to say. No more lies to spin.

"Now you'll see," were her last words. And as soon as they were spun from her mouth, she took me with her.

We were spinning, spinning, spinning . . . Until we weren't. At some point the blade piercing her heart, the hilt still in my hand, went away. And then so did she.

It was just me, standing over and under a black canvas. I squinted my eyes as I turned in a circle. If I concentrated, I could find stars twinkling in the distance; and if I tried really hard, I could see one of them twinkling so bright that it almost seemed to be growing. And that's when I realized where I was.

Light's End.

"Welcome to the tunnel, Makayla."

I spun around on my toes, my wings pointing in every direction. Facing me were three familiar faces: Avalon, Titania, and Dora.

Titania spoke first. "We've only brought you here to say good-bye."

"You've done well, and you may be happy to find out that the souls will be reset. Amantha and Miranda shall have a second chance at love," said Avalon.

Normally, I may have leapt at them—questioned the uncertainty of such an act. But as soon as the reflex fired, it was just as quickly usurped. It was the tunnel; it was speaking to me. Telling me that Amantha's soul could be returned to how it was before the tunnel changed her. Before her vibrations went haywire. The creation at my fingertips had made it so. If evil returned to the land I called home, it would not be because of her.

The light in the distance was getting closer. "Why light's end?" I asked, peering between the three cousins. Each a daughter of a different god or goddess. "It seems like it is the reverse. The end of darkness."

"'Tis all in how one sees it," Dora explained. It was still weird for me to see her this way. Darker skin, freckles strewn across her nose. Her scars were gone though, and her golden eyes sparkled in a way the blue ones never did. "Amantha saw the light's end because the magic she'd fed upon from her mother was twisting her heart beats. It wasn't the fault of one or the other; it was simply a grand misfortune. Amantha tasted something sweet when she was young and her brain only knew that it wanted more. Miranda was only acting on impulse. Saving her child from an abusive husband and doing what she had to do to survive."

I placed a hand over my stomach. As I did, I saw an impish grin grow in my mind. A face to match . . . a mix of mine and Toby's features. "I understand." I would do anything to keep her safe. "I just wish I had chosen both sacrifice *and* love."

"You did," Dora affirmed. "One always has a choice. It will make sense to you one day."

I started to shake my head. "But they said I only chose—"

"You chose the crown," Titania stated. "But you did so because of the love in your heart. You believed love could conquer darkness in a world where dark magic was doing its best to tear down any and all goodness. You desired the crown so that you could rule in the name of love, for you've always understood this is where true power lies."

"And we've no doubt you'll be a firm ruler for the greater good," Avalon added. Then, with a teensy-weensy bow, she added, "Queen Koehaias."

"Even if my love has been taken . . ." It was funny, how in this place, heart break didn't exist. Like, even as the words left me, it didn't hurt.

"Love is energy; therefore it cannot be taken," Titania stated. "Heartbeats that have been lost can always be remembered."

"And can be found in my next life . . ."

"Yes," Titania answered.

And then with one final smile, the three of them turned and began walking towards the light.

I bit my lip, thinking over everything they'd said. They were just about to disappear completely when I heard it.

Dora's last words to me: *You've earned it, faery. The tunnel is now yours . . .*

And then I was back.

The world was still stuck on pause, but only for another second before someone pushed play. I woke on the ground, sprawled next to my friends. Around my body, Dora's cloak.

The storm was over. I could never get over how a twister, something with the power to cause so much destruction, could just dissolve into absolute nothingness seconds after it had ruled the earth. It was still so unexplainable. The clouds had already parted, and the sun began to thirst for its first cup of tea in a very long time, as the bodies of my friends began to come back to life.

First it was Layla, a moan as she reached for her head. Then Heime, who grunted an irritated, "Oi," then Blythe— her wings gyrating from where she was laying over them on the ground.

My best friend turned from where he'd been facing the end of a bad curse. "You did it, Makayla." He had a somewhat tired, somewhat sad, yet genuine smile on his face.

I blinked away a tear then jumped into his arms, squeezing him with all my might. "Jeremy! You were so brave!"

He pulled away just enough so I could see as his lips moved around the name. "It's Bally now."

I bit my lip, tasting another tear. I nodded, "Of course it is."

Finally, a moan rose from Cee-Cee's lips. It took Jere— Bally and I about two seconds to jump on her. We were pulling at her arms, forcing her to sit up—hugging and squeezing her.

"Cee-Cee," I whispered, cupping her face.

I knew it was her, because if it wasn't, the trio of god and goddess droppings wouldn't have been sent home. But still, I needed to look into her eyes and see her soul; I needed to hear her voice and know it was actually hers. And then that spunky attitude that we all knew and loved came back to the surface.

"Dang yo, my head really hurts. What did you bitches do, like punch me out or somethin'?"

Bally and I glanced at each other, grinned, then clobbered Cee-Cee like we were toddlers trying to climb on top of one another.

"Oh my god, STOP," she said with a chuckle. "Kayla, your wings, girl! They are all up in my shit!"

I didn't care, nor did Bally. We couldn't stop hugging each other.

It wasn't until Layla spoke and we turned to find a sour grimace on her face that we stopped.

"I thought we had to kill the body that was housing the soul of the lich."

"We did," Heime stated, then balled up his fist and coughed into it. Bally fetched him something to drink from one of their bags and the elf drained it in one gulp. "Dora harnesses power like none other. She was strong enough to pull the lich into her body." He coughed again, his eyes widening. "Should've known she was more than a witch—in all my years, I'd never known a sorceress to be able to do such a thing. At least not without the work of extremely dark magic . . . Dora never smelled of rot. Her heart knew not the darkness of the witch who birthed her."

"She used the dragon breath." Every last one of us turned our attention towards Cee-Cee. She giggled as she said the next part. "It was in me this whole time. I didn't even know— like how can someone not know they have *dragon's breath* in their damn body?"

I scratched at the skin above my brow. "Wait—what?"

Bally reached for Cee-Cee's knee and squeezed it as he

explained, "In their past lives, Malina was given dragon's breath. The lich was going to use it to open that tunnel they all kept talking about, but obviously the Crone didn't get that far. When they reincarnated" —he gestured to Cee-Cee— "the dragon's breath was still with them. It's ethereal so it can't be erased until it's used. Dora used it to undo the binding curse the lich placed over Malina's, or as she is now, Cee-Cee's soul. It's how she was able to take just the Crone into her body."

It was quiet as we all absorbed Bally's speech.

As usual, I was the first to speak. "How do you know all that?"

He shrugged a shoulder. "Dora told me. She told me lots of things while on the way here."

Cee-Cee smirked and laid her hand over his. "Look atchu, Bally. Just a little witch charmer."

His weathered cheeks glowed and turned pink. And don't think it escaped me that my lanky friend who was no longer human held himself taller than he ever had. I didn't know what Cee-Cee would choose to do once we left this place, but I knew there was one thing I could count on: I would have at least one friend from my old world staying with me once we moved back onto Garlandian soil.

❧

The sun was fully out by the time we had finally all gathered our bearings. Looking around, there was a charm to the place that made me remember the witch in the wand named Miranda. Miranda who had wanted nothing more than to know love.

After discovering love for myself, I couldn't for a second fault Miranda for a single action. One would do almost anything to avoid heartache; and on that note, it hadn't escaped me that when all was said and done, we weren't just minus a witch, but there was someone else in our company that was missing. No, it hadn't escaped me . . . but I hadn't been ready to address it. Not at first.

Jeremy and Cee-Cee were crouched over a letter that Cee-Cee had found in her back pocket. Apparently, it was from her mom. I could tell by the way Cee-Cee's hand was placed over her lips that she needed her time alone with her first best friend to process whatever was between the words in that letter and the beats of her heart. Heime and Layla were busy building a fire, and I had decided to wander down to the beach before the lake. We were all far too tired to try and return to where we each belonged just yet. If it had been as easy as POPPING into the forest and settling our bones into 17 Serendipity Lane (because that would always be my first home in Garlandia), then we would have jumped at the thought. But none of us knew what was waiting for us. We could be entering right back into war. We needed a good night's sleep before we even thought about what laid before us.

"Hey."

I didn't need to look her way to know it was Blythe.

"How you doin', queenie?"

I was holding in my hands Dora's cape. I thought it had been gone to the cyclone, but after being where I'd been and seen what I'd seen, I knew what it represented. It had been sent to me, for the tunnel was now mine.

I wasn't sure how I felt about that.

"I don't know," I replied.

I saw her nod out of the corner of my eye. "You think all their souls were put to rest—the village, that is?"

Now that was something I was fairly sure of. "If Amantha was given the chance to start over, then I have a feeling those who became Cronies were too." I turned to face her. "I think you can consider your parents' souls safe."

She bit the corner of her lip with a sharp incisor, then nodded so quickly I almost missed it—the tear in the corner of her eye. For a fleeting second, I wondered if it would be inappropriate to hug her . . . because of what had happened while in the gray. But screw it. I threw my arms around her and pulled her in. "It's going to be okay." Then a little softer, I whispered, "We got this."

"I'm so glad to hear you say that," she whispered. When she pulled away, she opened her palm. As soon as she did my world shook.

It was the same necklace Toby had been wearing the whole time I'd known him, up until the moment Rally's sword crossed his neck. Except now it looked like the light inside of it had gone out. After everything had been said and done, it was the only thing remaining of Toby. My lips trembled, as did my fingers, as I lifted my hand to it. Blythe very gently handed it to me.

"You haven't said a word about him being gone."

I shook my head very slightly.

"Do you want to talk about it yet?"

Again, I shook my head. Covering my lips with my free hand, I asked in a voice that hadn't belonged to me since I was three, "Can I keep this?"

"Of course," Blythe replied. Her forehead was littered with words I didn't have the heart to read just yet. "The keeper's necklace keeps them bound to the land if something happens to them before their keeping has been fulfilled. It only reappears after the one they've vowed to protect has been avenged."

I nodded, if not a little too quickly. "I gathered as much."

There was no Great Beyond to run to. No mushroom within sight to dive into. But I'd seen the gray; I'd been in it.

I was no longer afraid to face my fears. And thankfully, I still had my friends.

Blythe caught me as I fell into her arms, shaking. "I loved him so much."

"I know, queenie." She stroked my hair as I soaked her shoulder. "I know."

$\maltese$ 43 $\maltese$

Makayla

While in the application process for Harvard, I wrote an essay. I didn't focus on what sort of law interested me or what I wanted my development to look like while I was progressing with my studies. No, I wrote about what my life would look like after I won my first case. Because winning isn't the end; if you are defending something or someone who you truly believe in, then that journey never ends. The struggle to maintain and stand up for what you believe in is something that should and will stay with you for the rest of your life.

As far as I was concerned, I'd won my first case. Actually, we'd all won. Every single one of us. Bally, Cee-Cee, Dora, Blythe, Layla, Heime, Toby, me, and all the creatures from all the worlds who had lent a hand—or a life—towards taking down the illness that had been rooted in our worlds for hundreds of years.

I'd slayed a lich, but the fight was far from over. Loral was still in hiding and none of us had a clue as to what the Garlandian grounds had evolved into in the short time we'd been away.

When the sun rose the next morning, we booked a flight back to Garlandia. Layla and Blythe were coming with us. We may have just saved the worlds, but in Lorelei, we were still fugitives. It didn't matter that I no longer had the sword— Layla assured me that the mer wouldn't care. They weren't about to see reason. In fact, we'd been sawing planks over thin ice just staying at Lantern's Edge for the night. Sure, nobody in their right minds, including the army of sea people, would venture over the cursed land leading into Forest Peak, but since I'd been here, the land was piecing itself back together. It would only be a matter of time before somebody decided to step a toe over the border, and when word spread that it was no longer cursed, there would be no fear of crossing over into it again.

I didn't know of a single mermaid in Garlandia. I decided that needed to change. Any of these weirdos had a home in the castle that would soon be mine. Any of them. And if that didn't please them, then they for sure were welcome on Garlandian soil for as long as their lives led them to it.

Layla and I called for the beasts as soon as we rose that morning. My heart wasn't in it, but I needed to start using my new skills. I was a dragon dancer after all, and at some point in my overly long life, the inheritance would probably come in handy.

"Once they're called," Layla had said just before we sang into the sky, "my people will feel it in their bones. They'll know it's us bringing the dragons forth. We will not have the luxury of stalling."

"Yes," I'd answered. My language had been nothing more

than short answers ever since that embrace Blythe and I had shared next to the lake's shore.

We gathered two dragons to take us back into Garlandia. Blythe, Layla, and Heime rode one, while Bally and Cee-Cee rode the other. I stayed on Petal's back. The old girl and I had some bonding to do. We hadn't spoken about our shared loss out loud yet, but we'd spent a lot of time in one another's eyes. We misfits, we stuck together.

It took us two days to get back to Garlandia. We stopped at the same island Petal, Toby, and I had on the way into Lorelei. Ate the same berries, caught the same breed of purple trout.

Blythe was by my side to make sure I ate. I hadn't let go of Toby's necklace from the moment she'd given it to me. Yes, I'd been too smart to believe my king was back forever. I knew—the second Rally took his head—I knew he was gone. It was why I'd been trying to escape into the Great Beyond.

"Loral is still alive . . ." I whispered while Blythe and I sat just before the shore between a handful of berries and cooked fish while the others sat around the fire, closer to the trees. "I thought Titania wouldn't rest until he was dead. Therefore, Toby wouldn't be able to . . . rest." I thought I'd have more time.

She'd been facing me, hugging her knees into her chest, when she let one of her fingers fall to the burnt-out light bulb in my hand. "It's a powerful bond, to be someone's keeper. And when I say that, I don't mean like a keeper who watches over finances and stuff like that."

My thoughts drifted to the memory of the Ardeen faery who had come to watch me sign off on the generation house I'd inherited. He was more like a family lawyer.

With her fingertip still on the necklace, she continued, "A necklace like this signifies a deeper bond. You are holding someone's life-long secret, and you will not pass on until you finish what that person couldn't. Or," she added, lifting her gaze to fit into mine—where it did so perfectly, "until you ensure the battle is won." She paused for effect. "The main event that Titania was here for was always the Crone. Loral was but a side act. She knew very well that as soon as the lich was taken care of, that his unnatural magic would dissipate. Toby's job ended the second you put out the Crone's light . . . or darkness."

I didn't have any more tears to cry . . . or so I thought. My tear ducts burned, and my voice trembled as I stated very slowly, "Toby always said his mother was Titania's keeper, but she must've passed it on to her son." I hesitated as I said what I knew was true. "She saw what Titania saw; that her son would be the only one who could bring out the warrior in me." I gulped. "And she knew that he wouldn't survive, that the necklace would be needed to bring him back. But it didn't bring him back, not really."

The necklace hadn't saved him. It's why he hadn't felt real to me. Why I began mourning him even as his arms had wrapped around my waist.

I sniffled and wiped my nose with my knuckles. "So um, are you and Layla going to try and, you know, get back together." My stomach turned as I said, "You can love one another in Garlandia. As soon as the crown is mine, that is."

Her face settled on an indifferent expression. "I don't think that's gonna happen, queenie."

"Why?"

"She's not my mate."

I held the necklace tighter in my hand, trying to squeeze what was left of my king into my hands. "How do you know that?"

Blythe held my stare for too many breaths. Too many heartbeats. Finally, she started to get up, but just before she walked away, she whispered into my ear. "Quit acting like you don't know all the things, Makayla. You've got more brains than all these funky misfits combined. Start owning it." When I attempted to narrow my eyes, she added, "You already know. You've known since our wands touched."

And then she was off towards the fire.

In an act I would find myself in for many future years, I looked up at the sky and whispered, "For you my king, I will not crumble." And with a hand on my stomach, I closed my eyes, feeling the day's end sink into my skin. "For her, I will not forget how to love." A new tear found its way down my cheek. "For Garlandia, I will be the best ruler there has ever been."

Shortly after that, just as I was reaching for my satchel so I could return to the fire, something caught my attention. Something in my bag was warm. When I opened it, I discovered that the secret stone Toby had made for me the day we first kissed, had in fact been heating up . . . and it was now changing colors.

My attention rose once more to the sky as I heard a previous conversation play through my mind.

When can I hear what it has to say?

When it's ready.

My chin danced up and down as I let the warmth from the stone fill my veins in with love and hope. I held it for another full minute before gently placing it back in the satchel.

It might've been ready, but I wasn't.

❦

From the essay I wrote: *Once I've won my first case, I will shake my client's hand then return promptly to my office. From there I will begin organizing letters and videos to go out to the world. For it's not really a win, is it? It's a small victory. Winners know that the race never ends. They know there are just moments of rest between this one and the next. That to keep achieving greatness they must continue to train and treat their bodies accordingly.*

They are also acutely aware that, like waves of the ocean, life can be unpredictable. They will have good days and bad—failures over successes. This is why they keep pieces of their wins in their pockets. When they celebrate, they break off a corner piece and bury it inside themselves just in case a tsunami attacks and wipes out all their current progress. That way, when everything else is gone, they have a memory of positivity to stand upon. Something to use to help themselves stand back up.

I will keep the memory of that first handshake from that first winning case in my mind. I will bury it, and I will bring it back out when the losses seem to outweigh the gains. And when it looks like I have nothing else to be proud of, I will relive that handshake with the first client I ever helped. And I will know that I am still worth a damn. I will know, that even if I've lost my wings, I can still fly.

44

Makayla

The dragons dropped us off behind the castle before flying back through the worlds. Dawn was breaking when we reentered Garlandia. Yet right away, we could all tell, it was darker. The sky was bloodred with orange undertones. Dust swirled from the ground to the sky whenever a light wind blew. There was no grass. Only dirt and blood. Even the castle walls had the stains of war strewn all over them. The air smelt metallic.

And here I'd thought my heart couldn't break anymore.

"Pure destruction," Heime stated.

"Yes," I said, a hitch in my voice.

"Let's get this over with," Cee-Cee stated.

We'd landed far enough away that we couldn't be seen, but in near enough proximity that we could scope out the going's on of the new leadership. Namely the Robes of Lorelei. I wondered, did they know their precious Crone had been sent back to the ether? That she was no longer evil as shit.

From there we marched, together, hand in hand. Heime to Bally, Bally to Cee-Cee, Cee-Cee to Layla, Layla to Blythe, and Blythe to me. Petal remained at my side. We trekked across the land in one straight line. As we got closer, we noticed signs of life. An elf sticking his head out from a boulder here, an old hag carrying a basket of supplies there. The skies were bare of air traffic, but who knew if that was because of the hour, or some other reasoning too terrible to bare.

"Look," Layla said, gesturing with her chin in the distance.

We followed her direction, noting a group of about twenty creatures—fey, gnomes, and elves. Some had shovels and rakes, while others were using wands. They were turning out the soil . . . repairing the land. As we grew closer, and our faces were recognizable, one by one they stopped from their work and began to kneel . . . and bow.

"What are they doing?" Bally questioned. "Aren't they going to get in trouble?"

"They aren't prisoners," came a piercing voice.

The pieces of my heart that were left dropped into my stomach and I gripped Blythe's hand so hard that she chirped.

"Rally," I said to the specimen who had seemingly come out of nowhere. He was as sickeningly pale and undead as I'd seen him when I'd POPPED into the Garlandian forest.

His wan expression didn't waver as he moved to stand directly in front of us. "They haven't been prisoners for a while. And those that have been sent away are being rescued as we speak."

An air bubble popped in the back of my throat as I stood

there with my mouth open. I looked up to Petal, who seemed just as confused as I was, then returned my attention to the foul elf (or whatever the hell he was) who had murdered my king.

"What are you up to, Rally? I assure you, you cannot undo me anymore than you already have."

A thin red tongue slipped between his lips, and he licked them. I could see his fangs. They were so white they could have blinded someone. "I cannot undo what has been done—"

With the deepest bravado I could muster, I shot back at him with verbal bullets, "No, you cannot."

Then Blythe whispered to me, "How does he stand in the sun?"

His gaze met hers. "Enchantments." He brought a hand, strewn with elongated fingers up to eye level, then wiggled a finger laced with a gold ring holding a purple stone. "Don't worry, only those worthy of the light may own one." He locked his gaze onto mine. "I've ridded the kingdom of any and all killers that I know of, minus one."

My tongue pressed against my back molar. If I was good at one thing, it was assessing the character of another—minus Helene. I might've let my frustrations and impatience blind me to her true motives. However, if I wasn't mistaken, Rally's energy was satiated. He was exhibiting a calmness that I hadn't ever seen in him before.

Heime stepped forward from his place at the end of the line we'd formed. As he gritted his teeth, he looked from Rally to me. "Do not listen to this spinster of lies, Makayla."

Tread lightly, I told myself. *Don't assume anything. What would my king do?*

My gaze lined back up with Rally's. "If you are being true, then answer me this: why the change of heart?"

His head fell slightly to the side. He didn't blink as he

stated, "We didn't get off to a very good start, nor did we get to know one another very well, but there are some things about me that you may not know. One of them is that I have some very serious mother issues, and because of that I laid my trust into the figure of a king who was the closest thing to a father I ever had." As he spoke, I directed my attention very casually to where Layla stood so still, she looked like she might crack in the sun. Rally, undeterred, continued. "When I was reborn, I had a few revelations. More than a few actually," he scoffed. Then he snapped his fingers and the same butterfly that had visited me just days ago, appeared. As soon as I laid eyes over her, my chest lifted, and my clavicles felt like they were going to snap. "Rasha came to me the day I rose. She said she belonged to a faery who had been waiting many years for someone to hear her message. I was the first one who could."

My breath delivered my next words. "What was the message?"

Rally looked to the butterfly and almost immediately the space was echoing with the same raspy voice that always seemed to come from these kinds of insects.

From the moment life enters the world, a mother knows—even if she runs out of milk, her babe will be saved if only she can share her love with that child. Love is just as important to survival as are other forms of nourishment. Hatred will never yield power, only damnation. The real power grows from souls connecting other souls together, growing as one. Raising the vibrations. It is how we ascend before we ever even leave our bodies. 'Tis not always the job of a god or goddess to ensure love is eternal. That, dear listener, is in our hands. It starts with our mothers and our fathers, and it trickles down to the smallest of creatures. My last frozen hope is that this backwards world finds its way again. That even when the milk runs out, love remains. That even when survival is having its bleakest moment, the survivors join hands and will themselves to live on. Because the earth knows when its inhabitants are true, and the earth will reward those who have earned it.

And there we were, all in a line, hand in hand. I was still turning the message over in my head repeatedly when Rally began speaking. "It's why I had to know, you see." My chin snapped up and I looked him dead in the eyes. "I had to know what kind of mother you were going to be." He looked to Rasha and nodded. When next the butterfly spoke, it was my own words that entered back into my ears:

I assure you that no child of mine—no matter who or what they are —will ever be considered a burden. I may not have planned this, but it's just one thing out of a million other things that I never accounted for. That doesn't mean I won't absolutely love her. And if she has fangs then I'll learn how to show her how to use them.

I swallowed a cry just as Blythe squeezed my hand a little tighter.

"Does this still ring true, queen?"

I batted my eyelashes and tried to sift through the static appearing from all corners of my vision. My tongue felt swollen as I answered. "Of course it does."

He called me queen.

"Then follow me."

The world was blurry as we each took turns looking at each other with twisted expressions. But my gut said to follow him, so I wiped at my saltwater eyes and nodded to my company. From there we followed the knight of the undead army over the broken grounds, nodding to those who knelt before us, until we came to a corner of the castle I'd never seen before.

I gasped when we arrived at our destination.

Rally had eyes only for me as he said, "I am under the impression you still carry Titania's gift."

My lips parted, but my voice was still hibernating in my stomach, where my heart was still in pieces.

When I couldn't speak, Rally said, "Dora assured me it will be with you all of your days."

"I—I would assume so," was all I could muster.

He jerked his head up then down, then snapped his fingers. Almost too soon after, Foxfire appeared—a gold ring with a purple stone around his own finger—and he was dragging behind him a black body bag. But whoever was in its folds wasn't dead.

"Dora was a friend to me when I'd ensured I had no friends left. She knew it was a risk, but still, when I showed her a man without a mother, she let me experience, even for the briefest of moments, a mother's touch. She made sure not to leave this planet without telling me where the last missing piece of this game existed."

I looked from Rally to Firefox, who incidentally made a point to lower his head in a brief bow, then to the squirming bag below.

"Go on, queenie," Blythe whispered, slipping her hand from mine and pushing me gently forward. "You've got this."

A guttural breath slowly seeped from my mouth as I placed my hand over my belly—my wand now taking residence in my other hand—just in case. *Yes,* I thought, sending my thoughts down into my womb, *we've got this.*

As Foxfire began to unzip the bag, Rally explained. "His power has been dwindling ever since you were born. All Dora did was bury his emotions deep inside, then filled in that space with some of her magic. All it took was the emotions seeping back, light between the cracks, to burn away his gift of being untouchable." As he spoke, Loral's face appeared out of the bag. He no longer looked like someone who was capable of such destruction. He had branches and berries stuck to his ratty white hair, his skin was dirty, and his clothes were nothing more than rags. It looked like he'd gotten into the ring with a bear and lost. Badly. "Fear has drained him, but he's still clinging to some of the witch's magic."

Rally paused, long enough for us to hear Loral whining as Foxfire stomped on his leg and caused him to cry out. Rally pointed at the statue he'd brought us to.

"I would assume that by now you've heard his story, and you have figured out your family's place in it."

I looked from the first statue Loral ever made back to the foul creature writhing on the ground. Then I bent down and put my face so close to his, it was almost as if I was inviting him to spit at me. "You were friends, all of you. You fell in love with my grandmother, but when she didn't feel the same way, you turned away from love altogether. You couldn't have her so you made sure no one could have her. And then you created a law so vile that it placed darkness in the hearts of those who could have been great." Helene's face lingered in my thoughts. "I believe in forgiveness, Sebastian, but I also know a dud when I see one." His eyes became tiny slits the likes of buttonholes and his lips pressed together. "Don't you have anything to say?" I blurted out.

He chewed on his lips for a second before growling. Foxfire kicked at his side and he yelled out.

"Stop," I stated calmly to the first knight I'd ever created.

Foxfire simply dipped his chin.

I returned my attention to Loral. "Well? Do you?"

His pupils grew then became small again. "I'd rather die than see an insect wear my mother's crown."

I inhaled a slow breath through my nose, then nodded. "Don't worry, Sebastian. I've never liked hand-me-down's all that much. I think I'll have my own commissioned, thank you."

As I stood apart from him and all the curses he no longer felt the need to keep contained, I noted as I stepped up to my grandmother's statue, that the world had started to come out from where it had been hiding in the shadows. Faeries and elves—gnomes and animals were gathering around us in hoards. I could have even sworn that I saw my grandfather walking through them. But as curious as I was to take a second look, I had other things on my mind.

My touch was lingering before the hand that had once cradled my mother's head when I looked to Rally. "Where are the Robes?"

Without a hitch, he answered. "They've taken the dragons back to Bathar. From there they've been instructed to wait for further instructions. They are under strict orders not to leave until they've gotten word." The closest thing to a genuine grin that I'd ever seen on Rally's face appeared. "They'll be waiting a while."

Heime all but snickered from behind. "Skin doesn't do well in Bathar, and one must have scales to breathe through the elements for an extended time."

"Too bad for them, then," Rally said.

I'd kept my gaze firm over Rally, and as I continued to do so, I asked, "And where do you plan to settle after all of this?"

"That is up to you."

I looked to Layla, who returned my stare. Dancer to dancer, we spoke through our minds as dragons do. When we were finished, I returned my attention to Rally. "You have my husband's blood on your hands. I would like to say the love and creation I carry can forgive you, but today is not the day for that. However, I see that you have changed, and I want to believe it is real. So once this is done" —I gestured to where Loral was still cursing on the ground— "I expect you to find a way to Lorelei. Once there, you shall find the temple of the sea. You are to do whatever needs to be done to keep the mer from crossing into our world. They believe we've wronged them, and this is false. I do not care or wish to hear from you unless need be. All I ask is that you keep that world peaceful. Perhaps one day, we may reunite, and I may shake your hand on behalf of a better country here and there, but I assure you, Rally, you must earn that handshake."

The half witch, half elf, full vampire, just set his eyes on me for the count of ten. Finally, he asked, "What in the world is a handshake?"

And though the world had done its worst to strip me of my love and magic, I grinned. "Something I hope we can manage in the future."

I was still grinning when I closed my eyes and set my hands on that of my grandmother's. "Welcome back, Cecilia," I whispered.

After that, there was a whirlwind of white dust, a lover's embrace as a man who had lost his wife caught her—living and breathing—into his arms, and a howl that could be heard in every world as the rest of Dora's magic evaporated from Loral and he felt his heart beat again. His love was now unfrozen.

I did not use my magic or my hands, or any of the swords that reflected my face, to undo the king who had tried so very hard to undo my family and all this land. Instead, I let those who had been wronged carry on with what they needed to do. And as the commotion grew and shouts of victory commenced, I linked arms with those in my company. New friends who I hoped to grow old around. And we continued our march around the castle until we found the giant double doors that led inside.

Petals' hooves echoed against the marble as we all stood there in a line.

"Welcome home, misfits," I said.

"Welcome home," each one of them echoed.

And so it was.

❧ 45 ❧

Makayla

One Year Later

Garlandia was free. Lauslin and the other surrounding
kingdoms were following suit. One of the first things
I'd done after accepting my title officially was to use Loral's
tracking system one last time before having it demolished.
With its help, I found every last statue and freed all of the
souls. About half of them came back to—the others returned
to the ether. I saved Helene's for last. I think some of my
peers expected me to leave her there, but it wasn't fair to
keep her soul caged. Even she deserved a chance to return to
the ether and start a new life. A life where she could choose
light over darkness.

When I finished with that task, I simply continued

moving down the list I'd written in my head. I no longer required Post-Its. Blythe was right, being royal meant I had people—and man did I ever. Wherever I went I was followed by assistants in the form of Ardeens. I found myself covering my body in stink charms now and again just to get some peace and quiet.

I'd picked rose gold for the color scheme in the bedroom and attached nursery. The rest of the castle exhibited neither a masculine nor feminine feel; I stuck with Garlandian blue but made sure it wasn't so in your face that you felt like you were drowning in a Greek restaurant. Also, there were no more dungeons and the throne room had just finished its remodel. At first, I'd fought to have the throne on equal ground, but my associates had argued that it should still be elevated.

"Come on, Kayla, even a judge sits up high," Cee-Cee had stated.

"True," I'd said.

So, we'd compromised by creating a small set up, a bit higher off the ground, and adding four thrones to the mix instead of just one. Because from here on out, there were no dictators. There would be a king and queen (or a queen and queen, or a king and king, or what have you) as well as two (or three if the leader remained solitary) other creatures who would be voted in and who would also have the right to make political decisions. We were still drafting a doctrine to live by, but so far, I was working my hardest to mimic the utopia Blythe had come from.

The day we'd wandered into the castle as a group . . . as a family, I'd invited every single one of my company members to live in the castle with me for as long as they wanted to. At first they stayed, but one by one, they began to drift.

Heime had a love for leather that he returned to, moving back to his forest dwelling with his new apprentice, Bally, in tow. Bally really was good at making shoes—I'd bought a few for myself. Layla was taking charge of helping Firefox with my new guard, but even she came to me one day and said it was time to leave the castle. I understood . . . Blythe's room was only across the hall from my own. I signed over the generation house to Layla and she accepted it with a smile on her face. She'd had an inground pool put in; it was a first for Garlandia. The mermaid hadn't been prepared for the number of guests she'd had show up on her doorstep, pool floaties in tow. I'd had to ensure that public pools were now a thing in this kingdom just so Layla could have some privacy.

Then there was Cee-Cee. I had a feeling this one was going to be complicated.

Jeremy's identity had been erased. His family didn't even know he still existed—he was forgotten to them. But Cee-Cee, she still had a father waiting to hear from his daughter.

"He probably thinks I'm dead," she'd said to me just days ago. "I can't stay in Narnia forever, Kayla."

I sniffled as I looked my best friend in the eyes. "You know you saved me right."

She'd laughed. "I think you have that turned around."

"No." I lifted a piece of pink hair from her eyes and tucked it behind her ear. It just looked better pink. "You and Jeremy were the only two kids—in all my life—who ever took the time to talk to me. I know I set myself up to be an adult from the time I was two, but even when I was in school, the others just looked at me like I was some sort of weird anomaly."

She'd rolled her eyes. "That's cause you are!" Her arms picked up and spread around me until she was hugging me tight. "And that's why I love you." After forever passed us by she pulled away and assured me, "I just want to go back and do all the things, you know. Go to college, get 'Makayla drunk' on wine, act stupid, fall in love. But I promise you I'll be back. Mort's already made sure I got the recipe for mud ice-cream. I can come back anytime."

"You better," was all I said.

And that's what had brought us to this day. It was a big one. All of Garlandia had been invited for the ribbon cutting of the new throne room and it was doubling as Cee-Cee's going away party. I was thrumming through my closet, trying to choose between a lavender pant suit or the new dress Esmerelda had just sent me when there was a knock at the door.

I walked over, clad only in a silk robe, my faery wings draped around my shoulders, and was about to open the door when it slowly swung open from the other side. Blythe's head popped in. "Can I come in?"

"Of course," I said, leaning in for a quick peck on the lips. She still slept in the room across the hall, but that was only because I wasn't ready for what was inevitably going to come next.

Swords didn't lie, that was the conversation I'd had with Tanker shortly after we'd been reunited. Toby and I had married but then he'd been taken back into the ether. My soul wasn't meant to cross over the Garlandian grounds alone. If it were, a new mate wouldn't have found me. And as Tanker said, "You couldn't have found a better choice if you'd scoured all the lands and all the worlds. Toby would want you to be happy, Makayla."

Blythe slipped through the door and dangled a bottle close to my face. "Time for the royal feeding."

"Right," I muttered. "She's awake—over there." I pointed to the cozy little butterfly cushion my swaddling preferred. As soon as she caught sight of the pink concoction in Blythe's hands, she started cooing—her little fangs hanging over her lips.

Toby Lala Koehaias was the name I gave to her. There

was no better name in the world. Though Contessa and Owen would argue that Benji Tobias was even better—I would never correct them. The fact that they'd named their little male swaddling after Toby also, well, it meant everything to me.

Toby fed on my milk mixed with blood; she would have a thirst for the rest of her life, for she was part vampire, part elf, and part faery. I suppose it was the elf in her that survived the poison in my veins. She also had the ability to show her wings whenever she wanted. One minute they would be there, the next they wouldn't. She was the funniest little thing.

It wasn't *her* fault that I couldn't look into her beautiful eyes.

"She's reaching for you, Mama," Blythe said as she picked up the babe.

I was busy holding up the two pieces of clothing as I said, "She's got her other mama, she's fine."

I could almost hear Blythe roll her eyes. I knew what she was thinking—that I needed to give up my grief and begin living. I would. I just had some other things to check off my list first.

"Your moms are here," she said as she stuck the nipple of the bottle into Toby's mouth.

I stared at the ceiling and scoffed. "Already! They're going to pounce on me before I'm prepared for all that energy. Where are they?"

"Uh," Blythe started, but never got the chance to finish. A second later, my bedroom door swung fully open and in came Naomi and Maude like a couple of fluttering butterflies.

"Lala!" they cooed together, coming around me in a rush of hugs and fluffing. They were pulling at my hair, holding my cheeks—looking at my teeth.

"Have you been brushing?"

"Are you sleeping okay?"

"I think she looks tired—what do you think, Naomi?"

"She looks tired."

"We should move in."

"NOOOOOOOO!" I screeched, pulling away, shooing them off with lavender and blue fabric. "Can you two, like, please just stop for one second! I can't even concentrate enough to find something to wear."

Maude turned to Naomi. "Well then." And as though she wasn't offended (which she nearly always was) she looked at Blythe. "What are you wearing, dear?"

"Oh, I was just going to—"

"Please don't say you're wearing that," Maude said in a condescending manner. Blythe was dressed simply in capri pants and a T-shirt. "You are practically royalty, dear. You must present yourself in a way that denotes—"

"*Mom*," I said causing Maude to look my way. "She can wear whatever she wants."

Maude's brows met the ceiling as her gaze veered to the right. "Well then."

I huffed an audible and irritated noise as Maude sauntered over to baby Toby and sat next to her granddaughter, choosing to mess with her hair instead of mine. That left Naomi. I gathered myself, rolled my shoulders back then looked to her. "Where's Dad?"

"Downstairs with Tanker. He's helping him pick out his players for this year's fantasy football."

It was all I could do to keep standing up straight. My birth father, who was convinced footballs contained rubies inside the leather (and that was why those giants kept trying to take the ball from one another—his words) was going to join my adoptive father's fantasy football game. And of course he was. If I could count on one thing to remain constant, it was that Tanker was the best person or faery that ever existed. Ever. He was born to make others smile.

With that in mind, I dropped the pantsuit. "I'm going to wear the dress. Tanker would like this more."

Out of the corner of my eye, I saw Maude smile warmly.

Soon the hour was upon us. Maude and Naomi had taken little Toby down to greet some of the incoming guests and I was putting the finishing touches on my make-up and hair.

"You look beautiful, queenie."

I glanced at where Blythe was sitting on the edge of the bed from the mirror's reflection.

I managed a smile. "Thank you. So do you."

She'd picked up the pant suit from the floor and tried it on. She looked fantastic. Lavender *was* her color, after all.

"I, um, I have something for you."

Using the balls of my feet, I flipped around so I could look at her. "Oh?"

She stood, walking closer to me, her hands in the pockets of the satin pants. When we were less than an inch from one another she pulled out her right hand to reveal a small box. One that could very easily be home to a ring.

All the air left my lungs.

"I know I told you I wanted to wait until things get easier for you, but uh—" She turned her cheek to me and bit her lip. "Anyway, I know how humans do this in the world you once knew and I wanted it to be familiar."

"Blythe—"

Her purple eyes leaned into me. "Makayla, shut up."

I slipped my teeth over my bottom lip.

"I'm not trying to be pushy. I just want you to know that when you're ready, so am I."

I sucked air into my mouth from the cracks of my teeth. And then I said, "Okay."

Very slowly, she shook her head. "I'm not done." She pulled her other hand from where it had been resting in the other pocket. I gasped—it was the secret stone Toby made me. It had been resting on my dresser from the moment we got here. Not once had I picked it back up. "It's time."

I just stared at her. Then my chest flung forward as a nervous laugh escaped, tears welling up in the corner of my eyes. "I—I don't think—"

She took my palm and placed the stone in my hand, then covered it with hers. "You're a mom now. That little girl deserves to see her mother strong. You can't stand up straight if you're still tethered to something that's pulling you down." She gulped. "Free your wings, Makayla, so that when the time comes, we can both show her how to fly."

She removed her warm hand from over mine and smiled at me before turning towards the door. "I won't go down without you," she said before she left, letting the door close behind her.

I stood there for a long time, like someone faced with a buffet of food when they'd long since forgotten how to eat. There was a time when I wanted nothing more than to know what Toby whispered into this stone.

My shaking fingers met my lips as I slowly sat on the edge of my bed.

How could I not remember his words to me just before he created this?

Would you rather taste the forbidden fruit and know how it feels on your tongue, even if you can only taste it once, or would you choose to live your life without ever knowing what it tastes like—because if you don't know, you might not miss it?

He knew. Toby knew the moment we met that he was facing death. He may not have known the ins and outs—the hows and how comes. But he knew that he was more than likely never going to meet his daughter while in flesh and bone. He knew my heart would find its ache, just as surely as my ignorance would be turned to wisdom.

The sun began to change positions in the sky as I sat there, holding that stone. Voices were getting louder, slipping from where they were entering the castle down below through the crack in my window. I knew Blythe was right. I needed to rip off this Band-Aid because this wound needed air to heal. It wasn't doing me or baby Toby any good under that bandage.

Finally, very slowly, I lifted the stone to my lips and whispered, "What's your secret?"

As soon as the words had been said, my surroundings changed. The tile I'd chosen for the floor turned to wood— my rose gold walls into a circle. Then trees began to trickle in. I guess every good closing scene needs an audience.

I was back in the forest, in the gazebo where Toby and I first kissed. And then I heard it, the voice that I'd been waiting to hear from the moment I lost it that day in the castle. The day my king was killed.

"You look beautiful, my queen."

The stone fell from my hands and I ran to him—my king. He was standing against the balcony, one leg crossed over the other, and when I collided with him, he nearly toppled over the side.

"Easy," he said, laughing as though it was the most natural thing to do in all the worlds.

He steadied himself and wrapped his arms around me while I searched his face with my hands. "Toby! I—I've missed you so much." I pressed my cheek against his chest and inhaled like I was trying to feed from his soul. He felt so *real*.

"I've missed you too," he whispered into my ear. His breath was hot.

I was taking breaths like I'd just found the surface after being under water for way too long. "How could you leave me —how could you love me just to leave me?"

He pushed me away just enough so that we could look at one another fully. "It was never a truth that I would have to go; it was only a possibility. One that my mother saw in the stars."

"Why didn't you warn me?" I questioned.

He grinned. "Have you met you? You would not have been able to do what needed to be done if you were constantly looking over our shoulders for a blade."

I chewed on the side of my mouth . . . because he was right.

"What did you name her?" he asked, a longingness in his eyes. Perhaps also a sadness living in there that he wouldn't ever hold the gift we made together.

"Toby Lala," I answered. "And I gave her your father's last name."

His lips curled up at the side. "You didn't want to add either of your names?"

My tongue danced over my bottom lip. "I didn't want to add a book to her formal address. Mine's bad enough."

"Touché. But in the end, is Abberwockey really all that bad?"

"No." I shook my head, taking in all that my king had to offer. "Not at all. It's regal in its own way."

"I think so too. Now then," he said, pulling at my hand and leading me to the inner part of the gazebo. "Let's get on with it."

"On with what?" I asked.

"Isn't it obvious, my queen. I've brought you here for one last dance."

My heart shrunk. "M—Maybe we should, like—I don't know—wait."

He looked down at me. "What for?"

"For it never to be over."

He held my gaze for long enough to convey through his eyes that he would always love me. But still, he leaned in and whispered, "Close your eyes."

I did, and then he began to lead me into a dance. I kept my eyes closed, just feeling his body against mine—his scent wafting through my nostrils, and eventually, his lips over mine. Tasting of ginger candy.

When next he spoke, he whispered to me, "We were stitched back together, therefore we will always be a part of one another. You must only close your eyes to come back to me. I am but a breath away—the ether is not far."

My head resting on his shoulder as we swayed to the music of the trees, I said softly, "My wand has bonded with another."

"I know," he said, as if it was the simplest thing in the world.

"I feel bad for loving her."

He pulled away, his hands over my shoulders. "Never feel ashamed for having love, Makayla. For love is the only reason for living."

"But I chose work over love—Titania herself told me this."

"You chose to accept sacrifice."

I blinked. "But she said—"

"What you could handle at the moment." He continued to grip my shoulders as he pulled me into him again, so that our noses were near touching. "There are no surprises in life. Not really. Your soul knows everything that is before you. 'Tis your heart that must learn to follow. And your heart is strong. This is why I know you will return to your role standing taller than you ever have. You will take the hand of your new mate and walk over the Garlandian grounds with your heads held high and our child in your arms. And when Toby Lala asks about her daddy, you tell her that he died so that she could have a better life. That one day we'll meet . . . in the ether."

I knew time was running out, the sparkles that had just started appearing moments ago were growing thicker. A moment like this didn't last forever.

Toby pulled away, sinking back against the balcony. I wanted to reach for him, to hold him for *so much* longer. But I knew I couldn't. That I shouldn't.

"Would you do it again?" he asked. "Would you taste the fruit?"

His scent was still in my mouth.

"Over again and again," I said.

Through the falling stars I saw one final grin. "Me too."

"Wait," I said, just as it was all fading into the ether. "What's the secret?"

One of his brows perked up. "Ah, I almost forgot." I braced myself, waiting for something that might shake my world. But then he said this, "Petal's allergic to peanut butter. Still, she tries time and again to go after it. Don't let her. 'Tis a pain to deal with afterwards."

My shoulders rolled forward. "Are you serious?"

"Quite, my queen. Now then, go on. Be mated. You've my blessing, and forever, my heart."

Moments later I was back on the bed, holding the stone, and chuckling softly at my king. Of course that was his secret. Garlandia was a place where one could rest easily knowing that it was okay not to take life too seriously. However, as I dried my tears and prepared to straighten myself out so that I could try and go out into the world and present myself as someone to lead all the others, I found myself stuck on that stone.

It had changed, an inscription over the top. One I immediately recognized.

Without pause, I jumped up and ran into the nursery where I'd stashed all the cards that faeries, witches, and elves had sent to congratulate us on the new royal bloodline. Still holding the stone stiffly in one hand, I rummaged through the cards until I found the one I was looking for. Adlar's.

Toby's cousin had made it through the war but had come back wounded. He was permanently blind in one eye and his wand still sent sparks whenever he tried to use it, but he was alive. That was all any of us really cared about. Definitely all Bally cared about—the two had been seen going to the Farmer's Market together. We were all crossing our fingers that there was more to the story than that.

Finally, I found it. The card Adlar had sent that had caused me a bit of confusion.

He and Toby had always found ways to communicate when it seemed there was no way of conversing. I should have known that Toby would find a way, even in his bodily death, to do so. I opened the card and sped read through the congratulatory remarks until my eyes met with the last line:

P.S. When the secret's out, hold on to its remains, for one day she will have the key to unlock that side of her she's always wanted to know. Watch for the inscription. 'Tis all in a name.

My gaze flitted back to the stone. And then I turned the envelope over to where Adlar had written Toby Lala's name. He'd written it in elvish. I didn't know elvish all that well, but I knew enough to know that, just as I knew enough to realize that the secret stone Toby had made me was now a key. A key with my daughter's name on it.

My head fell back, and I looked to the ceiling. "You left her a way to meet you."

Of course he did. She was his Lala.

I made sure my hair and make-up were back in order, that the stone was tucked away somewhere Toby Lala could find it when she was old enough to use it, and then I left my room. Blythe was waiting for me, patiently, at the top of the stairs.

"Are you ready, queenie?"

"Yes." I smiled.

"Did you do it?"

"I did."

She sucked her lips into her mouth. I could tell she wanted to ask—all the questions—but she didn't.

"Hey, I'd like my gift now."

Her wings fluttered quickly behind her back. "Seriously?"

"Yeah," I said, grinning from ear to ear.

"Okay, let's go down there and—"

"No." I shook my head. "Now. I want it now. Not in front of everyone—our lives will forever be transcribed before others. Let us keep this for us. This moment."

A sparkly tear hugged the outside of Blythe's eye as she nodded. And then she came down onto one knee before lifting up a black diamond hugged by little white ones.

I grinned. "It looks like a tunnel."

"'Tis," she said. "So what do you ya say, Makayla?"

I bent down so that we were nose and nose. "I say, thank you for being born. For being unafraid. And for loving my swaddling as though she is your own." A sparkly tear of my own ran down my cheek. "I say yes, queenie, for that title belongs to you now as well."

Her shoulders shook, as did her hands and lips, as she pulled the ring from its home and slid it over my finger. "I love you, Makayla," she said, holding my hand in hers. "I love our family. I will never turn from you or her."

I wiped at my wet face with my free hand and nodded. "I believe you, and I love you too."

So, I got engaged that night, for the second time. For the final time. My fated faery and I walked down the stairs together and greeted the faces of our kingdom, and when I saw Toby Lala beaming from where her grandparents were taking turns throwing her around—her wings fluttering as if she already knew how to use them—I sunk my arms into their circle until my hands came around her waist. I held her high and looked into her eyes. Oh, how they shone! And I said to her, "I love you, my heart, my soul. I love you so, my little Lala."

It really was a good name.

ACKNOWLEDGMENTS

Once more, thank you to CJM for seeing something in my weird little worlds. I must also give a shout out to my editor, my ARC readers and author friends who have been with Makayla Wood since the beginning of her journey. To everyone who boosts my posts and boasts about this series— I see you and I thank you again and again. And of course, I need to give a big thanks to my cover artist, Diana. You've nailed every one of my books with covers that seem to just get more beautiful with each new release.

It also needs to be mentioned that this book wouldn't have come full circle as well as it did without a little help from a couple of my closest weirdos. Sis, thank you for telling me your story about the killdeer, and to my best witch, my dearest Sarah—you didn't disappoint with the lich. You are both now immortalized in a Stillbrook.

And though some of you may think you have nothing to do with this book, I must admit that you do. You see, a book is nothing without readers, without souls seeking growth. There is more to Makayla than just a young girl who discovered she was a faery—more to Garlandia and any of the worlds found in these books. Makayla Wood is a light worker. A healer. A badass warrior with butterfly wings.

Like every one of us she is imperfect.

When I first started working on this series, I wanted to create a place where both young adults and adults could return to discover the simplicity of youth. Where faeries dress in frilly tutus and animals, trees, and flowers have the ability to cop an attitude. I wanted people to learn to let go again. To laugh. To raise the vibrations.

I know the world we live in isn't perfect, that it probably won't ever be. If only love and compassion was as important to some as power and riches. If only people could accept that even though we are all so very different, that love is love. If only . . .

However, if I've made one person laugh, cry—return to a magical forest where flutes are played and flowers gossip—and if I've made that person smile, genuinely, then that's good enough for me. And I thank you for being here for it.

ABOUT THE AUTHOR

Mariah Stillbrook, originally from Iowa, lives in Colorado with her white German shepherd, husband, and little girl. She graduated from the University of Colorado at Colorado Springs. She spends most of her days writing, reading, and enjoying the occasional hike. In her late twenties she realized that her writing was missing something, magic. She now focuses her writing on horror and urban fantasy in both adult and young adult genres.

Visit us online:
creativejamesmedia.com

@creativejamesmedia   @creativejamesm1   @creativejamesmedia   @creativejamesmedia